MW00563616

Always Darkest

By

Jess Flaherty & Keith Flaherty

Welcome to our world.

Published by

Crimson Cloak Publishing

©Jess and Keith Flaherty 2016

All Rights Reserved

ISBN: 978-1-68160-446-6

ISBN: 1-68160-446-9

This book is a work of Fiction. Names, characters, events or locations are fictitious or used fictitiously. Any resemblance to actual persons or events, living or dead, is entirely coincidental. This book is licensed for private, individual entertainment only. The book contained herein constitutes a copyrighted work and may not be reproduced, stored in or introduced into an information retrieval system or transmitted in any form by ANY means (electrical, mechanical, photographic, audio recording or otherwise) for any reason (excepting the uses permitted by the licensee by copyright law under terms of fair use) without the specific written permission of the author.

Publisher's Publication in Data
Flaherty, Keith and Flaherty, Jess
Always Darkest
1. Fiction 2. Fantasy 3. Angels and Demons 4. Good and evil

If a journey of a thousand miles in the real world starts with a single step, this journey of imagination began with the words, "So I read about this really cool demon. I think he'd make a good character in a story." We had no idea that conversation would lead to the creation of a whole new universe, and while we definitely couldn't do this without each other, there are others that have played such a vital role that we have to take a moment to thank them.

To everyone who continues to support us on this strange and winding road, and most particularly to Morgan K., Karla Karla, Deidre & Logan E., and Andy P., the Alpha and Omega(s) of all beta readers,

To our Logan who appreciates that Mom and Dad love their imaginary children too and need spend time with them sometimes,

To Ian (Butts),

And above all others, to Ben (You know what you did),

Thank you all.

And if we may quote the founders of the church of our hearts, *Wyld Stallyns*, "Be excellent to each other."

Or if you prefer, a quote from the church in which we are actually clergy, "Just abide."

Disclaimer

If we shadows have offended,
Think but this, and all is mended,
That you have but slumber'd here
While these visions did appear.
And this weak and idle theme,
No more yielding but a dream,
Gentles, do not reprehend:
if you pardon, we will mend:
And, as I am an honest Puck,
If we have unearned luck
Now to 'scape the serpent's tongue,
We will make amends ere long;
Else the Puck a liar call;
So, good night unto you all.
Give me your hands, if we be friends,
And Robin shall restore amends.

~ William Shakespeare, A Midsummer Night's Dream, Act V, Scene I

"In the beginning was the Word and the Word was with God, and the Word was God ... And the light shineth in the darkness and the darkness comprehended it not."

That's when things got complicated.

As Above

It was strange being surrounded by the glory of Heaven, knowing you had nothing, but trying to hang onto it anyway. Michael sat on the steps of the throne of the Most High grasping at what used to be. *Might as well chase a moonbeam.* He didn't know why he kept coming in here. The quiet was unnerving. Now it was just a room; beautiful, certainly, but not more so than anything else brought into being by the hand of the Creator. The emptiness always made him question their chosen course. He sighed. Uriel passed, avoiding his eye. Michael sat deep in thought, sandy-brown hair hanging in his eyes, realizing after a time that he was no longer alone. He glanced up to find the violet eyes shared in some fashion by all Angels of the First Order gleaming down at him. Michael thought God had done well in the creation of him and his siblings, and he knew he was so beautiful humans were usually rendered speechless in his presence, but at moments like these he was vaguely jealous. He thought that he and Uriel who appeared, in his mind anyway, to most plainly resemble humans, had gotten a little cheated in the looks department. The beautiful brown face of Raphael created a contrast that made his eyes shine like Heavenly amethysts. And then there was Lucifer, most hated and most loved, whose pale skin and dark hair made his powerfully compelling eyes look like coal being consumed by violet flame. Much like Lucifer, Raphael liked to tease his brother and sat mimicking his downcast expression.

Michael's face broke into a rare smile. "Raphael! What are you doing here?" Raphael almost never sought him out these days and he was truly pleased to see him. He relaxed almost immediately because the two of them could speak openly. Raphael smiled in return, all trace of teasing gone, and put his arm around Michael, thinking that such affection had once been an easy thing in Heaven.

"I thought it best to keep you informed of Enoch's activities." Michael said nothing. "He's been writing again, almost incessantly. The only thing he does more is ask when he might walk with the Lord." Raphael sighed. "A little bit ago, I brought him fruit and wine, thinking perhaps it would soothe his mind." Raphael stopped, looking up at the throne and then at Michael. "It didn't. He's been raving, tossing his papers, running around the gardens like an animal. I just finished picking up after him." He sighed again. Nursemaid to a madman was not exactly his calling.

Michael's voice was heavy with weariness, "What has he done now?"

Raphael decided it was best to be blunt. "The scraps of parchment I collected … All contain fragments of the Emerald Hill Prophecy."

Michael face contorted with frustration. "So he ripped up a scroll. That's not new."

"You misunderstand. He had written the whole thing over and over. He keeps whispering to himself. It sounds like 'she is born' and more concerning 'his return'." Raphael took in Michael's silent reaction. "I'm worried. He's been very astute about things unseen before …"

Michael stood abruptly and strode out of the Throne Room. Standing under a shining arch, an air of command settled onto Michael's shoulders like a comfortable and familiar cloak. "Summon Uriel, and see if you can find The Voice, as well. I may need him to go to Earth. Sandalphon probably knows where he's gone. Let's see what we can make of this nonsense!" Raphael set off, only just catching the words Michael spoke to himself, his voice like tempered steel. "If there is any choice in this Prophecy I will be the one to make it."

So Below

In a place about as far from Heaven as you could get, a demon reclined in a mountain of pillows, absentmindedly chewing his thumb nail, lost in dark thoughts. Even basking in the illusion of sunlight created by his enchanted lanterns did nothing to improve his mood. He did his best to make his home as much like Earth as possible, refused to suffer his demon form, surrounded himself with human souls, but some days his head was the only place he could stand to be. His servants, souls he had personally chosen to safeguard, quietly puttered around with their own endeavors, giving him a wide berth. Even his personal attendants, normally welcome company, kept their distance, understanding his silence as the wall it was meant to be.

The recent council had been grim. They always were. War with Heaven, blah, blah … burn the Earth, blah, blah … we want control of blah, blah … blah, blah, something pointless … and then everyone went back to torturing, or drinking, or screwing, or whatever they did when they weren't licking the King's boots or secretly cozying up to Lucifer. Irritating as the councils always were, his assignment to use his skill for language to examine some supposedly earth-shattering prophecy was a new addition as unexpected as it was unwelcome. He still had a bit of a grudge against prophets, since the seer in his little village was largely responsible for the fact that he'd become a demon. Well, maybe not that, but she was why he died with no family left behind to carry on his name, to be part of the storied history of the Isles with kings, and wars, and conquest. Besides, he could barely be bothered with maintaining the appearance of giving half a damn most of the time and tried to go unnoticed as much as possible. He focused on protecting his quiet corner of Hell and those he sheltered in it.

He stared into his golden goblet, brooding silently. It was clear from the building tension that a battle was coming. Not the *Battle on the Mount* nonsense the rest of Hell blathered about, but a proper war. He thought he could rouse himself for a real war, like in the old days when he held sturdy human weapons against encroaching clans and then the cursed Roman invaders. He'd been well suited to it and his people had admired him for his eloquence, bravery, and skill. Being strong and handsome hadn't hurt his influence any either. He supposed Hell wasn't so different for someone like him; still revered, powerful, a force to be reckoned with. His human life had lasted less than twenty years and had come to a brutal end at the hands of those interlopers from the Seven Hills. But he had known affection, beauty, and the honesty that characterized life as a tribal warrior. He missed the simplicity. That and fresh air. Damn, but the smell of sulphur was wearing on him lately.

Maybe a vacation would be just the thing: sleep on a soft bed, maybe seduce a young lady or two, have a decent meal, experiment with his supernatural alcohol tolerance. It shouldn't be remarkable and it might make this little corner of eternity bearable, or at least break up the discontent constantly buzzing around his head like a cloud of mosquitoes. He thought he would be granted leave if he could invent some reason his work with prophecy required such a trip. He was well-known for being able to talk equals or subordinates into nearly anything and to sway the King and even Lucifer in matters from completely trivial to absolutely crucial when he made the effort. The last time it had come up he hadn't even had to bother using his power to convince them. He'd enjoyed getting his way with nothing more than the charm he'd been born with.

A light touch on his shoulder broke into his thoughts. He glanced up at one of his beautiful souls, her silver hair and blue eyes making her exquisitely wrinkled face one of his favorite sights. Her clearly Celtic bone structure reminded him of his grandmother. He thought perhaps if he looked into it, they might actually be related. His sisters had survived, some of his nieces and nephews, probably. Of course he'd never bother to find out. His family obligations ended when defending them got him sent below. He studiously ignored the thought that he had the exact same pleasantly sharp chin and dimples that highlighted the bow-shaped mouth smiling down at him. "Lord Ronoven, a visitor."

He always found being addressed by his Hellish moniker a bit jarring, so it focused his attention swiftly. He could now hear for himself the hooves trip-trapping over the stone bridge outside this chamber, like a goat from the old fairytale. Arranging his expression and posture to convey a supreme lack of interest, he tipped his tousled blond head at his doorman, "You'll have to let him in, I suppose."

His visitor burst in self-importantly before the door was all the way open. This grotesque servant of the type nearly always preferred by the King sent a putrid stench into his nostrils as it approached. In its squealing voice, eliciting involuntary associations with fingernails on chalkboards or some other hideous sound of torture devised in the Pit, the creature squawked, "I BRING ORDERS!"

Ronoven took a drink and raised his golden eyebrows at the creature. Its rheumy eyes stared haughtily back. Always prone to a hot temper, Ronoven's displeasure boiled over. It was about time the King's minions remembered he was not to be ordered about like a mere servant. He was a Count and Marquis of Hell! He could be King if he so desired. He considered more than dabbling in

Hell's politics to be a good way to come to a bad end, but by the Fire his servants wouldn't make his nobles want to vomit! His voice, beautiful and deadly, cut through the room. "You forget yourself, Worm. I will have respect in my territory."

Heedless of the clear warning, the creature screeched, "I SERVE THE KING!"

Smiling now, the lethal smile of a true warrior and accomplished demon, he replied quietly, "As do we all in our own way. But this is my dominion. And in this house, I am Lord. Remember yourself hereafter."

The creature stood stammering and gibbering in front of him.

"Gareth, fetch my flenching knife so I might loosen the tongue of this pitiful excuse for a messenger." Undone by the mere implication of threat, the creature began to plead in a wheedling voice. Ronoven rose to his feet with deliberate slowness so his towering height could intimidate, his amber eyes glowing in rhythm with his golden aura. "Last chance, little pimple, before all your master has to show for his trouble is a bag of bones."

Groveling now, the creature mewled, "A thousand pardons, your magnificence. Golden Ronoven, of whom maidens still surely sing, the most beauteous noble in all of Hell ..." This went on for some time. Ronoven didn't bother to suppress the deep roll of his eyes. "By your leave, my gracious Lord, I bear a message of some importance," the creature finally panted.

Ronoven stood, arms folded across his broad chest, and smiled crookedly, "Get on with it."

Determined to complete his mission so he could go enjoy some tender new souls as payment for services rendered, the creature sputtered, "My Lord, the King orders, he wants, that is, he requests ..." Ronoven waved an impatient hand. "Your services are required, on Earth, with all due haste."

Concealing a smile, he spread his palms welcoming further explanation.

"The girl from the Emerald Hill Prophecy is born and must be brought into the fold. Our dread Sovereign requests your presence in the Great Hall tomorrow so you might share your expertise."

The creature handed over the orders to a servant, knowing Ronoven would take nothing from him directly. The boy bowed as he passed it on and faded back behind a statue, wanting as much distance from the blatantly monstrous messenger as possible. Ronoven skimmed it briefly. "Excellent. I will send word he may expect me." Ronoven beckoned to Gareth, who bowed his head and came forward.

"My Lord," squeaked the messenger, "I would be happy to deliver your reply."

Hell could use one less revolting torturer of the innocent. Sa'ir had given him the perfect excuse with his disrespect. Ronoven took a shining dagger from Gareth's outstretched palms. He turned it over in his graceful hands and it glittered wickedly in the firelight. "Of course you would. But I only require your skin for the task."

The creature's eyes widened and his words left him.

"Those pardons you requested are in short supply."

Chapter 1

"'Tis no sin to cheat the Devil."
~ Daniel Defoe

onoven approached the Great Hall with reluctance. He preferred to fly under the radar whenever possible and this level of unwanted attention could spoil his nicely private existence if he didn't manipulate perceptions with care. Understanding he would be called upon to speak to the masses rather than in the private audience he would have preferred, he had donned his preferred battledress. Clad in a traditional hunting drape and soft kilt over bare legs and feet, a sword slung across his back, he knew his simple attire highlighted his humanity, but also showed off his height and strength. It would serve to remind everyone of his daring and cunning in battle, not to mention how quickly and ferociously his soul had distinguished itself here before being imbued with any power, against demons and on his own merits. In life he had fought with legendary bravery and more than two thousand years hence was still spoken of by those who held to the old ways, even if they did so mostly in secret. Calling a full audience about a routine mission was unusual. This had to be another power play. Ronoven thought he would do well to distinguish himself as worthy of recruiting by all sides, since when it came to skins, he preferred his own intact.

As he approached the Hall, the door toadies (he came up with unflattering appellations for all the King's servants) parted the doors, bowing deeply. This demonstration of subservience usually reserved for the true royalty of Hell made it clear his response to the King's messenger had its desired effect. He stepped into the Hall with all the dignified confidence he could manufacture as the herald rumbled, "Lord Ronoven, Master of Expression, Gatherer of Old Souls, and Collector of the Unwanted."

The thunderous response to his introduction caused Ronoven's eyes to sweep the chamber more carefully than he might otherwise have done. The hall was carved from shining obsidian, stretching up past where the eye could see, containing vast overflowing galleries of demons. Those with title sat comfortably on the luxurious seats in the lower levels, while those of lesser rank were

11

relegated to the dizzying heights above, their eyes glowing dimly in the darkness. But marquis or messenger, soldier or slave, all called out loudly, stomping their feet and banging their chests. Ronoven was wise enough not to be overly flattered. The King had already whipped up the crowd. So … Castor wanted a show. Ronoven was more than happy to play his part and dissolve into the background, allowing the King and his inner court to soak up all the attention … and consequences. Following the expected protocol, he bowed, approaching the central platform. He noted, inclining his head, how the King and his most favored nobles occupied the far end of the table, a step up from their usual place. Most of them appeared in their demonic form today, something that Lucifer didn't permit at the table. But the fallen angels were conspicuously absent.

The hall quieted, awaiting the ritual of welcome.

"My dread Liege, I have come at your command."

"Lord Ronoven, you are welcome."

"I am here to serve." Ronoven dipped his head with convincing deference.

Completing the ceremony the King replied, "I accept your service."

Ronoven straightened and considered the situation. Only those in command of twenty legions or more were permitted a seat here and few with less than forty were even considered. He was a fairly minor dignitary and the complete omission of Lucifer's people might offer an opportunity to stage-manage things so he'd be free to do as he pleased. He adjusted the short cape signifying his position and sat at the far corner of the table next to an acquaintance he could tolerate, mostly because she, too, refused to go about looking like a fairytale monster. He plastered on a false expression of reverence and looked toward the stout little gargoyle currently known as the King of Hell.

The King held up his hands to still the crowd. "As you know, we are assembled to discuss the Emerald Hill Prophecy." The King paused and looked significantly at Ronoven. "Lord Ronoven has studied the documents at length and we would hear his thoughts on the matter. The time is upon us. The girl's protectors are gifted at spell work and her location is hidden. What say you, Lord Ronoven?"

Ronoven rose, his handsome face a studied mask, camouflaging his contempt for prophecy as well as his scorn for this self-important little demon who fancied himself a monarch. Lucifer barely tolerated the demons' pretention of holding real power and no one with half a brain had any illusions about who was really in charge. But the pretense kept the peace, such as it was, and as this demon was presently the nominal King, there was no reason for Ronoven not to make the most of his regard.

"Majesty, allow me to begin by expressing my awe. Your wisdom is unbounded." His dramatic pause allowed the throng to raise their voices in agreement. "You act, as always, Sire, with decisiveness and forethought. I see not one of the Fallen present to influence our plans. When Lucifer hears of this he will be enraged. But here sits our Sovereign, bold and unafraid." He knew he was banging it out for the cheap seats but they were eating it up so he doubled down. "The Prophecy is clear. The girl can truly free us to use Earth as our playground! As we deserve! With angelic magic in our way it could take years to find her! Our King acts courageously. I serve him proudly, as should all!"

The crowd became deafening in its adulation, lest anyone think them one jot less loyal than Lord Ronoven. *There*, he thought. *That ought to do it.* He glanced at the King, pleased to see his chest puffed with pride, face red, smile ready to split his skull. Style over substance was always effective when Castor's ego was involved. Ronoven seated himself, assuming a semi-subservient posture, hiding his inward satisfaction that he'd managed to speak without saying a damned thing.

The King vaulted to his feet. "Now we have heard the honest truth of things. Time to act for the good of demon-kind!"

The audience was eating out of his hand, primed as they were by the opening festivities and now Ronoven's encouragement. Even the nobles at the table were caught up in the moment, though they should have known better. He knew Castor, basking in the adoration of the masses, would go on a bit. Once Lucifer found out what the King was up to, the retribution would be swift, the King's fall long and hard. Lucifer was always good for an entertaining grandstand. The pretentious pretend king had earned a slapping down from the real ruler of Hell. *It's too bad I won't be around to see it*, Ronoven thought.

This pleasant daydream was interrupted by the thunder of the hall's massive doors slamming open. The heads of the doormen were tossed unceremoniously onto the table, rolling down its length and stopping with their clouded eyes and lolling tongues facing the King. The Fallen had arrived, a bit earlier than Ronoven had anticipated. The hall fell silent in an instant, the clamor quelled by the demons' well-founded fear of Lucifer and his most trusted warriors.

The frightened herald gathered his wits and squeaked, "The Archangel Lucifer, Morning Star, First of the Fallen and … guests." He stepped away, pleased to have retained his head. Scores of cloaked figures solemnly entered the room in a silent procession, each carrying a dark sword held aloft. These imposing figures filled the outer circle of the gallery, facing the legions, their heads bowed and identities obscured by silken hoods. They also lined both sides of the doorway and dropped to one knee. A low humming emanated from them, whether generated by their sheer collective power or some chant unknown to the rest of Hell was impossible to guess.

Lucifer entered; a figure of indescribable beauty and grace. He was dressed simply; red tunic, black sash, shining black wings furled at his back like an elegant drape. His sword, the gleaming blade of an archangel, swung from a jeweled scabbard at his hip. His regal bearing made clear what all of those gathered already knew; not all the demons in Hell could hope to make a stand against him. Without a word or sideways glance he crossed the silent hall. His purposeful stride covered the distance in less than no time despite the unhurried fluidity of his movements. He cleared his throat. The King meekly bowed out of Lucifer's seat, motioning one of his nobles to clear the way for him to sit at Lucifer's right hand. Lucifer spoke with quiet menace, his voice echoing throughout the hall.

"Dogs sit at their master's feet." As he took his seat he held out his hand and quirked his fingers as though beckoning a pet. Castor knew better than to disobey. He was not the first King of Hell and planned to keep his position as long as possible. Lucifer continued theatrically, "Your Highness, I was most injured at the lack of invitation to this gathering." His Tyrian purple eyes narrowed. "Well, more blindingly furious than hurt but I'm sure you take my meaning." He gripped the King's collar and glowered into his face. "This ridiculous prophecy is false. So a half-breed has been born. She is an infant, basically human, and poses no threat. It's not as though the Grigori are still running around siring Nephilim." He waved a dismissive hand. "Since she worries you so much, she will die. Your only concern is to find her. I will send my assassins when she is located." Lucifer's eyes swept the room. "It is hardly an emergency. When you find her summon Azazel. These rumblings of prophecy mean nothing." Lucifer stood and patted the King on the head. "Good doggie," he murmured quietly, but in the exaggerated hush hovering over the hall his voice carried. He glided out without another word, followed swiftly by his entourage.

Silence held for an endless moment. Then someone coughed. The King rose unsteadily, hand resting on the arm of a chair. "Well, you heard him. Find the girl."

Without any formal ritual of dismissal, the King scurried from the hall whispering brief instructions to selected demons as he fled. Ronoven smiled, well-satisfied. Rising purposefully, he headed to his chambers to prepare, thinking he could not have hoped for a more ideal outcome. Even Lucifer thought the prophecy was a sham, and the insurmountable task of finding one child among millions meant he could go to Earth on this so-called mission and no one would bother after him for decades.

Chapter 2

"It is better to rule in Hell than serve in Heaven."
~ John Milton

Lucifer strode into his private chambers, his contented smile making him almost unbearably lovely. He felt their admiring eyes skimming over his perfectly proportioned height and breadth, knew they were nearly mesmerized by the almost blue glints in his dark hair, and could see them all trying to catch their own reflections in his almond-shaped eyes. All the Archs had eyes tinted some shade of purple, but his were a deep reddish violet that were at times velvet soft, at others sharp like sunlight through a garnet. Of course, nothing made him more attractive to them than these little displays of power. There was nothing he enjoyed more than demeaning that squat little schemer Castor, the so-called King of Hell, unless of course he could humiliate the little pretend king *and* make him jump like a frog on a hotplate. It was all part of demonstrating who was really in charge of the nether realms. Without a war on, maintaining discipline among the Fallen was tricky. The average workaday demon was easy enough to manipulate, but Castor's eventual replacement was a steady source of information on the inner circles of Hell's hierarchy. Between the nobles maneuvering and the King's delusions of grandeur, he liked to reiterate his superiority to those with some semblance of power. It kept them mostly in line.

Lucifer's most trusted associates sat on marble benches waiting to hear his real plans. He mounted the mother-of-pearl stairs and arranged himself on his alabaster throne. Lucifer paused, gathering his thoughts, considering what was at stake. He slowly absorbed his surroundings, enjoying the illusion. The room appeared to be carved from white marble with silvery veins and tiny fossilized sea creatures. Edges inlaid with gold gleamed in the light of softly glowing orbs floating at intervals throughout the room. No sulphur tainted the air here, only the soft scent of flowers. In the corners, Fallen angels softly strummed golden harps, none playing the same music, but creating a rich tapestry of sound nonetheless; a potent antidote to the cacophony of Hell. It was a poor imitation of Heaven but it was as close as he could come. For now.

He was certain the prophecy could not be divinely inspired. Still, it was from a traditionally reliable source and, even well before the appointed hour, it had interested Michael enough to negotiate. Lucifer already confirmed the birth of a half-angelic child not long ago. That didn't mean this prophecy was anything but bunk, but considering the child's parentage and the timing, it was plausible. If the girl were not hidden by the powerful magic of the Guardians he would claim her now and see what unfolded. If the prophecy proved true he could command her and return to Heaven victorious, claiming dominion over all Creation. With so much on the line Lucifer was determined to proceed as though the prophecy were the Word itself. There was nothing left to lose. And everything to gain.

Azazel cleared his throat to break the silence. Lucifer turned his gaze to him, inviting him to begin. "My Lord, if I may ask?" His expression indicated that his question was impertinent.

Lucifer smiled. Impertinence was one of the things he enjoyed about Azazel's company. He smoothed his sleek dark hair away from his angular face, his lips quirking slightly. "Why am I allowing a bunch of incompetent demons to look for the girl?"

Azazel chuckled, the lines giving character to his intimidating countenance. "Well, yes, that." There was general tentative agreement all around.

"Demons draw little notice. Malicious possession is typically interpreted as madness or drug-addled raving. Purposeful possession is safe as houses. All of Hell's soldiers could dance around Earth in their monkey suits and leave the humans none the wiser. Besides," Lucifer scoffed, "the few nobles involved favor their human form even here." He paused and scanned the room. "Demons intermingle much less noticeably, protecting our secrecy. Angels are conspicuous. Our steps echo loudly. And anything noticed by those barely-sentient bags of meat is likely to be noticed Above. Particularly given Heaven's historical vigilance regarding our presence on Earth."

There was a collective shudder at the mention of drawing Heaven's interest. It had taken nearly all of human history to carve out the barely tolerable existence they had. No one wanted to jeopardize that by attracting celestial attention. Despite their outward compliance everyone attempted to hide their relief when Azazel voiced their secret thoughts. "Forgive me, my Lord, but I find putting such important work into their unworthy hands … distasteful."

Lucifer proceeded to explain but the edge in his voice let them know it was not open for discussion. "I have work I will require from your ranks. It should be limited enough to draw no notice. If you are not given an assignment you will aid your fellows." He regarded his second. "Bhaal, we will show our support to the king's mission by sending instructions to Castor regarding the signs. Remind him they are to summon The Assassin. They cannot discover we want her alive, and mustn't dare act alone. Put some fear into him," Lucifer smiled. "He's terrified of you."

Bhaal's wolfish grin was wicked, his face handsome and terrifying all at once. "That shouldn't be difficult considering what I did … well, am doing to his predecessor. His fear is not misplaced."

Lucifer indicated his most powerful mage. "Armaros will look into breaking the enchantments shrouding the child's whereabouts. Her protectors may make some mistake or the enchantments may somehow be vulnerable."

Armaros rose and bowed, leaving the chamber immediately. It did not pay to waste time when given a direct order. Pleased with Armaros' obedience, Lucifer frowned at the continuing expressions of dissent around the room. He directed instructions to Bhaal again. "When you speak with Castor have him order the demons to see what they can discover of potential magical solutions. They already know the girl's protectors are using magic and they may just stumble onto something useful."

Bhaal tilted his chin in agreement, thinking Lucifer had a talent for keeping people busy with trivialities and distracted from his motives. Lucifer turned his gaze formally to Lahash, inclining his head in admiration. Her particular power was beyond his understanding. Much like the gifts bestowed on humans, this one seemed like perhaps God hadn't thought things through. Lahash could see the hand of divine will and, in some cases, interfere with outcomes. She was not one of his original recruits, but her considerable powers and her willingness to obey his orders quickly made her a favorite.

"Lahash alone will go to Earth. She is able to move unseen by Heaven and most of the demons hop to do her bidding." Lucifer regarded her eager young face. "You know what to look for?"

She slowly blinked her assent with hooded pale eyes, pleased to have been chosen. "I do, my Lord."

She bowed her head, her platinum hair falling around her porcelain face like a curtain, concealing her expression of satisfaction as she chanted almost inaudibly, and vanished. Lucifer observed each of them, gauging their reactions. He saw one beautiful countenance appearing particularly peevish. He adored looking at her. She reminded him of his brother Raphael, could almost be one of the First Order, if not for her cocoa-colored eyes and thick dark blond hair. Amused, he chose to single her out. "Someone horning in on your territory, Lilith my love? Feeling slighted are we?" His mocking smile drew a strong reaction from one of his oldest associates.

"Of course I am. You want a child brought to you? That my *job*, Lucifer!" she huffed.

Lucifer steepled his fingers under his chin, weighing his words so as to reveal what was necessary without saying too much. "Ordinarily, Lilith would be justified in hoping for this assignment. The claiming of children is normally her purview. But when the child is from the Line, more subtle measures are required." He allowed his words to sink in. No one expected this particular wrinkle. It was mere chance he had discovered the information. Azazel shifted uncomfortably and Lucifer raised a finger, inviting him to speak.

"My Lord, in light of this new insight ... Does that not make it more critical ..?" He trailed off under Lucifer's flinty gaze.

"I understand your diffidence, but this more measured and stealthier tactic will be the best means to acquiring the desired end. We will be bold in due time." Most of the group appeared placated, but Azazel still seemed unconvinced. "Yes, Assassin? What now?" Lucifer was out of patience.

"My Lord, forgive me. I am only anxious to see us succeed," Azazel offered by way of apology. "But, Lucifer ... what about God?"

Lucifer stood to dismiss them. "My friends, rest assured it will not be long until we are once again in our rightful place." He opened his hands to indicate the meeting was adjourned.

He waited a beat.

"He is in no position to oppose me, I assure you."

His associates looked back in confused trepidation. He allowed a broad smile to spread across his face.

"God is not a factor."

Chapter 3

"There are three things all wise men fear:
the sea in a storm, a night with no moon,
and the anger of a gentle man."
~ Patrick Rothfuss

L ahash inhaled the damp night air, her wavy white blond hair billowing behind her. The stiffening breeze of an oncoming storm carried the tang of salt, and in the quiet of this sleeping suburban neighborhood, she could just make out the sound of the inexorable rise and fall of the sea against the shoreline close by. In the distance, Boston cast a pink glow into the sky above it. She knew her pale skin, nearly colorless eyes, and equally fair hair, made her glow like a phantom in the night. Still, she smiled. She was so close to her goal.

After several years of futile spell work and observing the general uselessness of demons, not to mention her own seemingly endless wandering without so much as a sniff of the girl, Lahash had the ghost of an idea. Her particular power allowed her to sense divine will and work with some aspects of cause and effect. This was a difficult power to use because it had to function over the background noise of all Creation, many chains of events large and small, conducting the symphony of the unfolding universe. Regardless, no amount of magic could veil true intention from one of the Line forever.

When the Fallen had accomplished some verifiable divination magic, they discovered the Templars had revealed themselves to the young family and offered their active protection. Lahash knew it was only a matter of time before the parents became consumed with her safety. It was risky for the Knights to have come forward but it was not outside the realm of possibility they were aware of the prophecy and Hell's magic seemed to indicate the mother could bear no more children. If that were true, and if Lucifer's interpretation was accurate, this child was definitely the one. It was best to collect her now so she could be brought up properly, knowing the way she should go. Surely the Templars had come forward thinking the very same thing. Lahash began to focus all of her power on sensing a specific intention. It had taken time to use this knowledge. At first, every time Lahash thought she had pinpointed the Scion's thoughts the signal would dissolve and disappear. Then Lahash had begun to feel a tugging on her awareness that grew into an undeniable echo of true divine will that held the clear, if inarticulate, message: *I will keep her safe.*

As time passed a detailed image formed; situated at the end of a cul-de-sac in a pleasant suburban neighborhood was a neat little house surrounded in privacy hedges on a well-manicured double lot. At first the image was maddening. It looked like any suburb in the Western world. Once the picture became so clear it was more like a memory she was able to expand its reach. Slowly, the smell of the sea and a flat-sounding stream of consciousness permeated her thoughts. Her efforts left her exhausted and unable to move for days. Over time she discerned the unassuming little house was in a middle-class neighborhood less than an hour from Boston. The physical searching had been daunting, but rather than relying on magic she had resorted to using resources in the local demon network which had further delayed her search. After a few unproductive expeditions amounting to fruitless real estate shopping, she had a strong sense this was the neighborhood and if she didn't move tonight this wonderful clarity would dissolve back into the blunted itching in her mind she had suffered for years.

Her eyes raked down the row of houses full of mostly darkened windows to the little white and yellow raised ranch at the end. The bright streetlamps illuminated the details from her vision as perfectly as the noonday sun, even on this dark night of the new moon and overcast skies. Then she saw something that made her success certain, a cage of magical wards against angels and demons alike surrounding the house; a complicated enchantment if the girl and even her magically-humbled father could come and go as they pleased. She would be wary until she saw the child, but this had to be the place. Lahash crept closer until she was at the edge of the silvery spell, only just visible to her magically enhanced angelic eyes.

In the shadow of the hedges she began chanting. The smell of sulphur filled the air as neighborhood dogs began to bark and cats screeched and ran from nearby yards. Thunder rumbled in the sky, lightning struck the middle of the street and several demons, gaudy and terrifying, emerged from the steaming pavement to join her. The rain that threatened all evening had begun, precipitated by her magic. The largest, ugliest, and most obviously powerful of the group stepped forward, steam rising from his scabrous shoulders as the rain struck him. He spoke in a low rumbling growl.

"Lady Lahash, how may we serve?"

Lahash pointed to the little dwelling, its security lights now blazing in the dark. "Seal off all exits and guard the perimeter. Let no one in or out. Until I give the command, do not advance on the wards. It would only injure you and sound their alarms."

The demons melted into the night. Shadows passed in front of the windows. For such a late hour there was a great deal of activity in the little house. Lahash took a moment to be sure none of the wards had been breached and then murmured the incantation to summon Azazel. His rasping softly menacing voice greeted her.

"Have we made some progress at last?"

"A thread of divine intention is radiating from right here." She motioned vaguely.

Azazel surveyed the scene. "There could be few other reasons for such warding." He paused looking sullenly at Lahash, who was Lucifer's chosen commander. He yielded to her, but grudgingly. "My Lady, what is our plan?"

Lahash felt a bit smug at his deference and grateful Lucifer had been unequivocal about the chain of command. Azazel had a heavy hand and this mission had to be precise. She gave him a feline smile. "Wheels are in motion, Assassin. The wards will be broken momentarily."

Azazel frowned, "All the activity? Could they be alerted to our presence?"

"No, but something has them stirred up. Your position is at the rear."

Azazel disappeared into the increasing drizzle. Lahash stood quietly, her head bowed. She began to pluck at the tiniest threads of universal divine intent. She soon saw headlights round the corner. Near the edge of the road, a woman in a raincoat so large as to be cumbersome was attempting to walk an enormous dog, straining against its leash. The car came up the newly wet road gathering speed. Lahash intensified her will and in a moment of dark serendipity the dog slipped its collar and ran into the road. The speeding driver swerved to avoid the animal, overcorrected, and bounced over the curb, through the bushes and the first ward, then crashed into the corner of the house severing the net of the second. The force of the crash and the iron in the car combined to break the wards. As human chaos threatened the night, the demons closed in, snarling and snuffling, with Lahash close behind. Completely unexpectedly, two men emerged from around the side of the house firing handguns. The demons fell, flesh smoking, writhing in agony. Whatever ammunition they were using was deadly to demons.

Enraged things were already running off the rails, Lahash gave a flick of her wrist, and was rewarded with a satisfying wet crunch as the men's heads twisted grotesquely, settling at a sickening angle as their bodies fell into a lifeless heap. From the other side of the house came a piercing wail followed by a terrible gurgling and a powerful voice shouting, "Maggie!"

Lahash teleported to the rear of the house where the danger in the air was a physical thing. On the muddy ground lay the body of a beautiful young woman, rain falling into her unseeing eyes, blood from the gaping wound that tore her from belly to throat washing around her. Her aura's power faded into the night like her blood in the water. By her side, on his knees, was a man, dark wavy hair plastered to his forehead by the rain. The subtle wavering shine in the air around him revealed him to be an angel, fallen certainly, but not corrupted as one of the Fallen of Hell, rather in a form that would one day force his soul to face judgment as though he were entirely human. In his arms, a little girl of perhaps three or four, with soaking dark strawberry-blond curls and dampening footed pajamas stained with her mother's blood, thrashed helplessly, wailing, "Mama! Mama!" over and over as tears and struggling reddened her cheeks.

Azazel, eyes glazed, right hand dripping blood, spoke with deadly threat, the rain near his face turning to ice and tinkling to his feet with the terrible menace of his power. "Give me the child and you may yet live."

The angel stood slowly, adjusting the girl on his hip. Tears streamed down his face, mingling with blood from a cut over his eye. He had only barely prevented this creature from taking his daughter, pulling her from her mother's arms before she could hit the ground. He knew there was no help for his wife since the beautiful glow of her aura now surrounded their child. Beginning to quiet, the little girl reached up and patted his cheek with her tiny hand. He brushed her wet curls off her forehead and kissed her. She stilled as if by magic. "It's okay, baby. I've got you now. You just look at me okay? Don't you look away," he whispered. She stared up at him raptly, and as she continued patting his cheek his bleeding stopped. Two more men advanced from the dark to come to his aid, but he waved them back.

"You cannot stand against us both," Lahash said in a hypnotically soothing voice. "We don't intend to harm your daughter. You can come with us and witness her rise to prominence in Hell! We will make her a queen!"

The angel stood his ground, his deep blue eyes narrowing.

"Give her to me, Arialon." Azazel's voice was like a blade. "Do as I say or I will take her by force and you will die here tonight next to her whore of a mother."

At the word *whore*, the angel's eyes flashed and a powerful explosion emanated from him, the shockwave visible in the rain. This display of force was surprising, as he was unimposing in appearance, muscular but not overly tall, handsome, with features that spoke of Mediterranean or Middle Eastern origin, but not particularly striking, just altogether human looking. Besides, he should have been limited by his physical form; but righteous fury made him powerful. The men threw themselves to the ground to dodge the full impact and Lahash was thrown back into the mud. Only Azazel, shaken by the blast, stood his ground. The fullness of his power augmented by every spell Hell could muster barely allowed him to keep his feet. Materializing next to Arialon and the child was a towering figure, appearing in the fullness of his Heavenly form, dark flowing hair billowing in the breeze, wings unfurled and white as snow. He put a hand on the angel's shoulder. "Ari, I'm so sorry. I just felt the call. I thought this was all well in hand. Something must have interfered."

Azazel hissed, "You!"

Without words, he turned his blazing silver-grey eyes on the Assassin. Tears of white flame began to run down Azazel's face. He struggled to make some argument or threat to prevent his final death but could only manage unintelligible choking sounds. The angel reached out and closed his fist and Azazel was consumed. Lahash stumbled back into the light. "Davidos!"

"Yes, Lahash," his voice was quiet, almost compassionate. "Mind yourself or I will be only too happy to smite another Deserter." She stammered for a moment under his gaze. "I require a messenger and you'll do."

She snapped, "You want to talk to him? I will call him to us and he can claim his prize!"

"Then I would be forced to summon Michael. We both know how that ended the last time." Of course, he had no intention of involving Michael, but he let a cold smile play on his lips anyway.

"You expect me to return empty handed and with news of the fall of Lucifer's chief assassin?" She was incredulous.

Everyone could feel Davidos's power building again. "That is exactly what I expect. Deliver it with a personal message from me, if you please." His tight smile made Lahash fidget uncomfortably, like a child caught with her hand in the cookie jar right before dinner. "Tell Lucifer the girl is hidden from Heaven and Hell and will remain so. This child has a life of her own to live, regardless of any prophecy or the wishes of angels or demons. Now, go."

He waved his hand dismissively. Lahash growled like a feral animal and vanished with a hiss of steam. Davidos surveyed the scene. In the distance, red flashing lights and sirens approached, responding to the crash out front. He would have to act swiftly. He obliterated the smoldering pile of wailing demons with a thought, and then the two men dispatched by Lahash were consumed by the white flames. He turned his attention to the body of the former Scion, bowing his head. Ari moved toward him, clutching the little girl almost desperately. All his anger evaporated in his sorrow, his raw panic. He only pleaded, "No, Davidos, don't. Please don't."

"Ari, she's already gone." Ari fell back to his knees beside his wife, the woman for whom he had given up Heaven, thinking only to put himself between her body and his friend.

"I'll get you to safety and see things are tended to here, but this body is a complication you cannot afford. Think of your daughter. Please."

Ari gazed up beseechingly. Despite her father's shaking, the little girl had begun to doze peacefully against him, her head tucked into his neck, oblivious to anything but the warm strength of his arms and the lateness of the hour. The two remaining men came forward; muddy, bruised, but ready to help. Davidos indicated the approaching police cars, speaking directly into their minds. Immediately they moved off to smooth talk some town police, prepared with a story of being house-sitters who knew little other than which insurance company to call. *Gunfire? No, officers, just an awful lot of thunder. Coastal storms are something else, aren't they?* The Knights Templar were always prepared to do whatever it took to aid the preservation of the Line.

When they were alone, Davidos spoke softly, sadly; "Ari, I'm so sorry to have failed you. All of you. But I must. You know I must."

Ari shook his head violently, denying the words, but moved back, just barely out of the way, sitting hard on the wet ground, rocking his little girl gently and whispering his wife's name like a prayer, as holy fire erased the last evidence of her existence. Assuming a more human scale and appearance, Davidos helped Ari up from the mud and led them through the bushes at the back of the house to the car the Templars had arranged, already packed with essential possessions, including things belonging to Maggie that Ari would come to treasure. It was not ideal, but because of the child they were constrained to travel in earthly fashion. He took the sleeping child from her dazed father and buckled her in the carseat. Her eyes opened just a little and he said softly, "Hey, princess." He brushed her wet hair back from her forehead and she was magically clean and comfortably warm and dry again. She smiled as her thumb found her mouth and sleep overtook her again in a moment. Ari stood staring into the rain, a man utterly lost, completely bereft.

Gently, Davidos guided him into the car and climbed in to drive. His friend's breathing was rapid, his hands shaking, but he was still holding himself together. Davidos could feel Ari's pain and felt responsible. He knew Magdalena had been a very special person and their love had been more than enough to draw him from his place in Heaven. That child's sleepy trusting smile in the face of all she had been through was all Davidos needed to know he would do anything as her Guardian to ensure she had an opportunity to grow into the person she was meant to be, free from the interference of those who would try to choose her destiny. As they drove along the tempestuous coastline, he thought no matter how difficult it was they would have to discuss what was necessary to keep her safe.

"Ari," he began gently. "We're on our way to the safe house the Knights prepared for you." He paused when he heard Ari's sharp intake of air, knowing he was feeling the full weight of events. "Don't take this all on yourself. It was my responsibility." Ari looked like he was about to speak, but Davi pressed on. "Once your affairs have been settled, we'll discuss how you can make a life for her on the move and what protections will be the most effective." When Ari didn't respond, he continued. "You know what needs to happen. Until we can determine what to do about this prophecy, it hangs over her like a curse. And she's only a baby, Ari. Until she can understand her own power and use it to defend herself, it falls to us."

Ari nodded, but was unable to trust, or even find, his voice. The silence continued for several minutes; the only sound was the rain pattering against the car and the rhythmic swish of the windshield wipers. Thunder crashed. From the back seat, the child stirred and murmured, "Okay, Mama."

This undid Ari completely and he began to sob, his grief, his pain, the crushing sense that he could have prevented Maggie's death, and the weight of caring for their daughter on his own tore at him; his entire being rent by grief. He turned into himself, head in his hands. At least he still had their baby. Their little girl was safe. They disappeared from their old life into the night.

Everyone had tried to get them to leave, had told them of the danger.

He should have listened.

By God, he should have listened.

Chapter 4

"Experience is simply the name we give our mistakes."
~ Oscar Wilde

In the blazingly white room a battered Lahash approached the throne on her knees, with fear her sole company. Only Lucifer and Lord Bhaal at his right hand were present, and the silence was eerie, deafening. Lahash sorely missed the musicians today although she normally found their pretense at heavenly harmonies grating and counterfeit. Lucifer's face was contorted with a wrath so intense it was physically repelling but she continued to crawl forward. Bhaal stood, his hand on Lucifer's shoulder, whispering softly in his ear. She hated even looking at her master's chosen assistant. It wasn't that he was ugly, in fact at first glance he was strangely beautiful, but then you started to see things moving underneath; like his tanned skin was really just a sack for keeping worms. She shuddered at the foot of the dais, but prostrated herself and waited.

Lucifer's voice, normally a mellifluous joy, rasped like cold steel on a whetstone. "Where is the child, and what of my chief assassin?"

She dared not lift her eyes, but rather spoke to the floor; her shaking making her reply nearly unintelligible. "Mmmmy Llllorrrd. Ffffforgive me, I bbbbeg yyyyou. Ththethhe chchchild issss hihihidden, aaannnd Aaaazazel slslslain." She waited for death by his blade, but instead a hard kick of Lucifer's heeled boot sent her sprawling. Dark blood stained the marble floor.

"From the beginning. I will hear every detail of your failure."

Lahash struggled to her feet with her head bowed, but when Lucifer cleared his throat, she dropped back to one knee and in a quavering voice recounted the events of the evening. When she finished, the silence hummed like the air before a lightning strike. Finally, Lucifer broke the tension.

"Davidos." He spat the name like a piece of rotted meat. "The Templars," he was more contemptuous now. "Failure cannot be tolerated." He paused. "You will stand as an example." Lahash cowered as she heard the deadly sound of his blade being drawn. Bhaal interceded, placing his hand over Lucifer's.

"She is mine to do with as I will." His voice was still the grating of metal against rock.

"Lucifer, be reasonable. Imagine the failure of one without her gift. In fact, you don't have to imagine, do you? Just remember on it a bit." Lucifer's eyes darkened, but he seemed to be considering his advisor's words. "Azazel's life was forfeit the moment he struck down the Scion."

Bhaal's quiet assertion and sensible tone infuriated Lucifer. "You forget yourself!"

"No, Lucifer, you forget. I was worshipped as a god by generations of humans after I stood with you at the gates of Heaven. That fight cost me power and leverage, and though I would gladly pay the price again, it doesn't mean you owe me nothing."

The silence was heavy.

"Very well then." Lucifer sheathed his blade. "Lahash, resume your efforts to locate the girl." Lucifer reached down and grabbed Lahash by the chin and forced her to face him. "But you will be supervised. I don't care how long it takes you or what sacrifices you have to make. Find her and report to me directly." He let go of her roughly, annoyed that one to whom he showed open favor had failed so miserably and forced him to punish her with a loss of rank. Losing face was something he had difficulty tolerating. Lahash sensed her survival still hung by a thread and she scrambled out the doors.

"Bhaal, take responsibility for overseeing our operations from here. Report to me at once if your augury shows even the slightest deviation from orders." Bhaal bowed solemnly and began to make his way out of the throne room. Lucifer's sharp order stopped him at the door. "Send me Lilith, as well. Time is I have need of her."

The noise from outside Lucifer's throne room faded as Bhaal made his way to the Hall of the Old Ones. He saw to the wounds Lucifer had inflicted on Lahash with a brief incantation and sent her on her way. He enjoyed her discomfort when she looked at him, wondered if she was one of the few who could see his true face. But he had more important matters to consider. *God was somehow not a threat to his position? Lucifer had become far too unstable and prone to rash action since the Dawn Wars and his subsequent exile. Had those experiences taught him nothing? Imagine killing his best hope to find the girl. Lahash was the only one who'd made a modicum of progress since the child's birth. Lucifer was definitely slipping.* He smiled.

Entering the Hall, Bhaal took his seat at the round table, truly the only place in Hell where he was among equals. Around it, in the room that reflected the character of a grove in a deep wood, sat his peers, the Fallen Gods of the Dark Ones. Many in Hell understood Bhaal to be their ruler because of his position as Lucifer's second, but nothing could have been further from the truth. The group was accustomed to plurality and thus did quite well without a formal leader. His position had been mutually agreed upon as he was able to tactfully tolerate Lucifer's ego and they needed a representative to protect their position. He was also quite competent in dealing with the lesser beings inhabiting this realm and had a terrifying gift for keeping them in line. After a chilling chant to the Elder Gods from Before the Dawn, their Dark Parents, Bhaal spoke. "Brothers and Sisters, I thank you for accepting my invitation to gather. I wanted to offer something for your consideration. I sense an opportunity."

Chapter 5

"I was 'round when Jesus Christ had his moment of doubt and pain."
~ The Rolling Stones

It was a large room for a small man but, appointed simply as he had asked, it was one of his favorites. He was looking forward to getting away for a few weeks to walk in the gardens, sit in the shade, and perhaps feed the birds in solitude. The heat wave had begun in the spring and continued to hold the city in its grip. The Tiber had become fetid and sluggish, making a retreat all the more attractive. Perhaps the world would listen to his message about the changing planet, perhaps not. All he could do was observe, listen, share what wisdom he possessed, and keep the faith. For now, he would pack the few papers he wished to bring and wait for his transport.

Unexpectedly, and without a knock at the door, his young chamberlain bustled in. "Your Holiness, that man Bishop Calderon wrote you about just arrived. Missed his audience by two weeks, and now he won't leave!"

"Well, I'll have to see him then, won't I?" The Pope wore the gentle smile that was quickly becoming recognizable to even non-Catholics the world over. New to his position, he was accustomed to people being uncertain how to take him, but was determined in his approach to the office.

His chamberlain couldn't quite hide his shocked expression at the Holy Father's disdain for protocol. Then he smiled as well. His adherence to detail was why he'd been chosen for this post, and the Pope had been elected largely due to his unique thinking and gentle manner. Actually, they made a rather good team most of the time. "I beg your pardon, Holiness, but I never requested the man's documentation. I've just sent a member of the Guard to the Archive."

The Pope stood from his desk and beckoned for his visitor to be admitted. It was rare for anyone to be welcomed into the Pope's private apartments, to say nothing of someone known only through a letter of introduction from half a world away, so it would have been natural for the visitor to be awkward or unsure. The man who walked confidently into the room was neither. His dark hair, lightly olive skin, and slightly aquiline nose marked him as an Italian. His athletic build, squared shoulders, sun-lined face, and sure measured gait, marked him as a soldier. The penetrating blue of his eyes was less common, though striking, and the sharp intelligence behind them was readily apparent. Despite the fact that the man had obviously shaved and was trying to put his best foot forward for this meeting, his cheeks were shadowed even this early in the day. Clearly familiar with protocol, the man dipped down and kissed the proffered ring. When he rose, he looked directly into the Holy Father's eyes, and greeted him in faultless Latin. Impressed, the Pope's smile broadened, and he put his hands on the man's shoulders in a gesture of inexplicable instant affection.

"You speak Latin like you were born to it!" he exclaimed, pleased his unexpected visitor was an educated man.

His visitor grinned crookedly and spoke in a pleasant gravelly voice, "You might say that, Holiness." He clasped his hands in front of him. "I hate to drop onto your doorstep looking for another favor from the Church, but I need a new identity, a new job. I've been recognized."

He appeared unusually relaxed for a Vatican visitor and was thinking the Pope, despite the newly minted nature of the man's office, was certain to grant his request with the efficiency he had become accustomed to over the years. The Pope motioned for the young man to join him at his desk. When they were seated, the Pope folded his hands and looked at the man kindly. "I'm sorry my child, but who are you that you should ask this of the Church?"

"Didn't you receive the Bishop's letter?" The Pope nodded. "I thought you'd be expecting me." A look of real worry was creeping onto the man's handsome face. Before the Pope could reply, a Swiss Guard opened the door for an elderly little priest wearing linen gloves and carrying an ancient vellum document encased in something like glass. The little old man placed the case ceremoniously in front of the Holy Father and bowed slightly.

Visibly relaxing, the visitor exhaled, "Ah, my *bona fides* have arrived."

"Forgive me, Holiness, for the delay. These old legs are not what once they were." The Pope smiled, dismissing the man. The guard glanced over his shoulder at the Pope and his guest, but followed the tiny priest out and closed the door. The Pope donned gloves, his wire-rimmed glasses, and began to read, squinting. His brow furrowed and his eyes tightened as he read and then reread the ancient document. In his own time, he looked up at this man, whose papers designated him Paul Romano, with an expression of pity warring with irritation, even anger.

"It appears I must render you aid, as have many before me if these seals are to be trusted, but I must ask ..." The kindness inherent to his character kept the words from leaving his mouth, but nonetheless the question hovered in the air.

"Why in the name of Heaven should you be rendering aid to the gatekeeper of Pontius Pilate? It's a fair question, Holiness." He paused and pulled a pendant on a chain from inside his collar; the immediately recognizable symbol garnered him an encouraging nod. "I've made my peace with what some call my curse; repented my actions. I made my confession to Peter himself, and he baptized me. I am a penitent man, in need of help only the Church can provide."

The Pope stared at him thoughtfully for a few minutes, silent. The man looked back steadily, head cocked slightly to the side, inviting further questions. All at once the lines of the Pontiff's face smoothed and he appeared mollified. "I understand now why I am to help you, my child, but I admit to being curious as to why you need it."

"Thank eco-tourism, Holiness. One of my former students came to Costa Rica to see the sights and, in the middle of a marketplace, he recognized me as unchanged from his youth." He paused and a small tired smile appeared on his face. "It was a trip to celebrate his retirement, you understand ... The shock sent the poor man to the hospital." The Pope, his face now entirely sympathetic, listened carefully. "The fact that he appeared to have suffered an attack of some kind was all that saved my secrecy." He paled slightly. "I think I should be relocated. I have a sense this could happen again if I stay too close to the places I've been lately, even with a new name. I'm seeing too many coincidences for my own comfort. And too be honest, I've had rather enough of the heat." He paused, "I think I'd enjoy going back to America, if that's possible. Someplace up north. Maybe I could go skiing, catch a hockey game?"

The Pope picked up the iPad from his desk and keyed in a few things, finding the man's file and making necessary adjustments. With a few taps on this wondrous device new papers and a new assignment would begin being prepared immediately.

"Peter gave you his promise." A broad grin appeared on his mobile face. "Who am I to unbind the word of the first Pope?" Chuckling almost to himself, he rose. They walked toward the door. "We are happy to help you, my child. And a new place, one with cool breezes and new faces is easy enough to arrange. If you wouldn't mind though, I have just a small request ..."

They always asked. He couldn't blame them. "He was gentle. But strong. Powerful. You could feel it. I heard Him preach a few times in my travels. As a soldier of Rome, you're trained to be hard. Like stone. But being in the presence of someone like that ... It changes you." His breath caught slightly. The Holy Father stopped walking and turned the man firmly by the shoulders, his

31

expression encouraging. The man took a deep breath and continued. "When I struck Him … I did it more out of fear than anything. I didn't feel anger or hate. But … I don't know how to explain. It's like most conversion experiences I suppose. He challenged everything I'd ever been taught, everything I believed. I was terrified." He let out a slow resigned breath. "If I could take back my words, stay my hand, I would. But I can't. So now I'll walk in the world for a spell. My act of contrition, so to speak."

The Pope wiped a tear from his eye and embraced him. When his arms closed around this seemingly young man and he was no longer looking into his face, the man spoke again. "I saw Him once. Risen." The Pope's eyes grew round, his own faith confirmed by this simple exchange. "He told me anyone can be forgiven if they are truly repentant and make repairs for their actions. His last act on this earth to the man who struck Him was to give me hope. Hope. And I will make those repairs."

The Holy Father released the young man and said, "It is my pleasure to help you, my son. We'll have your papers for you presently." He smiled slightly at his own sense of word play; while it was a small joke, he firmly believed life's smiles were where you found them, and he was sure his visitor would pick up on it instantly. "Now you will be known as Christian Guerriero." He opened the door and with one last embrace sent the Gatekeeper on his way.

Chapter 6

"Pleasure in the job puts perfection in the work."
~ Aristotle

Ronoven rolled onto his back with a contented sigh, the feeble spring sun just managing to warm his face through the cracks in the tapestry tacked over the window. After close to two decades enjoying Earth, he wondered if he'd ever get tired of the agreeable feeling of being human again. If anyone below caught wind of his activities here, he knew they wouldn't be pleased. He'd done far more good than harm. But he was going to forget about Hell for as long as he could. And there was nothing like the company of someone young and energetic, free of inhibitions due either to genuine self-possession or their poison of choice, to help you forget. Modern life had many things to recommend it and the endless variety of ways for a young man to entertain himself was one of them. He'd missed out on that in his own life, having begun training as a warrior when he was only a child, and his previous furloughs from Hell had been torturously short. This time he was drinking from the cup of youth and pleasure with abandon, and adventuring as much as he felt he could get away with; because the only thing that pleased him more than a good meal, some decent wine, and the company of a beautiful woman, was the feeling he'd earned them with some thrilling heroics. He hadn't exactly earned it this time with anything other than some witty banter and maybe flashing his dimples, but it had been a decent evening nonetheless. This morning he was thinking one of the greatest benefits of demonic magic was the absolute inability to get a hangover. Last night had been nice, but he couldn't remember hangovers well enough to decide if it would have been worth it. It was about average for him in most respects, so probably not.

College towns were a great place to blend in and partake in various diversions; this particular little college was well known for great parties, attractive rich kids, and exceptional chemical amusements. It was plenty of reason to visit the sleepy little town from time to time. Although Ronoven traveled around quite a bit to keep up the appearance of cooperating with his mission, he regularly came back to this area. The Northeastern United States was always his favorite spot for a number of reasons. He'd come here often to collect souls from among the discarded and forgotten. Vermont in particular was full of good food, good booze, well-educated people, and was easy for him to love. In many ways it resembled his homeland, and while he avoided going back there if he could, the similar appearance was a pleasant reminder that he had once known a life without Hell. And something just drew him here, regardless of where he was supposed to be, again and again.

Showing up on a Sunday made pickings dismally slim, even in the one decent bar close to campus. People were still waking up from the near hibernation of a hard winter. When three girls had stumbled in around ten he knew immediately which he would prefer to seduce. A fairly brief round of drinks and some half-assed flirting sealed the deal. It wasn't just her boundless vodka and Red Bull fueled enthusiasm, although that had its merits. She could have been a little archangel; well, one specifically. She had an athletic almost sexless build save for the generous swell of her almost-natural breasts, an artificial polish to her smooth skin, sleek dark hair, and strange dark eyes that looked like polished rubies next to the purple of her tight t-shirt. All this contributed to an amusing illusion of vicariously screwing Lucifer. She was also kind of a superior acting pain in the ass and that shored up the metaphor nicely.

Ronoven grinned and rolled over the rest of the way with a 'Good morning, beautiful' on his lips, when he realized the bed and the messy dorm room were empty. Not accustomed to waking up alone, he grimaced with the irritation of being surprised by solitude and the nasty taste in his mouth. He might not be able to get hungover but could certainly taste a night of smoking the local herb through dirty water chased by the training-wheel cocktails of those new to the habit. Oh well, his worst day on Earth was a damn sight better than what counted as a great day in Hell.

He stretched while his eyes searched for his faded jeans. They were wadded up in a chair across the room with his favorite tour t-shirt, which he now remembered was torn by his impatient inebriated companion and her fashionable salon-installed talons. Now that he'd moved a little, he realized his back had a few fading reminders of that as well. He was about to get up and see if the shirt was salvageable or if he'd have to deal with the distasteful experience of wearing one of the dirty ones in his bag when he heard the door handle turn. He waited for … Damn it, he couldn't remember her name to save his own skin … then just shrugged and turned up the wattage on his charming smile. Looking particularly fetching in her tennis uniform, Angela (memory came with a wave of relief) hurried into the room. Seeing him barely awake and still lounging in her narrow bed she let out an involuntary startled squeak.

"Christ, Ben! What are you still doing here? It's like noon!" Her surprise was replaced quickly by amusement. Caught completely off guard by her reaction he could only stammer self-consciously, which made him seem younger than he appeared.

"Sonofabitch ... If you lied about your age, I swear I'll kick your ass all the way back to high school!" Her rolling eyes told him to talk fast.

"Angie, I told you, I'm eighteen. My ID's in my wallet if you want to check. It's, um, behind the fake one I used at the bar." He put on his best sheepishly winning smile. When she responded with an amused grin of her own, his broadened into what he hoped was an even more appealing display of his perfect teeth. She shook her head and sat facing him with arms folded strategically under her already round breasts, raising an arched eyebrow.

"Do you need to call somebody for a ride? Gas money? Food maybe? You can borrow my cell if you need to ... Oh, and there's a vending machine in the hall and change in my drawer." The nearly pitying quality to her voice wounded Ben's pride. He could almost forget he wasn't the crunchy kid taking a year off after high school he'd been pretending to be for years. He briefly wished his magic would allow him to age himself up a bit without undoing other important protections. He wasn't baby-faced or anything, but his age got questioned with annoying regularity.

"Nah," he gave a casual shake of his head. "I'm gonna hitch up to Burlington. There's a throwback punk show this weekend and I've got friends who live around there."

"Old school punk. So sophisticated." She smirked. "What're you doing screwing your way around the world anyway? I mean, it's an obvious talent, but you seem like a sharp kid. College could be fun for someone like you."

College *was* fun for someone like him. He just didn't stick around long enough for the homework. He decided to just let that go and shrugged noncommittally. "So, hey, before I take off ..." He tilted his head, indicating the bed. Angela smirked again and shook her head.

"Look Ben, you're adorable. Seriously. I had fun last night. Repeatedly. But my boyfriend's coming to take me out to lunch before my three o'clock class." She saw Ben's unimpressed look. "He's a lineman for The Spartans and the off-season is making him cranky. He's been just itching to pummel somebody. So you probably want to bail. Just sayin' sweetie."

Ben's immediate impetuous response was that it sounded like some jackass who would casually mention a desire for real violence to his girlfriend could probably stand someone skinning their knuckles on his teeth ... and he hadn't been in a good knock-down-drag-out in a long time so maybe it would be ... Then his good sense reluctantly reasserted itself. While he would have no difficulty besting some college kid in a fight, footballer or not, it would draw undue attention, locally, and if there were cops involved, possibly otherworldly. Considering where he was supposed to be that was the last thing he wanted, because at the moment he could think of no good excuse to justify not being there.

"Okay, I get it. I'm going," Ben said with good humor. Then he remembered his clothes were under her Pilates-perfect ass. He was anticipating her heading to the showers and leaving him to disappear in peace. She smiled at the expectant expression on his face and settled more comfortably into her chair. He prompted, "So, um, are you gonna leave, or ..?"

A woman clearly accustomed to getting what she wanted, Angela gave him a devious smile as she eyed the whole length of him, mostly buried under her blankets. "Why would I want to do that? You've made a mess of my bed, not to mention my morning." She winked. "The least I deserve is a little show."

Ben heaved an eloquent sigh as he rose, letting the covers fall away. Angela smiled and dangled his ripped shirt off her manicured fingertip. He stepped toward her to retrieve it, feeling his face redden for the first time he could remember. This body was starting to get to him. He was uncomfortably conscious of her eyes skimming over every inch of him. He couldn't recall the last time he'd felt so naked. He thought whoever coined the phrase 'Earth girls are easy' should spend some time in Hell's dungeons. Just for a millennium or so.

Chapter 7

"Not all who wander are lost."
~ J.R.R. Tolkien

B en accepted the first ride that came along. Although it had taken him south rather than north, it was worth it to get out of Angie's room before it got any more uncomfortable or his presence caused a break-up or a fight. This trip was about having fun and enjoying being back in his flesh. And despite his brief discomposure back in the dorm, he had to admit that for the most part he was having a wonderful time. He kicked around Bennington for a couple of days, ate well, and drank copious amounts of good local microbrew. Then he made his way to the little town of Manchester over a series of long hikes and short rides, managing even in the chilly spring weather, and one fleeting unexpected snow squall, to enjoy both quite a bit.

The local music station was excellent. Being able to call in and request Flogging Molly or The Dropkick Murphys without having to explain himself was the mark of really fine radio as far as Ben was concerned. He remembered the bookstore from a past excursion and knew he could spend all day in some comfortable corner reading and drinking coffee and no one would pay him any mind. Ben loved to read. As a human, he had never so much as seen a single piece of writing that wasn't burnt into the seer's divining bones, but as a demon his gift for words always drew him to languages, literature, and books of all kinds. If you've got an eternity to study, there's a lot you can learn, and his broad knowledge was one of the things that made him formidable in Hell, not to mention kept him on the list for missions on Earth. By Thursday though, he'd seen all there was of the little town, and the girl he hooked up with seemed like she might be a little too interested in making more out of their pleasant fling. No matter how lovely she was, or how nice her warm little apartment with its soft queen-sized bed happened to be, he had no intention of starting a relationship with anyone. A tumble and a hot meal were great, but he couldn't afford attachments. That kind of shit was a good way to wind up getting busted blowing off work. Besides he did have a feeling he should to go to Burlington. He was certain he'd be glad he did it and he'd always believed in following those sorts of intuitions. They were rarely ever wrong. Besides, somebody good was bound to be playing Higher Ground or Nectar's, and the food and the booze could rival any city he'd traveled to. Hitching that far would be fun, too. He could have gotten himself a car long ago and easily gone wherever he pleased, but there was something cool about just bumming rides, being off the radar. It fit the clean-cut-kid-turned-vagabond image he'd cultivated for himself perfectly, and he often managed a satisfying adventure or two along the way. Manchester wasn't the best place to pick up a ride north, so after a brief note of appreciation left for the thankfully-still-sleeping Melissa, and an early headache-inhibiting coffee at a little brick gas station that was open at that ungodly hour, Ben headed out on foot in the cool grey mist before the sun was all the way up.

Even in the brisk morning air, hiking along the side of Route 7 out in the open, Ben was reasonably comfortable. The winter had been a particularly cold one in these parts but spring was looking promising. Today seemed like it would turn out to be quite pleasant if the last of the fog burned off and the sun made up its mind to shine. Ben had made decent progress in the few hours since sunrise but knew during the week at this time of day rides in any direction would likely be few and far between. He hoped the forecast of clear weather held because the clothes on his back were his only dry ones. His few other garments had been damp in the machine but he hadn't wanted to wait through another cycle so he'd jammed them into a repurposed grocery bag and tied it to keep the damp off his other belongings. Lyss had already repeatedly expressed her disappointment at his departure, and going through it again was more than his aching head could handle. He adjusted the straps of his battered Army-surplus backpack trying to more evenly distribute its weight. He probably shouldn't have bought all those books. The occasional breeze from the still-snowcapped peaks of the surrounding mountains provided a bracing counterpoint to the warming sun. The sound of the little frogs the locals called peepers and the damp verdant smell of this valley filled Ben with a sense of peace, but also a strange hollow ache deep in his chest to go with the one in his temples.

He knew where it came from. If he was honest, nobleman or not, Ben hated Hell. He hated the sounds, the stink of it, the coarseness, and most of all the abject cruelty and suffering that pervaded most of the under-kingdom. Ben knew his hands weren't entirely clean on that score, but in Hell survival took precedence over everything else. He determined early on he wouldn't suffer if he could avoid it. His time as a warrior had eased the transition somewhat. Life, after all, was cruel, and no one had ever promised him the afterlife wouldn't be. This ersatz mission offered a wonderful escape. Ben always longed for opportunities for absences from the Pit. These were few and far between and none before now had ever been longer than a few months.

Mostly his life had been rather small; short in mortality and focused on a certain standard of living since. If he went a long while without time away, he felt Hell's fires would consume him, put a final end to him, and he would welcome it. Not a good feeling for a survivor like him. Hell was one thing, oblivion something else. That was the thing you avoided at all costs; was the one thing he really feared. These times when he could come up, feel human again for even a little while, were saving his soul from giving in to the feeling that anything was better than eternal perdition. He was hopeful if he was gone long enough, maybe they might forget about him.

He finished adjusting his backpack and was considering taking off his heavy fisherman's sweater in spite of the wind when he caught his breath. Beside the road was one of the most beautiful things he'd seen in a terribly long time. Across some rusty train tracks was a swampy area teeming with life even this early in the season, and just beyond it, a tidy brick-red sugarhouse. With the yellow-green of the early leaves, the purply pink of the remaining buds, and the drifting silver mist, it looked like something out of a story where a good wizard might live who would come out and set everything to rights. That was a sight to sum up springtime in Vermont. Just a golden storybook morning full of beauty and promise that people who lived elsewhere would not believe existed and Ben wanted to believe in more than anything.

He had no idea how long he'd been standing there when his woolgathering was interrupted by the welcome sound of tires crunching to a stop on the gravely shoulder, but the sun had definitely made a little progress on its climb in the sky. He had become so caught up in the arresting sight of the little white-trimmed structure peeking out at the edge of the forest, and his own long thoughts, he was disoriented for a moment.

A deep voice called out and brought him back to himself. "Where you headed?"

As he turned to look at today's good Samaritan he squinted, hoping his answer wouldn't be a deal breaker, "North! Burlington, if I can get there."

"Well, you happen to be in a rather large amount of luck," the man called out good-naturedly. He waved Ben in through the window of his old Subaru station wagon. It was ancient but well-kept, hardly a spot of rust on the dark green paint. Grateful for this unbelievable windfall, Ben opened the back door and tossed his heavy pack onto the one space not taken up by books and boxes that seemed at first glance to contain even more books. Barring any big surprises, he believed he would enjoy this ride.

As he slid into the passenger seat the driver was moving another box into the back to make room, "It's been so quiet out here I thought I might be biting off more than I could chew hoping to catch a break this morning!" Ben gave the driver a very genuine grin. "Seriously, thanks for stopping."

As the driver edged back out onto the road, he glanced at Ben and smiled kindly. "Never hurts to help a stranger."

Ben got the vague impression this man should be familiar somehow. There was something here pulling insistently at Ben's awareness. When it hit him, his jaw nearly dropped. No, it couldn't be. His mind raced. Despite how much his name was bandied about, Ben had always wondered if his story was more legend than fact. One of the oldest human souls on the planet had just stopped to give him a lift. Despite his appearance of being in his early thirties and his youthful, fit, almost military bearing, the underlying soul, filled with countless decades of memories, was as apparent as fresh paint. This could only be Cartaphilis. The Gatekeeper. From the Prophecy. This *was* an interesting wrinkle. Ben decided to draw him out, see what happened. It might give him something noteworthy to report if he needed to keep his superiors off his case and if not it would make one hell of a story. You didn't run into a soul like this every day.

"You're heading all the way to Burlington?" Ben rubbed his hands together. There was more of a chill in the air than he had noticed when he'd been moving around and he couldn't exactly do a spell to warm up now.

"I live there." The man smiled, adjusting the heat for his passenger. "Name's Chris."

"I'm Ben. Thanks again! I never expected to get all the way from one hitch."

"I wasn't sure that's what you were doing, but you looked like you could use a lift. And like I said, it's never a problem to lend a hand." He glanced sideways at Ben who was already starting to look less like a teenaged popsicle. "What's taking you to Burlington?"

"I'm going to a show, then who knows," he offered with the unworried confidence of an experienced itinerant.

"How old are you, if you don't mind me asking?" Concern was clearly etched in the kind lines of his face.

"Eighteen," he replied. "Almost nineteen." An eyebrow was raised, so he added stridently, "I really am. I'm not a runaway or anything, if that's what you're thinking."

The last thing he needed was for his first day in Burlington to be a trip to the police department to prove he wasn't some errant kid. The papers he had on him were good, although the identity was kind of shallow, so it could be a huge drag. It had the added potential to make real trouble since there was an Office in Burlington, making administrative attention almost a guarantee.

"Relax, I'm just asking. You're at the age where it's difficult to tell. Based on my experience you could be anywhere from sixteen to twenty-six, and I try to make some effort to be a responsible adult." Ben relaxed visibly so Chris felt it was safe to press a little more. "You have a place to stay?"

This question sparked another strong gut feeling. Maybe there was something to this. The prophecy clearly named this guy and its description of emerald hills and little water made Ben think of here since he'd first visited. *Well, shit.* He thought fast and then answered in the same casual tone he'd used to mention the show, "Yeah, I'm staying at the hostel on Main Street so I can meet up with some friends, check out some music this weekend. I'll probably stay there until I find an apartment."

"Oh, you're moving to the area?"

Well, I am now, Gatekeeper, thought Ben. This was quickly followed by wondering just exactly what the hell he was going to tell his superiors. All he said was, "Yeah, I like the vibe. Lots to do, and I thought I had a place lined up, but it fell through, so ... whatever. You from there?" Ben was curious to hear the story that had been concocted for this man's life.

Chris chuckled and shook his head, "Not even close! I mean, I'm an American now, but I thought the remnants of my accent might give me away." Ben only appeared curious, not about to say, '*Well, duh, I know you're a Roman, like of the ancient variety*'. He almost choked on the gum he'd been chewing when Chris continued. "I'm Roman. I mean, Italian. I am from Rome ... originally." He looked moderately surprised at himself for phrasing things in quite that way. *Nothing like a little honesty to shake things up.*

"You don't have much of an accent, I guess. You sound American to me,"

Since Ben could sound like he was from wherever he chose he did a brief mental inventory of accents he knew. If he hadn't known better he would have assumed Chris was from the Northeast; the slight variations Ben heard weren't particularly remarkable even to his ear other than maybe harder than average ending consonants, so he just shrugged. He felt like he was doing that a lot. Then he figured he might as well lay on the kid routine thick as it was usually good for getting more out of adults anyway, and the longer he stayed in this body, the more it felt like his default position. Besides, Chris somehow made him feel like a kid someone might mistake for needing a helping hand. Seeing the concern in Chris's eyes, Ben thought the innate human protective instinct must be a real bitch; he knew he looked young, but damn.

Following his gut, he asked all at once, not pausing long enough between questions for Chris to really answer, "How long have you been there? Is it a nice place to live? What do you do? What's with all the boxes if you already live there?"

"I've been in town a couple of years. And it's a very nice place." He smiled broadly at Ben's enthusiastic manner. He liked this kid and he still wasn't sure he didn't need some kind of help. Chris's instincts were usually good. He'd had a lot of practice helping people. "I teach part-time at a little Catholic high school, mostly Latin. That's what I'm doing with all the boxes. We're on spring break and our sister school down in Connecticut is closing at the end of term, so I was picking up some useful books and papers from a friend. Actually my primary job is as a professor at one of the local colleges. Saint Thomas's. Ever heard of it?"

He hadn't, but he figured it was better to sound like he knew the area and he didn't think his knowledge of the local bars and sororities would impress his current companion much. "Yeah, I think so."

"I teach ancient languages and history there."

"Cool. I was thinking I might take some classes somewhere once I settle in. Everybody treats me like a stray puppy. Maybe if I go to school people will take me seriously."

Ben figured it couldn't hurt to open himself up to an offer of help from this man, who seemed naturally inclined to it anyway. He was now in no hurry to report this meeting. Realistically, he'd be called back to Hell to make a detailed accounting, and Ben had no interest in even a short trip in that direction. He needed to keep an eye on him though just in case there was something to this. Even if not, an actual place to live in a town like Burlington could be nice, at least until it snowed. Ben was reasonably dedicated to not hanging around anywhere it stayed cold for long. Too much like the long, lean, winters of his youth for his comfort.

"Well, I'd be more than happy to help. I'll give you my card when we stop." Chris smiled again, genuinely pleased at the prospect of helping him.

Ben grinned too. If the perceived age difference was too much, he thought he could get Chris to a place where he was willing to be a mentor; and damned if he didn't just like the guy even if he was one of the long-hated Romans. The miles were slipping past while they talked, and soon they stopped for lunch at a little place in Middlebury on the main road. The parking lot was jammed and once they had gotten their food Ben understood why. He definitely had no problem eating like a teenager anyway, but three orders of potato skins later he was almost embarrassed. It didn't stop him from eating his spaghetti or the butter dripping garlic bread it came with, or even the banana pudding which he could've honestly eaten about ten bowls of, though he wasn't normally much on sweets. He was a little bummed he'd never made it in there before. Holy hell, he loved being on Earth. Food was almost as good as sex, and frankly it was much less complicated.

Chris seemed to kind of get a kick out of watching him eat like he was in a competition, and made sure the server kept refilling his glass with delicious cold milk. They didn't talk much over the meal because Ben was too busy filling his face. It occurred to him that he hadn't eaten yesterday; he'd had coffee but that was about it. Then he'd spent half the night thanking a young lady for her hospitality and walked five or six miles in the cold this morning. You could really wreck a body if you didn't pay attention, and he knew it but he'd been distracted, in a hurry. No wonder Chris thought he was some kid in trouble staring off into the fog beside the road. It was unsurprising when the considerable check arrived, Chris wouldn't hear of splitting it.

"You're eating on my dime today, kiddo," he said as he waved off Ben's rumpled cash with a smile. *He probably thinks that's all I've got*, Ben thought, and he wasn't far wrong, at least until Ben got himself to another office. He hadn't stayed anywhere long enough to bother about a bank account in a while. Chris continued, "Besides Ben, you mentioned, I think, between bites, that you might want to take my class. I could use the enrollment. I can't have you starving before I get you onto the books, right?"

Ben shook his head and smiled as they headed back to the car, "I guess not, Professor." Maybe it was all the food, or the warm car, or the rhythmic sound of the tires on the road, or maybe it was being with someone he almost instantly trusted, but uncharacteristically, Ben fell asleep with his face pressed against the window. The slight grind of tires grazing the curb and Chris's hand on his shoulder finally ended his gentle snoring and mumbling.

"Hey Ben, we're here." Chris shook his shoulder lightly. Ben sat up, startled; sucking in his breath, rubbing the sleep out of his eyes.

"Holy crap, I'm so sorry. That was really rude of me!"

Chris's face creased in worry. "You okay? You feel kind of warm. You haven't been sleeping outside down in those mountains have you?"

"No, un uh. I stayed with a girl," he admitted with a shake of his head and just the right touch of self-consciousness at the implication he'd been with a girl for the warm bed and not herself. "I just kind of run hot." Ben had never seen a more skeptical expression. "I swear I never get sick. Healthy as a horse."

He threw Chris a winning smile as he opened the door, hopped out onto the pavement, and hurriedly reached into the back for his bag. Chris had a distinctly dad-like look about him, and Ben wanted to keep tabs on him, not get adopted. Besides it was mostly true even when he'd been human. He'd never gotten sick much, couldn't be slowed down long enough. Nope, never suffered a serious illness, was never even injured all that badly, though his particular run of good luck had ended on the field of battle with one Roman spear. At least the bastard had looked him in the eye.

He stuck his head into the open window and reached out his hand. "Thanks seriously for the ride, dude. Not to mention the lunch, no, the feast. And the nap. I really appreciate it."

Chris shook his hand warmly and then handed him his card and watched Ben carefully put it into his wallet. "I want to hear from you soon, Ben. If you give me a call next week, it's early enough to get you some financial aid, maybe even housing." He gave Ben an encouraging nod.

"Don't worry, Chris, you'll definitely be seeing me!" Ben smiled, waved, and then turned his back and headed inside the hostel.

He briefly considered using the last of his cash to pay for a bed and a locker to secure his bag, but decided, all things being equal, he'd probably better wait to see how this evening played out. He was going to need better papers if he wanted to immerse himself in a life here. This could get complicated. Maybe he'd just bail after the weekend. No one ever need know he'd encountered the Gatekeeper. As he thought about leaving, it made him feel anxious, twitchy. His intuition was strong he should stay involved with Chris and see what unfolded. Now, with a belly full of good food and a mind fresh from sleep, Ben had the beginnings of an idea about how he might negotiate a stay in Burlington. It was worth a shot anyway. When he was sure Chris had pulled away from the curb he walked back out to settle his situation.

See you next week, Professor.

You can count on it.

Chapter 8

"Knowledge will give you power,
but character, respect."
~ Bruce Lee

C hris pulled into the northbound lane, grateful as always that he'd made a downtown transition without incident. The pre-rush-hour jumble of automobiles and pedestrians was enough to take years off your life. It made him miss traveling by horse or even on foot, and he knew his mind wasn't entirely on his driving. Hours of conversation left Chris with more questions than answers. He liked Ben, an engaging kid who seemed like he could use a hand finding his way. There was something distinctly vulnerable about him, despite a veneer of worldly confidence. There was just no way Chris was walking away from someone in need, but he wished he could figure out what was bothering him. As he drove toward his little two-bedroom apartment in South Burlington Chris realized it was almost like Ben knew who he was, like he'd recognized him. The more he thought about it, the more reasonable it felt.

Chris shook his head as he hung a right onto Dorset Street, breathing a sigh of relief that he'd caught the light. Ben was just a teenager, barely out of high school. There was no way he could have even an inkling. Most young people Chris met had no idea who the person he had been was, even the Catholic school kids who had to take religion classes that made mention of him. Chris smiled to himself; he was a fairly minor character in a rather grand story filled with much more important figures.

Still, something nibbled away at a dark corner of his brain, like a rat worrying a secret store of cheese. He pulled into his favorite market and headed straight to their great take-out counter that frequently kept him from starving, trying to shake the nagging feeling. A memory of being recognized before hit him out of the blue, and he nearly crashed into a slightly disheveled young woman with a toddler in a shopping cart. She had been paying more attention to her little boy's displeasure with his elasticized glasses than her surroundings, but Chris apologized. He mulled over the memory while he waited for his order. Saint Petersburg. Rasputin. That had been an interesting adventure.

As Chris paid, wandered back to his car, and made his way the short distance to his apartment, he reflected that he had enough material from moving around the globe for a couple of thousand years to publish himself into quite a nice living, although his adventures would have to pass for fiction. There was also the small problem that he found writing even the expected scholarly articles arduous. Besides, he liked teaching well enough. He parked behind the building, got out and stood dejectedly in front of the collection of books and papers spilling haphazardly all over his car. He was tired and in no mood to deal with this mess tonight. Lugging and organizing all of this could be Future Chris's problem. Present Chris was going to head up the stairs with his sandwich, kettle chips, and late-season blood orange, settle in on the sofa, and relax; maybe have a beer and watch some TV. He thought maybe he was in the mood for some *Doctor Who*. Chris's own appearance never changed, of course, not by so much as a grey hair, but he could relate to the urge to help, time losing its meaning, and the constant ebb and flow of friends loved and lost.

He opened the hatchback to grab his dinner and a small leather-bound book fell out at his feet. He picked it up and read the gold-leaf script on the cover. *Prophecy of Enoch Concerning the Emerald Hills – Fragments with Translation*. He opened the first page to the text written in an esoteric language typically referred to as Enochian with a side-by-side Latin translation. His hands began to shake as he looked at one of the shortest most distressing things he'd ever read.

The Exile imperiled in the age of the Water Bearer ...

Child of rebellion ... angelic holy blood ... last of her Line ...

Her burdens, though great, will not be borne alone ...

The Gatekeeper will be her guide ...

Her journey will be long; the Wanderer ...

... The seventh sun shining light on the key ...

*The hollow of the Emerald Hills, by the Little Water,
a place to begin ... to return ...*

*... Climbing from the snowy beds of cold stone ...
heart of the mountain ...*

... A false choice rejected will all Truth lay bare ...

... A new beginning for ...

He stood and stared, turning the book over and over in his hands, his dinner quite forgotten. His mouth was dry and his head was beginning to ache. He needed to go inside and get to his own papers with this book. Tonight would unfortunately be much less relaxing than he had hoped. He puffed out a resigned sigh and murmured the other short and distressing words that leapt immediately to mind.

"Jesus wept."

Chapter 9

"The fishermen know that the sea is dangerous and the storm terrible, but they have never found these dangers sufficient reason for remaining ashore."
~ Vincent Van Gogh

Wandering around at night was usually one of his favorite pastimes, but as Ben walked along the sidewalk in the gathering dusk his feet felt heavier with each step. He knew if he wanted to stay here for any length of time, particularly if he was going to discover if there was any import to his timely encounter with the Gatekeeper, he would need help. To get it, he would have to go through Hell's official channels.

Almost grudgingly, he called on his demonic senses and was drawn by a peculiar acrid scent and distorted humming energy to a franchise of what most from below called simply The Office. Locations to access any of the network (otherwise known as Hell, Inc.), which facilitated doing official business on Earth, were located throughout the world. They served to collect and collate information, manage specific jobs, possessions, soul collections, and to keep tabs on souls under contract. They also furnished authentic resources and legends for Hell's undercover missions including identities, income streams, contacts, and in some cases rare or difficult to obtain magical ingredients. The Offices supplied a convenient place for demons and contracted humans to meet and be entertained as well. While this all operated like a corporation, or more accurately sophisticated organized crime, it was not new, in fact was as old as time. Business was done through various public and private institutions, guided if not by someone from below, then by a human on contract. Often if the human proved useful, their terms could be renegotiated. Demons found this whole arrangement much easier for the more banal matters of operating on Earth. Magic was to be saved for things one couldn't easily get otherwise.

Ben finally approached the local Office as the last little bit of pink faded from the western sky and true twilight was falling on the city. It was a good thing his vision was preternaturally strong because there was not a single working streetlight in this rundown neighborhood that seemed to be mostly bars, and one place that gave the distinct impression of being an underground strip club; at least the music thumping through the walls sounded stripper-ish to Ben. Good place to situate yourself if you didn't want decent people wandering in.

He hated this. It was probably run by some hideous sycophantic lackey of Castor's and he could wind up back in Hell tonight for not being where he was assigned. The only story he'd come up with to explain himself was paper thin. If he was lucky, all that would happen would be a loss of rank, and even that would hurt his ability to protect his people. He felt his shoulders tightening, his head starting to ache. He was never going to pull this off. *Damn.* He had to try. *Shit.* He made an involuntary face. *Shit. Do I really have to do this?* He thought again about leaving and his stomach flipped unpleasantly. He sighed. *Fuck.*

All too soon he found himself in front of another non-descript dive bar, a faded hand-painted sign over the door in childish block lettering designated the establishment The Pit. *How original.* The windows were so filthy only the barest glow visible to his demonic eyes convinced him he was looking at a place that was even occupied. The front door was heavily chipped and scratched. Another sign hanging from a piece of wire over a rusty nail read faintly 'Members Only'. This looked about as promising as it had felt on his walk. *Well, nothing ventured, nothing gained.* He reluctantly pulled the door open and entered a small vestibule nearly filled by a large man dressed in faded jeans and a tight black t-shirt straining to contain a massive chest and trunk-like arms sleeved in graphically violent tattoos. His bloodshot eyes held not the slightest trace of humanity and he seemed ill at ease in a human body but more than capable of breaking one into however many pieces he chose. Were he not a demon himself Ben would definitely have found this creature intimidating. He wasn't thrilled to occupy the same space regardless. However, business was business, and if he wanted to get out of this with his Earth privileges intact he had better get in character and focus.

He drew himself up, allowing experience to harden his youthful features and his unusual amber eyes to glow slightly, as he slipped comfortably into his well-worn persona as a Count and Marquis of Hell. "Sentry, I require admittance."

"Members only," rumbled deeply from within the man's chest, as though Ben hadn't spoken aloud. The creature seemed not to take in Ben with his eyes, nor move his lips much when he spoke.

Ben had nearly forgotten how good it felt to pull rank. His recent experiences left him feeling all too human. He raised one of his golden eyebrows and cast a haughty expression, which felt a bit comical here on Earth, but it got the creature's attention. More satisfying was his reaction when Ben spoke again, "My good man, I am the Lord Ronoven. Unless you'd like to spend the evening being sent back to the actual Pit in meaty pieces, I suggest you let me pass."

The giant sprang aside like a much smaller man. "Right away, my Lord." He held out his enormous steam-shovel hands, "Your bag?" Ben scowled with irritation at the idea of handing over all of the possessions he currently bothered to own. "It's policy, sir," he apologized with a deferential bow of his titanic head. Ben gave the creature his backpack along with an imperious glare. The guard made a show of hanging it up carefully and then opened the door. "Apologies, my Lord."

He released the lock on the inner door which slid aside on a silent track. Ben stepped over the threshold, feeling the magic of the place brush him like a curtain. As usual with one of the offices, the outside belied a decadent interior. Ben found the polished black floors and ceilings and the blood-red walls a little obvious and showy, but most demons seemed to prefer stereotyped and over-the-top and humans expected it. Plush furniture and small tables were scattered around the room, giving groups plenty of privacy. Music poured from hidden speakers, loud enough to keep the creatures at one table from hearing the business being conducted at the next. A well-appointed bar dominated the far wall. He scrutinized the guests in the room, nervous he might be recognized, but relieved when he found everyone unfamiliar. Only the bartender paid him the slightest attention, looking up and offering him a reserved smile as she polished a glass. Feeling much more at home, Ben approached the bar and greeted the lovely dark-haired twenty-something with a nod and an ingratiating smile.

"Get you something?" Polite, rehearsed.

"I'm Lord Ronoven. I need to see the Agent as soon as possible."

"Appointment?"

Ben shook his head. "I'm sorry. I didn't have time to make arrangements."

She keyed something into the computer behind the bar and peered at something, perhaps a reply. "The Agent is in a meeting with King Castor's representatives at the moment." Inwardly he grimaced, but kept his face carefully neutral. He thought she must have seen something in his eyes or maybe recognized his name because she smiled at him more openly. "Lord Ronoven, she may be some time. Would you care for some refreshments in the private anteroom?"

Relieved, Ben answered, "Thank you. A drink in relative peace would be great."

She indicated a red door to the left of the bar and without even leaving his order he proceeded through it, eager to avoid Castor's people. A definite improvement over the bar, this room was paneled in pale natural wood, had bright lamps in every corner, and in the middle was a luxurious velvet couch, a couple of overstuffed chairs upholstered in the same soft fabric, and a frosted-glass coffee table scattered with various local publications. It was also pleasantly quiet, insulated from the noise of the bar, probably by magic. He was just getting comfortable when the lovely young woman entered with a tray bearing a cut-crystal glass filled with perfectly clear ice and two fingers of above-average scotch, accompanied by the rest of the bottle. Exactly what he had planned to order. She placed it in front of him and without a word turned to leave. A bit wrong-footed by the whole experience Ben managed a hurried 'thank you' at her back. She turned her head to tip him a flirtatious wink as she went out the door and her brown eyes flashed a brilliant unnatural green. *A Reader. An actual natural Reader.* Holy hell, he'd been starting to believe they were just a myth. That explained knowing his order, and sensing his discomfort, his casual interest. He hoped he hadn't been thinking anything too licentious or frankly incriminating when she peeked at his thoughts.

He thumbed absently through a local newspaper and sipped his drink. What in the name of Hell was he doing here? He wasn't supposed to be this far north. He certainly wasn't supposed to be setting up shop and starting a human life! He was supposed to be looking for the girl and reporting anything even possibly related to the prophecy. This little lark would be over eventually and he should be thinking about advancing his position, not hiding things from the boss and fraternizing with mortals. He was gambling with his life here, no denying it. In fact, if what he was actually doing was discovered, the final death was kind of a best case scenario. Lucifer took even the slightest deviation from orders rather personally. And then there was his right hand man, Bhaal. Ben shuddered involuntarily and tried to force the thought from his mind.

He sighed and poured himself another generous drink, hoping to take the edge off his nerves. He knew what he was supposed to be doing, but he also knew what his gut was telling him to do. He needed to get to know the Gatekeeper before deciding on any course of action. Besides, there was no way he was ready to give up on what he had here right now. Earth was much too pleasant. A warm hand on his shoulder startled him into swallowing his drink in one burning gulp.

"Ronoven! It's so good to see your face!" Ben grinned and jumped up, throwing his arms enthusiastically around one of his favorite demons, a true friend for countless years.

"Aife! I wasn't expecting to see you! I thought you were in Australia!"

"Well, love, you know how I hate the heat." They laughed comfortably. It was an old joke between them. "Actually, this whole operation was cleared out top to bottom a few months ago over a contract issue. I suppose that's what happens when you don't make your quotas, and then top it up with bad excuses." Ben looked perplexed. "Not enough souls pledged to Hell, love."

"This isn't a very populated area though, Aife."

"I don't know if you've met the boss, sweetie, but he doesn't much care for excuses." Ben laughed. "Besides, we're on important borders here. So I got reassigned. It's nice. Reminds me of home a bit." She sat on the sofa and patted the seat next to her, producing another glass from her apron. Her light green eyes sparkled and she tossed her long fiery braid, giving Ben a beguiling smile. "Share a drink with an old friend?"

He moved everything over and poured for both of them, sitting companionably next to her. They were quiet for a moment and Ben reflected on his good fortune. Aife was one of his clan and although she had come to Hell around a hundred years later than he had, she too had found her way there courtesy of Rome. Of course she had been a leader, the wife of a fallen warrior, and an accomplished woman in her own right. Ben knew he had been little more than a boy with strong arms, and perhaps more courage than good sense. He had plucked her from the Pit, claiming her for his legions. Arguing for imbuing her with demonic power was easier than for some of his other cases. Her bravery and savagery in battle were excuse enough and Lucifer himself had been impressed, called her a real spit-fire. Like him, Hell didn't seem to change her much, or not nearly as much as some. A few centuries ago, Ben had won the honor of placing an Agent as a reward for service to the previous King and had immediately chosen Aife. She was astute in the arts of war and politics, not to mention trade. It was easy to justify and he was pleased to spare her any additional time in Hell, if a bit jealous he couldn't go himself. He had missed her terribly, had seen her only occasionally when she was summoned to report or he came up on assignment with an excuse for a detour, but life above clearly suited her. Looking at her relaxed smile now he was glad again he'd had the chance to free her a bit from the eternal grind of life in Hell.

They talked casually, catching up. Although Ben had little interest in traveling there himself, he loved that she still naturally sounded a little of home, even after all this time. Ben knew she still made her way there frequently to see about the various branches of her living family all over the Isles, though they were far removed from her human life. It was so like her to try to look after her people in her own way. Despite the fact he was technically her superior and was vastly more powerful, she'd spent ages looking after him, too. The woman was a caregiver down to her bones. He reminded himself that his affection could not replace caution now. Even if she were willing to conspire to flout orders, he had no right to ask, especially since he had no idea why he was behaving this way. It was important to proceed without endangering Aife.

She was no fool either. She clasped his hand, her dazzling eyes puzzled. "Don't misunderstand, I'm thrilled to see you, but what are you doing here? Last I heard you were ordered to Richmond to search for that half-breed, and Castor's men are checking on that mission with annoying devotion. Some of the Fallen are involved now, too." She paused at his dark look and then continued, not quite probing but certainly encouraging, "It's not like you not to be where you're expected, at least not so openly."

Some truth was necessary for both their sakes. "I was there, but it's crawling with other demons, so I was just covering old ground." He sighed, still unsure his story was good enough. "I'm following a hunch. Just this feeling in my gut ... I can't explain ..."

"Well, you crossed the threshold, so your position has been reported to Hell via the building's core enchantments." She bit her lip thoughtfully. She knew there was more going on here; but her impulse was to help, at least as much as she could without jeopardizing her own status. "Your 'feeling' seems an inadequate reason." She tapped her fingers against her knee, thinking. "It'll be better all-around if I can report you came to me with information you dared not leave Earth to share." She waited a beat. "That's why you're here *isn't it*?" Her question had an edge that let him know she wanted to be his ally but rightfully would not risk too much. To gain time to think, Ben refilled their glasses and offered his in silent tribute. She raised hers in response. They both drank deeply. She put down her empty glass and tilted her head.

He acknowledged her maneuvering with a wry smile. "Please tell the King I have been focusing on locational aspects of the prophecy. I believe the reference to small water to be an inland lake rather than the coves he prefers. Lake Champlain occurred to me because I've traveled here before. It's all emerald hills and water here." He grinned. "I would suggest that he rearrange his forces to focus on territories surrounding lakes. New England, of course. The lakes region of Maine seems promising. The Pacific Northwest, especially Oregon, definitely Minnesota. Maybe California." Ben racked his brain for more. "There're places outside of the United States, but I assume someone else is assigned there." Ben paused and took a casual sip of the drink Aife had poured while he talked. "As for me, I'm following a lead suggesting our materials were translated incorrectly or incompletely. I've come to you for resources relative to that." He glanced up over his glass, his face a silent question.

"Well, my Lord, you do have a gift." Her mouth twitched at the corners. "You've thought of everything this office needs to offer you whatever you require." He was relieved she thought his story acceptable and she was obviously satisfied with their words. "Well?" His face was a little blank. Maybe he was just a little too softened by the excellent spirits, so she prompted, "What *do* you require?"

Ben smiled at his own distraction, trying to order his thoughts. "I'll need a complete identity, with high school transcripts and all of that, because I need to enroll in college. Grad school would be nice, but even if my lead hadn't already asked my age, nobody would believe I'm old enough no matter what you put on paper, even if I stop shaving. I guess it's accurate to say I'm following a person more than a hunch." Aife raised a questioning eyebrow. "I found a real expert in ancient languages. He's a teacher. I need to get close to learn what he might know, see what resources he has. Taking his classes seems the best way to work the angle I'm on. This man is all for helping a kid in need, so something that would justify some financial aid ... I honestly don't know how that works. Some modest means of support, maybe a place to stay and a part-time job for if anybody asks seems like it should cover all the bases." Had he said too much? *No, Aife was too comfortable.*

She pulled a Smartphone from her pocket and typed with her thumb, almost too fast to follow. "I'll have my assistant begin processing your request. It shouldn't take too long. Ciara is remarkably efficient." Aife smiled indulgently. "She brought your drink." Ben looked askance as to why the cute bartender was significant. "She's part of my direct line, and she was going to sell her soul to one of the King's little pukes over her student loans, but I horned in on the deal. I just keep extending her terms." Ben's eyes widened. "I rather enjoy the privileges of being an Agent." He would not have thought Aife capable of such subterfuge, but here they were, too full of good whisky, and secrets spilling out left and right. She laughed at his shocked expression.

She thought for a moment. "I could use a cook or server a night or two a week, for as long as you want, and you can always use it as a cover. I feel like based on past experience you can drop food into a fryer or watered-down drinks in front of demons without any trouble, and I'll have your official papers to you just as soon as I can in case you'd rather find something further removed from the Boss." He nodded; as far removed as he could get would probably be smart. "If you're interested, there's an apartment upstairs. Couple of Fallen just moved out, but I did what I could with the smell." She wrinkled her nose dramatically and he laughed. "You can move in tonight if you'd like."

Ben felt like another piece had fallen into place. "Aife, you're the best! My bag's out front!" He bolted from the room to get his pack, barely noticing the empty club or the late hour.

She stepped up behind him with their two glasses, the bottle, and a key dangling from her pinky. She smiled fondly. She could easily see the boy he'd been. If he stayed in his body much longer, he might forget himself and the gravity of his position. He was up to something and she liked the idea of keeping him close, protecting him as he'd once done for her. She checked a text from Ciara. "We'll have your papers by end of business Monday. I'm sure we can find something to occupy your time until then." She winked, pushing past to lead him to the side stairs. "Come on. I'll help you break in the place." She went ahead of him, calling over her shoulder, "Anything else I should know, Lord Ronoven?"

"You know I couldn't care less about Hell's hierarchy. That Lord Ronoven crap is their thing. I wish you'd just call me Ben."

She just gestured for him to follow; he grinned, taking the steps two at a time.

He did seem to keep falling into shit and coming up smelling like a rose. He was pretty okay with that. Who didn't like roses?

Chapter 10

"When you are in the eye of the storm, you are often not aware of the whiplash around you."
~ Hugh Bonneville

L ahash stared morosely into her glass. Not a day went by without that awful night dominating her thoughts at some point. What had Azazel been thinking? It occurred to her more than once since watching the Assassin weep holy fire and melt like candle wax that Davidos must somehow be directly connected to the Line. His effortless displays of power and how quickly he had been able to appear in spite of their spells made that a distressing idea given her current assignment, not to mention Lucifer's impatience, but she had little choice but to pursue it.

She scowled. Davidos was younger than she, barely a few thousand years old by her reckoning. His powers far outstripped the norm for one of his age or rank. Perhaps he was a special Guardian created for the preservation of the royal Line. No matter, of course. To spearhead this mission, she was partnered with Lilith, a terrifying and ruthless Fallen angel. Not only was Lilith powerful and ancient, but this time they had been promised hundreds of demons and ten of Lucifer's personal guard when they located the girl. Overkill certainly. But Lahash didn't mind overkill, not after their last disaster. Lilith approached the table and tapped her fingernails on its surface.

"Time to go, mopey. It's been a long time coming, but we finally have a possible lead."

The *'finally'* was clearly meant as a dig at her past failure, not to mention being addressed as *'mopey'*, but Lahash knew better than to rise to it with Lilith. "Where? How?"

"The *'where'* is the United States; Vermont specifically. The *'how'* is Ronoven of all demons. Apparently he hasn't just been drinking dry every tavern in the world and trying to determine if there's a Hell-resistant venereal disease. We're going to go have a little chat."

"Where have you been? I suspected I'd see the end of time before you dragged yourself back here."

Lilith smiled broadly, her pointed teeth making Lahash uncomfortable as they always did. Lilith was beginning to change, either because of her efforts in dark magic or her habits. It was a disturbing metamorphosis. "My, but aren't we testy, little girl. If you must know, I've been having a lovely time. There was a fat little baby being ignored." Her sinister smile broadened even further. "Father's face glued to his phone." She sighed with obvious pleasure.

"And?"

"And what? You know my particular means of inflicting pain on these pathetic creatures." Her voice was heavy with disdain.

"So you took a child in broad daylight?"

Lilith gave a throaty chuckle. "From a park. Beautiful place. All the disgusting meat bags do is sit with their eyes stuck to those tiny screens. So much for Daddy's little favorites."

Lahash couldn't stop herself; she'd always wanted to ask. "What do you do with them?"

"Well I don't set them on the doorstep of an orphanage," Lilith replied archly. "Enough talk. We need to see a demon about a girl."

Chapter 11

"Pearls do not lie on the seashore.
If you want one, you must dive for it."
~ Chinese Proverb

en stared at his phone, hoping this was the right way to proceed. He was fairly sure he could pull this off. He'd spent Monday evening looking over the materials he'd picked up from Ciara, Tuesday planning exactly how to use them to his best advantage ... and maybe he'd been stalling a little. Mostly he'd decided to just be himself and use what Aife had drummed up to fill in the gaps if anyone asked too many questions. Given the fact that he'd held back his real motives, Aife's instincts were impeccable.

Through various means she had obtained a birth certificate, a Social Security number, a lifetime of medical records, a short work history, and school records going all the way back to kindergarten. He was pleased to see she'd decided he was an exceptional student and accomplished athlete. While he didn't particularly relish the idea of joining a team, it would keep him around campus, and challenging himself physically was how he kept his head on straight anyway. His fictitious parents lived in Seattle, and if anyone called to check up on him Aife would get the message and make the call back. Her office would receive any inquiries regarding other aspects of his history and she would handle it accordingly within her local network. She'd also included a current passport and driver's license making him nineteen on August 1st. He smiled at that. His human life had begun around that time of summer and it was a time of power for him still. It had also been a significant harvest festival for their people, his favorite part of the year. He was sure he'd said so at some point, probably when he was waxing nostalgic after too much of whatever was on tap on the rare occasions they got together. He was more than a little amused by the name she'd chosen and her reasoning. Ben Brody. The alliteration was meant to make his new identity easy to remember and she'd teased him that now he had a mild-mannered alter-ego to go with his superpowers. He'd laughed, saying he'd never pegged her for a comic book geek and an obvious Stan Lee enthusiast to boot. At least she didn't think he looked like a Ben Grimm. He didn't think his ego could take that. She'd winked and said in her best bedroom voice that she thought of him as Ben Brody by day and the Dashing Demon by night. He was rendered flushed and speechless and Aife looked like she'd never let him forget it. Whenever he thought about it for nearly a week his face felt warm. Damned body; making him feel all human.

Sighing deeply without even realizing it, he entered the number on the phone that came with his identity package. It wasn't his first, but even after all these years, he was still trying to like cell phones. The constant buzz in a pocket from someone who wanted your attention was too much like being summoned. The internet on the other hand, easily accessed from his phone or tablet, was something he loved; the whole world's information practically at the speed of thought. If he was going to pretend to be a student he supposed that was a good thing. He tapped send and held his breath.

The phone rang a number of times and Ben was preparing to leave a voicemail when a weary sounding Chris answered, "Hello?"

"Hi, um, Chris? This is Ben. You gave me a ride last week …"

Chris's voice became more animated. "Ben! I'm glad you called! I was getting worried maybe you'd decided to disappear instead of putting that sharp young mind of yours to use!"

Ben smiled at the genuine relief and affection he heard. This was tough; he already liked Chris and didn't care much for lying. It always sat badly with him. Fortunately, being convincing was survival skill he'd developed that augmented his considerable natural charisma. "I thought about it. It sounds like a lot of work; but what've I got to lose? You seem like a good teacher."

"Well, I hope so," Chris chuckled wearily. "Would you like to meet at the registrar's office tomorrow to see what we can do?" Hopeful, but not pushy.

"No, well … I just found an apartment …"

"Already?" Chris interrupted. "I don't mean to pry, but I got the impression you were on a tight budget, and this isn't the most affordable city." His voice was full of fatherly concern. "Are you ready to pay rent so soon? I know some organizations that could help if you need it."

Ben was relieved Aife already devised a story for this. "Oh yeah, I mean, more or less. I've been kind of bouncing around taking odd jobs and traveling because when I told my folks I wanted a break from school they kind of flipped out. They, you know, cut me off and whatever. Mom's a doctor and Dad's a lawyer, and I was good at school, so they're awfully invested in my education. They kinda wanted me following in their footsteps."

"Nothing wrong with that, Ben. You strike me as someone who's bright enough to excel at anything you choose. Do you have any interest in law or medicine?"

"Not even at all. Screwing people over just isn't me and I've got kind of a weak stomach for all that blood and guts stuff. You wouldn't believe the lengths I would go to avoid that crap. Why do you think I bailed?" Ben startled himself into a genuine laugh. Those were actually more or less the reasons he'd been stretching his time away from Hell. "I don't know what I want to do, but I love to travel and write. I like history. I'm decent at picking up languages, too."

"Sounds like you have a lot of promising options, Ben."

"Yeah. I hadn't even called in months. My folks are so happy I'm okay and I'm even trying to figure it out, they're helping me a little. Not as much as if I toed their line, but better than nothing. And I already found some restaurant work, so I think I'm good."

"That's wonderful, Ben." Chris paused; he was glad Ben called and was hoping to pin him down about starting school. Kids that age were nothing if not changeable, and Ben struck him as particularly impulsive. Chris already had so much on his mind he didn't want to add more worrying about Ben to his list. Thinking that he'd like to know the boy was eating regularly, he offered, "Listen, why don't you join me for dinner Sunday? We can chat and see if we can get you sorted out before the aid applications close. I have a good relationship with the Diocese so a reference from me wouldn't go amiss. I could give you a ride."

Ben didn't relish the idea of Chris picking him up outside his apartment because he thought the appearance of the building might set off a whole new level of dad-like lecturing, but he agreed and gave Chris his address. They decided on a time and said goodbye. The conversation was easier than he'd expected. Chris had actually sounded kind of frazzled, distracted. Something was up with the Gatekeeper. It was a good thing he would be around to find out what. Now, if he could just get through this meeting with Lahash and that godawful creepy bitch Lilith, he could relax.

Chapter 12

"If you are going to sin, sin against God, not the bureaucracy. God will forgive you but the bureaucracy won't."
~ Hyman Rickover

The meeting had been mercifully brief and for that Ben was grateful. He hadn't had much previous experience with Lahash and, while she looked at him down her sharp nose with her mirthless colorless eyes like something she'd found on the bottom of her shoe, she didn't leave much of an impression on him. But the sinister Lilith was about as close to a fairytale monster as you could come. Even her appearance spoke of an embrace of the darker aspects of her temperament. She had once been almost forbiddingly beautiful, but whatever she had been doing had corrupted her exterior and she was beginning to resemble her true nature; her former rich colors fading to grey, her teeth sharpening, her skin starting to crepe and sag. She had all the warmth of a pit viper and made no secret of her contempt for demons. The unblinking way she stared at him made Ben certain she was fantasizing about turning him inside out and leaving him hanging from a tree at midnight.

Alive and screaming.

Ben offered a meticulously disinterested suggestion that maybe they should head to New Hampshire or Maine, but Lahash had gotten strangely quiet, saying this area *'felt right'*. It gave him the creeps something awful. He did succeed in convincing them to go south when he remembered a small body of water conveniently named Emerald Lake sitting in a bowl shaped valley. They'd behaved as though that was all very promising, decreed his endeavor appropriate as well, and then dismissed him with all the purposeful apathy he'd come to expect from the Fallen. He'd gone home, downed a handful of Advil, and flopped on his couch, covering his face with one arm. Knowing they remained downstairs for the evening drinking and talking with the locals made his skin crawl. He decided he'd avoid reading the paper for a few days. If he saw a missing child story he thought he might have to pluck out his own eyes. Lilith had commented on the number of young families in the area, and since he'd always believed she ate the children she took, he couldn't stand knowing she'd done it while she was here meeting him.

He would rest easier when he knew they'd left. Aife had promised to text him, or perhaps come up for a drink after they were gone. Although the south of the state would be too close by half, it was certainly better than deciding to stay in his backyard. At least he could probably avoid direct contact with them for a while. Lilith had shared Lucifer's instructions regarding communications. He was to send word through Aife, who was now the only one in the area authorized to summon them. *Typical bureaucratic bullshit, but then, that was Hell for you.*

Chapter 13

"So do the shadows of our own desires stand between us and our better angels, and thus their brightness is eclipsed."
~ Charles Dickens

Metatron sat at the table opposite his brother, looking out over the garden to the corner where Enoch was scribbling away feverishly under a fig tree. Of all the places in Heaven Metatron frequented, this was the only one he found any peace lately. Michael was constantly trying to send him to Earth to search for the girl from Enoch's prophecy, but so far he'd stood firm. No one knew better than The Voice that it must have come out of Enoch's addled brain, and he wasn't about to complicate the life of some mortal simply because Michael's unfortunate pet human was burdened with instability and an overabundance of imagination. He took a long drink of wine and sighed eloquently. Sandalphon glanced up, squinting, determined to find out what had his brother's darkly handsome face looking so pinched and vexed; he gestured with his gracefully slender hands for him to pass the bottle.

"What has you in such a humor today, Voice?" He knew already, but it was better to let Metatron talk things through. His thinking was generally clearer when he spoke. He had likely been chosen for his position because his words brought clarity to himself and others.

Metatron's sigh was resonant of discontent, his pale orchid eyes sad, missing their pleasant crinkle at the corners. "I don't know, Sandy. I suppose I was just thinking about Earth and missing humans a bit."

"You're in *Heaven* for pity's sake. Do you *honestly* remember what going to Earth was like? Seems rather like an unpleasant dream to me."

"I suppose I do; perhaps being sent so often to speak with its people gave me an affinity. Maybe *that's* what I'm missing, talking to people."

"I can't imagine missing that either. If you ask me, being human seems smelly, and painful, and boring. Now that you mention it, I find talking to them much the same."

Metatron shook his dark slender head. "They're actually lovely creatures for the most part. I don't think we're nearly as nice as some of the ones I've met. The ones who aren't so pleasant seem to sort themselves out eventually. Besides, *God* loves them."

Sandalphon, always the more boisterous of the two of them, lighter in both moods and appearance, laughed out loud. "Yes, well, God loves everyone, doesn't He? Even Michael!" They had a good laugh at their brother's expense.

Michael had been making himself increasingly unpopular with a certain element, sending angels this way and that, and telling everyone God wanted one thing or another. You'd think He'd walked off and handed Michael the keys to the Kingdom the way he was throwing his weight around. As far as Metatron was concerned, if God wanted him to do a thing, God would tell him Himself. If God needed the humans to know His will, He sent Metatron. Whatever was going on, Metatron didn't like it one bit.

"If you miss it so much, go talk to a human," Sandalphon gestured toward Enoch, wiping his streaming lavender eyes with the back of his hand.

"That would hardly be talking." Metatron was dismissive. All Enoch did was yammer about the girl and her choice. Mad as a drunken monkey as far as Metatron could tell; as bad as Michael going on about her. The whole thing just rubbed Metatron the wrong way.

"It's been years since Lucifer's bunch almost snatched that little girl. Michael hasn't dropped it yet, and we've not heard from the Lord on the matter at all. If it bothers you, why don't you just contact her Guardian, have a chat with the two of them, and put an end to this?"

"What does Gabriel say about it?" Gabriel had a much finer sense for politics than her brothers and Metatron was unlikely to interact with Michael unless Gabby thought he should.

"What she usually says, of course." He chuckled. "Michael is being a brat … But she does a fair job of humoring him, or seeming to anyway. It keeps the peace." He arched a dark blond eyebrow and took a significant pause. "You might try it some time."

"Oh go on then!" Metatron waved his brother off in irritation, stood, picked up the bottle and stalked off into the garden drinking directly from the neck. Sandy had always been the least likely to rock the boat, not one to question the status quo. As the eldest, not to mention the chosen Voice, it had never bothered Metatron a bit. He supposed it made him rather a poor soldier, but that didn't bother him much either.

He wandered around for a while, occasionally plucking leaves to strip or fruit for a bite from random trees, kicking stones off the path to watch their brilliant colors blaze in the glow of Heaven. Eventually, he found himself standing over Enoch, who scribbled away, happy to be left alone, mumbling to himself. Against his better judgment he sat down on the ground with Enoch and offered him the bottle. Enoch immediately dropped his quill and grabbed it with both hands and took a long slow drink. Raphael had been distant from Enoch lately, more keeping guard than caring for him. And Michael had forbidden him wine the last time he'd torn up the garden. Looking at him now, Metatron just felt badly for the little man. The little brown grizzled creature gazed earnestly into his sharp eyes.

"She's going to choose, you know."

"Yes, Enoch, you do keep saying so." Metatron sighed. What had made him subject himself to Enoch's company?

"*God* said so, Voice. He said so." The little man bobbed his head fervently.

Metatron became annoyed. "Nonsense! I'd know because He'd have had me tell you! Or it would have exploded your tiny human brain!"

Enoch bobbed his head again vigorously. "But Voice," he tapped his wild-haired head with his finger, "He spoke in here ..." For a brief second, Enoch's eyes burned, and it was clear what had undone his mind. Seeing that spark of divine light altered the landscape quite a bit.

He put a pitying hand on Enoch's shoulder, left him the bottle, Michael's dictates be damned, and rose to find their fearless leader. His own feelings were no longer important. There was a true Divine prophecy and a young woman, barely more than a child by modern standards, was caught in the middle of it. Gabriel probably had the right of it. He would volunteer for a mission to Earth. It was only a matter of time before Michael made a real bother about it. At least this way, his new secret could be kept and he could hold Michael at arm's length. Metatron knew well the angel that had been involved in the protection of the Line from the beginning, even when other Guardians were assigned. He'd taken a particularly strong personal interest in more recent years. Lord knew Metatron had shielded this brother of theirs from Michael enough times in the past. Even though he was the superior officer, he thought they could come to an arrangement of trust. Time was slipping away and someone would have this girl for their own, removing her choice, despite the free will the humans were supposed to be blessed with. Metatron had never thought much of that approach, and he felt in his heart the time had come to make a stand on the issue.

Chapter 14

"Home is where the heart can laugh without shyness.
Home is where the heart's tears can dry
at their own pace."
~ Vernon Baker

Malin Alina Sinclair woke slowly with a sleepy smile and gave the luxuriant groaning stretch of an over-sized cat. She was in a room of her own for the first time in what seemed like forever. Having a bed big enough so she hadn't had to sleep curled on her side in a tangle of her own limbs was paradise. God, she loved it here. She'd be the first to admit that growing up the child of a free-spirited silver-smithing artist, traveling the world, staying wherever seemed like a good idea, sometimes with relatives or old friends of her dad's, other times in their big RV, was downright idyllic. It was even fascinating to help run his business at little traveling fairs between longer stays for gallery shows. She had especially enjoyed that her dad had mostly chosen homeschooling since she was terribly independent and the sorts of constraints school imposed were difficult to tolerate, to put it politely. When she was younger, Mal didn't think she'd ever get tired of it.

Her eighteenth birthday looming over the summer had changed her perspective on things somewhat. College, making her own permanent home someplace, maybe a relationship that amounted to more than a couple of weeks' worth of casual … whatever … were on the horizon. They'd had a nice enough life and she loved her dad a lot, in a way that was often fiercely protective, but she'd finally reached her limits on continuing such a weird roving existence. She needed a home base, someplace stable from which to approach her future. She'd been afraid her pronouncement would hurt her father. He seemed strangely fragile sometimes and often worried. But when she sat him down over coffee near Sedona in the spring and just asked for one normal year, the chance to be on a team, join a club, have a guidance counselor … it could be boarding school if that was easier for him … he had just smiled and said, "After all this wandering you deserve a chance to give a normal life a try. Who knows? Maybe we'll both like it."

Before she knew what happened, he'd packed everything into the RV and they'd traversed the country while he made about a million phone calls, until he found out about some gallery space and a small house right on Lake Champlain in the little town of Charlotte near where he and Mal's mother had met. Mal couldn't remember much about her mother but her dad loved it here, said it made him think of her. She spent some of her early years around New England, was born in Boston, but she had no memory of real time here, save for a vague sense she would like the smell of a fresh Christmas tree in the house, and she might want to try her painfully underdeveloped artsy side by painting with her dad when the leaves changed. The yard was big enough for a garden and a chicken coop, and the barn had more or less come with a fat black cat that was friendlier than he had any right to be.

In a little more than a month Mal would be starting her senior year at St. Augustine's, a prestigious parochial school in Burlington. She would have preferred public school, but her dad felt strongly about Catholic school for some reason, and she decided since he'd humored her about putting down some roots she could humor him about uniforms and boring religion classes. For now she was enjoying sleeping on a regular schedule and not taking over driving in the middle of the night to help get them to the next show on time or whatever else cropped up to keep them on the road. Eating food cooked somewhere other than a microwave or on a stovetop was another perk she appreciated. Her dad was secretly just about the world's greatest cook and now he had a real kitchen with an oven big enough for things other than individually wrapped frozen meals. So if he wasn't working in his studio, he was baking bread, frying chicken, or making something else warm and delicious. In fact, she thought she could smell scones, though the grey light coming in her west-facing window told her it couldn't be four a.m. yet. Hot buttered scones, jam, and strong coffee were better than dozing back off any day.

Swinging her feet onto the floor and sitting up in one graceful motion, she had to resist the urge to duck her head. Mal was tall for a girl at nearly five foot ten but she thought a gnome would have had to duck in their RV. Or maybe it just felt that way. The cramped conditions made everything seem more difficult as she got older. She untangled the intricately engraved necklace she'd had since she was a child from her slightly wild curls and smiled. When she told her ex in Sedona, if you could call someone you dated for three weeks an ex, that she was leaving, the response, instead of goodbye, had been the whisper, "Your hair reminds me of a wheat field on fire caught in the wind." An obvious line designed to get into her pants one last time, sure, but it still made her feel pretty when she thought of it.

The one disadvantage to living here was the slight dampness in the morning that seeped into the old farmhouse off the water, even now at the end of July. It made her hair an unruly mess that she referred to ruefully as Medusa-head. She'd always had nightmares about the ocean and when her dad had first showed her this place on the internet she'd been worried the dreams would start again. The lake was so big. But all this water did was project peacefulness. She even liked swimming in it, although her dad would have nothing to do with it. He only eyed the dark water doubtfully and stayed on the shore.

Mal wrestled herself into a shabby college sweatshirt and began making her way down the dim hallway and staircase. By the time she reached the creaky second step at the bottom she could see the single overhead illuminating the kitchen. The smells of coffee and cinnamon warmed the air almost as much as the old oven. Already, this place felt like home to her. Her dad's back was turned and she had practically tiptoed down and through the living room but her favorite mug sat steaming on the checkered tablecloth in front of her chair.

"Morning, Sunshine," he said from almost inside the oven as he bare-handed scones off the baking stone onto a warm plate, comically held by a hot pink rose-patterned oven mitt. Mal smirked as he turned around and put it on the table trivet. Between his camouflage cargo shorts, faded red *Late Night* t-shirt, yellow flip-flops, and some grandma's oven mitt, she thought he might want to quit being an artist and see if he could get into Clown College. Misreading her expression, he looked worried. "It is morning, right? I didn't wake you with all my banging around down here did I? I thought I could smell the sun."

She shook her head. That was just the odd kind of thing he came out with sometimes. Mal thought maybe it was purposeful, something to keep up the whole artist mystique, or maybe he was a little crazy. But it was a good crazy; a homey and predictable crazy that came from his big heart and the unique way he saw the world. Mal was already buttering a scone and stuffing it in her mouth before her giggles got the better of her. Crumbs sprayed everywhere as she laughed and choked out, "No Dad, look at yourself, seriously. It's hilarious!"

His bemused smile as he sat down with her, tossing the oven mitt into the middle of the table, told her it was going to be a good day. He could be overly serious and was sometimes so quiet and still it was like sharing the house with a living statue. But once he'd made up his mind to get silly, he was practically like having a kid brother. He flicked one of her crumbs back at her precisely. "Such table manners. My daughter, the delicate flower."

Gaining control of her early morning giggles by swallowing the huge mouthful of half-chewed scone with some volcanically hot coffee, she grinned, "You bet. About as delicate as concrete, and I have my dad's fashion sense to boot," indicating her pink leopard-print leggings and ratty grey and red hoodie. "Which is the perfect segue for the favor I wanted to ask …" He just raised his dark bushy eyebrows at her over his coffee mug. "I was kind of hoping if you're done with that piece you were working on you'd maybe take me into town and drop me off at the mall. I'd like to do a little school shopping with the money Uncle Davi sent me for my birthday." His eyebrows inclined another fraction of an inch. The expression highlighted the little scar running through one eyebrow and drew attention to the slight asymmetry of his deep blue eyes. She'd asked him about it once and he'd said it happened in the accident. Then he'd slipped into one of his quiet pensive moods for most of the day. She never brought it up now, but she thought it made him kind of more handsome. Every woman they met of even remotely similar age to him appeared to agree, although their attention always seemed lost on her dad.

"Okay, so I have my uniforms, but honestly Dad, would you want to spend your life in one of those tacky abominations? Besides I get the feeling it's going to be cold so I want get some insulated leggings, too." She knew she was rambling, but didn't seem to be able to put the brakes on. "Also, I'm kind of thinking cross-country might be a good sport to try since I like to run anyway, and the coach seems nice, but I need some new shoes ..."

"And this has absolutely nothing to do with the cute little brunette with the nose ring you were flirting with at the jewelry kiosk last week?" Amusement tinged his gentle question. Mal had agonized over coming out as bi for a while, but had kept things to herself, thinking she was never in one place long enough to have a real relationship and there was no point in causing conflict with her Catholic father if she didn't need to. She stammered a little. Ari just smiled. "Mal, I'm your dad. I notice things."

"I ... I just ... I mean ... I don't know what I mean ... I like boys too ... you probably ... I just ... I figured ... church ... and ..." She rehearsed this conversation a thousand times and not once had she considered this scenario. She had friends who'd been kicked out the second their parents suspected they weren't straight. She had another friend who was bi like her and he had a particularly hard go of it since there were so many stereotypes and it was hard to fit into the fabric of different people's expectations and still be yourself. Leave it to her dad to blow all that out of the water.

"Mal, you are how God made you. I love you for yourself. I like going to church mostly because it makes me feel close to your mom. But churches are made up of people and ... people make mistakes." He shrugged. "As far as I can tell, God doesn't make mistakes, Princess. He makes plans. I want you to always feel free to be who you are."

His smile let her know, if she wanted it to be, the subject was closed. And it was obvious he meant what he said. Wow. Acceptance like that was such a gift. Everybody should have it, but not everybody did. Despite her weird nomadic existence, she had to admit, her life was pretty damned good. First he dropped everything to move here; now he had come out *for* her and told her it was great. She got up from her chair, went around the table, and hugged him hard.

"I love you." She said simply. She was on the verge of tears, but if he wasn't going to make a big deal of this then neither was she. She made her voice purposely light, "But seriously, all I was thinking about was some clothes and maybe new shoes. My old ones reek. I don't want a relationship right now, no matter how cute somebody is. I just want to look like a normal person, plus I'm kind of going stir crazy in the house. I know I asked for it and everything ... You probably don't get it."

"Sure I do. It's weird for you to be in one spot, and even though it's what you want and you kind of love it, you're bored. This is brand new. It's been so long since we've stayed anywhere, it feels peculiar. For me, too."

She raised her own eyebrows in response. It was almost eerie how much conversation they had without talking. If you didn't know better, you'd think on some level they were reading each other's minds. Her dad's smile lit up his golden brown face. "We can go into town. I'd like to hit the bookstore near the mall. I need something to do while I'm sitting around the gallery. Maybe this time, *I'll* flirt with somebody!" Mal knew he never would, never did, but it dissipated any seriousness that might have been lingering.

"But," he stood up, "we've got hours before anything opens." He kicked his flip-flops off under the table. "I'm going to feed the chickens and go for a run." Without waiting for any response from Mal, he bounded out the door in his bare feet like a little kid, another scone in his hand.

Mal slowly finished her breakfast and cleaned up the kitchen. The man was a genius with silver, paint, even clay, and definitely all things food, but there was never a time when his creations didn't lead to an outrageous mess. After the last of the crumbs and dishes were seen to, she went to have a bath, her guilty pleasure since they'd moved in. The RV only had a smallish shower. After a long soak, she got dressed and put on a little make-up. Standing in front of the mirror scrutinizing her face she noticed the coppery tint in her hair was more prominent, probably from all her time outside lately. She had a tan now too, since while she wasn't exactly dark like her kind of Mediterranean-looking dad, she turned a pleasant golden color anytime she was outdoors much. She'd always liked her eyes. She definitely got those from her dad, although hers tended more toward grey than his, and they had funny little silver flecks that she'd never seen on anyone else. More than once when they'd been in bigger cities, modeling agents had given her their card, remarking on her long graceful limbs and unusual eyes. Yeah, right, like she'd put up with that kind of crap. Looking in the mirror now, she decided with the tan and lightened hair her eyes looked a little weird, almost fake. Swirly. Like the ocean. She pulled on her blue sundress, hoping they'd pick up the color from it. Instead it just made them look stormier today.

She lay on her bed, thinking for a while. Her dad was right, this was what she wanted and she did kind of love it, but it was so much easier to not give a damn what other people thought when you knew you'd leave in a few weeks and never see them again. She heard the screen door bang shut and after a while she could hear her dad rummaging around in the kitchen drawer for his keys. Mal got up, mentally adding a few items to her shopping list. She cast one last glance at herself before heading down the stairs. *I can do this*, she told her reflection. *I have a whole year to figure out how to make it work.*

Chapter 15

"Watch with glittering eyes the whole world around you because the greatest secrets are always hidden in the most unlikely places."
~ Roald Dahl

T he Pope sat on a simple wooden bench in his private garden. The flowers and ornamentals appreciated by his recent predecessors had been replaced by rows of vegetables, trees, and shrubs that fruited at different times of year. The bounty of the garden was distributed to poor families around the countryside. The early morning sun danced on the dew-drenched leaves, tiny rainbows and blinding pinpoints of light sparkled everywhere. The fresh clean smell of the place was always welcome.

Whatever peace the Holy Father had hoped to find here was sadly not forthcoming. The cause of his troubling thoughts that followed on after a sleepless night was contained in the letter hanging from his hand. The Bishop General of the Order of the Temple of Solomon had sent him word in his closely written scrawl about the Scion. She would end her wanderings for now, in the northeastern United States. In fact, she would apparently be attending the school where he had secured a position for the Gatekeeper just a few years ago. He was somewhat comforted by the fact that her father had chosen a Church-sponsored school and was open to help protecting her, although after what had happened to the child's mother, her father had rejected direct involvement with the Templars. Fortunately, they were reliably circumspect these days.

The prophecy was unfolding. The final secret of Fatima, not the one revealed to the public, the real secret, known only to a select few members of the church hierarchy. Himself, the little grey man knew the words by heart. Not that he'd pass them on to the Templars. But he had to do something. While the Order of Solomon was not officially associated with the Church, they had deferred to it for some time. The Pope had no idea how to respond, be of help, or even where to begin. Unsure how best to proceed, with all of these signs appearing together in his sight, he determined some fasting and prayer to clear his mind was the best next step.

Chapter 16

"Memories are the key not to the past,
but to the future."
~ Corrie Ten Boom

Mal drove into the city with the radio blaring and windows down so the short trip was turning her curls into an unruly jumble. The glorious freedom of having a car of her own was as unexpected as it was appreciated. She'd never had much room for 'stuff' growing up. Rather than tangible gifts, birthdays usually involved a meal at a nice restaurant and a unique experience, like the Falls in Niagara or the Van Gogh exhibit in Amsterdam. This year, she'd asked her dad to just cook for her at home. She figured he'd already given her a huge gift in agreeing to be here, so after breakfast on her birthday when she'd gotten up from the table to go feed the chickens and her dad had said, "Think fast!" the last thing she had expected to catch was car keys.

Granted the brown Volvo was about a million years old, but to Mal that just meant it was reliable and she and her dad could keep it in repair themselves. And after driving around the RV from the moment she'd been able to reach the pedals, and handling ill-kept rental cars in some legitimately strange places, this car was a breeze. She couldn't love her dad any more than she did; in fact, she adored him. But considering they lived about ten feet apart for most of her life, the simple act of claiming some space and independence was like Heaven. Just the chance to take off and meet a couple of the girls she'd connected with over the summer and do a little shopping, maybe grab some lunch, was a luxury so new she was positively reveling in it. She was looking forward to checking out Church Street Marketplace. Everyone talked about it but since they'd been busy setting up her dad's gallery in Shelburne and they did most of their shopping there or in South Burlington she hadn't yet made it there. Mal often formed close friendships quickly, and her new almost constant companion was no exception. Besides Petra was a daring little punk rock waif who, in an effort to piss off her wealthy board-of-director parents, always knew where the best parties were and where to have the most fun. With Petra's directions, navigating downtown was easy. She pulled into the parking structure on Cherry Street, left her ticket on the dash, locked up, and made her way through what was known locally as the Underground Mall, to what everyone assured her was the best place to meet up in the whole city, Queen City Buzz, or sometimes QCB, or just The Buzz if you were being cool.

The mid-August air was hot and hazy, dampening her skin and frizzing her hair, and the skies over Lake Champlain promised storms later in the day. Mal smiled in anticipation. Watching the summer storms roll across the lake, rain falling in decorative sheets, from their little porch swing had quickly become one of her favorite pastimes. She normally didn't like rainy weather; it usually made her feel inexplicably jumpy, but the show thunderstorms put on over the water here usually drove her anxieties away.

When she pushed out of the doors and caught her first glimpse of the large open-air pedestrian mall full of visitors from all over the region, she grinned. Vendors, food carts, and street performers filled several blocks. Diners at various establishments sat outside on the cobblestoned street enjoying the late summer scene while grabbing some lunch, and most likely a cold beer. The noise, the intermingling music, the smells of food, the pleasant crush of people, reminded Mal of years traveling to carnivals and fairs with her dad in the best possible way. It had all of the glamour and excitement, but none of the rundown tiredness. Mal made her way south through the crowds toward the courthouse looking around for the sign for the coffee shop. Emily's voice caught her ear over the noise of impressed spectators *ooing* and *ahing* over some half-naked guy juggling flaming sticks.

"Mal! Hey! Over here!"

She saw her new friends, as well as quite a number of unfamiliar young faces, crowded around a smallish table under an awning. There were more people than she had expected but that was fine by her. Mal had never been shy. Her dad often said, given an audience, she'd go on making up stories and entertaining until she lost her voice. All the traveling and helping her dad with his business had only served to make her even more comfortable meeting new people, so she quickly joined the group, introduced herself around, and did her best to commit the names to memory. Teddy was easy enough. He was an adorable baby-faced ginger with freckles and a quiet pleasant voice. She knew he couldn't be as young as he looked since he was built like a miniature prize-fighter, and although they hadn't had a chance to talk, she recognized him from the pre-season seniors-only meeting with the cross-country coach. She was sure they'd speak more soon since practice was starting Monday ahead of school. There were so many new faces Mal quickly jumbled up all the names in her mind. The only other one she could remember after was a boy who turned out to be Emily's younger brother, because she might have asked him out if he were a little older. Mal thought he must've gotten all the cute genes in the family because while Emily was a lovely person, she was overly thin, a little mousy, and just kind of beige all over. Little brother reminded her of her favorite TV show hero with a beat up Army jacket, broad shoulders, and big green Disney-Princess eyes. Unfortunately, she knew he was only about fifteen. Emily introduced him as Toby, but he'd thrown a dark look at his sister and said in an overly deep register clearly meant to make him sound older, "Please, call me Rob."

Petra and Emily led her inside the beautiful air conditioned shop and insisted on buying her a sweet, frothy, blended iced coffee and a giant cookie. While the barista fixed her drink, Mal checked out what was sure to be her new hangout. This was a nice place; a mix of soft inviting furniture and more utilitarian tables and chairs made it a great place for everything from casual socializing to serious studying. As Mal scanned the interior she noticed a young man at one of the back tables situated in a secluded corner. He was almost offensively good-looking; a strong jaw paired with an almost elfishly sharp chin, dimples, and even though he was hunched over a book, she could see broad muscular shoulders, advertising an exceptional physique. His tousled butter blond hair was long enough to be wavy but not quite hang in his unusual eyes, which she could see, even from a distance, were a beautiful deep golden color. Not to mention his outrageous long pale paintbrush lashes. *Dear God.* Mal was sorely tempted to just go sit down at his table and introduce herself. He looked a little older than her, although he'd obviously been a few days without shaving, and the thick books stacked in front of him screamed studious college boy but, what the hell, she was eighteen, right? She willed him to look up at her, even cleared her throat not so subtly. Not so much as a flicker. He just continued to read and scribble notes, pen cap between his teeth, scratching absently at his jaw.

Then her coffee was ready and they went out to the crowded table and everyone sang a loud and boisterous happy birthday since today was the first time she'd gotten to take the car out just for fun. Mal was so happy she almost cried. This is what it was like to be normal. Friends, and food, and songs. This was what her heart had been aching for, and what her father was working so hard to give her. For all of his efforts to hide it, it was clearly difficult for him to stay in one spot, so she was determined to truly appreciate it for the gift it was.

After too many treats, the sweaty, sugared-up, caffeinated group decided to walk around. It was the only natural thing to do even in the oppressive heat. They wandered in and out of shops, ate dripping *Ben and Jerry's* ice cream cones, and dropped change into musicians' cases. Mal seriously considered getting her eyebrow pierced. Her friends, especially Petra who had several piercings of her own, were more than happy to egg her on. She decided against it, imagining her dad's face if the first time she went out with the car she came back with a facial piercing. He'd tried to hide his shock when she'd shaved her head on one side a few years ago, but she'd seen it anyway. Then she considered a tattoo, but the wait was long in the little parlor off the main drag, and the pinched expression on the face of the girl in the chair made her want to think it over a little longer. Her friends booed good-naturedly when she came back out onto the sidewalk.

"You try to overdose me on coffee and chocolate and now I have to bleed for you too?" she joked. Still, everyone was determined to find something interesting and unusual to mark the day.

As they wandered, dark clouds began to gather more rapidly over the water. They did pop into a salon and several of them, including Mal, came out with a bright red temporary streak supposedly to honor their school's colors. Mal thought the day was already as exciting as it needed to be and suggested she had better head home. At this time of day Charlotte could be better than a half hour from town and she never liked driving in the rain. Everyone insisted on one more pass before letting her go. They came upon a table they hadn't noticed earlier, covered in dark velvet and tacky metallic moons and stars. Behind it sat an older woman, at least forty-five, and she must have once been truly beautiful. She was still kind of sexy in an intentional way with heavily lidded eyes and interesting dramatic makeup. Her dark hair shot with silver was mostly covered with a purple silk scarf, and her blood-red fingernails were at least two inches long. This theatrical display could only mean one thing. A fortuneteller. Mal clapped her hands. In their travels, Mal had seen many similar booths but her dad was always dead set against them. If anything could make this memorable it would be sitting for a reading with a forbidden mystic. Petra, her still 'in the broom closet' Wiccan friend, was so enthusiastic about it she slapped down the five dollars required by the sign. Mal sat down in the folding chair on the street side of the table, unsure of what to expect, but thrilled to be doing something new.

"What kinda reading ya want?" The woman's pleasant voice and Brooklyn accent ruined the mystique a little bit, but in the gathering gloom, with the flickering candles on the table, it was still sufficiently fun and spooky in a silly way.

She giggled, "A good one? I don't know! I've never done this!"

"Do Tarot," encouraged Petra, "you'll like it." Mal dipped her head in assent and the fortuneteller, whom Mal noticed was called Madam Meredith from a business card propped in front of her crystal ball, pulled a deck of oversized cards from a black velvet pouch, shuffled them, asked Mal to cut the deck, and spread them out in a pattern resembling a plus sign and a capital 'I'. The pictures were exceptionally fine, even though they were a little bizarre. Mal waited to hear what they were supposed to mean. The woman's expression clouded and her head tilted as though she was confused, but then her face smoothed and she began her practiced spiel.

"This is an interesting spread, my dear. Your present is represented by the King of Pentacles. This is very good. It's saying where you are right now is lucky and everything you do is going to go the way it's supposed to." She looked expectantly at Mal, who just smiled encouragement. "Your position in the cards is represented by The Empress and this is most beneficial with your Present card. It means you are a creator. You're choosing your destiny."

"Well, that's pretty good!" Mal liked that a lot. *The Empress. Hell, yes.*

"Your immediate future is sure to include romantic love capable of lasting forever." She tapped the card. "The Ace of Cups in this position is nearly always predictive of happy couples, especially considering your own energies and the energies of your present." Mal was getting skeptical. This all sounded a little too lovely, a little too canned. She had no interest in falling in love right now, but she suspected that's what many teenagers who sat in this chair were hoping to hear. Sensing she might be losing her audience, Madam Meredith pressed on.

"Influences in your life include the Strength card. I am sensing a strong association with the lion symbolism in this card. Does that mean anything to you?"

"Wow, weird. My dad's name literally means lion. He's pretty much the biggest influence in my life." Mal laughed a little nervously.

Madam Meredith's eyes skimmed over the rest of the cards and moved on to the Outcome position. "Here we have the ultimate outcome in your situation represented by The World, which suggests supreme peace, happiness, and union." She projected professional satisfaction. You couldn't ask for more than that. Besides it was starting to rain and what she wanted to do was get things inside before they got ruined.

"Yeah, okay," Mal frowned, oblivious to the fat raindrops falling almost in slow motion around them. "But what about all this other stuff? There's like ten cards here and you haven't told me about even half of them. Like what's this one?" She put her finger on a card depicting a man holding bamboo or some kind of staff.

"That's the advice card. It's the Seven of Wands. It is a sign you'll have to face your fears to attain your outcome."

"What about this one?" This time she pointed to a terrifying card depicting a bleeding body riddled with swords.

There was a forceful note in her voice she didn't like, but she wanted to know.

"It doesn't affect your outcome, my dear." She would rather have spared her this card. But then maybe it was nothing.

"Seriously?" Mal's tone conveyed her disdain flawlessly. *Fine*, Meredith decided. *If she wants it, she's going to get it.*

"This is the card signifying your past. Someone was taken from you violently."

Mal frowned. "My mom died in a bad accident when I was a kid. I guess that makes sense." Mal felt a little ashamed of making such a big deal. This was the one card that had been scaring her and even if it was accurate it was something she didn't remember and it wasn't painful to her. "Sorry, you probably want to get out of the rain."

Before she could stop herself, Meredith continued, "No, not an accident. Deliberate violence was done to this person and it ended in tragedy. This card represents someone made to suffer for something beyond their control."

As if on cue, thunder crashed and the skies opened.

Cries of dismay and some colorful cursing went through the group and they ran for the doors of the mall. When they got inside everyone wanted to hang out and maybe grab a pizza but Mal felt weirdly unsettled, her heart beating much faster than a little run from the street could explain. She begged off, saying her dad would already be worried because she hadn't been in touch and she didn't dare use her phone because it had gotten wet. Everyone offered to walk her to her car, but she waved them off, telling them they'd better get in line if they wanted a pizza because people from the street were now funneling into the mall to wait out the storm.

She walked through the parking garage feeling edgy. It was pouring now, the rain sounding like the end of the world on the metal roof, and it was kind of dark in there. She got to her car and, when she moved to unlock her door, dropped her keys. Her hands were shaking. *What the hell?* The fortune teller's reading had been a frivolous game and nothing she'd said could be true. *Magic and mysticism are make-believe, no matter how convincing the woman sounded.* She took a deep breath, picked up her keys, and hurried into her car, eager to be home. She wanted to tell her dad about her day and stuff her face with some of the French bread he'd been rising on the table this morning.

Her drive home was unbelievably stressful with sheets of pelting rain destroying visibility and cars appearing stopped abruptly in front of her, all while thunder rumbled overhead, and lightning flashed in all directions, disorienting her several times. God, she hated thunderstorms. She should have just stayed home. She was so wound from the commute, which took far longer than it should have, she'd more or less forgotten how unsettled she'd been after her strange encounter.

Her dad was more than a little happy to see her when she slammed the screen door looking like a drowned rat and was totally sympathetic. He'd been ready to go out looking for her given the severity of the storm. He made tea and didn't even insist they eat a real dinner. They took a couple of loaves of warm bread into the little living room, along with the butter dish, swiping pieces of bread through it as they tore them off the loaf, heedless of the crumbs they were scattering everywhere. They sat on the beat up old couch in front of the TV watching *Star Trek the Next Generation*; all the Q episodes, which were their mutual favorites. Mal laughed until her stomach ached. Sci-fi and carbs were a sure cure for all the ills of the world, and they miraculously didn't lose power all evening. By the time she was ready to go up to bed she was so full of good bread and tea and pleasant thoughts of her day, her weird experience and terrible drive were all but forgotten. For now, at least, the worst of the thunder and lightning had passed so all she could hear as she laid down to sleep was the steady thrum of the rain on the roof and the wind blowing around the water on the lake.

During the night the storm rolled back into the area with a vengeance. Thunder, lightning, and trees tossing in the wind created such a racket that it leaked into Mal's dreams. At first it was a strange random flashing and noise in the periphery of her awareness while she wandered an empty Church Street alone. She had a sense she was dreaming when actual tumbleweeds drifted over the stones in front of her. Then lightning struck about ten feet away and out of the smoking pavement Madam Meredith emerged, her body pierced with many splintered pieces of wood.

"I'm the Ten of Swords. I don't affect your outcome," she choked, blood bubbling from her mouth.

Mal closed her eyes in horror. She felt a jolt and opened them to find herself the middle of the lake, or maybe it was the ocean, in a ridiculous little inflatable yellow boat like she'd had when she was little for playing in the pool. Rain blustered around her obscuring everything but the angry waves. She was soaked and freezing. She couldn't remember ever being cold in a dream before, even in her worst childhood nightmares. *What if this was somehow real?* Her sense of panic quickly escalated with her growing discomfort. She was so cold now her extremities were burning and her teeth chattering.

A wavering light penetrated the downpour from far away. Desperate to be heard and pulled from this terrible place, she screamed for help until her throat hurt. A huge wave crested in front of her and she saw a raft balanced on the top. Her father was there, on his knees, crying, bleeding. Her mother, who she knew best from pictures and scattered pleasant memories, was lashed to the mast, head lolling against her chest, insides spilling out through a gaping wound in her middle. There was a monstrous creature standing between her mother and father with glowing red eyes and blood dripping from its enormous mouth and claws. Mal was too terrified to scream anymore. Out of the tempest, her Uncle Davi walked calmly toward them over the waves. She tried to call out to him, but found she had no voice left. He reached out toward the raft and her father was tossed into the deep. The raft began burning, the horrible bloody man melting. As she was also consumed by the flames, Mal's dead mother lifted her head, eyes glassy and unseeing and she croaked, "You will have to choose, Malin."

Mal woke up screaming hoarsely just in time to see her father crashing into the room with a flashlight in hand. He was sitting by her side, holding her, just like he had when she was small, before she'd even struggled all the way upright. He rocked her like a child, smoothing her hair away from her tear-stained face.

"Honey, what is it? What's wrong?"

"A dream ... you ... mom ... the blood," she sobbed, in a strained whisper.

The power had finally succumbed to the fury of the storm. He helped her out of bed and led her downstairs in the dark and silent house. He put the flashlight in her shaking hands and moved around the room lighting every candle and kerosene lantern he could put his hands on until the living room was bathed in a comforting glow. Then he disappeared into the kitchen and she could hear him rattling around but couldn't bring herself to go see what he was up to. She couldn't even make her trembling hands turn off the flashlight. Her father came back into the room carrying a glass and a dark bottle. He put the glass in front of her on the coffee table and poured out a generous portion of a dark golden liquid. When she didn't move, he pried the flashlight from her hands, turned it off, and replaced it with the glass.

"You'll probably think this tastes awful, but it will help calm you down."

She sniffed it. It burned her nostrils. She sipped it and it burned her tongue and throat, too. Even when the opportunity came up, Mal wasn't much of a drinker, but she sort of liked this. In a strained voice, she croaked, "What is it?"

"Brandy. It's the best I can do with the stove off." She looked at him questioningly, and he shrugged his apology. "No tea."

She took another long sip, still shaking, still cold actually, but after a few minutes she could feel a pleasant diffuse warmth starting to spread and the sharp edges of her jangling nerves softening. When she spoke again she sounded much less like she was recovering from strep throat. "No, it's good."

"You haven't woken up like that since you were eight." As she settled down, she could hear that her dad was kind of shaken too. She supposed hearing your only kid screaming like someone was killing her in a dark house would be enough to unsettle any halfway decent parent, and her dad was way above average.

"I could go another ten years, or you know, forever, and be totally okay with it." She emptied the glass and before she could put it down he refilled it. Finally, her shaking was subsiding and her throat no longer felt so raw, so she accepted it without comment.

"Can you tell me what it was about? If you don't want to, it's okay," he said quickly.

"No, I can tell you. Maybe it will seem more like a dream if you hear it." She curled her feet under her and leaned against him, still shivering a little, and recounted the horror of her dream. She could feel him getting tense. When she finished talking she sat up, saw his expression, and just passed him her glass. He drained it in one swallow. "I shouldn't have told you. You were with her when ... I can't imagine what it must have been like. I'm sorry."

He shook his head, as if to clear it. "Don't be sorry, Mal. I always want you to tell me when something upsets you, even if it's hard for me to hear."

"I'll try," she hedged quietly.

"Look, we'll just sit here on the couch like the old days and if you go back to sleep I'll be right here with you. Okay?"

She gratefully curled back up against him, burrowing her feet under the cushion. As warm as it had been all day, she just couldn't shake the bone-deep chill she'd felt while she was being tossed around that nightmare sea. As she dozed off, she sensed her dad fishing his cell phone out of the pocket of his sweatpants and start texting back and forth with someone. Who would you text in the middle of the night just because your kid freaked out on you? *Maybe he finally has a girlfriend*, she thought as she fell back asleep to pleasant dreams of birthday songs, sweets, and friends making sure she was happy.

Chapter 17

"Go fast enough to get there, but slow enough to see."
~ Jimmy Buffett

Sitting in the grass, stretching tight hamstrings, Mal was grateful for how well her dad had chosen for her last high school experience. Cross-country was turning out to be the highlight of the Fall. She had natural speed and endurance and had picked up some decent running habits from her dad to begin with, but now that the year was gearing up she was getting to find out why St. Augustine's had such a formidable team. Because it was affiliated with Saint Thomas's College through the church, many high school activities that had a college counterpart paired students up with grade-equivalent peer mentors at the college. Cross-country was one of those lucky teams. They practiced together as often as their schedules allowed. Mal's mentor was a thin speedy senior named Trish who was dialed in to everything happening on campus, and was a wealth of information about running, school, and life in general.

"You might want to practice with your breathing and pacing a little for competition. I've noticed that you spend all your air early by starting so fast. It slows you down at the finish."

Trish was an insanely even athlete. "Mmmm. I'll stick with your pace group next time."

Mal was not really paying attention. She liked to watch the others, measure her own skill against theirs in her head, although right now she found herself boy-watching. Rounding the last bend on the endurance course the coach set for them was the second wave of runners, or at least the first of them. The rest of the pack was far behind this boy so she was getting a good look. She hadn't seen him at practice before. She would have remembered. He was tall, fair-haired, deeply tan, and ridiculously attractive in his red and white running shorts and sleeveless shirt. It was clear his workouts went well beyond cardio, although he didn't look like a gym rat either. He had a flexible strength that looked much too functional to be purely vanity lifting. He waved at the trainer who was timing the group as he passed, still moving like he was fresh off the line. He slowed his pace as he approached the water fountain on the corner of the brick building. He seemed kind of familiar. That was probably wishful thinking though. Maybe she just wanted him to *be* familiar. He peeled off his shirt and wiped his sweaty face with it. *Holy abs! And holy ink!* Emblazoned across the center of his chiseled chest was an extremely cool tribal sun in reds, oranges, and yellows. He was gorgeous and shining in the late September sun. Then it hit her; *this was the stupidly hot guy from the coffee shop this summer.* Her thoughts had wandered to him frequently since that day, mostly regretting not introducing herself when she had the chance. *Damn*, she'd been right; *he* was *well-built.* She must have made some sound because Trish laughed and patted her shoulder.

"So, you've noticed Ben."

"Wha? Um, no … Well, maybe." She was mildly embarrassed she'd been caught ignoring her mentor and more or less drooling over someone she'd never met.

"Yeah, *everyone* notices Ben Brody. He's kind of noticeable." She gave a sigh and a doleful shake of her head. "Good luck to anyone who can get him to notice them back."

"Why?"

"All he does is run and squint at dusty old books. You'd think he was a monk."

"*Please* tell me he's not a divinity student." Mal sounded horrified at the very idea.

Trish laughed, "No! He doesn't even go to mass when they let out classes for it." She smirked at Mal's look of relief. "He's just a real book worm; kind of Dr. G's little protégé. He's in a bunch of advanced programs and all kinds of independent study stuff. He's an unreal runner, too. He's set a bunch of school and division records. And he runs for charity, of course, because being smart and gorgeous isn't enough. Like last spring he did the local marathon in his bare feet for the food basket program and raised a ton of money."

"He must be crazy! Although come to think of it, my dad's a terrific runner and he'd rather be barefoot, so maybe shoes are overrated."

"Or maybe they're just masochists," Trish shook her head in open disapproval at the idea of hitting the pavement without shoes. "Oh, and my God, you have to see him sprint. He's like lightning on the track. The kid runs like he's trying to get away from the devil himself. And he never seems to tire out."

"I'll bet." Mal sighed, maybe a tad wistfully, "I'm sure he wouldn't notice me anyway since I'm still in high school."

"You're eighteen. Besides he's only a sophomore, so he might if he ever took his nose out of a book! To be fair, he does a *few* other things. He's a pretty good actor and he destroys people at debate."

"I'm rubbish at theater, but I'm on the high school debate team. I was picturing somebody kind of bookish, but he must be the '*Ben*' Dr. G was telling us about. He's never made it to one of our joint discussions though."

That sounded all kinds of promising.

"I guess he works a lot because he's on the outs with his folks. And he's Dr. G's research assistant. Or whatever."

"Oh. So hey, I'm thirsty," Mal got casually to her feet. "Back in a sec."

Trish grinned. They both knew what she was up to. She covered the distance to the fountain at a light jog, her ponytail a swish of tangled curls down her back. He was looking right at her. She was about to speak but he brushed past almost running into her, calling out to Rob, Emily's baby brother, whom he was apparently supposed to be mentoring. *Damn it!* She thought she looked cute today, too! She filled her water bottle anyway and rejoined Trish with an almost comically disgruntled expression. Trish was laughing, practically reading Mal's mind.

"See, I told you! Oblivious! Don't let it get in your head. He's just that guy."

Well, '*that guy*' would be around for at least a few more practices and maybe, if she got lucky, a debate meeting or two. She didn't think she wanted a relationship with anyone before today, but damned if this golden-headed speedster didn't make her question her judgment. Besides, she could use a distraction to get her mind off all of her weird dreams, and he could probably be very pleasantly distracting if she gave him the chance.

Chapter 18

"A true friend is someone who lets you have total freedom to be yourself ... That's what real love amounts to – letting a person be what he really is." ~
Jim Morrison

Ben sat drinking his third coffee of the afternoon, anticipating the arrival of a few seniors from the high school debate team along with their coach and maybe a couple of other kids from St. Thomas's. After everything that happened over the last year, he was glad he and Chris were still friends; glad and surprised. Certainly, they'd always had a connection. Ben reminded Chris of what it was like to have someone around that grounded him, someone to care and worry about, and Chris reminded Ben of what it meant to be human, to be looked after. Chris often made him forget he wasn't just a kid without much of a rudder. It was that momentary forgetting that led them to the present state of their relationship; one more beneficial, if much more complicated for both of them.

It began innocently enough as a History 101 assignment, right before winter break last year. Chris, or Dr. G, as all his students called him, had assigned a short paper to culminate their Ancient Rome unit – *The Gifts of the Roman Empire to the Modern World*. Ben had set out to get another 'A' he could pretend to call home about. But *GODDAMNIT* the more he read the assigned materials, the more it dragged up unpleasant memories; and the more the scar on his chest (which he couldn't seem to get rid of no matter what magic he tried) bothered him. Vivid images filled his head, of his whole family, even the young woman who had been his intended bride, torn apart by Rome's ambition. He could almost forgive the spear that had burst his heart. He was a warrior, after all. He could even forgive the deaths of his father and brothers for the same reason. All those villagers though, those children? None of them were fit for battle, nor had any particular quarrel with Rome.

The whole thing gave him a terrible headache, and Aife complained he was intolerable to work with and had pissed off half her clientele within a hundred miles. But he'd written the damned paper and he'd tried to give Chris what he asked for. The next Friday however, the man who'd been feeding him Sunday dinner and checking up on him for better than half a year, passed back papers during the final exam, the last class before the holiday, and instead of a graded paper, all he placed in front of Ben was his cover page with the scribbled note, *Please see me in my office before you leave for break.*

Ben had gone through the motions for the rest of the day, thinking only of that paper and how it had made him feel to write it. He was pretty sure he'd bombed his math exam as a result, which only increased his irritation. By the time four thirty wound around, Ben was in knots. His shoulders ached, his stomach churned, his teeth felt brittle from clenching his jaw. *What the hell was the problem?* He'd done the stupid paper! So if he didn't like it, why didn't Chris just fail him? That was easy enough and it wasn't like one bad grade would even hurt his average all that much. He'd still probably make an 'A-' for the term. Maybe a 'B+' but that wasn't the end of the world, not really. *Why the cryptic note, the private meeting? This is starting to be more trouble than it's worth.* He hadn't gotten anywhere with this prophecy and there didn't seem to be anything particularly remarkable about Chris either. He was in a state of total male adolescent pique by the time he dragged himself to Chris's office. All his years in this body should probably have tempered the throes of fading adolescence, but Ben found himself caught in the full force of his biological age.

He hadn't even knocked when he'd arrived. He just banged the door open, kicked it shut noisily behind him, and dropped gracelessly onto the leather couch opposite Chris's desk with a loud sigh, looking completely put upon. Chris glanced up from the late paper he'd been grading, and raised an eyebrow. "Hello, Ben," he greeted in a measured voice, "How are you this afternoon?"

Ben, unable to contain himself any more, snapped, "What the hell Chris? I have to work this afternoon. If you want to fail me it wouldn't be the first time I ever sucked at something! Just do it and let me go earn my fucking rent!"

Ben's choice of words and heated tone let Chris know immediately his instincts had been correct. *This paper touched a nerve, but why? What possible nerve could discussing things like public sanitation, a professional military, clean water, and maintained roads touch for a kid from a privileged family in Seattle?* The answer was, of course, none, so Chris was determined to find out what was going on.

"Ben, son, calm down." Chris spoke like Ben was a frightened animal and poured tea into a spare cup, passing it across his desk, the way Ben always took it; Earl Grey, brewed strong, served plain. Ben grudgingly took a sip and scowled at Chris.

"I am calm," Ben frowned, sounding anything but. "But seriously, what do you want from me?"

"It's a well-written paper." Chris paused thinking how to phrase his thoughts, especially with Ben's indignant expression asking what he was doing here feeling totally called on the carpet. "You've earned another 'A' if worrying about a grade is what has you so upset. I should have put that in my note."

Ben puffed out a frustrated breath. He'd probably earned a 'C' on that math test today; if he was lucky. Twenty percent of his goddamned grade. And all because he'd been worried about this paper. *Sonofabitch.*

Chris had certainly dealt with more than his fair share of first time college students who had trouble managing the demands of school, life, and outside work, so he could practically read all of this in the lines forming on Ben's forehead. He quickly went on to explain, "I just found it unusual and I wanted to talk to you about it as your teacher. I found the tone a little concerning, so I also wanted to ask you about it as your friend."

The defiant set of Ben's jaw suggested he should come quickly to a point. Chris often thought Ben was in danger of just walking off campus and never being heard from again. It wasn't the work; Ben was a straight 'A' student most of the time and that didn't seem to tax him much. Nor was it extracurricular activities; he was a star on the track, in the theater, on the debate team. But even the most casual observer could tell he was frequently on edge. He was often distracted, never really still for a moment. With most kids his age it was usually something simple; girl trouble, a fight with mom and dad, a broken down car. But with Ben it seemed much more complicated, although Chris couldn't have said why. There was just something about him.

"Ben, it was just a silly little paper. I wanted you to sum up what we've covered and I didn't want anyone to have to work too hard the week before finals, but you took it awfully seriously. Your paper was almost political. It seemed very," he groped for an uninflammatory word and had to settle on, "angry."

Ben drained his cup and set it down quite a bit harder than necessary on the end table. "Yeah, well, maybe I don't think it was such a good topic for a light paper. Maybe I wanted to treat it with the seriousness it deserves." He folded his arms obstinately. The headache that plagued him the whole time he'd written the paper was throbbing at his temples, making him narrow his eyes against the light.

"Ben, honestly, I'm concerned for you. We were just talking about what Rome brought to the world, things we can still appreciate. You included an awful lot from outside sources. It must have taken hours. Why go through so much effort?"

"A lot of what happened wasn't in the assigned reading!" Ben's belligerent tone increased Chris's concern.

"I'm sorry I made such a production out of this. You're right of course, but you just seem to feel this so deeply. I'm trying to understand why you're so upset about discussing the high points of civilization." Chris folded his hands and sat back quietly, waiting for Ben to fill the silence.

"High points of civilization?" Ben was incredulous.

"Ben, certainly you can see the contributions ..." Chris trailed off as he noticed Ben's hands involuntarily clenching and unclenching.

"Look, the Romans did a lot of horrible things, too," Ben spat, red in the face. Under his breath he added, "You of all people should know that, Cartaphilis!"

Chris stiffened and looked almost confused.

Ben sucked in his breath. *It just slipped out.* He knew Chris had heard him in the quiet office, too. Now, he'd done it. *Shit.* "I'm sorry. I shouldn't put that on you ... I ..." Ben closed his eyes; his pounding head was making it hard to concentrate and nearly impossible to access any of his powers.

Chris felt cold all over and was telling himself half-heartedly that Ben was just cracking under the pressure of starting school and he just needed a rest over vacation, but he was beginning to process what had actually been said. Denial was easier.

"Ben, I want to help, and this isn't an accusation, but are you taking drugs?"

After his brief fit of temper, Ben calmed down enough to analyze the situation. Maybe it was time. There had to be a reason he was drawn to this guy. Chris might be acting like he thought Ben was just some kid having a freshman freakout, but Ben knew he was in too deep and something in Chris's eyes told him it was now or never. *Well, fuck it.* He looked at Chris levelly and took the leap.

"Cards on the table, Gatekeeper?" Chris blanched as reality dawned. "We're both more than we seem." Ben rose from the couch and took a careful step toward the desk. "*I* know who *you* are. So, it's only fair I introduce myself properly." Ben allowed his eyes to glow subtly and the last of the color drained from Chris's face. "I'm known elsewhere as Lord Ronoven, Master of Expression, Gatherer of Old Souls, and Collector of the Unwanted. Not to mention Count and Marquis of Hell, Commander of Twenty Legions." He sketched a little bow, thinking it was probably overkill, but sort of wanting to do it anyway. He had a dramatic streak he couldn't always quash.

Chris sat in stunned silence, studying him with a kind of slow growing horror. Ben flopped back down on the couch, his usual slightly coltish grace absent.

Every inch the lanky teen that hasn't quite figured out how to manage his limbs, he huffed, "Prob'ly don't wanna shake hands, huh?"

"You're a *demon*?" Chris was ready to work up a professorial frenzy and Ben already knew he could lecture himself hoarse; with his painfully pounding temples, he couldn't cope.

"You've done your share, Centurion." Ben's voice was cold, flat. Chris's stunned expression looked like he'd been slapped. Hard. Ben immediately backpedaled, feeling badly about his verbal attack on a man who'd only ever been kind to him. "Shit, Chris I'm sorry. I had no call to bring up your old life." *Damn it. Things just keep slipping out.* "I mean, we're friends right? At least we were up to now. We don't need to be miserable to each other just because I've cleared the air some."

Chris didn't know what to make of this. How could this boy sitting in front of him, whom he had come to truly care for, be a demon? Ben was a gifted student, a thoughtful person, a genuine pleasure to know. All that came to mind was the hesitant question, "What are you doing here?"

Ben sank back into the couch, rubbing his forehead. "Well, what I'm supposed to be doing and what I'm actually doing are kind of two different things. Which do you want first?" Chris looked back with blank shock, so Ben continued. "Look … there's this prophecy …"

"The Emerald Hill Prophecy?"

Ben nodded soberly.

Chris's voice hardened, "Are you here for me?"

"No!" Ben wanted it clear right up front that he would never attack Chris. Not only was the idea objectionable to him, he didn't want this man, whose energy broadcasted that he was a talented mage and an adept fighter, to jump the gun and come after him. That would be all sorts of bad news. He continued, "Not exactly anyway. At first when I met you I did kind of follow you, but that's not what I was sent for. Hell doesn't even know I know you."

"So … what? You're on a mission to kidnap or murder a girl?"

"Jesus, Chris, you think ..? Never mind, we'll get to that … I'm glad you know. Telling someone they're named in some doomy sounding prophecy is the least fun thing ever." He paused. "What I'm *supposed* to be doing, along with half the other demons in Hell, is looking for the girl, and if I find her, I'm *supposed to* summon Lucifer's latest assassin." Chris gasped. "Oh yeah, Lucifer's a real thing, and he's a total fuckwit, too. He says he wants to kill her because apparently being half-angel is the worst thing somebody can do." Ben laughed nervously. "I guess if they're all like him, I get where he's coming from."

Chris had to smile a little. Always effortlessly charming, Ben often unintentionally drew people into agreeable moods. "If you're not doing what you're supposed to, what *are* you doing here? Are you possessing some poor kid, Ronoven?"

"Please, don't call me that," Ben said abruptly, looking hurt. "Look, I'm not possessing anybody. I'm not *evil*. A couple thousand years ago I got a Roman spear through the chest before I'd even had a chance to start a family or have anything like a real life of my own and I found myself in Hell. I did what I had to do to survive. But it's not like I ever *liked* any of it … Well, maybe some of it, but not most of it! I'm just not stupid enough to choose to suffer for no good reason. Like maybe the stories you've heard don't do it justice, but AC/DC was full of shit … Hell sucks." Ben stretched his neck, trying to loosen the tension making his headache worse. "Chris, I hate to ask, but do you have some aspirin or something?"

"Demons get headaches?" Chris was skeptical, but began fishing around in his messy top drawer anyway. When he found it, he tossed Ben his bottle of Advil, stood and retrieved his cup to pour him more tea, a strangely familiar ritual between them.

Ben caught the bottle and dry-swallowed four pills, grimacing slightly, before answering. "Well, not specifically, but whenever I'm in this body I do."

"Tell me again how you're not possessing anyone. I know how to perform an exorcism, you know." Chris sounded almost normal, like he was making one of his trademark bad jokes.

"This is a real body and it's as mine as it ever was. There's a ritual demons can do to make their real human form back up to live in. It's kind of tricky magic, and definitely frowned upon, so it's not a popular choice."

"Why?"

"Well, for starters, if someone from above catches you, and you're not on the job?" Ben drew his thumb across his throat with a choking sound. "Also, most demons think high-jacking a human and crushing a soul is the highest form of entertainment. They see living as a human as weak, too. This body has a lot of the same problems any human has. I have to eat, sleep … you know … all that human stuff. And I can get hurt. Like when I trashed my ankle racing back in October? I didn't do it for show."

Chris's inquisitive nature was starting to get the better of his outrage. "Are you truly human?"

"Not exactly. It's a real body, but there's magic involved. And magic, which I'm sure you have more than a passing familiarity with, is pretty fucking cool.

Demon magic makes a body a lot less vulnerable. You can definitely get hurt, but not as easily."

"Example?" Chris was starting to be genuinely curious.

"Like I said, when I wiped out, without magic I probably would've needed surgery. In the moment it looked pretty bad. Coach made me go to the hospital and the whole nine." Ben rolled his eyes at the memory of Coach Dawson bypassing the campus infirmary and dragging him to the ER, sure his star athlete's running career was over. Ben grinned. "By the time anybody got around to looking at it, it was mostly okay. Took a couple days to fully heal though, and I used crutches for a week or so, to keep my cover. It sure as hell didn't stop me from racing the little shit that tripped me at the next meet. Kicked his ass, too." Chris stayed silent, but gave an encouraging nod. "Other cool thing? Spellwork I've done … I can have basically endless fun with no consequences."

Chris frowned. "Meaning?"

"I heal pretty fast. I don't age, can't get anybody pregnant. I could do any drug and not overdose. That doesn't come up much. I like booze well enough and I might take a couple bong rips, but the rest of it seems kind of stupid. I can't be poisoned because of that magic either though. Also, I never get a hangover and I can't get blackout drunk. Believe me, I've tried a few times," he chuckled, maybe a little stiffly. "I don't get sick, which is top-notch in general and especially given the other stuff … I have poor impulse control and a short attention span."

Chris looked confused and Ben laughed again, more naturally this time.

"Demons tend to get around some."

He continued to look perplexed and Ben gave him a significant knowing look. When his implication dawned on Chris, Ben was amused to see him blush a little.

Ben grinned, "Wow, you *are* a real book guy, huh?"

Chris managed to smile back.

"But, you can be killed and then you find yourself back in Hell, getting chewed out because you were stupid enough to let some human get over on you. That's never happened to me, thankfully."

He let it all sink in.

"There's magic to leave it and go back, but the longer you stay the more human you feel … At least that's how it is for me." He took a deep breath. "I'm more prone to things like anxiety, insomnia, being moody as fuck, which I guess you've noticed." Ben exhaled slowly. "It's usually no big deal because I'm not allowed to be here long enough for it to matter, couple months at most ... I've been back about as long as I lived this time."

"If you can get hurt or killed, why do it?"

Ben sighed. "There're only three ways demons can interact with the living."

"Which are?"

"Well, there's your demonic form." Ben wrinkled his nose in disgust.

"That's bad?"

"Chris, it's repulsive. It's like the present you get for becoming a demon, only because, guess what, it's Hell, it's more like a curse."

Ben was so appalled it made Chris curious. "What's it look like?"

"Nice. Thanks for asking." Ben's voice dripped sarcasm. "It's humiliating!" Chris just waited. "Picture the total opposite of me." Chris sat in silent expectation and finally Ben heaved a resigned sigh. "Fine! Short, fat, bald … Well, not all bald. Hairy … but in not a good way." He frowned. "And the icing on that particular shit cupcake? Goat legs. Who *does* that to people? Seriously? I won't even wear that form in Hell. I think if that had been a requirement, I'd have opted for just being tortured."

Ben shuddered dramatically and Chris gave another slightly reluctant smile. "Sorry I asked. What else?"

"Well, you know about possession, at least a little if you know exorcism." Chris waved impatiently for him to go on. "It has a lot of advantages. You can't feel pain. You can come and go between worlds with no effort at all. There's no difficult magic and it's easier to use your powers. Even if the human dies because of whatever you were doing with it you can keep it going for quite a while before the rot sets it."

Chris looked like he might be sick and Ben shrugged sympathetically.

"I know, it's pretty bad. Plus it hurts the human, a lot. Even if you ever give them the body back they're usually too damaged to be much good to themselves or anyone else. Apparently you can feel their suffering the whole time, too. Lots of demons get off on it. I won't do it. I never have." He paused. "Then there's my way. Worth the drawbacks."

Chris seemed to consider this for a moment. Then he got up from his desk, brought Ben his cup of tea and sat down next to him. Ben took the cup but put it back down almost immediately, grateful not so much for the drink, but rather the gesture.

"So are you going to tell me what you're doing here?"

"I was getting to that, but my head hurt. Still does, but it's getting better, so thanks." He rubbed his hands over his face, realizing he'd forgotten to shave, and then thought distractedly that as nasty as it felt at least it made him look less like a kid. "Look, I was just taking a freaking vacation, kind of feeling bad about it, but trying to enjoy myself. One major advantage of a body? Pleasure."

"Pleasure?"

Ben grinned, "Food, women, and wine, my friend. That was life before I met you."

"Why did you feel bad?"

"Because here I was, as one lovely young woman put it, screwing my way around the world and I didn't know what was going on with my souls back in Hell." Chris looked alarmingly like he might start lecture mode again so Ben quickly continued. "I collect souls as part of my duties. It's not a choice or anything. I don't do it for fun. I try to keep as many of them with me as I can. I have them act as servants because I need to have a reason for them to stay, but mostly we just do our best to avoid the rest of that shitheap."

Ben wondered if Chris would accept what he was saying and felt the thoughtful way Chris was watching him was a good sign he wasn't going to spike his tea with holy water.

"Anyhow, until I met you, I figured the prophecy was bullshit anyway. As far as I knew you were a legend! How do I know if half the shit people talk about is true? I figured I might as well get myself a break while I convinced the guys in charge I was a good little soldier. Then you come along, right in the place I was drawn to and it's all freaking green hills and water … and you know about the prophecy which I wasn't sure …"

"I found it in my friend's papers the same day I picked you up hitchhiking. It actually fell out of a box at my feet." Chris sounded uncomfortable.

"Doesn't this all seem a little convenient to you? A book about a prophecy you're named in just falls on you, literally. The whole thing makes me feel like a goddamned piece on a chessboard. I don't like it; feeling like someone else is calling the shots. It makes me awfully nervous. I spent my whole damned life just serving someone else's purpose. That's sure as shit not how I'm gonna spend eternity!"

"Well, what are you doing now that you think there might be something to this?"

"I'd like to try to find the girl; well, woman by now. It's been a long time." Ben paused. The Professor was getting ready to pontificate. Ben hurried on. "Look, Chris, think about this for a minute. If you were me and you found out this prophecy was real and you knew what Hell is like, would you want those bastards using some innocent kid to end Lucifer's exile?"

"It's not like you can have much choice."

"Sure I do. I didn't sell my soul. I don't even know why I went to Hell!" A look of pure frustration passed over his face briefly then disappeared as he ticked off his options. "I can do my job, or pretend to do my job and have as much fun as possible until someone else does it. Or I can act like a decent fucking person and try to help you so I'm not responsible for allowing Hell on Earth. Why else do you think I've hung around?" When he said it out loud, he realized that was the real reason he had stuck this out. He'd subconsciously decided to act against orders. "Seriously, other than some minor demon stuff, and some magic you might not know and I'd be happy to teach you, you already know me. What do *you* think I'm gonna do?"

Chris contemplated him in silence. This went on long enough that Ben got uncomfortable. He stared down at his hands, fidgeting nervously.

"So Ben ..." Ben held his breath, not sure what to expect. "Would you like to come spend Christmas with me, talk this whole thing over?"

Ben frowned at him, one eyebrow cocked in skepticism. After a moment's consideration, he decided that the offer was genuine. His face relaxed into a boyish smile and he nodded.

That was when they'd become real friends. It was also when they'd decided to work together to figure out the implications of the prophecy and what to do about them.

Chapter 19

"The beginning is the most important part of the work."
~ Plato

When Chris walked through the door with the debate team's four senior kids, fresh off a competition prep session, Ben's first thought was one of genuine fondness. After a moment, he noticed there was a young woman next to Chris chatting away like they were old friends. She reminded him of someone, or maybe he knew her from somewhere. She was tall, nearly as tall as Ben, and gorgeously classically proportioned, nothing slight or gawky about her, with large almost hypnotic eyes, and wildly curling dark strawberry-blond hair that was nearly auburn in the sun and clearly had a mind of its own. She was, as far as Ben was concerned, a complete tearing beauty. He hadn't spent much time recently enjoying anything other than his own solitary company, thinking that even a casual relationship was too much distraction, but this young woman's presence resulted in immediate electric attraction. Then he noticed her cross-country jacket. *She's a runner. Wait; how the blue hell have I not met this girl?* he thought. Determined to meet her now, he joined the group at the benches by the window. Chris had been after him to meet with the team since the beginning of the year and it was practically Thanksgiving.

"Hey, Dr. G! Bet you didn't think I'd make it! Got out of work early and everything."

"I'm glad you're here! We have some new students that have been hearing the Legend of Ben the Silver-Tongued Sophomore since our first meeting."

Ben gave what felt to him like a humble smile but which anyone could see meant *I hope being a smooth talker is impressive to pretty girls.* Chris directed everyone to get comfortable and introduce the new folks while he went to get food and drinks. The boys, Blake and Tim, whom Ben already knew, each gave him a nod, and were immediately immersed on their phones. A mousy bookish girl was new to the team. Ben recognized her as Rob's sister Emily who picked the kid up from practices. He couldn't imagine how someone who seemed so shy would fare in a debate, but she did hold his eye for a minute and tell him she'd attended a St. Thomas's debate last year with her public speaking class and his performance was what made her want to push herself to try the team. He gave her a friendly grin and she blushed and quickly turned to chat with Alan, the college freshman of the group who was nearly as reserved as she. As Chris came back with a teapot, cups, and a plate of cookies, the other young woman held out her hand, perfectly poised to properly introduce herself. Ben reached out his own, saying, "Ben Brody," and was gratified to notice her pupils dilate slightly. Good, this was mutual. Then she clasped his hand and things went a little sideways.

"Sssssss." Ben pulled back like he'd touched a hot stove, grimacing with unexpected pain and holding onto his hand, surprised.

Chris peered at him with concern. "You okay?"

Ben widened his eyes, shaking his head, as he sat down, replying, "Yeah, no." He did his best to cover his reaction. "Hey, I'm sorry. I got my hand slammed in the dishwasher at work. Didn't realize I'd actually hurt it, I guess," he finished apologetically. In spite of the pain ratcheting up by the second, he was ridiculously pleased when the striking young woman whose weathered wooden ring had just scorched him like a poker straight from the Pit sat down deliberately across from him. "What was your name again? I didn't catch it while I was busy being a wuss."

"I'm the one who should be sorry! People say I've got a handshake like a vise grip. You poor thing." She reached across the table and touched the back of his throbbing hand. The contact sent a brief painful jolt through his whole body and the room spun a little. Then the ache working its way sickeningly up his arm vanished like smoke in the breeze as the room righted itself. He breathed an involuntary sigh of relief as she said, "I'm Mal Sinclair."

The burn was weird enough but its disappearing at her touch was firing off all kinds of alarm bells. Part of him had this feeling he should get out of there as quickly as he could. The other part of him wanted to stay until time stopped. The 'stay' part won. "Good to meet you, Mal. That's an interesting name for a girl. Bad," he laughed and shook his head. "I mean, in Latin."

She laughed, too. "That hadn't occurred to me, but it should have because I think all Dr. G likes to do is assign Latin homework!" She glared at Chris playfully. Ben found her obvious confidence that she was a social equal of her teacher, in this situation at least, extremely appealing. "It's short for Malin. It's a family name and it's so icky and old-fashioned I never go by it."

"I think Malin is a nice name. My name is *actually* icky and old-fashioned."

"Benjamin?" He shook his head and wrinkled his nose in a way she found instantly adorable and that communicated clearly he wasn't about to tell her what it was. She smiled. "So stick with Ben. You look like a Ben. I've always thought so."

"Always? The whole two minutes we've known each other?" She blushed prettily.

"No, I mean, I've seen you at cross-country a bunch of times. You kind of stand out." Her voice was confident, but she blushed again, a little brighter. "I mean, you know, Trish told me about all your records."

Still vaguely aware of the other people sharing the long table, Ben's entire attention was focused on Mal. His charbroiled hand hadn't done much to dissipate his attraction, and oddly unable to help himself, feeling his own face warm with an unexpected flush, he replied, "Yeah, well I can't believe you've been at practice and I never noticed you. You kind of stand out, too."

She rolled her eyes and gave a rueful shake of her head. "You've been looking right through me for months, you big flirt! A few weeks ago you bumped into me hard enough to make me drop my water bottle and you didn't even look up."

Ben shook his head. It had to be some kind of powerful ward, or possibly an obfuscation spell. Maybe it was both. He needed to talk to Chris alone. He hadn't even been able to see Mal at first when they'd come in, and there was his burned hand, the weird sick feeling, and the desire to run away, not to mention that her aura didn't strike him as altogether human now that he was paying attention. *Damn it all.* The first person he'd bothered to think was cute in over a year and she had to be the freaking Prophecy Girl. With such powerful magic around her, it was the only thing that made sense. And there was something more he couldn't quite put his finger on.

He was being too quiet.

He needed to get out of here and think.

"I'm a lout. Clearly no one ever taught me my manners." He paused and grabbed his phone from his pocket and glanced at it like he'd gotten a text. "Crap; it's my boss." He pulled off a sincere sounding apology despite his distraction. "I'm sorry you guys. I guess they can't do without me after all. I'll come to the competition Tuesday. I'll be on break and I'm supposed to be off work then."

Everyone seemed agreeable enough.

"Sure you should go back to work with an injured hand?" Chris's face showed genuine concern, not misplaced, since they both knew he no longer worked at anything other than helping Chris put together as much information as possible about the prophecy.

"Yeah, it feels totally fine now." He glanced significantly at Chris who tipped his chin ever so slightly. Ben felt better. Chris was probably already three steps into trying to figure out what was going on.

"Alright, but you know I'm going to call and check up on you later, make sure you filed an accident report."

Ben just smiled and gave a little roll of his eyes, "Yes, Dad."

The entire team laughed. They'd played that just right. All the kids knew Chris's parenting tone.

As he put his phone in his pocket Mal said, "You should give me your number."

Surprised, but unable to help feeling a little pleased, he rattled it off. Mal keyed it into her phone and snapped a picture of him, looking extremely satisfied. "This way I can text you the next time I'm at the track and you'll know to look out so you don't run me over again."

Ben gave her a charming smile. "That'd be good. If you texted me."

Chris appeared to be paying no attention while checking his email, but Ben felt his pocket buzz. He slung his bag over one shoulder. "See you later."

He hurried out onto Church Street as soon as they'd finished saying good-bye and pulled out his phone to check the text from Chris.

You alright?

What's going on?

Ben texted back.

I'm okay.

Need to think.

Then he did what he always did when he needed to focus and work something through. He started walking. Running would have been better, but he had his backpack with him, and just the rhythm of his feet on the ground always helped him concentrate and sort things out. He meandered through the streets not intent on any particular destination, just letting his mind turn over the problem. He eventually found himself sitting in Battery Park on one of the marble benches, looking out over the lake, watching the sun disappear into the trees. He was alone, it was cold, and the breeze was kicking up quite a chop on the water. The ring, the warding, those fathomless eyes. He was certain after spending some time alone with the thought. He was considering texting Chris when his phone rang. Ben answered abruptly, "Hey. Can you pick me up?" He didn't have to say where; he was here so much Chris would know. "We need to talk. Mal's the one, Chris. No question about it."

Chapter 20

"Three things cannot be long hidden: the sun, the moon, and the truth."
~ Buddha

"Chris … hey, wake up a minute." Ben was answered with a snore. Carefully, so as not to upset his materials, Ben stuck out one of his large bare feet to jostle the books on the coffee table, sending one thumping to the floor. Chris, having succumbed to sleep scrunched over in his chair hours before, just after dawn, now jolted awake. Ben was on the sofa, his long legs folded lotus-style, a book balanced in his lap, one on each knee and his tablet in his hand, surrounded by takeout containers, stacks of papers and books, with a pencil forgotten behind each ear.

Chris stood stiffly, rubbing his stubble-covered face wearily. "Sorry about that. Guess I couldn't keep my eyes open anymore."

"No worries. You need to sleep."

"So do you, I seem to recall."

"I wish. I told you already, insomnia just happens. I'll rack out eventually. Glad I didn't though. I think I might have found something kind of crucial, but my Old Enochian isn't great."

Chris gave a knowing nod and his face got that teacher look to it. "Bring it to the kitchen table; we'll look at it together."

Ben began to move his carefully arranged books so he wouldn't lose any of the places he was open to. Chris went into the small adjoining kitchen and in moments Ben could smell coffee brewing. As he began carrying his materials to the table he realized there was another mouthwatering smell filling the apartment.

"Are you cooking? I want you to look at this first."

Chris called from around the corner, "No, I ... Oh ... it's Thursday. Normal people are probably starting their turkeys." Ben got to the table and Chris continued, "As for us, right now I can offer you some stale donuts and some reasonably decent coffee."

It hadn't occurred to Ben to be hungry while he was immersed in his reading, although when Chris set a cup and a plate off to the side he began unconsciously shoveling in donuts that if you were only half paying attention tasted okay. And he loved coffee; it was almost as good as dark chocolate. Chris sat down next to him with his own cup.

"Show me what you think you've found."

Ben showed him the Latin translation of the prophecy. "See how it says '*holy blood*' here?"

Chris gave a wry smile. "I've read that a time or two."

"No, listen." Ben slid another book in front of Chris. "Here's the piece of scroll this translation was made from."

Chris had spent plenty of time staring at this as well, but added, "I just want to be clear Ben. I know you think this is important, but I still don't think this can be about Mal. Half-angels, Nephilim, are monstrous creatures, usually enormous and often just unhinged."

Ben shook his head. "Maybe so, if the parent was one of the Fallen who disobeyed God. But they haven't been allowed to just be on Earth for a long time." Chris frowned, wondering if Ben would elaborate. "The Archs got pretty smitey about it I guess, wiped out most of the Grigori." Ben shuddered. Archangels were bad news as far as he could tell. "Since it hasn't all happened yet, it's much more likely this kid was born to an angel trying to live as a human. It's uncommon, but it does happen. That would change the magic involved ... probably enough to avoid some monster. Besides, these days, you know a Nephilim would be all over the internet."

"I suppose," Chris hedged. He'd heard of angels living as humans but had yet to meet one.

"And I haven't gotten to the interesting part, the part I need your help with. It's what I suspected but I didn't want to say anything until I had something to back me up. It would kind of explain a lot." Ben slid his tablet in front of Chris. On its brightly lit high-definition screen was an image of a crumbling scroll, dated by the time stamp in the corner as coming from the early first century. He couldn't imagine what Ben had made of this since his Old Enochian was truly terrible, "As you can see, it's a fragment of the Emerald Hill Prophecy."

"Where did you find this? And how do you know? You can barely read the language."

"I've been working on it. I feel like the older documents are going to be important. Primary sources and whatever. Not to mention there's some damned useful spells I've heard about written in it." He paused, distracted again. Then he caught up with his original train of thought. "This was on the Archive-thingy you logged me into last night, or was it Tuesday? Anyway … doesn't matter. What's important is it's the oldest known copy of this part of the prophecy I can locate."

"Go on."

"You see this piece?" Ben's finger hovered just above a character on the tablet.

"Mmmhmm," Chris mumbled.

"That's the same line, but that's not the character for '*holy*'. It's *really* similar, but they're not identical." Chris looked a little skeptical and Ben moved the tablet next to the copy they'd been using for direct comparison. "Look. Really look."

Studying it more carefully, Chris saw the subtle variations between the characters. He'd never found this fragment before and supposed he might have noticed it eventually if he had, but he was grateful for Ben's subtle and rarely openly displayed powers. The sooner they solved this puzzle the better. Chris studied the images. He used Old Enochian so rarely; before the prophecy came to his attention he'd only ever bothered with it for certain protective magic. He didn't immediately recognize the symbol and was about to say so.

"Chris, I did a bunch of digging around and I think this means '*royal*' not '*holy*'." Chris peered at it more closely, as Ben's suspicion jogged his memory. He nodded slowly. He could check a few sources to be sure, but he was fairly certain Ben was correct.

"What do we do with that? Could you be wrong about Mal? Maybe we're looking in the wrong place. Plenty of places have royalty and match the description in the text."

Ben shook his head. Leave it to someone tied to the Church to ignore the correct conclusion. "Chris, no, pay attention. We are looking at a prophecy of biblical proportions right?" Chris's whole face folded into a thoughtful frown. "SO …" Getting no response, Ben continued, "Biblically speaking royalty can only mean one thing." Still no response. Frustrated, Ben's voice rose. "The King of Kings, Chris! The Line! Mal Sinclair has *got* to be the Scion."

Chris frowned silently for a moment then got up from the table slowly and went to the counter to refill his coffee. He paused, reached up into the cupboard, and pulled out a bottle of whiskey. He poured a generous amount into his cup, studiously stirred in sugar and cream, and came back to the table and sat, this time facing Ben. He took a sip of his coffee and grimaced. Then he took a longer drink and looked at Ben seriously.

"Ben, the Church maintains it never happened. Jesus never married, never had children. I've never seen a single official reference and I've had access to the Vatican Archives for years."

Ben laughed; the kind of spontaneous laugh that surprised him enough it made him laugh even harder. After a minute, he managed, "Oh, Chris, you crack me up sometimes. You and the Church. You think God went and got himself a body and didn't bother do any real human stuff with it? Dude. Human stuff is the whole point of a body. Besides, you think the Church never makes mistakes, or covers things up? Oh, that's good, seriously."

"I'm not saying that at all." Ben continued to snicker, then when he tapered off he contemplated Chris's coffee cup and went and got himself one of the same minus all the nasty sugar while Chris was formulating his thoughts. Ben sat back down, still amused at the disapproving look on Chris's face at the suggestion that maybe, just maybe, God wanted to eat, drink, and be merry, too. Chris finally continued. "The thing is I've done an awful lot of research into it."

"Why? If you don't believe it?"

"That day." Ben froze and his laughter dried up. He had never asked and never expected to hear, but that could only mean one thing. Confirmation from Chris's own lips made Ben glad he'd poured himself a drink. "In the crowd, I saw this beautiful woman, richly dressed, long dark red hair. It was so unusual, I really noticed. The way she looked at Him … the way she wept … and the way she was swept away by what had to have been bodyguards …" Chris stopped, swallowing hard. Ben prompted him with a wave of his hand, wanting to hear the rest. "She was obviously expecting."

"You remember a glimpse of some cute pregnant lady in a crowd in the middle of everything after all this time? Must have seemed important." Ben was hoping Chris realized he'd just made his point.

"Ben, I'm unlikely to ever forget anything about that day." His solemn expression made Ben want to move him along quickly, back to Mal.

"See! You gonna believe the Church or your own eyes?" Chris shook his head like he didn't quite know what to say. "Besides, everyone in Hell knows it's more than a legend because it is strictly forbidden to harm or try to contract with any member of the Line." Chris opened his mouth and then closed it again quickly. Ben thought maybe he didn't trust his voice so he went on. "And there's another thing … It's second hand mind you, through the underworld grapevine; but when Prophecy Kid was little, Lucifer's crew almost snatched her. I guess it was a big operation, even though they were acting like she was a run of the mill contract hit and they could leave finding her to schleps like me."

"They got that close?" Chris was horrified.

"So I hear. Like I said, it's a 'friend of a friend' story. I was already topside when it happened, so I can't say. But the rumor is they killed the little girl's mom and some Superman angel shows up and burns Lucifer's chief assassin with holy fire, just turns him to ash. Bunch of demons got the final death, too."

Chris interrupted, "Final death? You've said that before … what does that even mean?"

Ben glanced away for a second, and when he looked back, he wasn't exactly meeting Chris's eyes. "Um … well … a soul can live forever, right?" Chris nodded, frowning at the expression on Ben's face. Ben swallowed and went on, "But it doesn't have to … there are things that can end a soul, sometimes beings even gain power from doing it, quick as a hiccup."

Chris quietly said, "Oh," and then looked like he wanted to say something else. Ben took in the look in his eye and hurriedly went on.

"So anyway, the dude who offed Azazel? Obviously a powerful Guardian. Only one of Hell's crew made it. This creepy fallen angel who can sense divine will, and she only survived because he let her go to play messenger."

"Did you ever hear the Guardian's name?"

"Nope. I know it wasn't one of the Archangels that are Lucifer's version of scary bedtime stories for demons. But word under the street is he just kind of eyeballed the assassin, and *poof*, gone. Dude was clearly a legitimate badass."

"Who was the one who survived?"

"Chris, I don't know if you know this, but … never say the names of underbeings. Especially hers. She's in charge of the search and she's on my ass now all the time; close by. Imagine the fun." Chris's brow furrowed. "You could call her, invite her, without meaning to. Don't mean to either. All those creatures are a ticket to misery. Above or below."

"Is that why you don't want me to use your demon name?"

Ben was indignant. "No! I want you to call me *Ben* because that's who I am!" He was thoughtful for a moment. "Well, there's power in it, too, of course. You know how magic and names go together. I told you so you'd know you can trust me … You have the name Hell gave me. It wouldn't take much for you to kick me out of my body and send me back below, metaphorical hat in hand, hoping I wouldn't wind up a sentient doormat for the next couple million years."

Chris looked at Ben intently, realizing just how much trust had been placed in him. "I wouldn't do that, Ben."

Ben's face turned serious and his eyes avoided Chris's for a moment. "Good. I'd make a terrible door mat." Then he grinned and waved off whatever he'd been thinking. "Anyhow, my baggage isn't the point. The survivor insisted she might have been successful if the Templars hadn't interfered. The official story was it was just the Knights butting into otherworldly affairs, but we all know the Line exists because of the ban."

"The Templars." It wasn't a question.

"With the mistranslation, the involvement of the Knights, the incredibly powerful Guardian … I'm just putting two and two together here. That kid in the story is the Scion. I imagine there're big implications if Hell decides to try to use the however-many-greats-grandbaby of the Big Guy for anything." Ben paused. "After what happened the other day? It's gotta be Mal."

Chris noticed the familiar way Ben used her name. He felt oddly protective of both of them. "Have the two of you spoken since the coffee shop?"

Ben looked away for a second, like maybe he was a little embarrassed. When he'd told Chris about what happened the first time, he couldn't hide his interest. Chris had pointed out the obvious age difference and Ben assumed an air of complete innocence and said, "What? She's a senior and I'm only twenty," which had earned him a dirty look and an hour of the cold shoulder. Then Chris had seemed to come around. What Ben didn't realize was Chris almost always thought of him as little more than a kid, regardless of how long he'd been around. Some souls are born old; some stay young forever, no matter what they've been through. Chris thought maybe that was why Ben liked old souls so much; the contrast.

"We've texted some," he admitted. "She wants to have coffee this weekend."

"Coffee?" Here was the dad voice. It had been a while.

"Yeah, coffee. I've got to get to know her right? I mean we can't figure this all out, be any good to her, if we don't know her."

"And you've got a crush." Chris seemed more amused than worried.

"Maybe I do! Have you actually seen her? I mean when you guys first walked in I couldn't see her at all, but then once I did? Just, wow. Honestly, she's all I can think about. Then there's the thing with my hand …"

"I thought you said it was alright."

"It is, but … When it happened, I thought my hand was gonna start smoking. And like I told you the other night, this weird ache was moving up my arm, almost like it was poison or something. I felt sick, too, which doesn't happen, ever. Then, when she touched me again, it was gone like it never happened. That was the first thing that made me think about the Line thing. Healing. She obviously didn't even know she was doing it, just knew I was hurt and wanted to help. That's power."

"Maybe it wasn't a physical burn. I couldn't see anything when you showed it to me."

"I told you before; it was a real burn, like serious Ben-bacon. Extra crispy. I don't know how I didn't just pass out, demon constitution and all. But when she touched me the second time, it felt normal again. Well, no, it hurt worse for a minute and I felt super weird. Then she just … fixed it."

"I believe you. But I'm getting the impression you haven't told me everything yet."

Ben shifted uneasily in his chair, uncomfortable. "You're not gonna like it."

"Tell me anyway, Ben."

"The whole first day, every once in a while where I was burned … got warm, tingly. Not a bad feeling or anything, just it was kind of intense so it's not like I could ignore it."

"Well, your body has nerves. Even if she healed your immediate injury, it could have been some lingering damage or part of the normal healing process."

"No, that's not the weird part." Chris's eyebrows lifted. "I got the impression it was because she was thinking about me." There, he'd said it.

Chris looked like he was about to form a question, but Ben interrupted. "It wasn't something of mine, like some demon-mind-trick-power-thing. It was coming from her, some connection. It was strange but … nice, too. I kind of miss it now that it's stopped."

"It seems you've formed some intense feelings for Mal on extremely short acquaintance. It's hard to believe you never even noticed her."

"Trust me Chris, there has to be some heavy mojo involved for me not to notice someone like her. I've apparently been looking right through her for months. But now I've noticed, and I want to keep noticing." He paused, eyes intense, face hard. "I'll tell you right now, if I'm right and Mal is the half-angel from the prophecy? There's no way I'm letting any of those bastards near her. I'll burn the whole fucking thing to the ground before I let them screw up her life."

Chris could hear something of the warrior Ben must have been in his voice. He could also see how he could command legions of demons. But this was more than a young man infatuated with a beautiful girl, more even than a demon bent on upsetting Hell's applecart. Chris decided to share an observation, allowing Ben to make of it what he would.

"Something I've noticed about Mal is she seems to draw people to her. Everyone likes her, just about instantly. Her peers, well, if I'm honest, the teachers and even the clergy at school would just let her talk their ears off all day. I'm a bit guilty of that myself. She's taken over class more than once with some idea or story of hers. She brings out the best in people, or at least makes them feel their best is worth sharing. She has power over people, Ben."

Ben smiled, and gave a little nodding shake of his head. "She surely does." They were silent for a few minutes, Chris lost in thought and Ben surreptitiously texting Mal under the table to wish her a nice holiday and confirm the time for Sunday. He was interested in any excuse to talk to her and was actually starting to like his phone. Then Ben broke the silence. "So, it's starting to smell really good in here."

"Do you ever not think with your stomach?" Chris smiled.

Ben could smell roasting turkey, baking bread and all sorts of other good holiday smells wafting from the other homes. It was worse because they'd been eating like impoverished students for days. "It's Thanksgiving. Dude. Embrace local customs. Didn't anyone ever teach you how to blend?"

"Yes, well ... I think there are exactly three beers and maybe half a stick of butter in the refrigerator. We've gone through everything else. There might be some mustard left. I'm a brilliant scholar, I was a solid soldier, but damned if I've ever learned to cook."

"I could teach ..." Ben trailed off at the look Chris gave him and then tried again. "Chinese food? I'll buy. The place around the corner delivers and it's never closed."

"Fine with me. I'll order. You clean off the table. We'll have an early dinner."

Ben was already on his feet moving papers around, happy that Chris agreed with his translation and he'd won his point. Also, it seemed like Chris was not freaking out too much about his plans with Mal. He was positively beaming by the time Chris got off the phone. "German beer. Chinese food. Ancient Enochian texts. I love a good American holiday."

"As do I, Ben. After dinner we can make plans for our research over the rest of the weekend. I'd like to see if we can locate any other versions easily. We know what we have isn't complete, and if you're right, we need all the information we can get."

"Agreed."

Chris's left eyebrow went up, "We can discuss your budding relationship, as well. You've read the prophecy. If her mother was the royal part of it you know her father must be an angel, right?"

Ben sighed.

Chapter 21

"I love you as certain dark things are to be loved, in secret, between the shadow and the soul."
~ Pablo Neruda

Mal waited impatiently, playing with her phone and trying to look casual. She'd been in the warm shop for almost fifteen minutes but she gave a little shiver. She was still trying to shake the chill from the stone church and her walk to the cafe through the chilly parking garage and down the windy street. She might need a heavier coat. They usually spent the winter in milder climates and the black wool she'd bought last year out west was inadequate for the northern cold. It wasn't December yet and here late fall felt like the dead of winter.

She thought she was dressed pretty conservatively in a grey shift dress, black tights, and a red cardigan, but her dad had given an amused raise of his eyebrows when she'd come downstairs before church. Of course, she never bothered to wear make-up to Mass, and she'd kind of gone the extra mile; liquid eyeliner and everything. She'd also put on high-heeled boots instead of her usual flats or sneakers, mostly because she thought they might make her nearly as tall as Ben, who was about six foot three, and she kind of liked that idea. She had arranged to take her own car, too, saying she was hanging out with friends afterward. She guessed she had been acting a little weird. He must know she was meeting someone but bless his heart he hadn't said a word.

She couldn't wait to see Ben again. It had been killing her since she'd first noticed him not to meet the boy who seemed to be made of gold, right down to his unbelievable eyes. Their color made her think of dark topaz or tiger's eye, but prettier, deeper. She'd gone to all the cross-country events she could, never missed a practice and all she'd ever gotten out of it was bumped into like she didn't exist. It's not like she'd never set her sights on somebody really attractive or older than her, but before catching sight of Ben her interest had always been immediately reciprocated. Mal attracted partners effortlessly when she wanted them, but before last Saturday he'd never even *seen* her. It wasn't that, of course.

She wasn't insecure enough to give a damn if someone wasn't interested in her, regardless of how outrageously damned sexy they happened to be. And even though everyone told her how intelligent and accomplished he was, she didn't think that was part of the allure either. There was just something about him that defied reason, like a craving.

When she found out she was going to finally meet him last Saturday she'd hardly been able to tolerate sitting through practice. Debate was easy for her anyway. She could almost always convert people to her side without trying. She'd heard the same was true of Ben. When they'd met, the attraction was obviously mutual. His smile and the way he angled those smoky gilded eyes at her had told her everything she needed to know. She regretted that he'd had to leave so soon, especially since she felt badly about squeezing his injured hand. She'd never had to ask for someone's number before. They were usually just pressed into her hand or messaged to her the minute she thought she might want them. She'd texted him the next morning, too. She was sure that was totally uncool and maybe came off as desperate to a college boy but she didn't give a damn. Besides, he didn't seem to mind. This was her year of getting what she wanted, and right now what Mal wanted was Ben Brody.

When he walked through the door, the sight of him made her breathe a little faster, feel a little warmer. He searched around the restaurant, uncertain, and even looked right through her a couple of times. She stood to get his attention. His expression when she caught his eye made her feel like the only person in the world. He closed the space between them quickly; his cheeks were flushed an appealing apricot color from a long walk in the cold wind.

"Mal, I'm so glad you made it." He sounded relieved.

"I'm glad you made it, too. I was afraid Dr. G would monopolize you for his research project over break."

Ben was pleased to hear she'd asked enough about him to know the story he and Chris had invented for the amount of time they spent together. Smiling, Ben waved to the woman behind the counter for table service, gestured for Mal to sit, and lowered himself into the swiveling chair opposite her.

"Oh, your hand! It's been over a week! You must have really hurt yourself!" she exclaimed. "I hope I didn't make it worse!"

Actually Ben had wrapped it up in an ace bandage to avoid shaking hands again, just in case. "It's fine. My boss is just super fidgety about injuries. And Dr. G called me twice to make sure I filled out an accident report; called my boss, too. They've been driving me nuts. I didn't even go to the infirmary. I just said so to get them off my case."

Her expression was almost reproving.

"Okay," he fibbed, "maybe it still hurts a little, but I don't need to go to a doctor for some bruises. It's really fine."

She eyed the heavy wrapping on his hand, "You sure about that?"

"Totally sure. Doctors are first class pains in the ass. Besides, I'm sure you've heard from Trish I run marathons for fun. This is nothing, honest."

She smiled coyly. "I've heard all sorts of Ben stories from Trish."

He rolled his eyes; the college rumor mill. He didn't want to open up that can of worms. He didn't want to reinforce the fictions of his life any more than he had to, and he was afraid if he was right about Mal's true identity he'd have to keep things from her to keep her safe, at least for a while, until he figured out what to do about Lahash and her ability. The idea was already bothering him. He deflected, "I haven't heard many Mal stories. Tell me about you, since you've already heard all about me."

Ben had expected maybe some self-consciousness since most people that age were still growing into themselves a bit but Mal didn't seem to have an awkward bone in her body. What followed confirmed what Chris said. She regaled him with tales of her travels, of her father's art, of the places and people she'd seen, through several cappuccinos. She didn't just talk at him either. She involved him, asked him little questions about himself. He racked his brain afterward trying to remember if he'd said anything that might sound off because she was awfully distracting in her good looks, her stimulating conversation, and the happy contentment spreading through him just sitting with her. It was an unfamiliar set of feelings he thought might prove dangerously addictive.

They'd sat slamming coffees through lunch time, so as afternoon gave way to early evening, Ben told Mal honestly that he was starving and she told him she could always eat, so they ordered some soup and sandwiches. She said she felt like she was talking too much and asked him to tell her about himself; something real, not a Trish tale. He'd come prepared with his usual story, but it caught in his throat. He couldn't look at this woman and outright lie, just couldn't do it. He could omit and even maintain his cover story when he had to, but to be asked a direct question by Mal Sinclair begged for some form of the truth. He breathed slowly in and out, catching a faint whiff of her perfume. Lily of the Valley maybe.

"Not much to tell, to be honest, Mal. Your life sounds awfully glamorous by comparison. I'm kind of a simple guy, making my way in a complicated world, far from home. I've worked hard, studied hard, gotten lucky along the way. I've met some special people. Recently, for example." His sideways smile was both flirtatious and sincere and it charmed her completely. "My past is actually kind of rough. I'll tell you about it if you want, but it's sad and boring."

If she'd asked him then, while he was still bowled over from his first real time with her, he might have, at least a little, consequences be damned, but she shook her head, not wanting to make him uncomfortable. She'd heard something about his parents kicking him out just because he didn't have any interest in the career they'd picked without consulting him. The idea of a parent who didn't support what you wanted for yourself made her inexplicably angry at his faraway family. Everybody should have a choice about the direction of their lives.

"I'm good at some stuff, like running, writing, talking a blue streak … and I'm terrible at other stuff. Nobody should have to tell a woman what they're bad at on their first date."

"So this *is* a date? Good. I was afraid you wouldn't think so. I've wanted to have a date with you since September."

"Stop, I'll blush," he said, smiling in a way that meant don't stop at all.

"I wanted to meet you the first time I saw you at practice … well, actually …"

"What?" He liked the way the color was intensifying in her cheeks.

"I think I might have seen you here, sitting behind a pile of books a while back, over the summer. I thought about just sitting down at your table, but I chickened out." Her eyes flicked away from his for a moment, wondering how he'd feel about how long she'd had her eye on him.

"If you saw some tired dude full of too much coffee behind a stack of books about the size of the entire library it was probably me. But I can't imagine why you'd remember me sitting here all studious and squinty." He laughed, shaking his head, and she thought he must have no idea how handsome he was.

"I don't want to sound creepy or anything, but I thought you were all kinds of good-looking. I thought about you, after. I regretted not introducing myself all summer. Then I saw you at practice; it was that warm day, it was almost October. You took your shirt off and wiped your face like you didn't care if the world was watching. I saw your tattoo and … I liked that. It was like you were all alone. And nobody gets a tattoo in a place like that to impress anybody. That's a personal piece of art. I like people who are themselves for themselves, you know?"

"Wow," he breathed, thinking about how to respond. "You're probably right. I never pay much attention to what people think. And my tattoo is really personal. I like it a lot."

"I've been thinking about getting one. Did it hurt?"

"It wasn't as bad as I thought it would be; it stung quite a bit." Ben, who'd always had a high pain tolerance and had the added benefit of demonic magic, thought it best to use the honest words of others to describe it to her. And it wasn't like it had been pleasant, so he added, "I mean, if you're afraid of blood or needles you'd probably want to pass."

Mal laughed, "Neither one bothers me even a little. I've wanted to go into medicine since I was like four. I still want to be a doctor, maybe even a surgeon."

Ben crinkled his face and she realized she found nearly all of his expressions instantly irresistible. "Is it too late to take back what I said about doctors?"

She just laughed and raised her eyebrows in a playful provocation. "Maybe."

He grinned in response and gave another adorable disgusted wrinkle of his nose. "I don't much care for either one, so if a big wimp like me didn't mind, I'm sure you'd do great."

She gave a coy grin. "You don't look like a wimp … Big maybe, but …"

Ben gave a self-deprecating laugh. "Looks can be deceiving …"

"Maybe you just didn't have the right person there to hold your hand." *Was that a wink?* He couldn't be sure, but he thought it might have been.

"If you want to get one sometime, I could go with you. I could hold *your* hand … if you want," he almost stammered, but she just grinned. He liked how frank she was and thought she might be looking for someone who would respond in kind, with no inept flirting or adolescent games.

She decided she liked the idea of him holding her hand quite a bit. "Why did you get it if it hurt? It's huge; the whole middle of your chest. And it's right over bone. That's the worst!"

"Like I said, it wasn't too bad, and I'm covering a scar. It bothered me way more than anything about the tattoo." It felt unbelievably good to say something that was the absolute truth. No matter how many times he came and went from Earth that ugly scar was still in the middle of his chest, calling up incessant thoughts of his former life. Nothing he found in his research could explain or get rid of it and whenever he noticed it he got angry and depressed. It made it even harder to sleep; and that was saying a lot. Getting inked allowed him to look in the mirror without constantly replaying troubling memories. One less thing to remind him of how he'd wound up a demon was worth feeling like he had poison ivy for a couple of hours.

"That does sound personal. I shouldn't have asked." She had a lot of friends with tats; they were kind of ubiquitous here.

"It's cool. It was from a long time ago. I had a heart thing." That was *kind of* true. It was a spear, but still. "I'm fine now. I just didn't want to think about it every time I took a shower." When she reached for her coffee, he added, in as casual a voice as he could manage, "That's a neat ring."

She smiled, twisting it around. "I guess it was my mom's. She died when I was little and my dad wanted me to have it."

Well, that confirmed one part of the story and it certainly explained a lot; enchanted heirlooms on top of other magic. "Mal, I'm so sorry. Way to make it awkward, Ben."

"Don't even worry about it. I don't remember her much. But my dad? He really loved her. I can tell. He still wears his wedding ring and he's always wanted me to have a little piece of her with me, too. It's super important to him." She toyed absently with her pendant for a moment then she dangled it off her fingers so he could see it better. "He made me this when she died, too. I guess it has something to do with my name and my mom's name in some old language ... or something."

Ben smiled as he thought, *Yeah, angel alphabet, even older than Enochian. I wonder if Chris will ever get tired of me being right*, but all he said was, "It's gorgeous. Your dad must have quite a business with talent like that."

Over their meal, they talked of inconsequential things, school, running, music, how good the food was. The shop had gotten busy, so after dinner Ben walked to the counter and ordered the Buzz's wonderful drinking chocolate and a chocolate croissant to share. He found himself even more distracted than usual. It had never happened to him before but this was more than just attraction. He was utterly caught up in every detail about her, from the curve of her jaw and the silver flecks in her irises, to the slightly husky sound of her voice and her easy laughter, even the clear challenge in her eyes when they had both reached for the last piece of their pastry. Then there was the delightful weightless feeling he got whenever he felt her eyes so much as graze him. He was wondering if something was wrong with him when he realized this was what happiness felt like. It was almost painful in its strangeness. He was convinced he was both the smartest and unluckiest being in all Creation. He knew with certainty now she was the Scion, child of prophecy, and here he was falling for her like a teenager. *Son of a bitch.*

Finally, when she checked her phone for the third time, she put it in her purse with an apology. "My dad's texting me like it's his job. I've got to go help him get ready for a new exhibition he's starting tomorrow. Some museum thing. He's awful at the numbers stuff and I'm good at math."

"It's getting late anyway." He paused and texted Chris. "I did tell Dr. G I'd work on his project tonight." They sat silently for a moment. "Could I walk you to your car?"

"If it's not out of your way. I'm in the garage on Cherry Street. I like to park there and sneak out of town the back way so I can avoid all the lights."

"I'm meeting my ride near there. It's totally on my way."

They split the check, left a generous tip, and walked through the mall to avoid the cold, talking like they'd known one another forever; sharing little pieces of themselves and delighting in what they learned. Chris was right. Mal just drew you in. When they got to her car, the protective side of Ben was happy he'd accompanied her. It was darkish in here and he could see better than humans in low light, although she seemed to be able to see just fine and she moved with an almost feline confidence he wished he could match. He thought maybe she had other unseen powers that hadn't occurred to him, or maybe it was just natural to her because she knew she could take care of herself. She told him in addition to running and yoga she did martial arts and liked it a lot. Unlocking her beat up old Volvo, Mal stood with one hand on the door.

"I enjoyed talking to you in person, Ben. Texting was nice, but sometimes it's different IRL. You know?"

"I had a nice time, too." *Ask to see me again*, he thought desperately, his mouth dry at the thought of asking and being refused.

"Want to get together again this week? Maybe go for a run? The weather is supposed to be nicer."

Oh thank everything, she feels the same way. When he replied in the affirmative, she reached out to brush his arm with her fingertips. Her hand lingered for a moment. His eyes widened, but he managed to stand there with a smile fixed on his face.

"See you soon." There was a note of anticipation in her voice that made his heart practically skip a beat.

He forced himself to sound natural as she climbed into her car and he responded, "The sooner the better."

He raised his hand to her as she pulled out of the garage. Instead of walking to the park to meet Chris as they'd planned, he sank down heavily onto the curb, fumbled for his phone, and hit the call button with trembling hands.

"Ben?"

"Cherry Street parking garage, okay?" He sounded reedy and strained.

"I'm almost to the park. Can I just wait for you? Traffic's a nightmare."

"I think I might pass out ... I feel really sick." He let out a low, involuntary groan.

"*You* don't get sick. What's going on?" Chris asked, alarmed by Ben's shaking voice.

"Mal touched me ... more magic."

115

He ended the call and put his head between his knees. *Holy shit.* As the world spun around him, he had a terrible thought. Did he break the spell? Why didn't he think of that possibility before? *Damn it!* That made him feel even worse. He had never been so grateful to see headlights in his life than when he recognized Chris pulling up. He tried to stand and stumbled, had to drop down on one knee to keep from just sprawling on the pavement. Chris got out quickly and took his arm, helping him into the car, the lines of concern on his face adding at least a decade to his apparent age.

Chapter 22

"Nothing you do for children is ever wasted. They seem not to notice us, hovering, averting our eyes ... but what we do for them is never wasted."
~ Garrison Keillor

A ri sang along with the radio, window down enough to let in the crisp late autumn air, but not so far as to make the interior uncomfortably cool. He had the heater on, blowing pleasantly warm air on his shoeless feet. Ari only ever wore shoes grudgingly and as soon as he'd gotten back to the car he'd kicked off his loafers and stuffed his socks into the toes. Mal was always teasing him about his habit of running the heat, or the A/C for that matter, and driving with the window down at the same time. Ari just liked the sound of the rushing air through the window and the subtle smells riding on the breeze.

He was smiling to himself, pleased with how happy Mal seemed. The nightmares began again not long after her birthday and she seemed almost perpetually tired these days, but she wasn't letting it spoil things for her. She'd seen a doctor when he'd expressed concern, and been assured sleep problems at her age were not atypical and she was very healthy. She'd been confident that was the case, but was happy to reassure him. She was going out quite a bit, which on one hand made him nervous, but on the other he was glad that it seemed to be the normal hanging-out kind of activity common to people her age. He was glad he could pay her for all the bookkeeping and her help running the gallery because the idea of a job that would keep her location predictable for some casual observer without the magic he was used to employing to keep her safe made him want to crawl out of his skin. He chuckled ruefully to himself, thinking he'd have to work on his protective streak because her outing today had a date-like feel to it. It wasn't like her to keep things from him, but he couldn't be upset. She'd certainly had flings before, but he'd never seen her like this. She'd been distracted lately, on her phone much more than usual, and she'd come downstairs this morning dolled up like it was New Year's Eve. All she offered was she was meeting 'friends' after church. She was obviously smitten and keeping quiet about it, so it was probably a college kid. But she was eighteen and he trusted her to make good decisions, so he didn't ask. Although he did perform a little early morning magic to ensure there were no immediate threats to her safety. It wiped him out, but was worth it for the reassurance it offered his troubled spirit.

Ari had worked hard to make sure Mal would be a strong independent adult. He'd always given her the freedom to express herself, making sure she felt in charge of her own person. Funky hair color? Why not? Wild hair style? At least twice. Eclectic wardrobe? He'd have been surprised if it wasn't. *You want to go skydiving for your birthday? Sure, I'll watch. From right down here on the lovely ground.* He smiled thinking about overhearing her and her friend Petra talking about piercings and tattoos. She was worried what he'd think if she got one, didn't want to disappoint him. *As if that were possible.* He'd have to think of a way to bring it up. He wanted her to know exactly how he felt about her marking herself like that. Namely, it didn't matter what he thought. He loved her. Period. Full stop. She was in charge of her decisions. His job was to respect the ones she made and pick her up if she fell.

Ari pulled into their long dirt driveway with his thoughts extremely focused on his fresh bagels, smoked salmon, and cream cheese. He always tried to observe the tradition of fasting before church in Maggie's honor. Some days he wondered why he bothered since it seemed only to amuse Mal, who obviously went because it was important to him, not out of any real religious feelings. Not one for self-denial, she usually scarfed down leftovers with a big cup of coffee and then had to suppress her giggles at his grumbling stomach through the service. As he rolled to a stop, Ari's face broke into a brilliant smile. A familiar figure sat on their porch swing, rocking it gently with his heels. Ari finished parking, grabbed his bag from the bagel shop, and hopped out of the car, still barefoot. The man stood and jumped down off the porch to greet him. Ari could never quite get over the sight of him in his earthly form; always dressed casually, tall, lean, with dark hair that looked in need of a trim, and always the shadow of a beard that never really got started.

"Ari, it's good to see you."

"Davi, the same. What brings you? Should I call Mal?"

"No need. I'm just here to see you and then I'm off."

"She mentioned missing you just this morning."

"She'll see me soon. I plan to come for the holiday."

"I'll be sure to tell her. She was ready to put in the tree last week." Davi smiled. Ari waved him up the steps. "Come in, join me for lunch." Davidos followed him into the house, holding the bag while Ari unlocked the door.

Ari moved around the kitchen, getting down plates and cups, a bit preoccupied. "So, this isn't a social call."

"No, Ari, I'm afraid not."

Ari began to make coffee, his tension visible; hunger entirely forgotten. *When a Guardian showed up on your doorstep to see you and not their charge it couldn't be good news, no matter how long you've been friends.* When the coffee was poured the two of them sat together at the small table, food spread out in front of them. Ari set his cup down, "Alright, Davi, you know I'm just winding myself up now. Mal's dreams have been getting worse. I'm afraid they're wearing her out. Is that what brings you today?"

Davidos gave an understanding nod while spreading a large amount of cream cheese on the onion bagel he'd sliced for himself. "Partially. Some other things, as well."

"I appreciate your help. I'm already so much in your debt."

"Ari, this has never been about what either of us owes the other. It's about how I feel about you and Malin. You're my family. I love you both."

"We love you. Thank you." Ari made an elaborate show of fixing himself a bagel, but it sat untouched on his plate.

"Besides, Ari, we've been friends a long time, and if we *were* to talk about the balance of that friendship … You stood with me when no one else would. I questioned Michael. He took my unwillingness to obey him without speaking to our Father somewhat to heart." He shook his head, smiling wryly. "If you hadn't summoned Metatron ..."

Ari remembered the day well. It felt almost fated. Michael was furious and responded by demoting him, passing him off on the Guardians, who eventually sent him to Earth to replace someone at the end of their term with their charge. Things hadn't turned out the way any of them expected. "You stood for me once, too," Ari said distractedly. He was thinking not of his own trial but of her; so lovely, so bright, so sweet; that profusion of mahogany hair, her quick wit, and a smile that could stop the turning of the Earth. Ari sighed, his expression wistful.

Davidos laughed gently. "You're remembering meeting her, I think."

Ari blushed. "I think of her often." Then he sighed again. "I can hardly help it. Mal is practically the image of her mother, especially when she flashes her dimply smile or gets stubborn and pours on the charm to get her way."

"She favors her father as well, my friend," was offered with a wry smile.

"She's such a gift." Ari missed the implication that there was plenty of stubborn to go around in their little family. "She's doing so well, Davi. I guess I never realized what she was missing with all our moving around. She's so happy.

It's like she's truly come alive, like she knows who she is and who she wants to become."

He smiled, "I'm glad to hear it." Davidos became more serious. "Have you met Mal's teachers?"

Ari thought about it. "Most of them. Why?"

Davidos paused, certain this would be difficult. "The Gatekeeper is at her school."

Ari, who had finally picked up his bagel to eat, set it back down. "What?"

"Do you think you'd know him if you saw him? Could you have met already?"

"I'm not sure. I mean, he's human. Anything particularly special about him?"

"Well, he bears the mark of the curse that gave him immortality. You'd be able to see it with some spellwork, if you had a mind."

Ari took a drink of coffee, quite unable to force himself to eat, but needing something to do with his hands. "Come to think of it, there's only one of Mal's teachers I haven't met at some point. Dr. Guerriero. He's her debate coach, teaches Latin I believe. He's always busy after the competitions and he's only at Saint Augustine's part time. He teaches history and ancient languages at St. Thomas's, as well, so we've never managed to cross paths."

"Latin and History? Well, that would be a little on the nose, wouldn't it?" Davidos smiled. "But perhaps you should make the effort."

"I will. But if they've met …"Ari trailed off.

"Meet him, Ari. According to all I've discovered, he's an ally. But you'll be the best judge of that I think."

"What about the nightmares? What can I do to help her?"

"There's nothing you can do to make this easier. And her dreams are bound to become prophetic. Nothing earth shattering for now, but encourage her to keep a dream journal. It may help spot patterns and head off trouble."

Ari's voice rose with a tinge of true anger, "She has to be a prophet, too?"

"Nothing like that … you may want to keep a journal, too. And keep an eye on her close friends." Ari looked momentarily confused. "This is all just part of being caught up in prophecy. The connections to the other plains of existence may cause any number of hardships … Look, I know this is difficult, but I do believe good will come of it eventually, although it may not come easily."

"Davi, there must be something ..." Distress strained his voice.

"You're doing it. Love her, encourage her, be her father." He stood. "Tell Mal I'll see her in a few weeks." He squeezed Ari's shoulder in reassurance. "I won't be far. Thanks for lunch. Now you eat something. You're going to need your strength."

Davidos disappeared, leaving Ari alone with his thoughts.

Chapter 23

"Love must be as much a light as it is a flame."
~ Henry David Thoreau

They'd been reading all night again and Ben felt his eyes might dry up and fall out if they didn't find what they were looking for soon. He and Mal had gotten together a number of times and it was always the same. If they touched he felt like he'd been hit by a bus. When he thought about it, a while back he'd taken a nasty spill during practice and gotten a rotten headache. He'd gone back to his apartment and slept for half a day at least. That could easily have been when he'd bumped into her. She put her hand on his arm yesterday at the water fountain and while it wasn't as bad as before since he'd been expecting it, braced himself for it, when he got home he'd gone directly to bed. He couldn't even eat dinner. He was grateful he was on holiday break and that Chris, instead of discouraging his interest in Mal, was trying to help him figure out a way to fix things.

Almost worse than how lousy he felt was that everyone kept asking if he was coming down with the flu, including Mal. Even Aife made a crack about it and she knew damned well he couldn't get human illnesses. He supposed it should've come as no surprise since the magic protecting Mal was incredibly powerful and they were already seeing a lot of each other. He was supposed to see her again tomorrow. She was going to lunch with her dad after church, but then they planned to meet, do some Christmas shopping, and have dinner at that little place near the parking garage; it was named after a wild mushroom or something. Mal loved that. He knew he couldn't keep this up much longer and what was he supposed to say to her? *Sorry, I'd love to be around you but I think you're killing me?* He sighed with frustration and tossed aside the huge volume he'd been thumbing through. Chris glanced up. Ben made a sour face and went to put on the kettle.

Ben was so relieved when they confirmed that the magic didn't seem breakable like a typical warding spell. It appeared the enchantment was specifically meant to make Mal difficult for otherworldly beings to notice, to make them want to get away, or to weaken them; an angelic charm neither of them had ever encountered. Here was poor Ben, a moth to a flame. When he came back with steaming cups for both of them, careful to pass Chris the sweetened one, Chris was balancing a legal pad on the arm of the chair and jotting down notes while looking intently at his tablet.

"Find something?"

Chris smiled kindly at the hopeful question.

"I think maybe I have."

Ben's expression of relief at the mere possibility would have been comical if he didn't look so wretched.

Chris shook his head. "Sit down before you fall down, Ben."

"It's worn off. Just show me," he snapped. Patience was never one of Ben's virtues, and since meeting Mal and being affected by her magic, his emotions had been especially volatile.

"Glad to hear it, but when was the last time you slept?" Ben's brow puckered in response. "Just sit. I'm still reading."

Ben sat down, folding and unfolding his arms restlessly. He was fine, great even. Well, maybe not great, but he would be as soon as they figured this out. He sulked a little while, staring at Chris, mentally trying to hurry him up. After what felt like hours, Chris finally put down the tablet and tossed Ben his notebook. On it was a sketched an unfamiliar intertwining symbol that reminded Ben vaguely of Pictish, along with a list of spell ingredients and some illegible instructions.

Ben frowned, "I'm not familiar with this. I've never done much symbol magic."

"I came across an old book about various magical marks in the online Archive. This is old. Magic at its most basic. You mix the ingredients, do the ritual, and embed the symbol on your body something like a tattoo. You want it someplace hidden from easy view because someone determined could cut or burn it off and the effects of that are unpredictable. If the ritual is successful, the spell becomes part of you, telling other magic you're safe, or invisible to it. Something along those lines."

"And if it's not successful?" Ben raised an eyebrow and Chris couldn't tell if it was skeptical or apprehensive.

"Best guess?" he asked, and Ben nodded. "It'll just hurt like hell."

"But you think we could do it?"

"I can't see why not. It's not complicated."

Chris expected Ben to be pleased, but instead he reacted with concern. "Could just anybody use this?"

"Certainly. If they found it."

Ben uttered the foulest curse he knew under his breath and paced around the small apartment. After a while, he slumped back into the chair, "Anybody can just … whatever?"

"You didn't think we'd find some solution special to you did you?"

"No, but … goddamnit!" Ben was not feeling particularly clear-headed. Actually, he was kind of missing being able to go pick a fight and randomly kick some demon's ass to vent his frustrations. "What do we do about it?"

"Well, for starters I was thinking we could do this magic so you stop looking like you've got the plague."

"Ha ha," he said flatly. "Obviously we do the spell." He gave a little shake of his head. "I guess I'm just realizing how complicated this is going to be."

"Before we knew it was Mal and who she really is we knew this wouldn't be easy. All we can do is keep working, trying to discover what we're missing, what we're supposed to do, how to keep that fallen angel off her back maybe. For now we'll just do our best to watch out for her."

Ben read the list again. "I can get all this relatively easily."

"Are you sure? Some of the constituents are fairly rare. This isn't TV. There's not a well-supplied wizards' warehouse on every street corner."

"Yeah, well, I've got a guy."

"Oh, so you've just got 'a guy' for rare spell ingredients?"

Ben, always good for a pop-culture reference, dropped his voice into its deepest animated secret agent register and smirked. "What? You don't?"

They both broke out laughing; their mutual weakness for cartoons had been one of the things that cemented their friendship, and the tension of Ben's situation made it feel necessary.

"Your demon friend?"

Ben shrugged noncommittally.

"Okay, if you can get the ingredients and you really want to try it, I'll help you. I'm a decent enough spellcaster after all these years that I think I can make it work."

Ben got out his phone and began texting Aife the list. She'd learned not to ask too many questions and he couldn't imagine Acquisitions would make much of it either. It was pretty obscure. Chris picked up his tablet and continued reading. This book had some fairly fascinating information, interesting also in the things it omitted. Chris was finding the things that were missing were often important pieces of information. Ben was turning out to be a wealth of knowledge about things deemed unfit for general consumption or the Church simply didn't know. Chris was amused to see that with a solution to his most immediate problem imminent, Ben was leaning back in the chair almost dozing, looking like the cat that got the cream.

"Hey, Ben, can I ask you something?"

Ben's eyes opened slowly. "Sure. Find something else?"

Chris shook his head. "I'm just curious about something." Ben gestured for him to continue. "I know we've talked about how the Bible isn't literal, and obviously given our present predicament, there's a lot it leaves out or glosses over."

"Like completely omitting billions of years of history and being wildly inaccurate," Ben snickered. "Yeah."

Chris frowned, trying to be disapproving, but knowing Ben wasn't exactly wrong. "Reading all this lore got me thinking. What about Cain and Abel?"

Ben thought for a minute. "Well … it's not like the '*sons of the first man*' or whatever. The Bible is just a loose history of one group of people told mostly by their patriarchs, who obviously had an agenda." He stopped for a moment, trying to separate what he knew was true from what conjured the smell of bullshit. "I don't think I've met anyone in the *Genesis* lineage, but all those begats bore me to death anyway. You'd have to take it on faith, or maybe ask an angel, although they'd probably just talk you to death about how great they are."

Chris smiled a little. "You telling me I'd be better off picking up a tabloid at the supermarket for some facts?"

Ben chuckled, "Half the time. But the Bible isn't all crap. You exist, and we know other things in it exist. Like me." He paused for a breath, considering. "Actually, now that I think about it, I do know of a soul who fits the general description … Last I knew he was living in a monastery up in Quebec. He's a bit of a curiosity for everyone who operates on the other side. Thousands and thousands of years old. I couldn't say if he was his brother's keeper though. Never met him."

"You could have led with that, oh Master of Expression," Chris scoffed good-naturedly.

"It's been a rough couple of weeks." Ben's grin was sheepish. "Besides, that's one of my powers, so I have to focus on it."

"Wait a minute, you mean to tell me when you destroy someone's argument in a debate, or give one of your Oscar-worthy theatrical performances you're using a demonic power?" Chris's voice was an odd blend of amused and horrified.

Ben laughed dismissively. "It's not like that ... Wait; it's exactly like that. But, it's kind of natural. I was always good at all that. My powers are mostly just more Ben. It's not like I was a complete idiot as a human."

Chris tipped a wry smile. "Hey, you're the one who couldn't even stick around the planet long enough to reproduce, kid." Then he regretted saying it; the fact that Ben hadn't had a family of his own seemed to be something of a sore spot. Ben's response let him off the hook.

"That's about enough out of you, Roman." Ben frowned at him dramatically then laughed again. "If it makes you feel better, my *Hamlet* was all me ... well, except for maybe the fencing. I'm not naturally all that graceful ... Too tall." Chris glared at him. "Okay, so it's a little demonic. Sometimes. But it's not like I'm up there hurling furniture or fireballs with my brain."

"*What?*"

Ben laughed at Chris's scandalized expression. "I said I have powers."

"Minor demon stuff. You specifically said *minor*."

"Give me a break. It's just telekinesis and pyrokinesis. Humans can do those."

"Really? I've never seen that."

"Sure. More than you'd probably expect."

"What about running? Are all of your records because you're a demon?"

"I'm not a cheat! Remember how dinged up I was after that obstacle race?"

Chris raised an eyebrow and said, "I also seem to remember you jogging over here from your place the day after that like nothing had happened. That's what, five or six miles of mostly hills?"

Ben shrugged. "I guess how fast I heal is kind of an advantage because I love pushing myself and I hate being sore, but the running is all me. It clears my head, helps me think."

Chris was getting impatient. "Okay. But what else, Ben? *Now.*"

"Okay, jeez. Relax." Ben shifted uncomfortably under Chris's stern paternal gaze. "I can see spirits; identify supernatural creatures on sight usually ..."

"Supernatural creatures?" Chris's eyes were serious.

"You've met some?"

Chris nodded, frowning.

"Don't worry; most of them just variations on your basic demon and the ones that aren't are usually just corrupted souls, barred from the Netherrealms. Those are no big deal to slap down. I've heard about others, but they don't want anything to do with this dimension as far as I know ..." He thought for another minute, "Some precognition, but I've kind of always had that; even as a little kid. So that's probably a 'Ben' thing and not a demon thing ... What else? Hmmm ... If I concentrate I can pick up surface thoughts." Ben put up his hand to stop Chris's question. "Not a mind reader. Just, what else are ya gonna ask? There are real Readers out there, but they're rare. I've only ever met one."

Chris started to look slightly less horrified and more interested. Ben understood he would need some time to adjust, but it was probably good to lay it all out so they both knew what he could do to help Mal. His powers might be good for more than entertaining himself for a change.

"How deep can you go?" Chris's tone was merely curious now.

"Well, like I said, it's not easy. I have to concentrate to use any of this stuff. Proximity helps. I can do it when I'm talking with someone. If I focus I can pick up their intentions, maybe the odd word. I can almost always tell if I'm being lied to. Actually, I tend to pick up emotions, even if I'm not trying."

"What am I feeling right now?" Chris threw out as a challenge.

Ben laughed. "A little wigged out because sometimes you forget where I come from and ... a little irritated by me checking my phone while we're talking."

"Scarily accurate, although you could've just guessed that last bit as just part of what it means to be a Twenty-first Century adult." Chris was smiling a little. "Is there anything else?"

Ben thought for a moment, squinting, and then shook his head. "Not really."

Chris cleared his throat and prepared to change the subject. "So, anyway ... about Cain?"

Ben stood up and stretched. "I don't know. You may have noticed there are quite a few things I'm clueless about." Ben checked his phone again. "My source is having those ingredients delivered by messenger a little later."

"Good. Should be simple enough, although I don't imagine it will be very pleasant," Chris warned. "It's an old spell and symbol magic can be quite nasty."

Ben just shrugged again. "I'm hungry."

"Color me surprised."

"I'm gonna walk to the market. You wanna go eat?"

Chris stood and got his coat. "Sure, I could eat."

Ben opened the door and jogged down the stairs, wearing no jacket as usual. He called over his shoulder, "Besides, if you're gonna stab me with magic later, you definitely need to buy more beer."

Chapter 24

"One of the most beautiful qualities
of true friendship is to understand
and be understood."
~ Lucius Annaeus Seneca

When Ben finally woke the next day, he was on the couch under a heavy quilt, with the exhausted Chris across from him playing an elaborate hand of solitaire on the coffee table. Chris's whole manner, down to the carefully concealed tightness around his eyes, broadcast his worry. Ben forced himself slowly upright, rubbing burning eyes, taking stock of how many places he hurt, unsure if he was awake or if this was the start of another nightmare. Realizing he was finally conscious, Chris brought him a glass of water and Ben downed the whole thing almost desperately, so parched he thought his mouth might absorb it all before he could swallow. Looking like maybe he was afraid of the answer, Chris asked how he was feeling.

"Gross. Like I need a shower, maybe a shave, and literally all the coffee. I bet this is what a hangover feels like. How do humans even drink?" Ben said with forced nonchalance. Then, pulling at his damp t-shirt and wrinkling his nose, he gave a weak smile. "Bet a Bloody Mary would go down pretty smooth about now." Making an obvious effort to avoid real conversation, he got gingerly off the couch and headed for the bathroom down the hall. When he returned, he began to slowly put the room back in order.

"Ben, don't. I'll clean up. You've been out for ages, something like seventeen hours." Chris hadn't had the heart to straighten up after the spell. He'd just sat watching Ben, weary from working the magic, and dozing between bouts of Ben's fevered sleep-mumblings and occasional sharp cries of pain and terror.

"Nah, I'll help. It's kind of my mess." Ben was moving stiffly, his eyes narrowing occasionally, but all he said was, "After all that, I hope it works."

"Ben, son, please sit. I've never seen anything like that. It was …" he trailed off, not wanting to add self-consciousness to Ben's list of problems. Ben gave a one shouldered shrug. His other side felt stiff and aching and didn't seem to want to cooperate with what he was telling it to do, but he wasn't about to admit it. Then he bent to pick up a cold smudge pot and the whole room tilted wildly, forcing him to sit down hard on the coffee table.

"I'll be fine," he reassured Chris, grasping the edge so he wouldn't just slide off, and keeping his eyes squeezed shut until everything stopped spinning. After a minute he moved carefully back to the couch and, sinking heavily into the cushions, pulled the quilt around his shoulders. He sighed, "I'm thinking I'd better reschedule with Mal though."

He thought about what to say since he didn't want her to feel like he was blowing her off. He decided on a story with an element of truth, confirming something she already suspected. He texted her, telling her she'd been right; he had the flu and he felt like hell. She replied almost immediately saying he should go right to bed and he should have gotten a flu shot like a grown-up. He told her he was lying down already and that he was pretty sure being a grown-up was totally overrated. She'd responded that she had acted like a grown-up so she could come over and take care of him and not get sick. He felt badly enough about bullshitting her; the idea of faking actual symptoms was too much, so he said she should stay away from his germs, just in case. He assured her that Dr. G, the world's adultiest grown-up, was letting him stay at his place and was fretting on her behalf. She was busy with her senior project, so they agreed to go out next weekend as long as he felt better. He smiled at her concern, feeling vaguely guilty for lying, and promptly drifted off with his phone still in his hand.

The next time Ben woke, Chris made him promise to stay until he felt better. He even called in to work Monday because Ben was still feverish and not himself, not exactly delirious anymore, but not quite all there either. Despite wan assurances that he was fine, Ben didn't mention going home or even move off the couch much all week. He slept off and on during the day and most of the night in some borrowed pajamas, still aching all over and dreaming badly. Most concerning, he had no appetite, was only picking at his food, and was awfully moody, too. On Saturday Ben insisted he could get back to their research but he kept dozing off and seemed ready for an argument at the drop of a hat. Chris quickly put an end to any attempts at productivity, brought him tea, and encouraged more napping by putting on a PBS history series he knew bored the boy nearly to tears.

Sunday was another matter entirely. Ben had shown up for dinner over an hour before Chris was expecting him. He sailed into the apartment carrying a large canvas bag full of groceries, blithely saying Mal had dropped him off at the market and he'd wanted to walk from there because it was so nice out. Ben had then revealed another aspect of himself, moving around the kitchen with practiced ease. He knew how to cook. He was no chef, he said, but you couldn't like food as much as he did for as long as he had and not bother to learn how to make it. Chris sat at the table with a book, half watching Ben, periodically offering to help and being waved off, and listening to him quietly sing cheerful Christmas carols in an unpracticed but very agreeable tenor. Maybe all the snapping and churlishness yesterday had been Ben's anxiety it wouldn't work as much as it was the aftereffects of the spell. Either way, since Ben had spent most of the day with Mal and he was positively buoyant, Chris had to assume they had been successful.

Ben noticed his expression when he reached for a tasting spoon and grinned, "What are you smiling at, Centurion? Set the table. I'm not doing all the work in this outfit."

Chris was more than happy to oblige and pleased to have a reason to take his real plates out of the cupboard. Left to his own devices he would probably live on takeout. Even their usual Sunday dinners were more often than not eaten directly from cardboard containers. Ben plated up their meal, grabbed the gallon of milk Chris always kept for him, and came to the table, still humming to himself. Ben might claim to only 'kind of' know how to cook, but he'd blown most restaurant meals Chris had ever had right off the map with his version of meatloaf, sautéed garlic green beans, and buttery mashed potatoes. Ben sat shoveling in more food than one person should be able to hold, beaming in between swallows of milk at Chris's reaction to his efforts. Finally Chris decided it was time to pry some information out of him.

"You certainly seem to be feeling more like yourself," seemed like a safe observation.

"Um, yeah, great. Awesome," he agreed, mouth still half-full, cutting himself another slice of meatloaf.

Apparently, this would require slightly less subtle interrogation. He let Ben hear the obvious prompting in his question, "So how was your day?"

All week, Ben had found Chris's fussing over him maddening. He'd felt like six shades of week-old refried room-temperature death, which was taxing for someone who hadn't been sick in a couple of thousand years, and barely ever before that. Worse, when he let himself remember the spell it took a supreme effort to keep from shaking like a leaf in the goddamned rain, which just annoyed him even more. He was a warrior for fuck's sake. It's not like he'd never been hurt before. But, the way this had laid him up was infuriating, and the pain, the hallucinatory fevered dreams, made him sure he was being unmade down to the fiber of his soul. He knew he'd been miserable to be around and if he'd had to watch a friend go through that, he'd probably have been worrying and asking if they were okay every five minutes, too. He felt badly about being so difficult and knew he owed Chris for his help. Talking about today would just seal it in his memory and it was the least he could offer to assuage Chris's obvious concern. He grinned again. "I had a lovely morning, a lovely lunch, and a lovely lady on my arm. What more could a guy want?"

"On your arm? Literally or figuratively?" *Come on Ben, spill*, he thought.

Ben looked like he might float out of his chair. "Literally. Chris, it worked." His sunny smile said all his pain and illness had been forgotten in one touch. "I saw her the second she walked in, which I figured was a good sign. She brushed against me when I handed her her coffee and I was waiting for that awful feeling to hit me and ruin everything, but nothing happened. She took my hand while we were walking into the mall and I swear she didn't let it go all day!"

When he talked like that, looked like that, it was difficult for Chris to believe Ben had seen even more of this universe than he had. Often when he spoke of Mal he sounded even younger than he looked, which was to say, only barely a man with plenty of boy left over. He was dedicated to assisting Chris, but his focus had shifted entirely to protecting Mal, finding better magic, trying to cut his ties with Hell, no matter what it cost him. At school, Mal was not much different, often smiling to herself, texting under her desk, and staring out the window. He was fond of both of them and it would have taken a fool not to see they were falling in love. He could only hope there was some possibility of a future for them, somehow. In his long life he'd seen enough to believe it was at least possible, no matter how unlikely it seemed.

Instead of discussing the uncertainty of their situation, Chris went to the cupboard and produced the cake he'd picked up from the bakery around the corner. Ben normally didn't care much for dessert, but Chris had discovered he would nearly fight you for anything chocolate, and if there was some cinnamon involved, Chris could expect to get much less of whatever it was than usual. In the event Ben showed up dejected that the terrible spell hadn't been effective, Chris had ordered a chocolate spice cake with orange cream cheese frosting, not too sweet. He put a huge slab of it on Ben's dessert plate as Ben poured another glass of milk. The boy dug in immediately, eyes rolling with pleasure. Chris was happy to see him eating so heartily since he thought Ben had probably lost ten pounds this week, and he had to admit that, regardless, this was a fitting end to their meal. As their dinner came to an end, they fell into their habit of more leisurely talking. "Have you thought about what you're planning to do this week? I'll be in class at St. Auggie's, and finishing up semester grades at the college, but I have some new books being delivered tomorrow."

"I'd love a chance to dig deeper on mystical weapons." Since Ben didn't need to maintain the illusion of holding down a job he was dedicating any time he had off from classes to their work together. Chris wasn't sure why Ben stayed in school now that his secret was out, but he got a sense Ben was doing it because he'd discovered he liked it, was good at it. He seemed to be gravitating toward literature and writing, which having read some of his work, particularly his poetry, came as no surprise to Chris. "I'll come over in the morning. Maybe I'll run. All I did was sleep all week. I feel like a lump."

Chris responded with the almost inevitable fatherly brow wrinkle. "Ben, you still look like hell. If I didn't know you were a demon I'd be dragging you to the campus infirmary, if I had to knock you on the head to get you there."

Ben gave him a wry grin.

"You take it easy until you're sure you're okay!" Chris admonished. "Do you want to pick up the materials and take them home with you? You could take a cab ... I'll feel better if I know you aren't overdoing it."

Ben shook his head, frowning thoughtfully. "It's too loud, living over the bar, and it's hard to concentrate there. The energy's weird. You know?" Then he grinned again. "I'll come over here ... but I'll take a cab. I promise."

Chris, thinking he knew more than he liked about Ben's apartment at this point in their association, considered thoughtfully, "You know you'd be welcome to move into my spare room. You sleep here half the time anyway. I mean, I'm sure you'd want to move those boxes of papers, but I'm not picky. I'd happily store them in the living room until I sort through them. Besides, with you seeing so much of Mal do you really want her offering to drive you there?"

Ben's eyes widened. The idea of Mal going anywhere near The Pit was enough to give him a panic attack. Also, if he was honest, he sensed Aife might appreciate a little distance with Castor's men coming around more frequently and Lucifer's cronies within spitting distance. She was as helpful and loyal as she'd always been, but plausible deniability was probably welcome in their case. Chris was looking at him kindly, his face full of parental concern. The question popped out of Ben's mouth before he could stop himself. "Chris, did you ever have kids?"

Chris smiled almost sadly, and shook his head. "Never managed a family."

Now that the question was out there, Ben found he really wanted to know. "Not even back in your old life?"

"Ben, I was a soldier. Honestly, I had the comfort of a woman beside me whenever I chose, and I was young."

"How old were you? You know, when it happened."

"Oh, sometimes it's hard to remember. Not very old by today's standards. Early thirties, I think. How about you?"

"I don't remember even keeping track. I don't have much to go on. Probably seventeen or so. I mean … most of my friends were already married, had a couple of kids, but I …" He frowned. Ben spoke about his past infrequently and when something was revealed accidentally, he quickly rerouted the conversation. "So, never?"

Chris's smile was patient. "Why do you ask?"

"It's just the way you are with kids, even college kids, hell, with me," Ben hesitated for a moment then went on, "you just seem like pretty good dad material."

"No." He paused, then said more forcefully, "No, Ben, it's hard enough watching people pass in and out of my life. I don't think I could stand losing a wife. I know I couldn't bear to lose a child."

Looking at Ben, a shadow danced across his features. Ben swallowed hard. To give Chris a moment, and to distract himself from his own surprising near loss of composure, Ben cleared the table, stowing leftovers in the refrigerator. Meatloaf sandwiches for lunch tomorrow were already on his mind. Maybe he'd make bread in the morning. It felt good to be hungry again, to feel normal. That spell had been like Hell itself. He'd still felt awful this morning. All his clothes were too loose and he felt kind of like someone had been beating on him with a pillowcase full of oranges, or possibly baseballs. *Was that being sick?* He honestly couldn't remember, but he hated it. Maybe it was all in his head, but when Mal had taken his hand and asked how he was doing, her eyes full of concern, he'd felt better immediately, and over the course of the day improved until he felt more or less like himself. He scraped off the plates and stacked dishes in the sink. He took the dish soap and put it on the table.

"What's this for?" Chris asked, eyebrows climbing.

"Well, I'm gonna move some boxes. I think I like the idea of a roommate." He shrugged, pleased to find both shoulders painless and once again entirely under his command.

"This explains the dish soap, how?"

"You're on KP duty, soldier." He grinned. "I cooked. That means you do the dishes. Get used to it."

Ben headed down the hall humming and hearing Chris's soft laughter followed by a rare full-voiced expletive when he got a good look the culinary destruction Ben had wrought.

Chapter 25

"I often regret that I have spoken; never that I have been silent."
~ Publilius Syrus

Ben sat at the black enameled table, drumming his fingers, exasperated about being expected to justify his actions to anyone. He supposed his bullshit reports should have been more detailed, but nobody else was making any progress either so he thought it was safe to just let things slide. Aife brought him a drink and gave him a significant look. She knew he wasn't following orders, he could tell. While their past was as friends, occasionally with benefits, she been his self-appointed caregiver more than once. When she behaved with such anxious unease it was nearly as bad as when Chris hectored him with his most practiced voice of parental concern. Being called to account the day after he'd spent time with Mal made him extremely nervous, feeling like the angels would sense his betrayal like bloodhounds after a fugitive. Ben just shook his head. It's not like he could avoid taking risks like this. *The only way out was through ... or some bullshit like that.* He knew Lahash and Lilith had entered The Pit from the sinking in his stomach and the fluttering in his chest before he even picked them out of the smoky gloom. He plastered on his most loftily detached expression as they approached his table.

"Ronoven, there you are! Your reports have been so woefully inadequate we thought perhaps you wouldn't bother." Lilith's voice put him in mind of an open crypt, a rotting corpse reanimated in a nightmare.

He knew they expected him to stand, but as usual when he felt circumstances were working against him, he put on his boldest face, assuming the practiced swagger of Hell's nobility. He waved them grandly into their seats, signaling Aife to bring them drinks. "You must have known I was here. The building reports whoever passes through those doors straight to Hell and I know you have a direct line to the boss."

Lahash gave a throaty chuckle. "It's interesting you should mention that, my little *human* friend."

Ben's heart took off at a gallop and it felt like it might be trying to climb into his throat. *What is she talking about?* He struggled to get on top of his panic while maintaining his neutral expression. Aife bustled over with a tray, depositing drinks in front of them. Lahash appeared to be drinking champagne, but Lilith held a goblet that Ben tried to tell himself contained red wine. Unfortunately, he could smell the blood from across the table and was inexplicably certain it was human. Aife gave the barest apologetic shake of her head. She'd been trying to get him alone all evening, but things kept coming up. Business had picked up over the last few months because there were so many more demons in the area. Obviously there had been something she'd wanted to tell him. He should have pulled rank on the crowd and found out what was going on earlier.

"Surely you must know," Lilith hissed, eyes boring into him, her snake-like pupils barely dilating in the dim club.

Lahash took up where her sister left off. "Don't be coy. All those rare ingredients you requested. Acquisitions was intrigued immediately. Unless I work to see your aura, you appear utterly human. Even this office's enchantments read you as such. What clever magic! So ancient and dangerous."

"Oh that," he remarked offhandedly, buying a moment by taking a drink. He hadn't known the spell would go that far. *No wonder it was a nightmare.* Ben's mind raced, trying to think of a convincing justification, and then he remembered with relief that Lucifer had sent orders early on to make useful magic a priority in this mission. "Some of my research led me to a spell to overcome personal wards. In the event we locate the child, I thought it best to pursue it after Lahash's," he paused to let her hear the word 'failure' in her own mind before he finished, "experience." He gave her a tight smile.

"Well," Lilith observed, "I'm impressed, I must say." He frowned at her slightly. "You always were bold as brass." The lines on her face deepened. "You must know since that magic belongs to the old gods you shouldn't have survived."

She could tell from the slight widening of his eyes he had known no such thing, and took a satisfied sip from her glass.

What he said was, "I thought it worth the risk."

"Now that he knows a demon can survive it, I'm sure Lucifer will think so, too."

Ben thought of demons able to see and touch Mal without consequence, and the smug expression on their faces, filled him with seething rage. Fortunately, before he could reply with the vitriolic response percolating in his chest, Lahash spoke.

"I understand it's terribly painful," she commented with obvious eagerness. "Of course, I've also heard you're impervious to that sort of thing. How did you fare?"

"Well, I'm glad it's nothing I ever need repeat," he remarked in his most casually disinterested voice, as though he hadn't died a thousand deaths in the hours following the spell, and suffered miserably for days besides.

Oh, how he wanted to throttle her, or just lop off both their murderous heads and have done with it. Fortunately, he had learned some restraint in his latest time on Earth. "I am pleased to have been of service," he said formally. "Unfortunately, I truly have nothing new to report. I am continuing with the work I described when we spoke last. Your impatience deprived you of observing my adherence to protocol. I was about to report my success with this shield spell when I received your message. I assure you, if I discover anything else that might be of use, I will impart it immediately through the Agent, per Lucifer's orders." He thought he sounded haughty enough to be consistent with their experience of him.

Lahash stood, appearing satisfied with the encounter. "We feel our position is promising. We will summon you should we require anything further." She threw him a superior glance, and motioned for Lilith to come away with her. Lilith leered at him pointedly, revealing her whole mouth stained red and gruesome. It was a shark's smile, displaying no emotion, only the promise of pain and a wrenching bloody end besides. She could tell he found her repulsive and reveled in his distaste. She drained her glass and placed it on the table directly in front of him. The reek of blood bathed his nostrils and he could feel his throat constricting, the contents of his stomach threatening to make an appearance. He leaned back in his chair like he didn't have a care in the world and tipped them a sarcastic salute. They strolled out of the club into the night.

He suddenly remembered Mal mentioning that maybe he could come over and meet her dad some weekend, and he thought at least now he probably could without getting killed on sight. Then the idea of gaining any advantage through this magic, despite what its discovery by Hell might cost Mal, made his face feel hot and his chest tight. Ben couldn't get enough air in this stuffy crowded place, but didn't want to leave too close on their heels. Aife spotted his distress from across the jam-packed room and, unable to extract herself from the three-customers-deep crush at the bar, sent Ciara over to tell him he was welcome to wait in private until she was available.

When Aife finally had a moment, she found Ben sitting on the sofa, elbows on his knees, head in his hands, drink untouched. *Poor Ben.* She'd never seen him like this. He mattered more to her than her position or anything waiting below. She sat down and he jumped, startled. He saw her sympathetic face and sank back into the cushions, at a complete loss, eyes darting around like he was trying to find an escape. She put her hand on his arm, her face shadowed with concern.

"Ben, look at me." He was looking everywhere else. "Ben!" He grudgingly met her eye, unmistakably miserable.

His expression was desolate and he barely whispered, "Aife, what have I done?"

She looked at him steadily. "You tell me what's going on. No more of your faerie stories, either. I want to help you."

He shuddered with tension and emotion and haltingly unfolded his story.

Chapter 26

"Who's to say that your dreams and nightmares aren't as real as the here and now?"
~ John Lennon

Mal sat up in bed, slicked with sweat and gasping. Everything else was lining up as she'd hoped … why wouldn't these awful dreams stop? Her entire childhood had been plagued by terrible nightmares, but she never expected to be eighteen and still spend several nights a week curled up against her dad on the couch because she'd screamed them both awake. Lately, she dreaded going to sleep for fear she'd wake up breathless and weeping in the dark with her dad standing over her looking like he might cry. When she didn't wake him she was grateful, but she was still keeping a journal like he suggested. Her dreams were constantly about things she knew weren't real, but it was like they were trying to convince her otherwise. It made her jumpy and a little paranoid whenever she left the house. It was like maybe she was going a little crazy, and the idea of losing her grip on reality was at least as terrifying as the dreams themselves. She'd been casually leaving her journal on their coffee table in the morning so she could share it but not have to live through the retelling. Her dad wouldn't let her go off the deep end without stepping in to help, so having him monitor what was going on in her head made her feel safer.

Tonight's dream had been particularly upsetting so she was thankful that, while her cheeks were wet along with her pillow and her breath came for a few moments in irregular hitches, she hadn't disturbed him, because she knew she couldn't talk about this one. He never fell asleep behind the closed door of his room anymore. He'd come to favor their lumpy couch, which Mal suspected had more to do with her regular nocturnal terrors than his Netflix addiction. She was glad she'd finally told him she was seeing Ben because he figured prominently in several of her most frightening dreams lately and something made her want to share these with her dad. Sighing, she turned on her dim bedside light and made an entry in her journal.

12/2, 02:45 a.m.

I'm in the Underground Mall meeting Ben to exchange Christmas presents. I have the cool old coin Dr. G gave me and the nice pen I got him wrapped up with a bow. He has this cute little package all wrapped in white paper with too much tape and a lumpy red ribbon I can tell he tied himself. I'm thinking about just throwing my arms around him. I haven't done that yet and I want to know what holding him feels like. He always smells so good. I don't know what cologne he wears, but I can smell it in the dream. The lights go out without any warning. The skylight isn't letting in any light and we can barely see. Ben looks at me and his eyes are so big it's like they're taking up his whole face and so bright I could swear they're glowing and he's yelling RUN as loud as he can but there's no sound. From the big Christmas tree down on the lower level comes this woman, really beautiful, but all ghostly. She's glowing in the dark and Ben tries to take my hand to run away with me but she grabs him and twists his arm and he yells in pain and I can hear that. Then right in front of me there is this awful woman but she doesn't look like a real person. She has long spiked teeth and her skin is hanging off her body and she's wearing a grey robe covered with blood stains. She puts her hands on my throat. Her nails are digging into my skin. I can't breathe and I'm on my knees and the tile floor is so cold. She leans toward me and I hear this disgusting sound like when Dad cuts up a chicken and I realize she's actually unhinging her jaw like she's going to swallow me whole and then Ben is there fighting with her, trying to get her to let go of me even though I can see his arm is broken and his hand is bleeding. I'm about to die when everything gets hot and I see Ben and now his beautiful eyes are on fire and the thing lets me go and falls down bleeding icky black gunk everywhere. Ben helps me up and we're getting away, and then I feel her hand on my ankle and I know she is going to pull me down into where she came from. But Ben throws himself at her and I see her tearing into him with those awful teeth and dragging him into that hole and I hear him scream over and over like he'll never stop and ...

Mal thought she could just write it down and go back to sleep, maybe with the light on, but as she wrote her weeping intensified and she found she was shaking, then she felt like she might throw up. She wished Ben were here and was glad they had plans today. She was definitely going to throw her arms around him, and maybe kiss him, too, right in the middle of the mall, no matter how shy he was about it. As she thought about how it would feel to be in his arms, to know he was safe, she calmed enough to dry her eyes. She tossed her journal aside and decided she'd sneak downstairs for some tea. When she turned the corner she could see her dad's dim light on. She crept down quietly in case he had just fallen asleep with the TV on but he was waiting for her on the couch with a steaming cup of chamomile tea (heavy on honey, how she always took it). The quilt she liked was next to her usual spot. He smiled at her gently, reaching out his arm to let her know she was welcome. She was determined to be okay, but when she sat down and he covered her with the blanket and handed her the tea, her tears began again. He took the cup, put it back on the table, and held her.

"Oh Daddy," she sobbed. She hadn't called him 'Daddy' since she still sucked her thumb. "I just want this to stop. Why is this happening?"

He didn't ask; he knew the dreams were terrible for her, whatever they were about. She could feel his tension, almost as though he wanted to answer her, but he just held her close. "I'm sorry, princess. I'm just so sorry."

Chapter 27

"You don't get to choose what your nightmares are.
You don't pick them;
they pick you."
~ John Irving

iles away, having dozed off in the wingback chair that had become his favorite because it offered such easy access to the coffee table for his feet, even though the habit drove Chris nuts, Ben was also having a nightmare. At first, though he didn't know it, his dream was similar, except Lucifer was dressed like Santa Claus, hanging from the Christmas tree, and laughing like some cartoon villain. As Ben was grappling with Lilith she bit his hand and his whole body burned with the poison of it. Mal screamed, an awful keening wail, terrifying in its anguish, its hopelessness. At the apex of that sound, Lilith burst into gruesome confetti, covering everything with fine droplets of black blood. Ben saw Lahash moving toward Mal and he put himself in the angel's way, fighting against the sluggishness from her sister's venom. Ben dispatched her with a strange unfamiliar blade and Mal was helping him away, but he fell, woozy with supernatural poison. Lahash crawled toward them inexorably on stiff dead hands, dark angelic blood oozing from her mouth and eyes. She grabbed onto him and began pulling him away from Mal, her rotting flesh sloughing off against him and as he wrenched himself away he could feel her bones. Chris appeared and pushed the fallen angels back with some powerful spell, and Ben managed to get to his feet, between Mal and Lucifer. Lucifer jumped down out of the tree, still laughing like a madman, pulled out a sword made of ice, and ran Ben through. He grabbed Mal and the two of them disappeared in icy blue flames. Ben could only watch, blood dripping through his hands, as he fell to his knees, thinking with growing alarm that it hurt. And he knew he was dreaming. Why the hell was he hurting in a dream? His vision went dim around the edges and then dark.

When his eyes opened again, he was lying on a cold block of roughhewn stone that dug into his skin; he was secured to it at his wrists and ankles with sharp barbed wire. Everything pained him. This was too purely physical to be a dream. They'd caught up to him at last, must have found him while he was sleeping. He hoped desperately that they'd left Chris alone. Feeling almost drugged, his thoughts hazy, he tried to get his bearings so maybe he could figure some way to escape. The barbs were cutting into him and he could feel slick blood where the wire was biting into his flesh. There was an intensely bright light above him. It burned his eyes, made his head ache. A wound, not unlike the one Lucifer inflicted in his dream, gaped in his abdomen and he could feel thickening blood pooling under his back. As he lay there cold, naked, and helpless, a dark hooded figure appeared above him.

"Did you really think you could hide from us?" the figure hissed. It was unmistakably Lilith.

Trying to clear his head enough for some fast talking, he pretended confusion, "Hide from you? I work for you!"

She chuckled, a sound like bones rattling in a bag. He could hear the muffled sounds of her moving around him and then she was beside him. She began dripping holy water out of a heavy clay carafe from above so he could see the light catching in the droplets as they fell into his wound. Excruciating fiery pain sparked in his belly and spread through his blood. The smell of smoking flesh filled the room. A scream built up, but he bit it back, gasping.

"Where's the Scion, traitor? What's her name?" rasped from somewhere near his head.

Bhaal, Ben realized. *Ohshitohfuckohnononono.* How could he have let this happen? There was no talking his way out if the god was involved, and there was only so long anyone could resist Hell's chief inquisitor before they either cracked or he just killed them. *So this would be the end then.* Hopefully he could bait them into getting it over with quickly.

He forced a dismissive puff of air out of his nose and tried to look around so he could glare at Lucifer's right hand. He saw only a circle of blackness outside of the ring of cold light around him, but he made an angry face anyway, sure Bhaal was watching him closely. "How the fuck should I know? You're the ones who lost her! Couldn't even hold onto a toddler!"

Bhaal's strangely handsome terrifying face was next to Ben's ear. "But you do know. She's gotten under your skin. Perhaps that's where I should look." Bhaal used his sharp clawed nails to slowly pare strips of skin from Ben's shoulder to his hip.

It wasn't all that deep, but more blood trickled down and pooled under him as his nerves sang. "I don't. I don't know shit," he asserted, sounding adamant but also managing to sound annoyed. The nails were drawn across his stomach and back up his other side and he sucked in his breath.

"And if you did?" Bhaal baited him with a grin.

"And if I did, you're the last asshole in all of Creation I'd tell," he spat. *Shit. Never give the prick the satisfaction. That was the first goddamned rule of being interrogated.*

Then Lahash was standing over him, leering in anticipation. In her hand, she held a curved dagger. It looked dull. *Wonderful.* "I've always wondered if the rumors were true. Is there no amount of pain you fear enough to bend to?"

He glared up at her, eyes defiant.

"Shall I stop this?" She smiled her chilling smile at his silence, and the empty resolve he saw on her face made him clench his teeth.

Ben steeled himself, his breathing shallow. Then Lahash began her slow exploration of his nerve centers with the hooked tip of the dark polished stone. He squeezed his eyes shut. Time became another instrument of torture in her hands. It might have been minutes, hours, years; Ben was lost to its passage, wrapped in his suffering. His resolve strengthened by unintentionally rising to Bhaal's taunt, Ben was determined to resist long enough for them to put a frustrated end to him. Although they kept asking, kept cutting, he hardly made a sound, refused to speak again.

The knife tugged across his belly, then dug deep into nerves over his solar plexus. Lahash began to draw the knife lower again, deeper, then lower still. Ben made some incoherent sound and heard an order given, but couldn't quite make it out over the ragged noise of his own labored breathing. The pain intensified and strangely that made it easier to draw inside his mind, to see the sensations as far away. Finally, after an eternity of being carved on like a roast, he heard Bhaal's irritated command coming from the periphery of the light, "If he won't talk, just cut it out of him. I'll dig her secrets out of his heart myself."

The blade was thrust in and drawn up.

Ben fought his way out of the dream, thrashing. He knocked his leg solidly against the underside of the coffee table and he was immediately, blessedly, free from the last tendrils of the dream and fully awake. He was cold all over and damp with sweat. He was unsurprised to find Chris wrapped in his tatty grey bathrobe, standing over him, his hand on Ben's arm in the act of trying to wake him, looking worried. Ben thought when they first met that he didn't want to get himself adopted and now realized it had gone and happened anyway. Instead of chafing at having someone fussing over him like he would have expected, Ben was grateful for his presence and almost perpetual fatherly concern.

Ben sat gasping for a few moments and then he pulled an uneven but deliberate breath as he massaged where he'd hit his leg. "Sorry, Chris, another rough night, I guess. Did I wake you again?"

Chris didn't answer right away, just searched Ben's flushed face for a moment, noticed his shivering, and silently went to the kitchen. Ben was chilled through, and still felt utterly exposed even under the layers of his bathrobe, sweats, and a t-shirt, so he stood, grabbed the quilt off the back off the couch and wrapped it around himself. Chris came back and held out a small glass. Ben took it gratefully in his unsteady hands and he took a long burning sip of Chris's good Irish whiskey. Chris despised ice in his drinks, a prejudice Ben didn't normally share, but he didn't complain. Never a great sleeper, he'd been having terrible nightmares since the spell and they seemed to be escalating in their intensity lately. This was the worst one by far. He never should have done it, damn it, should have left well enough alone. Now half the demons in Hell were probably marked with ward-shielding magic. And they'd find her, find both of them, he couldn't convince himself they wouldn't. He sighed heavily and took another longer drink that made his eyes water.

Chris sat down on the edge of the sofa near him and finally responded, "You didn't wake me. But, the sounds you were making. Jesus, Ben. I thought someone was torturing you out here. What kind of dream were you having?"

"Pretty much that. At first it was Lucifer. I watched him take Mal with him and all I could do was bleed. Then I dreamed I was in Hell ... Being interrogated." Those were all the details Ben could bring himself to share. He forced a little laugh, like the whole thing was ridiculous. "Wasn't sure it was a dream until I smacked my shin and woke up."

Chris eyed him carefully. Ben was typically pretty convincing, but this performance was not up to even his minimum standard, and what he had obviously hoped sounded like a brush off came out broadcasting how shaken up he was. Thinking it would be better for him to get it off his chest, Chris asked, "What's really bothering you?"

Ben took another sip, thinking about what to say. "I guess I'm still kind of wound up over having to let," he paused, consciously stopping himself from saying their names, "those Fallen know about the shielding. Now any of them can probably just walk right up to Mal and ... Doing that spell was almost as bad as just giving her up to them."

"Ben, you know that's not true." Chris's voice was reassuring. They'd been on this particular merry-go-round several times since his meeting at the bar. "Besides, they knew about the magic anyway." Ben tried to interrupt, but Chris pressed on. "All you revealed is the potential for survival. If I'd known it was a question we wouldn't have done it to begin with." He paused, "Have you considered that maybe you're responsible for countless demons being consumed by the potency of that spell? Not everyone has your mental fortitude."

Having been too busy beating himself up about what might happen, too exhausted by his fractured sleep, he hadn't, so he shook his head. Then he thought about it ... No one else had ever won their way into the aristocracy the way he had either. Maybe his will was something to be reckoned with. Momentarily pleased with the prospect, he gave a small smile.

Chris smiled back, "You see how I didn't say general pigheadedness. In magic being stubborn is actually a bit of an asset."

Ben tried to hold on to his smile, but was not someone who let himself off the hook easily, and his dream had the disturbingly familiar feeling of premonition. "I guess. But if bad dreams are the worst that happens I got off pretty fucking cheap." He gathered his thoughts, then asked, "How about you? Usually you sleep like a dead man. If it wasn't me, what got you up?"

No matter what the boy said, his magical ordeal was about as far from getting off cheap as Chris could imagine. He was reluctant to share his dream with Ben looking so rattled, but felt compelled to tell him since it also involved Hell coming for Mal. "I had a pretty nasty dream, myself. We were somewhere sunny and green, in the park maybe, just out for a walk. Then a terrible man grabbed us, tried to get us to tell Mal's secrets, and when we refused, he cut our throats so deeply it separated our heads from our bodies. Slowly. I might as well not pretend I don't know it was Lucifer even though you've never described him ... I couldn't just go back to sleep. Then I heard you."

"Good thing we can just hang around here all day guzzling coffee," Ben remarked with calculated calm, hiding his badly trembling hands by keeping them on his lap.

"I remember seeing the ground roll by before I woke up. It was so real, I could smell the grass. What if these dreams are prophetic in some way?"

Ben's voice was bitter when he responded. "You'll be fine. Don't let it trouble you so much."

Chris's head tilted and his brow furrowed

Ben sighed. "The curse. You don't need to let thinking about the future get to you."

"Of course it gets to me!"

"Look, no matter what, you get to live," was Ben's brusque reply.

Chris, upset by their dreams, was infuriated by Ben's tone, and found he felt unusually querulous, "If Lucifer comes along and lops off my head I get to live?"

"No, of course not, but it's not even possible."

"Of course it's possible, Ben. I can ... I don't know ... get hurt ... sick. I'm completely human, believe me."

"You're missing the point. You can get sick or hurt sure, and you don't even get to heal fast because *mostly* you're just a regular guy, but ..."

Chris interrupted, "A while back when I was living Central America, I was at the local beer joint on a Friday afternoon, just having a drink and complaining about work with a couple of other teachers and a fight broke out at the end of the bar. We broke it up but one of the men had a knife. I thought he was aiming for my chest but he got my shoulder instead. There is little to recommend tangling with drunken tourists," Chris frowned, unconsciously scratching the spot the wound had been. "Took about a million stitches to close it up; left one hell of a scar, too."

"That dude was *absolutely* going to stab you in the chest, but light got in his eyes, or maybe he slipped, and now there you are with a scratch instead of a heart turned into shaved pastrami. And if circumstances can't fix what's happening, someone else will have to. Every damned time." Chris frowned in confusion. "It's the mark. Didn't anybody ever explain this?"

"What do you mean *mark*? Explain what?"

"Some angel must have told you about your curse, right?" Chris's face grew solemn at the memory. "What did it say?"

Chris was thoughtful. "Just that I had sinned against God and was cursed to walk the Earth. He touched my forehead and there was this brief bright light, a burning pain, and then the angel and the pain and the light all vanished. And here we are."

Ben leaned back in his chair, laughing spontaneously, and this was a genuine boyish laugh, not forced out to minimize or change the subject. "Oh, it almost makes me happy that it's not just Lucifer who's a dick." Chris sat watching him, so pleased Ben's terrible tension seemed broken that he was trying not to be annoyed. Despite streaming eyes, Ben saw his tacit irritation. "I'm sorry, I'm not laughing at your situation, I swear. But all the 'holier than thou' bullshit angels get up to ... it's so funny ... They're no different from anyone in Hell. Heaven's just got air conditioning and a better PR department."

"Ben, try as I might, I'm not sure I'll ever find anything about this amusing."

Ben rolled his eyes, still snickering. "Anyhow, the burning you felt was the angel putting a mark on you. I mean it's mostly for a Reaper ..."

Chris interrupted. "There's a Grim Reaper?"

"No … Well, I guess maybe, but it's nothing special. There used to be like *THE* Angel of Death who worked plagues and wars and stuff, or sometimes collected important souls personally." Chris signaled for him to go on. "For a while though, there's just been Reapers. It's what everybody in Hell calls them. Heaven calls them … Shepherds or some shit; who the fuck knows why?" Ben frowned. "I guess it's kind of like Heaven and Hell are these big shitty office buildings and if the department heads are busy, they have to have petty functionaries to send a memo or whatever … I've done that, you know, been the petty functionary; the collection stuff. But there are all kinds of beings who do it for both sides. Sometimes it gets super competitive, like occasionally angels and demons will really throw down over somebody. I won't fight. If Heaven bothers to show up, they can have 'em."

"Don't you get in trouble for that?"

"Telling convincing stories is one of my skills. Remember?" Ben shrugged. "Besides, not everyone in Hell is an asshole. There're plenty of demons like me, just trying to squeak by."

"I suppose that's good, all things considered."

Ben shrugged again, this time like the possible consequences of his choices were the least important thing in the world. "But anyway, your mark tells everyone you can't be collected."

"Can you see it?"

Ben shook his head. "I can sense it's there. If I were here on the job, my magic would make it visible. Magic is the other thing the mark is there for." Chris shifted in his seat. Ben guessed this was the part he was both interested in and afraid to hear. "It's a spell, too. You're cursed to live. So the mark will make sure that you do."

"What do you mean?"

"Okay, say we walk over to Dorset Street and stand beside the road at like three in the afternoon with University Mall in total Christmas traffic mode. Some jackass jumps the curb at the light …" He paused to make sure Chris was still with him. "So if the guy didn't just get a flat or something, some poor bastard who's *not* marked and it would probably be me knowing my luck, would just be compelled by the magic to jump in and shove you out of the way. And if the car did hit you, you'd break some bones or maybe rupture something you could live without, spend a couple of weeks in the hospital with every cutie in scrubs fighting over who gets to take care of Professor Ruggedly Handsome and then you'd go home with some cool new scars."

Chris raised a single eyebrow, smiling wryly.

"Okay, I'm sure it wouldn't exactly be oceans of fun, but if I get hit by a car it most likely flattens me. Squish. My magic is nowhere near as good as yours. So there I'd be, back in Hell, getting yelled at for saving you."

"Yelled at?"

"We'll go with that. You might want to sleep again sometime. Ever."

Chris raised an eyebrow.

Ben shifted uncomfortably, "Why do you think I'm not telling you more about Hell, about my dreams? You don't need to hear that crap."

"You can talk to me about anything you need to Ben. You know that, right?"

Ben waved off the offer. "Your curse doesn't seem so bad from my perspective. You know that in this fight you can't die, Chris, and if they ever let you, you know it means you're forgiven and where you're headed." Ben's voice dropped, his face grew serious, "No matter what I do there's only one way this is ever going to end for me."

Chris was concerned by the return of Ben's dark mood, "What do you mean?"

Ben swallowed hard, his face creasing for a moment. "Just a feeling. Those've happened to me often enough so I know when they're real. I'm going to help Mal, no matter what but … there's no way I make it outta this. Hell's going to know I betrayed them …"

Chris interrupted, "You said you have friends …"

"Most friendships below are pretty damned shallow. I know people who would maybe not rat me out, but there's nobody below that's gonna wade into this mess on my side … There's no 'happily ever after' for anyone who crosses Lucifer."

Chris paled. In his mind everyone could be forgiven, find Heaven. He had always assumed it was true for Ben, too. But Ben was taking Mal's part expecting to eventually be sent back to Hell, sure he would not be returning with the privileges of a nobleman, and just as sure the final death was waiting at the end of a long and terrible road. Chris, feeling cold, had to know, "Ben … Son, if you honestly believe you're condemning yourself, why in God's name are you doing this?"

"I already told you. I'm just doing the right thing." He gave a sigh that was almost a moan. "Fuck. And I'm doing it for Mal, and for you, but mostly I'm doing it because every goddamned time I think of taking the easy way out I feel like …" Ben tried to continue, but after a minute just shook his head. He put down his glass and rested his face in his palm, elbow propped on the arm of the chair.

Chris knew there was nothing he could say that could even begin to be a comfort, so he just sat looking at Ben's troubled young face. His eyes were closed and Chris suspected, from the way his throat and jaw were working, he was trying not to cry. Ben did a good job of keeping up a brave front, trying to stay in the moment, but Chris couldn't imagine what it was like living with that hanging over his head, nor could he imagine how someone with a heart like Ben's, a soul that could make this choice, ever wound up in Hell to begin with.

Chapter 28

"It is a fine seasoning for joy to think of those we love."
~ Moliere

The morning of Christmas Eve found Ari picking his way around the enormous tree Mal had chosen almost immediately after getting out of school for the holiday. It took up a ridiculous amount of space and stuck out awkwardly in front of the television, but he wasn't about to say no. She hadn't had a proper tree since she was little. She'd excitedly insisted they stop at the craft store and get materials to make ornaments, then spent hours at the kitchen table. Almost a week later they were still finding glitter everywhere. Now he accidentally knocked down one of the glass ornaments Mal had painted and expected to hear it shatter. Instead it just rolled a few feet on the floor, reflecting the twinkling lights. Pleased he hadn't broken it, he was getting it settled back on the tree when the tap came at the door.

Davi was on the other side of the glass carrying his annual armload of gifts for Mal. "Don't spoil her much, do you?" Ari observed, laughing.

Davi said with joking solemnity that it was in his job description. They went into the living room and began trying to place the packages under the huge tree without upsetting the entire room. Mal was still sleeping after another difficult night. Ari was explaining the worsening nightmares and how they'd be going to the early Mass since Mal was worried she'd doze off during the midnight service, when they heard an exclamation of delight from the top of the stairs. Mal bounded down, nearly tripping over the Christmas tree to throw herself into her uncle's arms. In her elation at having a real holiday she barely thought about her dreams. She was happier to tell her uncle all the little details of starting school, share the plate of cookies Ben had sent home with her yesterday, and brag about his cooking skills, mostly because she found them so genuinely impressive. It was difficult to learn to cook properly growing up in a camper. Mal thought if she lived alone she'd be reduced to Ramen and Pop Tarts for survival. Or maybe Kraft Mac and Cheese if she was feeling fancy. She told them Ben said she was worse than Dr. G and that, if you thought about it the right way, cooking was just science. Nobody who wanted to set bones or cut people open for a career ought to be intimidated by something as mundane as preparing food. She was sort of interested in learning. Ben had told her that if she wanted he'd at least teach her to roast a chicken and scramble some eggs, even if it killed him. She laughed as she was telling them about it, saying that if Ben was planning on eating her cooking, it might do just that.

When her uncle asked if her dad had the privilege of meeting this famous chef yet Ari said they would both get to meet him tomorrow. He'd encouraged Mal to invite him and Ben had enthusiastically accepted. They'd only been seeing each other for about a month, but anyone who was around either of them could see it was already getting somewhat serious. While Ari wasn't quite sure how he felt about that, he realized that it wasn't his call to make and wanted to be as supportive as possible. He knew it was the right call after seeing how thrilled Mal was at the prospect of having all the important people in her life together for Christmas. He was also happy to offer Ben a chance at a family holiday since his family was far away and Ari got the idea that the relationship was strained. Mal passed on Ben's repeated thanks all week.

They spent a pleasant afternoon eating too much and watching holiday movies. Her dad's favorite was *White Christmas* which Mal usually found way too cheesy but this year struck her as kind of nice; and she thought it was sweet the way her dad got choked up when the General came down the stairs at the end. She preferred *The Grinch,* and was a chorus to Boris Karloff through the whole thing, amusing her dad and uncle greatly. When it was time, she disappeared upstairs to get ready. It gave Ari and Davi a moment to talk alone.

"So," Davi began, "Have you met the Gatekeeper yet?"

"I made a point right before their break. The teacher I mentioned, that's him. The mark is plain as day. I barely had to do any magic. I didn't approach him as anything other than a concerned parent, but he knows who we are. I could tell. I just trusted him, Davi."

"He's trustworthy. I've done my homework since my last visit."

Ari continued, "He was very reassuring; making certain I know he's looking out for Mal, he's noticed how tired she is … that sort of thing. He clearly cares for her and he's obviously not walking into his role blind."

"If there's anyone who can help her figure this all out, he's the man to do it. Certainly, his debt is steep, but that's not what motivates him. According to the records I've seen, since the beginning, he's wanted to help people, to find a place in the world. He's spent all of this time learning." Davi felt it important to stress the man's goodness to his worried friend.

"About what?"

"Everything he can."

"He wanted to reassure me about Mal's boyfriend, too. He knew we hadn't met, and Ben stays with him, so perhaps he mentioned it. Says he's a good kid, he's had a hard road, and he fairly worships Mal."

"Well, she would be easy for him to feel that way about," Davi observed. "I think if the Gatekeeper approves, it's probably a sign you don't need to worry much. In fact, it's encouraging to know she's been able to start a real relationship with someone."

Ari was quick to agree. "I've always worried she'd have trouble with that, bouncing around the way we did. She's certainly never lacked for company … but connecting with someone is different than just filling up empty time."

Mal came downstairs a short time later, make-up subtle, hair a loose jumble of curls, wearing the dark green velvet dress and high silver heels she'd bought especially for the holidays. Her dad and uncle whistled and applauded, causing her smile to light up the room as she took a theatrical bow.

"That's awfully fancy for church, Mal," her uncle said with what could only be called an amused and approving tone. "What's with the 'I'm ready for my close-up' look?"

"Well, it's Christmas Eve. That's about the fanciest church gets."

"And?" her dad prompted, knowing fancy wasn't her style.

"I was kind of hoping we could leave early and stop for a second at Dr. G's. I want to remind Ben about tomorrow."

Her dad smiled, amused. "Sure. Why not?"

Uncle Davi grinned. "You can't just text him?" Then he added, "I think you just want to show off how dazzling you are when you wear something other than your atrocious sweatshirt."

Mal stuck out her tongue. "He thinks my total lack of fashion sense is adorable. But you're not wrong. What's the point in getting all dressed up if the person you want to look good for doesn't get to see?"

Shortly after, they were pulling up next to a row of townhouses giving off a well-lit homey appearance with holiday lights representing a number of winter traditions shining in many of the windows. Mal was almost out of the car before it stopped. "Back in a sec!" she called and was up the front steps in a flash, as though she wasn't wearing dangerously high heels. The door opened and Mal disappeared inside. She was only gone about five minutes when she skipped back down the steps with a festive looking bag covered with ribbons hanging off her wrist. She slid into the car, the color in her cheeks high and lovely, a bit of flour on her nose, her pink lipstick slightly smudged. It was not hard to imagine another face close by smudged with it, and perhaps a little flour, as well. Uncle Davi teased her gently about the obviousness of her infatuation.

"That's quite the smile, Malin. Did you win the lottery in there or something?" her uncle prodded.

"Ugh, don't use my whole name, Uncle Davi. I hate it!"

Her dad tried to help, "So what are Ben and Dr. G's plans for the evening?"

"Trying to eat all the food in the whole city apparently. Ben's cooking like a Christmas elf!" Mal laughed. "I think he feels bad about leaving Dr. G on his own tomorrow since, you know, he's kind of stepped in to be Ben's family." Then she gave a self-conscious giggle. "Honestly, he was wearing an apron and he had flour all over himself. I don't think I've ever seen anything more adorable in my whole life ... Except for maybe how red he turned when he realized I was there to see him!"

"At least that explains what happened to your nose," her father observed, glancing in the mirror. She blushed furiously and began trying to see herself in the glass to fix her face. They chatted casually for a few minutes as they drove along in the lightly falling snow, commenting on just how clean and lovely the city looked, covered in freshly falling powder and lit up for the holidays.

"So," Davi said over his shoulder, leaving off teasing for now, "what's in the shiny bag?"

"I don't know. Ben said I could take it and put it under the tree, but I had to promise not to look until he gets there."

"Of course you're going to keep your promise," Uncle Davi was back to teasing already.

They were pulling into the parking lot and the need to peek overcame Mal's fidelity to her casual pledge. She got quiet after that. Neither her father nor her uncle commented on it. Neither prodded her when she forgot to respond during the service. She was quiet all the way home, too. When they got there she kissed them both good night and placed the little gift bag under the Christmas tree. Then she said she was sleepy and disappeared upstairs. Sensing her strange behavior was related to her gift, Ari went and picked it up, wondering what could be wrong. He reached into the green and red tissue paper and withdrew a small white box taped up like it held the crown jewels and tied in rather amateur fashion with a curling red ribbon. He sighed and sat down heavily on the couch, placing the box in front of him on the table, massaging his forehead. Davi sat down next to him.

"What is it, Ari?"

"She had a dream last week she was too upset to even tell me about. She let me read her journal though. I'm sure she'd show you if you asked."

"Go on."

"The boy, Ben, gave her a gift in the dream, right before something dragged him screaming into a pit. It was in a box; she described it. It was just like that one."

Chapter 29

"The spirit is the true self."
~ Marcus Tullius Cicero

Christmas morning dawned like a fairytale; cold, white, and sparkling under a clear azure sky, the likes of which are almost never seen that far north after mid-fall. Mal shuffled downstairs in faded leggings and even more faded sweatshirt before seven. Uncle Davi and her dad were waiting for her with a strong cup of coffee and purposefully light conversation. When Mal looked marginally less bleary-eyed, the three of them opened their gifts.

Mal had made scarves and hats for her dad and uncle. Emily had been teaching her how to knit since it was something you could do to keep your hands warm in the drafty school building that didn't get you into trouble. Despite how lumpy and uneven her work was both of them praised her efforts effusively. She admitted that she'd tried to make mittens too, but was stymied by the thumbs. Ari had made Mal several pieces of jewelry and painted her a picture of their preposterously large cat Anakin, Mal's accidental first pet. She fruitlessly tried to get the cat, who was sitting in the middle of the coffee table, complacently batting around a piece of shiny wrapping paper, to be still for a picture with it. Uncle Davi, as usual, had outdone himself with stacks of books to read, journals to write in, and all manner of pens and clips and notecards she might want, as well as a generous stack of decorative postcards with a note saying he expected to hear from her more often and texting didn't count.

When all that was left under the tree was the little gift bag from Ben and her present for him, which after her dream she had rewrapped in a scarf she'd originally thought too lumpy to give him, there was finally a knock at their door. Mal leapt up from the pile of wrapping paper and ran to the front of the house. She opened the door so abruptly Ben nearly dropped the foil covered plate he was holding. She pulled him inside and put the plate, which she knew held a spice cake he'd been making last night, on the table, noticing that, as usual, he had not managed to put on a jacket. She figured if he wasn't going to keep himself warm it would be up to her, so she pulled him into her arms and kissed him soundly. They'd only managed to kiss for the first time a few days ago but had spent an awful lot of time perfecting their method since.

Almost predictably that was the moment when her father and uncle chose to walk into the kitchen. Ben flushed scarlet as she pulled away to introduce him. As he'd noticed when they'd first talked, there was almost never anything tentative or embarrassed about Mal. Ben put down the shopping bag, unwinding it from around his wrist, thinking he wished he could manage such unaffected confidence after all this time. Of course there was nothing that was going to make meeting her relatives right after they'd seen her with her tongue in his mouth even slightly less uncomfortable. Her dad grinned at Ben's sudden awkwardness, liking him immediately.

"Hi Ben, it's nice to meet you." Ari extended his hand.

Ben reached out to take it as Mal said, "This is my dad, Ari."

He noticed a slight sheen to Ari, almost a glow. He was about Mal's height, dark, and handsome in a self-deprecating way. Ben knew he was an angel by creation but he'd never met one who'd chosen a fall for a human life before. His aura wasn't quite human, but it wasn't much more than human either. He realized if he'd run into Ari on the street, he might never have noticed. Ben wasn't sure if using the familiar Ari was okay unless he was invited and he realized he had no idea if they shared a last name, so he began uncertainly, "Nice to meet you, Mister …"

"It's Sinclair, like Mal. I took her mom's name actually. Kind of a family tradition."

Ben smiled. "I like that, Mr. Sinclair."

"You can call me Ari."

"Thanks, Ari. I'm Ben Brody."

Mal raised her eyebrows at him, "He knows your name, Silly."

"I'm just being polite. It's too early to pick on me." Although his voice was light and teasing, he had circles under his eyes. He'd been so worn out since he'd been sick a couple of weeks ago. She and Dr. G were already conspiring to get him to stop spreading himself so thin, and she was determined that next year she'd drag him to the school's flu clinic by the ear, no matter what his excuse was.

"Sorry, Ben." And she was, but she was also grinning a little at how her subconscious had just informed her that she'd be at Saint Thomas's next year and Ben would still be an important part of her life. Then she batted her eyelashes dramatically, affecting an air of saccharine innocence, "I promise I'll behave myself." He already knew from experience, and the mischievous twinkle in her eye, she wouldn't. "This is my uncle and no matter what he says just call him Davi, because his name is almost as absurd and anachronistic as mine," Mal laughed.

Davi reached for Ben's hand, winking at Mal. He had a powerful aura, immediately visible to Ben, so strong he wasn't sure how Mal could fail to see it. "She's absolutely right, Ben." There was warmth in his grip and for a moment Ben felt like his hand was caught in an electric current. He looked into Davi's silvery-grey eyes and felt a brief moment of panic but Davi's expression was kind and all he said was, "Glad I get to meet the young man Mal has been telling us so much about. I don't get to visit as often as I'd like."

Ben gave him a small nervous smile.

"So Ben, what's in the bag? You already sent my present last night and you brought dessert. Who do you think you are, Santa Claus?"

Ben, distracted from worrying about the angels by the excitement in Mal's voice, grinned and took out the surprise, a festive looking box Mal immediately recognized.

"Crackers! Oh I love crackers!" She grabbed his arm with both hands and then took the box practically bouncing she was so happy.

"I know. You said so when you told me about your *BBC* obsession … along with your many other enthusiasms." His smile was huge.

"I didn't know you could get Christmas crackers around here! We'll have to have them every year!" Her dad and uncle smiled at her uncontained glee, at Ben's thoughtfulness.

After everyone poured themselves coffee they went into the living room so Mal and Ben could open their gifts. While Mal further decorated their tree with the bright paper favors, her cat arranged itself gracelessly in Ben's lap and began nudging his hand to be petted. Mal was so obviously pleased about everything Ben felt his face might actually crack from smiling. When she finished, she sat so they could exchange presents. All the strangeness had gone out of the little box now that she was seeing it in the same room with Ben in the light of Christmas morning. She opened it while Ben watched, his expression terribly uncertain. Inside was a vintage *Star Trek the Next Generation* communicator pin.

"Oh my God, Ben!" Mal squealed. "*TNG*'s been off the air since before I was born."

She peeled it out of its packaging and ran to get her cross-country jacket to pin it to, testing the authentic chirping sounds it made as she came back. Ben was relieved. He hadn't been sure if she was a collector or just an enthusiast, but he did know she was a proud geek so he felt it would probably be a good present either way. He'd been nervous though. The first thing you gave someone and how they responded said a lot about a relationship.

"Where did you even find this?" She was pretty clearly impressed.

"I went to the comic book store on Church Street and just waited for something to speak to me … Then the dude behind the counter saw my desperation and helped me find that online," he admitted honestly.

"It's so great!" She threw her arms around his neck again, dislodging the cat, and planted another kiss firmly on his mouth. He guessed maybe he'd better stop blushing every time she did that in front of her dad, because she didn't seem likely to stop and his cheeks felt like they were on fire. She handed him his present, biting her lip.

He first unwrapped the forest green and golden yellow scarf she'd knitted for him from the small package it enveloped. It quite coincidentally matched his sweater, and he immediately draped it around his neck, almost absurdly touched that she'd made him something with her own hands. It set off his unusual eyes in a way that made it difficult for Mal to remember there was anyone else in the room, and lumpy or not, she was glad she'd given it to him. Next he opened the nice little refillable pen and smiled almost shyly. He took it to mean she liked the poem he'd written her and that she took his constant scribbling seriously even if he just saw it as a way to manage his restlessness. The final little box had a sticker that said '*From Dr. G and Mal*'. His head tilted in a question.

"I wanted to get you something interesting, and since Dr. G knows you better than anyone, I talked to him before break. He told me … well, open it first."

Ben struggled with the tape on the little box, mostly because he'd bitten his fingernails to shit the last couple of weeks, and when the top finally popped off the immediately recognizable contents fell onto the floor. He picked it up, trying to suppress the slight trembling in his fingers. "What did you guys do? This is priceless."

At first, Mal grinned at his reaction. "He knows you like old coins and he had one from a period you're interested in. He said it could be from both of us." As she looked at him his expression actually troubled her a little. She went on, "It's a … oh it's in the lid," she picked it up and read aloud, "It's a *Celtic Britain Atrebates Gold Fractional Stater* from around *Fifty-five B.C.* It's cool right?"

Ben forced a smile, and then looked into her eyes and it became more genuine as he answered, "It's the coolest thing anyone has ever given me. Where'd you find it?"

"Oh, Dr. G just had it in some musty old box but we both thought it was neat. Do you really like it? You look a little freaked out."

He put a self-conscious arm around her. "I like it a lot. Just it's a piece of history, another life. It's kind of overwhelming. I feel like maybe I should have done a better job shopping for you."

Mal punched him playfully on the arm. "Don't be dumb. I love my pin." She was thoughtful for a moment. "And the crackers, and the cake, and the fact that you're here with us." She let out a small tired sigh. "And that the view outside the window's not changing at sixty miles an hour." She was smiling, but the set of her chin and the shine on her eyes told Ben she was almost ready to cry. "This is the best Christmas I've ever had," her voiced cracked.

Completely unselfconscious here for the first time, Ben took her in his arms and held her until he felt her shoulders relax. Then he tried to lighten the moment by pointing out that her cat seemed a little obsessed with him. The cat obligingly batted at the tassels on his scarf. Ben wiggled his fingers over its head, saying, "Hey, how do you get this thing to stop trying to eat my present?"

Once all the initial excitement of the morning was over, Mal realized she was still in her pajamas and had basically just rolled out of bed. Despite Ben's sincere insistence that she needn't change on his account she excused herself to go put on some clean clothes and brush her teeth. Ari also stood and said he was going to put the roast in the oven. Ben offered to help but Ari wouldn't hear of it, waving him off with a laugh saying he didn't want to get them both in trouble with Mal by conscripting him for the kitchen. That left him and Davi alone. He knew this powerful angel could see through his human façade. He'd known the moment they shook hands.

Davi said pointedly, "Tell me about yourself, Ben."

There was no point in pretending with someone like this. Better just to be honest and hope for the best. "Not much to tell that you don't know, I expect."

"You're as perceptive as you look." He raised his eyebrows. "I sense no danger from you. Quite the opposite. That makes me ... I think you'll agree ... understandably curious."

"Look, I don't know what you know, but I ... I'm not here for Hell. I want to help ..."

"Just help? That's deep magic you've got there, Ben. Those sorts of spells cost the kind of suffering that can end someone. You're lucky to be here." His voice was a little wondering.

"Some pain is nothing to be able to be with her, I don't care how much." He swallowed hard. "I love her, okay? I know I haven't known her long enough, but I do," Ben confessed, his face growing hot again while his hands went cold and clammy.

"I believe you. Seeing you together, it would be hard not to. You do realize though, you'll owe her the truth of what you are eventually, don't you?"

Ben glanced around nervously; he worried someone might come back while they were talking. "I hate lying to her. I'd tell her now ... but Hell is really after her ... there's this fallen angel ... If I tell Mal ... if she gets upset, like intensely emotional about it, which I imagine she will, they might be able to use it to find her. I'm not sure exactly how it works, but I just didn't think about it when we got involved, and now I'm responsible." He paused, troubled, but with determination growing in his eyes. "I don't have a weapon yet that would be any good, but I'll get one. I won't let her pay for my mistake, I swear," he said finally.

"You want to be careful trying that. There aren't a lot of attractive options."

Ben frowned, "Like what options are there?"

Davi shook his head sympathetically, "Nothing I'm going to direct you to. It's dangerous. And I already like you too much to wish any of that on you ... But I must say I appreciate the sentiment. I'm her Guardian." Ben's face drained of color and he was momentarily surprised to be alive. Then Davi said, "So, I know who you mean. I have some regrets on that score myself."

Ben didn't comment, just swallowed hard again.

"You mind if I do something to make myself feel better?"

Voice tight with apprehension, Ben answered reluctantly, "I probably owe you whatever you ask since you're letting me be here, and if half of the stories I've heard about her Guardian are true, you could do anything you want to me."

Davi sat down next to him and placed a hand on either side of his face. Ben didn't resist, rather just allowed his head to be positioned until Davi was looking into his eyes. He gazed back, open, guileless. After a minute tears trickled down his face. He couldn't imagine why that was happening. He thought maybe he should be afraid, but as strange as this was, he felt oddly serene. Davi let him go, patted him on the shoulder, and moved back to his chair, talking almost too himself, "Such a long road. Such strength. Hardly seems possible." Then after a moment, "Ben, your lady-love is coming back."

Mal came into the room while Ben was still drying his eyes and blowing his nose. Before anyone could think too deeply, Davi said, "Mal, I think Ben is allergic to Anakin."

Grateful for the cover story, Ben gave her a sideways grin, glancing at the fluffy black cat sitting next to him purring and gazing up adoringly with yellow-green eyes. "But I'm super manly about it."

She collapsed onto the couch, looking even prettier than when she'd left with her face scrubbed pink and wearing green and red stripped leggings and the world's most impressively ugly Christmas sweatshirt. She laughed, shooing the cat away, and snuggled against Ben's side in its place. The rest of the day was spent relaxing, eating, and laughing together. They took turns pairing up with the crackers and Mal had an uncanny ability to win, but she insisted Ben wear her green paper crown because it matched his scarf, and then came up with a purple one for herself. They read the jokes, exchanged the cheap little trinkets, and enjoyed the silliness of it as much as if they'd been children. They ate too much, sang too loudly, and periodically Mal danced around the house pulling Ben along with her. He didn't know quite what to make of all of it, but when it was time to leave, he just felt glad he'd been there to see Mal so happy.

Chapter 30

"A problem is a chance for you to do your best."
~ Duke Ellington

Ben paced around the apartment, his face a battlefield of love-sick smiles and fretful self-doubt. He'd had a wonderful time but the experience with her Guardian had been disconcerting, and he didn't know what to make of what he'd heard him mumbling afterwards. Ben was sure Davi wasn't going to say anything to Mal but the possibility was making him crazy. He hated lying to her, was worried to distraction she'd find out before there was a good way to protect her from Lahash. He was also anxious that whatever solution he found would be even more difficult and dangerous to get than he'd previously thought. He went round and round, fidgeting and mumbling under his breath.

Chris looked up from the book he was skimming and shook his head sympathetically at Ben's back. He casually reached for his cold turkey leg. While he'd tried to explain it wouldn't be his first holiday alone, Ben had been determined he would have a decent meal today while he was gone. Making another lap, Ben was pleased to see Chris eating after all the protests about him cooking yesterday. He made himself go and sit down at the coffee table, noticing his gift to Chris sitting on top of a stack of papers. "Thanks for letting me use the car today." Chris only waved it off, his mouth full. "I feel like I unloaded on you the second I got home. So, now I'll be polite instead of crazy. What did you do while you were stuck here all day?"

Chris swallowed and took a drink of his tea. "Mostly I plowed my way through those delicious leftovers. I won't tell you not to do that anymore, I promise. Anytime you want to fill the refrigerator with whatever it occurs to you to make, you go right ahead." Ben's smile brightened his whole face. "I also opened my beautiful gift. I like it a lot, but I was hoping when you got home you might explain it a little."

He paused, feeling like his gift to Ben, several sets of flannel sheets, was insufficient by comparison, although Ben had looked thrilled and put a set on his bed right away. Chris picked up the golden object. It had clearly been a coin at some point along the way but had been fashioned into what looked like a single elongated eight-sided die with no numbers.

Ben had been hoping he would ask. "Well, for starters it was one of those old coins you told me I could play around with because they'd slid around too much to be worth anything. I could show you how to store those like the people do, you know." Chris waved a dismissive hand. He wasn't much of a collector, more of a packrat, and he didn't concern himself with their monetary value at all. "Anyhow, think of that as the real currency of the universe."

"Now I'm even more confused, although I'm no less intrigued." Chris was interested to hear what Ben had to say.

"You're always asking me if I have a choice, if you have a choice, does anyone have a choice, right?" Chris inclined his head. "And I'm always telling you, of course we do and it's more than anyone usually thinks. See, most people think of making a choice like flipping a coin." Chris gave an encouraging nod. "Fuck that. Nothing is that simple. So I made my kind of coin. It's so you remember this isn't a yes or no proposition. We can steer this. We just need to figure out how."

Chris thoughtfully picked up the coin again and began turning it over in the light. Although Ben had insisted he was still too full from Christmas lunch to eat when he got home, he wandered into the kitchen for milk and came back with a tall glass accompanied by a mighty stack of oatmeal butterscotch cookies. "Well, thank you again, Ben. I liked it when I thought it was simply pretty, but now that I know it means something so important to you, I think it's one of the nicest gifts I've ever received." Ben flushed slightly, pleased he'd been able to offer Chris something unique. "How did you manage it? We don't exactly have metal working equipment lying around."

Ben glanced away almost nervously. Chris got weird about his powers sometimes. "It's the whole pyro/tele-kinesis thing I can do, some magic. I practice a lot. That's why I was interested in those old coins; well, mostly. Old coins are just kinda cool. And metal work isn't too hard, especially if it's soft like gold."

"What about steel?" Chris looked at his book on ancient weapons hesitantly. "This translation I just found seems like it might be worth a look."

"I'd need tools but we wouldn't need a forge. I can generate an awful lot of heat. What is it?" Ben got up and moved to the edge of the couch closest to Chris who spun the book toward Ben so he could read the translation. This sounded all kinds of promising. Then, lips moving, he gave the runes on the page before it a cursory glance.

The Dark Blade

The angel to slay,

On Brigid's Day

Stoke Hell's fire high,

Iron from the sky is needful for them to die

Sinner's bone turned ash will burn and sigh

Murderer's blood to quench the cry

Forge your blade in Hell's fiery heart.

Quench the hot death in a bucket of the life's blood of a killer on the turn of the day.

Etch upon it the symbols of sacrifice.

Consecrate it to those from before the dawn of the now.

"Well, the translation is a little hokey, but the original spell looks rock solid."

"You can read ancient Gaelic?" Chris asked with some surprise.

"My people come from there … those runes are one of the first things I learned." Ben smirked, a little pleased that there was something scholarly he could do that Chris couldn't. "I thought you could read everything."

"It's never come up." He tried not to smile at Ben's obvious pride. "Does the translation seem accurate?"

"First blush? Not bad. Not complete, but you get the gist. This actually sounds manageable." Ben didn't want to get his hopes up after what Davi had said, especially before carefully reading the whole spell.

"Well, it certainly sounds …" He stopped. Something in his gut was telling him this was a bad idea. "Look, I know you want to help Mal, protect her, but those ingredients are ghastly."

Ben was grinning a little. "I was thinking I kind of like this one. It doesn't say 'stab Ben with pointy things and burn him from the inside out for days.' So far, this might be my favorite spell ever."

This was the first time Ben had managed to just say something offhand about the shield spell so Chris decided to hear him out before breaking into a fresh lecture. "The ingredients, Ben? Are you just going to call your 'guy'?"

Ben shook his head, momentarily uneasy. Aife was more than willing to help but he didn't want to draw attention to himself again. Besides, this list might sound bad to Chris but the ingredients were reasonably simple. "Brid's is in early February," he considered, absently lapsing into the pre-Christian reference for it, already thinking of the spell's origins. "We have plenty of time. Hellfire's no problem." Chris raised his eyebrows, thinking that hadn't been the part that worried him. "Iron from … Fairbanks Museum might be easy enough to get into."

"What are you talking about?"

"You know, the natural history place over in the boonies. This obviously means meteorite, but it's ancient and even this translation is antiquated so it's all superstitious mumbo jumbo."

"You want to break into a museum?"

"Well, yeah, if I need to. I'll do whatever it takes to keep Mal safe." Chris raised his eyebrows about into his hairline but Ben pressed on. "'Ash of a sinner's bones' might be a little harder. Depends on how we do it."

"You're not talking about just torching someone after they rob a liquor store or something, right?" Chris now looked like fatherly lecture mode was imminent. Ben sighed.

"Chris, calm down, I've got this. Since the rules say all people are sinners, any dead guy will do. We could just steal an urn from a funeral home. Going all *Mission Impossible* looks like it's gonna give you hives though … We could find an old grave and just dig somebody up, magic the ash part. Well, you could dig somebody up. I can't go into the cemetery."

"Why on Earth not? Afraid of ghosts?" Chris chuckled.

"You're hilarious." Ben's face went almost blank and his voice grew serious. "It's consecrated ground."

"So? You have your shielding magic."

"No, Chris, there's a big difference between a magical '*keep out*' sign and ground consecrated to God. Unfortunately, I'm still a demon. No magic is going to thwart the power of God for long, no matter what anybody tells themselves."

Ben's forlorn expression made Chris want to say something comforting, but he could think of nothing adequate so he asked, "What about '*killer's life's blood*'? I don't care what someone's done in their past, I'm not about to murder them for a spell, no matter how noble the reasoning for performing it."

Ben laughed. "It's a good thing you have me around. Remember when we talked about different magical marks?"

Chris mumbled some agreement, thinking Ben was lucky to be around to remember it.

Ben continued, "So, Old Soul Guy who's probably Cain? Murderer who can't die. And Quebec's not far. Road trip."

Chris was thoughtful. "You've made me very aware of the fact that I can't die." He paused. "It's not like there's no blood on my hands."

Ben shook his head. "You were a soldier. That's different. Besides, I think that kind of blood loss would hurt you, weaken you for a long time. You're basically human and I hear Cain just isn't. I don't know exactly what he is, but I have a feeling he'd be safe."

"You're sure?" Ben's furrowed brow indicated he wasn't going to elaborate. "You think Cain is going to give you his blood?"

"I could convince him, I'm sure, if you can get him to come out." Chris was confounded. "Monastery equals consecrated ..."

Chris interrupted, "Not that. It just seems unlikely he'd ..."

"Oh he's gonna want to deal. Nobody's gonna just let you bleed 'em for free. But there's gotta be something he wants that I can get." Ben's eyes glittered, thinking not of any difficulties the spell might pose or what it might cost him, only of putting an end to Hell's best chance at finding Mal.

"Alright, we should start gathering those ingredients and making our plans."

As Chris spoke, Ben pulled the book closer, reading the original words more thoroughly, deep in thought. As he studied it, a line formed across his forehead and he was glad Chris couldn't read the full text. His head began to ache as he confirmed his suspicions. Unfortunately, it seemed Davi was right about this type of weapon. "I want to get the details ironed out as soon as possible. Spell this complex, things can go south in a hurry."

Chapter 31

"Sometimes, only one person is missing,
and the whole world seems depopulated."
~ Alphonse de Lamartine

Mal stretched, head hanging over the edge of Petra's bed, staring at the abstract glass sculpture on the nightstand lit from beneath with sparkling multicolored lights. She was pretty sure she'd been staring for a while, but she was discovering their chosen form of recreation for the afternoon caused time to do some strange things. Emily was out cold in the overstuffed chair in the corner and Teddy was lying on the floor holding up his freckled hands, fascinated by the patterns the sun was making on them through the fancy tulle curtains. Her quasi-concentration was broken by Petra coming back with refreshments. Even if she hadn't noticed, Teddy's enthusiastic response would have gotten her attention. He launched himself up from the floor in a smooth motion that only a competitive wrestler could manage.

"Duuuuude, pizza rolls!" Teddy was all over Petra.

Mal turned herself right side up, the room spinning slightly. She held out her hand for an icy cold Diet Coke. She knew the stuff was terrible for her, but sometimes she just had to indulge, and she sighed as it bathed her dry tongue and throat. She rolled her eyes at Teddy who had already powered through most of the pizza rolls.

"Stand back Petra, the Ginja Ninja's got the munchies." Petra reached to retrieve the tray and Mal couldn't resist adding, "Don't put your hand in there! He's an animal!" They laughed a good deal more than it probably warranted and then just as that was slowing down they made the mistake of looking at each other and dissolved into giggles again until neither could sit up and their eyes were streaming. Then they were almost paralyzed by the strange snorting snore Emily made as she turned over in the chair and pulled the blanket on the back down over her head. When this bout of mirth receded, Mal got up to get a snack just as Teddy was going for the last chocolate cupcake. She slapped his hand playfully, "Bad Teddy! Mal's cupcake!" Then he was off in a fit of his own full-mouthed, crumb-spewing giggles.

Mal flopped down into Petra's computer chair so she could swerve it back and forth. She sat eating her cupcake, lost in thought. Her forehead creased. Petra shook her head and pulled on the wheel of the chair with her foot to disrupt Mal's brooding. Petra frowned, positive she knew what Mal was thinking. There was no fun left in this girl. "No, Mal, nope, nopety, noooop. No sulking."

Mal heaved a deep eloquent sigh. "I *feel* sulky."

"Because Ben's working today?" One eyebrow went up.

Mal shrugged, licking crumbs from her fingers. "Mostly I was thinking I'm seriously PMSing and we don't have enough chocolate because Teddy ate it all."

"You used to be so much fun before you met Ben." Petra was obviously not about to start a Ben fan club.

Now Mal was irritated. She hadn't brought up Ben at all, trying to be sensitive to the fact that Petra didn't care for him and that she hadn't hung out with them in a couple of weeks. And she wasn't grumpy because Ben was working; she was grumpy because she had cramps! She was about to say something to that effect when Teddy piped up, mouth full of Doritos, "I like him. He helps me with my homework when we all go to the coffee place." Mal smiled at him, and then gave Petra an exaggerated frown.

"What's your deal anyway? Ben's never mean when I hang with you." Mal was almost angry, but it was somewhat blunted by the new and not altogether unpleasant feeling that her head was stuffed with cotton.

"Sweetie, you used to go to parties, do stuff after school, and hang out with us on the weekends. You never do any of that anymore. Kind of feel like maybe he's got something against your friends." Petra was daring her to defend how she'd been spending her time.

"Ben always asks what I want to do, and he likes you guys fine! Just, he's in college … There're kids in the regular group who are like fifteen. Honestly, that's not much fun for me either." As though she'd let some boy boss her around! It was just when she and Ben were together there never seemed to be any point in including anyone else. They were sufficient unto themselves and liked it that way, even if all they did was sit quietly on the couch, Ben writing in his battered notebook and her reading an article on some interesting scientific development, maybe doing some homework, or digging into the pre-med reading list she'd scored from a friend already off at college.

"Okay, tell you what, I'll give Ben a chance. My parents are leaving for Paris over February break and Alex and I are planning to throw a little party for my birthday. Nothing big, just a few of us seniors and some of his hockey buddies from UVM, various boyfriends, girlfriends, whatever. Ben can't object to what is basically a college party unless I'm right."

While Mal didn't care much for Petra's implication, she thought it might be nice to go to a party with Ben. Besides, Petra's older brother was an English major, so he and Ben were bound to have something in common. After a moment's consideration, Mal nodded her agreement. "Is it dress up, or anything goes?"

Chapter 32

"And Cain said unto the Lord, 'My punishment is more than I can bear'."
~ The Bible

Much to Ben's relief, things had gone surprisingly smoothly in planning the magical weapon to address the threat posed by the Fallen. By mid-January they'd managed to purchase meteorite fragments through the school, supposedly for Chris's new foray into ancient metallurgy research, and although Ben had thought *The Great Museum Caper* might have been fun, he supposed this was safer, and Chris was certainly happier. The bone ash had been easier than he'd thought, too. Chris had been skulking through cemeteries in the freezing cold, sometimes at night, trying to find a crypt or grave old enough to not be sealed and that he thought they could get away with disturbing, and one such evening Ben had an idea. He called someone he knew at the medical school and asked how much a real classroom skeleton would cost. It turned out while they were expensive, they were readily available, and Dusty was more than happy to help a library buddy, who'd scoured the stacks with him looking for obscure books many times. Ben shelled it out of the money Aife deposited in his bank account every month and texted Chris that the solution was on its way by FedEx in the morning.

Chris had come home pale from the cold and swearing under his breath. Ben had to pretend to be tired and go to bed because, between his own nerves and Chris's expression, he kept cracking up and knew he was just pissing Chris off. They had also managed to contact the monastery and speak with the man in seclusion there. The man who was unapologetically calling himself Cain seemed intrigued. Since Ben had discovered the blood had to be fresh, they'd arranged to meet him on the afternoon of January thirty-first. It didn't give them much time to negotiate or prepare, but Cain wanted something or he wouldn't have agreed to meet, and Ben didn't want to give him too much of a chance to change his mind once they'd made the deal.

Ben tried to spend every spare minute with Mal but found most of his time taken up by preparations for the spell or keeping Hell off the scent of what he thought of as his real life. He felt so badly about how little time they had together he'd even agreed to try to go to a party in a few weeks for Petra, although he prevaricated slightly, saying he might have to work. He knew Petra didn't like him. He suspected it had to do with his cracks about her attitude toward magic. She'd abandoned the spiritual aspects of her professed beliefs early on in favor of just dabbling with spellcasting and Ben knew she was playing with fire. He wanted to talk to her but couldn't think of a good way to bring it up. She made him nervous as hell. Of course, if going would make Mal happy, he'd do it, would do anything she asked of him.

They'd driven for hours through what, as far as Ben was concerned, was just another side of Hell, ice-covered and barren in the chill of deep winter. Chris found the austerity of it beautiful, but Ben, edgy and fed up with the cold, couldn't be bothered to notice. The most he engaged was to get out occasionally to translate the area's throaty French for Chris, who got muddled by the accent, but thought it was disrespectful to expect people to speak English for a tourist's convenience. He wasn't particularly interested in food but he'd finally accepted some Tim Horton's coffee and donuts because Chris kept asking him if he wanted to stop and eat and at that point he knew it would seem odd if he didn't.

Now Ben sat alone, waiting for word from inside the large stone structure. They were parked on the shoulder of the public road, as close as Ben would allow with no clear answer about the extent of the monks' consecration rituals. He was trying not to be irresponsible and run the car the entire time, relying instead on some hand warmers he'd bought at a gas station, but periodically the cold got the better of him. These long frigid winters were almost more than he could take.

He read for a while and then managed some preoccupied dexterity exercises with the coin he'd gotten for Christmas, wondering about spending some magical energy to either warm up or distract himself. He decided it wasn't wise with what was in front of him, but he hated sitting for this long regardless of the circumstances, and these were less than ideal. He didn't want to check the time again. All his clock watching seemed to be making it worse, but the sky was going from fading light to genuinely dim. *Hurry up*, he pled silently, staring at the building. *We only have until midnight, damn it.* And a small selfish part of him wanted to back out, even now. They needed a solution sooner rather than later and this was the only one they'd found; but contemplating the consequences filled him with a fatalistic creeping dread. Ben was starting to get visibly anxious and was ready to send an impatient text when Chris finally emerged with a companion.

Ben didn't know what he'd been expecting but what he got, dressed in a lambskin coat, faded jeans, and deer hide boots, was a man of early middle age in appearance, solidly built, with a good-natured twinkle about his pleasant face that was entirely surprising given Ben's preconceived notions. Chris and Cain talked convivially as they crunched across the frosty ground. Ben climbed out of the car and stood on the edge of the road, glad he'd finally gotten a decent jacket instead of stubbornly telling himself the same tired story about going somewhere warmer as soon as he had a chance. Now that he and Mal were together he knew he'd never leave unless she did, and as much as she hated the cold, he knew she loved Vermont. He raised his hand in an impatient wave. Then he jammed both hands into his pockets, wishing he'd bought gloves, too.

They approached, looking too relaxed for his liking, and having lost all patience for niceties in the cold and in his trepidation about the spell, Ben blurted, "Did you really kill your brother or not?"

Cain smiled, his long experience telling him an awful lot Chris hadn't revealed. "Yes, son I did, and I'm not sayin' it was right, but believe me, it doesn't say so in that book people 'round here are all so fond of, but I was sorely provoked. Never have you ever met a more self-centered preening peacock of an ass-kiss in your life."

Ben smiled wryly in return. "Bet I have," and he raised his eyebrows significantly.

Cain found this uproariously funny and laughed bending over, resting his palms on his thighs. "Minute I heard your story I knew I's gonna like ya. Damned if I knew I'd like ya this much."

Ben shivered in the bitter wind. He wanted this over with. "So you like me. Cool. You seem plenty likeable yourself. But I know you're not just giving away something so valuable because we could maybe have a beer together. What's your price?"

"I want a blade for myself."

"*Tabarnak!*" It was the first curse that came to mind after all his translating. He decided there was nothing like a Quebecois colloquialism to feel like you'd cursed properly, and he could do so in quite a number of languages. "I *need* this. I have a friend in serious danger."

"It's clear *you're* serious; I'm familiar with this spell."

Ben answered with a dirty look, casting a furtive glance at Chris.

"Seems like we can both get somethin' outta this. You have enough materials for a sword, right? We'll just divvy 'em up. Seems fair, given what you want from me. Besides I can't say as I see much sense in only havin' one weapon. Makin' a couple daggers is a lot more practical. Didn't you ever hear of not puttin' all your eggs in one basket?"

Ben thought about it. Several weapons, easily concealed, might be better, although consecrating more than one was not something he'd planned on. *Damn it. That'll probably complicate things.* He gave Cain a reluctant nod. "Why do you want one?"

"Got me a grudge with some angel folk. I'm allowed too, ain't I?"

Ben forced a laugh. "Suppose you are. Is there someplace we can go? I ... um ..."

"You'd just as soon not be the thing catching fire?" He laughed easily and pointed up the road. "There's an old barn up there a ways. Fella who owned the farm died a while back. His kids want nothin' to do with the place; just lettin' her fall apart. Worst you'll find up there is kids smokin' weed or maybe findin' love and all that means is they'll have a good fire goin'."

"Okay, good. We should probably get going. It's getting late, and we need to get everything ready, not to mention a bucket of your blood by midnight."

"Relax ... See that little square buildin' down the street there aways?" Ben nodded. "It's a clinic; serves the monastery and all the locals. It's closed for the evenin', but I got a key. I help out when they're shorthanded. Short of brain surgery, I know what I'm doin' more or less. It's the Twenty-first Century, boy! I'll getcha whatcha need, but civilized ... Dirty knife and a bucket in an old barn ... I look like Sunday dinner to you? Shoot."

Cain sauntered off. Ben was leaning against the car staring off into the trees, trying to get a peek at the last rays of the setting sun, looking remote. Chris was clearly enjoying their little adventure. "So far, so good. It's quite something to meet someone so old; he's a bit of a character." He turned to follow Cain. "You coming? I'm sure there's decent heat."

Ben climbed back into the car, turning the key to warm up again. "Nah. I'm gonna stay and study the spell. We've only got one chance at this." Chris nodded and Ben closed the door, speaking to himself, his sense of foreboding a cold tight knot in his stomach. "And we're running out of time."

By the time they returned Ben had become somber and still. Chris had noticed his odd behavior since that morning and hoped to draw Ben out. He tried to get a conversation going on the short drive but Ben responded in monosyllables, staring into the gathering darkness. Cain, apparently unfazed by the loss of blood, and determined to protect his investment, kept up his end of the exchange, glancing at Ben and thinking the kid obviously hadn't been honest about what he was up to, at least not the details. Before long they were too caught up in what they were doing for Ben's reticence to be remarkable. It was still the middle of the night when Ben uttered the final words to seal the spell. Looking grim and much older in the dim red light of the hellfire, he had drawn the three knives in quick painful succession across his palm. His blood disappeared into the dark metal as soon as he set them down. Chris immediately asked what Ben had done.

Ben answered glibly. "Signed an I.O.U."

Ben's face puckered as he wrapped his hand in a clean cloth and Cain stepped in to close the ritual. *Fuck that hurt. More than it should've.* Chris began a steady stream of questioning that escalated in intensity, as he tried to pry what had happened out of a laconic Ben. He was answered with a tight-lipped shake of Ben's head as the boy applied pressure to the wound, trying without much success to slow the bleeding. Cain didn't let much time pass before he pointed out that the injury was caused by enchanted weapons and was unlikely to close on its own. He offered to see to it saying, other than some potion magic, it shouldn't be too difficult. Ben gave a curt nod. It hurt like hell and he was irritated he hadn't anticipated this. With the dark sorcery involved, things would probably go beyond the simple trip to the emergency room he'd resorted to on a few other occasions when his magic had been inadequate. *Goddamnit.*

They traveled back to the monastery and Cain retrieved books and supplies from his room. Then they went to the clinic. Cain had Ben sit in an exam chair so he could look over the injury under a good light. After squinting at it for a few minutes he shook his head apologetically and said, "Sorry kid, you jobbed it good. Those blades are bad juju and it's deeper than I thought. Little surgical glue won't cut it. We'll need to suture."

Ben shrugged. It wouldn't exactly be his first set of stitches, and medicine had come a long way since he'd been a stupid kid who couldn't stay away from a fight, or out of a tree, or think about what he was doing before he leapt in and did it. Besides, Cain seemed to know what he was doing, and it wasn't like he had much choice. "I've had worse."

Cain knew something about the magic performed tonight, and wanted to sort Ben out as soon as possible. He didn't like Ben's color and set about dealing with his hand from both magical and practical perspectives. He gave Ben another look of pure speculation. Maybe the kid didn't know. Or maybe he knew too much and that's what was bothering him. The unpleasant pinching as Cain infiltrated the wound caused Ben to glance over and his stomach did a slow left roll. He pursed his lips, telling his stomach very sternly to behave itself.

Cain asked, "You alright?"

"Feel kinda weird. I'm okay." Ben shrugged. His face was the color of day-old oatmeal.

"Need some water or ..?"

"It's plain stupid to look." He gave Cain another hard stare saying he didn't want to talk about the spell in front of Chris.

175

Cain nodded. He waited for the anesthetic to take effect. Once Ben was looking away, he poked around the edges of the wound, peering at Ben's profile, trying to decide if he was feeling anything. When he was satisfied his patient was numb, he squinted at the ragged cut as he washed it out more aggressively with saline, and mumbled to himself, "Probably need to trim the edges."

Ben let out along slow breath. *The heat of battle was one thing. A place that reeked of antiseptic, staring at your own insides leaking out, preparing to be darned like a sock, was something else.* But he'd been sewn up plenty of times under much less pleasant circumstances, so it wasn't that. Not really. Seeing the strange spidery appearance of discoloring blood vessels around the wound and how the phenomenon was spreading up his arm ... *This was bad news. No denying it.* He'd known it was dangerous, but he hadn't expected any physical after-effects. He felt something shift in his aura, dampen his power, and Ben turned an ashen shade of green. He began to read the posters around him as a distraction, taking shallow cautious breaths. Chris knew he avoided violent or gory media and had made some assumptions about why. It's not like Ben was having fun, so that was probably a smart card to play to cover his unease about the magic, since he couldn't handle that conversation. Chris cleared his throat, hoping to get Ben to look his way. The whole situation worried Chris in a way he couldn't articulate.

Ben asserted again, with a hint of embarrassment, that he was fine. "It doesn't hurt." He wrinkled his nose, "I just don't wanna watch." That wasn't a lie, which helped him sell the rest. Ben threw his best sheepish grin. "It's alright if you never let me live it down." His eyes flicked to Chris for less than a second. "I'm really okay."

Cain contemplated Ben, knowing he was deflecting Chris's attention. He'd rather claim a squeamish streak than touch even the edges of what he'd done. Intrigued, Cain decided to play along. If the boy wanted to play this close to the vest that was his business. "Big brass ones like yours, I guess you're not likely to keel over on me, but if you're gonna puke, try an' miss my boots. These're my favorite pair."

Ben managed a laugh, looking away again when Cain picked up a scalpel. Chris resumed trying to get Ben to talk. He responded with the most general of reassurances while trying not to look at Chris either. He found himself looking at the ceiling an awkward amount, giving himself a crick in his neck on top of everything else.

When he finished with more practical matters, Cain held out a cup full of the potion he'd been simmering and after Ben got a whiff, he said if Cain wanted puke-free boots the potion was an epically bad idea. Cain said seriously, "Using your own hide to consecrate a dark blade imbued with power by the Watchorder has immediate consequences, kid. And you did it three times. You think you feel bad now? That's an exceptionally nasty mystical poison. Not just the kick-you-out-of-that-body kind either. Works pretty fast, too. Those fellas like to collect as soon as they can."

Ben was furious Cain had said so much about the spell and with the almost patronizing tone he was using. He could feel a stubborn line forming across his forehead and he opened his mouth for a hot-headed reply but was interrupted.

"You need to get on top of what this magic is trying to do to you, kid," he said in a matter of fact tone. Ben frowned, but stayed silent, then took a breath like he was about to speak again. Cain looked him squarely in the eyes. "If you keep taking your time, you'll pass out. I got no problem just starting an IV, but you gotta be gettin' tired of me poking you with sharp things." Ben grumbled something and Cain put the cup into his hand. "Why don't you try doin' things the easy way for a change? Just hold your nose and cowboy up."

Ben swallowed the sickly plum-colored liquid, taking deep breaths to keep it down. He wondered darkly just how many times he'd have to force down the vile concoction before Cain was satisfied. Ben's opinion of most potions was they tasted like toxic waste mixed with cat-sick and it made him wonder resentfully why, if they were magic, they couldn't disguise themselves as chocolate or beer or something. The minute he'd emptied the cup his numb hand started tingling and the room swam in front of him. He closed his eyes and leaned back in the chair against the crinkling paper on the headrest, feeling seasick. "Sonofabitch," he mumbled as the room pitched and heaved.

Chris began again, "I just …" Cain, thinking the boy had earned a break from being interrogated, gave Chris a look that said clearly he should back off. Chris responded with worry, "What happened out there? Why is it so dangerous? What did you *do*, Ben?"

Ben just shook his head, immediately regretting the movement.

Understanding Ben was tired from the spell, not to mention feeling a little green around the gills, Cain kept Chris distracted, asking for his help wrapping Ben's hand in potion-soaked bandages. Then Cain, putting his hand on Ben's shoulder to get his attention and pass him more of the potion, said, "That was deep magic, Gatekeeper. You know that costs."

Ben opened his eyes and took the cup, but made no move to drink it; just sat trying to gauge Chris's reaction. Chris had fallen silent, looking intently at Ben's grave resolute expression. Cain was sorry to have revealed details, but was unable to disguise his admiration.

"Cost is dependent on power, of course. Sometimes it's just pain. Sometimes it's blood. Sometimes, often even, it's a life; a soul …"

Chris looked like he wanted to speak, but he cleared his throat several times and didn't seem able.

Cain nudged Ben so he'd start the next dose of potion before more drastic measures were necessary. He looked at Chris coolly. "No matter what, our friend here is willing to pay."

Chapter 33

"I must not fear. Fear is the mind-killer ...
I will face my fear ... Only I will remain."
~ Frank Herbert

It was disappointing that February vacation was almost over, even though Mal had never been happier to think about a month ending. It was so cold here! Ben at least wore shoes to run this time of year, and after she'd bugged him about it he'd bought a real jacket, saying he supposed Hawaii was off the table for the moment. For Valentine's Day she'd given him heavy running socks and silicon-tipped gloves so he could keep his hands warm and still check his running app without stopping. Nothing could convince her to go outside when she wasn't forced to and she told him until it warmed up if he wanted to run with her it would have to be on treadmills in the student center. Ben revealed his gift of passes to the indoor track downtown, purchased so they could still race despite her aversion to the cold and his insistence that they weren't hamsters. They were making almost daily use of his gift and she'd even beaten him a couple of times, although he'd been having kind of a rough winter so she wasn't about to gloat. Well, maybe a little. Even on his worst day Ben was crazy fast.

She thought the running was good. He'd been kind of wound up since the end of Winter Break and the track visits seemed to help. She thought maybe he'd been nervous about the paper he was presenting with Dr. G because since he'd returned from the successful trip to the Université de Montréal he'd been more relaxed. Despite his good mood and the slightly reduced responsibility of his research project, he was still jumpy and distracted. He had managed to cut himself at work and he kept getting quiet and thoughtful in a way that made her worry a little. Dr. G assured Mal he was finding Ben a safer job on campus. Then she'd informed Ben that he needed to take better care of himself. He'd just smiled and said since he obviously couldn't adult with adequate skill he would place himself in their more capable hands.

She was pleased they were getting a chance to go out more now that he was working less. Petra's birthday promised some low key fun and even though Ben wasn't a big party person, the Knapp family home was in a beautiful spot on the waterfront, Petra was her best friend, and her parents always hired a good caterer and had a top-shelf liquor cabinet they had the maid restock, no questions asked. Petra's parties were legendary at school and he'd told her agreeably that if she wanted to go to her ritzy friend's he was game as long as she wasn't embarrassed by how much he was going to eat.

They didn't talk much on the way. After the dream she had early that morning, she wasn't feeling chatty. They had all been out in the middle of the lake skating, having a wonderful time, and a hole had opened up in the ice, all the water below turned to blood. Steam rose off it and even though it was a dream she could smell it, metallic and sickening. Teddy was skating like a champion, doing all kinds of flips and spins and then she realized he was on strings like a marionette. A huge twisted tree of a creature was acting as the puppet master, blood dripping off its claws into the ice, and it had looked right into her eyes and pulled the screaming Teddy apart. Then, it had snatched Ben up, thrown him in the hole, and held him under. She'd woken up crying and hadn't been able to stop until eventually she'd thrown up, but fortunately she hadn't roused her father. That had been the worst dream in a while and she didn't want him to feel like he had to cancel his business trip because of her. She didn't even write it down.

Ben had brought along his tablet and speakers so he could stream some music because her car had a crappy old cassette player that only worked intermittently. He seemed to sense that she wasn't in the mood for conversation because he was softly singing along to *Sorrow* by Bad Religion. Mal wasn't terribly musical but thought Ben had a beautiful voice, although she suspected if she said so he'd get self-conscious. Their tastes in music meshed nicely, expanding their shared interests. Ben had familiarized Mal with Celtic punk and she had gotten him hooked on a couple of regional bands. They'd thought it was hilarious when they both revealed their closet appreciation for pop music, and Ben joked that Taylor Swift was a gateway drug.

Over the last few months they'd discovered they had many little things in common. They each had a rapturous enjoyment of chocolate, especially cupcakes, loved comic books and superhero movies, never seemed to get enough of the other's company, and even shared the same birthday, which they'd thought was a delightful coincidence. Petra had proudly told them it was a pagan holiday and Ben had encouraged her to go on by saying, "Pretty good one … harvest festival, right?" Petra had been so pleased she'd even smiled at him for a change. Mal figured Petra would warm up to Ben eventually. Everybody liked him. Besides, Mal felt she was already leaving 'like' in the rearview and she was almost certain he felt the same way. She was full of wishful thinking tonight anyway. With her dad out of town she was supposed to be staying with Petra for a few days, and Ben had the little apartment he shared with Dr. G to himself because the professor was speaking at some symposium over in New Hampshire. Neither she nor Ben had mentioned their arrangements more than casually but Mal was sincerely hopeful that when she took him home tonight the opportunity to move their relationship along would present itself. Some people were so pushy about making things physical, but Ben was obviously disinclined to make the first move. She found his more measured approach kind of sweet, but Mal had never been in a relationship that lasted months before, so she'd certainly never waited this long. She didn't want to say it like that because she worried he might think that sex was all she was interested in, but she definitely felt like it was time.

When they arrived there was the usual new acquaintance awkwardness, but Petra passed around drinks and food early so things quickly loosened up. Mal stuck to Diet Coke since she was driving but was surprised when Ben opted for ginger ale. She was going to encourage him to go ahead since Petra had some high-end whiskey she knew he liked because he'd split a bottle with an unusually relaxed Dr. G on New Year's Eve and laughed all the following day about the big head his roommate woke up with. But she could see that even though he was trying, this noisy social situation was not his scene. He did hit it off with Alex as she'd hoped and they got into quite the discussion analyzing the work of Pablo Somebodyorother. As far as school went Mal found she was best at math and science and had always dreamed of studying medicine.

She was glad they had other shared interests because neither could see the attraction of the other's professional aspirations. When she'd offered to take out his stitches, saying she'd already had lots of practice since her dad did something dumb in the kitchen or the shop at least once a year and she didn't mind the head-start on her studies, his reaction had been dubious. She'd laughed and said if he didn't mind being her practice patient there was potentially a lollipop in his future. He shrugged saying it might as well be her because he couldn't quite manage it himself and he hated the campus infirmary. She went and got her well-stocked first aid kit and gently and efficiently took care of it, cleaning the remaining small scratch, and securing a sterile bandage over it because what was left seemed to want to start bleeding again. She asked if he'd really left the stitches in as long as he was supposed to, and he'd shrugged, looking a little guilty. She'd given him an elaborate disapproving frown. Then, as promised, she produced an orange lollipop, saying they were supposed to be for kids, but he was a worthy exception. He grinned exactly like a kid and stuck it into his cheek, with a muffled, "Adulting is lame." He'd been impressed with her work and declared her already worthy of being Chief Medical Officer on the *Enterprise* and at least four times as beautiful as Beverly Crusher. He'd thanked her by cooking cassoulet, which was her favorite thing and she hardly ever got to have, saying she'd rescued him from having to wait around for hours, see some intern who'd do a shit job, and definitely not get a lollipop. He added that she could play doctor anytime she wanted. She raised her eyebrows suggestively and he flushed an amusing shade of pink, mumbling that she knew what he meant, but, you know, maybe that, too. His disinterest in blood and guts was okay by Mal since he didn't seem to take it personally that other than his writing and maybe a little fantasy or horror she mostly stuck to non-fiction.

As Ben and Alex earnestly talked about the nuances of translating verse while maintaining the poet's intent, she went to see what everyone was up to and track down Alex's friend Ross to congratulate him on his acceptance into med school and interrogate him about the process.

Mal had just wandered back and sat down next to Ben when Petra came out of the other room with an oblong box. "Game time!" she called, obviously a few drinks in, although she was so small and thin one could put her under anyway.

Ben went rigid beside her, "Mal, I don't feel well all of a sudden. Can we go?"

She gave him a searching look. "You look okay to me. What's the matter?"

"Um, I have kind of a headache."

She raised her eyebrows. She'd massaged his shoulders through enough headaches in the last couple of months to know that couldn't be the problem.

"Look, I'm sorry. I just … I can't stay." He shifted in his seat, pale as milk and visibly uncomfortable. "That's a Ouija board."

"Ben, that's …" Then Petra took the board out and confirmed what he said. Ben was jittery, unable to sit still. Mal felt a brief warning flutter in her stomach but dismissed it as ridiculous. "You're not even religious! What do you care what lame crap my friend wants to do for her birthday?"

"Those things are bad news. You're the one who watches horror movies. Guess what? Art imitates life." He sounded angry and his eyes were wide like a frightened child. Mal didn't think Ben was really afraid of anything, and they never got angry with each other, had never had a fight. *What could be wrong?*

"Ben, honey, I'm sorry. I shouldn't have dragged you here. We'll just stay a little while longer to be polite, then I'll take you home. We're gonna do cake soon and then it's no big deal to leave."

Unable to tolerate staying another minute, Ben stood, grabbing Mal's arm. He'd done it more forcefully than he intended, so he let go and leaned down until their foreheads touched. "I need to go … I'm sorry."

Mal was disturbed by his reaction, but couldn't imagine what was causing it. "Come on. It's Petra's birthday. You don't even have to play. Don't be such a kid about something so silly." His eyes flashed.

"I'm being a kid? Great. Allow me to demonstrate a tantrum." He grabbed his coat and walked out.

She followed him. "Ben, come back inside. I'm your ride and I'm not leaving!" She hated ultimatums.

He didn't turn around. He knew his eyes were glowing and he didn't seem able to pull back on the energy. He just answered her coldly; fear making him aloof, "Fine. I'll walk. But if you're not going to leave, you need to go take that thing away from those kids and burn it before someone gets hurt, especially you!"

"Ben, c'mon! It's like twenty below out here!" Staying for cake was not too much to ask and she didn't intend to back down because he was in a snit. He responded by darting a wide-eyed glance at the house that she saw enough of to have the fleeting thought that he looked strange. Then he was stalking off across the back yard, his long legs covering ground quickly. In less than half a minute he had disappeared around the corner of the house into the near-arctic dark.

She knew better than to think she could live with him walking home in this cold, even if he was being childish. She went back inside to get her coat and keys and apologize to Petra for needing to leave. When she walked into the dining room it was dark, save for a few flickering candles. Everyone was around the board, about half with fingers resting lightly on the little pointer. There were guilty Catholic-schoolkid glances, some nervous giggles, and everyone was ready for some old-fashioned spooky fun. The room felt cold and she glanced over her shoulder to make sure she had closed the door behind her as she pulled out her phone to text Ben.

Come back.

I'll drive you home.

That's too far.

She sat on the bench near the table and waited. He always texted back right away and when he didn't she was immediately worried. He'd finally bought a jacket but it was just a wool pea-coat. Those weren't meant for weather like this and the wind off the water was like knives. He didn't have a hat and she didn't think she'd seen his running gloves on him either. She could picture him collapsed beside the road from hypothermia, extremities black with frostbite. People weren't rational when they were afraid and Ben had obviously been scared stiff, for whatever reason. She was ready to just leave and look for him when Emily cried, "OHMYGOD! What's wrong with Teddy?"

Mal's head snapped up and Teddy was staring intently at her, but instead of his softly grey-green irises, there were only bloodshot whites and his normally tiny Cupid's bow of a mouth was spread into a wide grin that stretched his round face unnaturally until the corners of his lips bled. His fingers curled around the edge of the table so tightly there was no color in his hands. A monstrous roaring, so different from Teddy's earnest not-quite-done-changing-voice, came out of his mouth.

YOU WILL ALL DIE IN FIRE

Mal felt as though her blood had been replaced with liquid nitrogen. *Oh my God, it's exactly what Ben said, just like in the movies. What do I even do?* She racked her brain, wishing Ben had stayed. Then she realized that not only had he been afraid this could happen (petrified was probably closer to the truth) but whenever she wanted to watch those sorts of movies or TV shows Ben would just go talk with her dad in the kitchen or outside to sit on the swing looking at the water. He had no interest in horror movies, didn't care much for violent entertainment in general. He said there was enough scary horrible shit in the world without making any up. The creature was looking right at her and even though everything she had ever heard told her not to engage it she knew it would have to be her. There was no one else. People were running from the room or sitting stupefied and she was not about to let this thing turn Teddy into its personal sock-puppet.

Mal stood up from the bench without knowing what she was going to say. She asked the first thing that occurred to her. "What do you want?"

I KNOW YOU, MALIN, WHORE'S CHILD

Mal's eyes widened with unexpected anger. "Don't you *dare* address me." She was surprised to hear the calm command in her voice.

A quailing cry of denial came from some hidden assertive part of Teddy and whatever had hold of him bounced his head off the table until bright blood began to flow from over his eye down his pale unseeing face. The collective paralysis broke and she could hear the few people left scrambling from the room. Mal could picture Teddy being ripped to shreds just like in her dream if she didn't figure something out soon. Teddy's hands gripped the heavy table harder and flipped it on its side, its edges tearing into his palms. Petra, cowering in the corner, wild-eyed with panic, short spiky black hair literally standing on end, was the only witness left. The creature stood in front of Mal, not eight feet away, its arms hanging slack at its sides, its head angled forward strangely, mouth sagging open, drooling. Teddy's skin glowed deathly white beneath his freckles, his form thrown into sharp relief by the candlelight, the blood on his face and hands terribly red.

She clamped down on the fear pricking the edges of her consciousness. This thing wanted her afraid and she was no good to herself or to Teddy if she let it win that point. She knew she needed all of her wits about her and was awfully glad she hadn't been drinking. "Leave him alone!" she ordered sharply.

It took a shuddering step toward her on clumsy feet. Its bloody hands began to reach out as it said the thing it expected her to fear most. *THIS BOY WOULD HAVE YOU NOW I WILL TAKE YOU FOR HIM*

Mal was galvanized with fury. Teddy was the sweetest most innocent person she knew and there wasn't a violent bone in his body. Besides, there weren't too many asses she didn't think she could kick. Her martial arts teachers over the years had always said she was one of the best pupils they'd ever had and that her instincts were near perfect. It took another step toward her. Instead of stepping back, she advanced on it, shoulders squared, eyes a thunderstorm of rage. On impulse, and because it knew her name, she demanded, "Who are you!"

WE ARE LEGION, it snarled. Mal knew the story of Legion from church and she felt it was just something picked conveniently from her thoughts. What kind of fool did this thing think she was? She was done playing games.

"Well, I haven't got any pigs to send you into," she said coldly. "TELL ME WHO YOU REALLY ARE *NOW*!" She could almost feel her words put a grip on the thing's throat. Mentally, she squeezed. The world became utterly silent. In the quiet following her command there was a whisper that barely moved Teddy's lips.

iambhaalreleasemeplease

Mal's eyes narrowed, as she filed away the knowledge. "You get out of my friend now. Run back to Hell. GET OUT! *GO!*"

Teddy howled, then screamed, and then fell forward onto the floor, thrashing for a moment. Then he stilled, empty and himself. Mal dropped down next to him, stroking his unconscious head, and began giving orders like a battle-hardened officer. She got people to pick up, put away the booze, and get the hell out. Alex and Petra scrambled around trying to do as Mal directed. Petra knew starting this had caused a fight between Mal and Ben. She'd done it knowing full well her cavalier attitude toward the paranormal irked him. And now this happened. She remembered how Mal had been wigged out for days after the fortuneteller last summer and thought Mal would probably never speak to her again after this fiasco. The house had mostly cleared out and Petra stood beside Mal, who was still trying to rouse Teddy.

"Mal? What can I do?" She sounded apologetic and afraid.

Mal didn't look up; her entire focus was on Teddy. She thought he might need stitches when he came around and if he didn't come around soon he was going to get a ride in an ambulance as well. She was hoping to spare him as much of an ordeal as she could; he was extremely squeamish. He'd been the one who'd passed out when she'd donated blood at the school's drive over Christmas, to his endless embarrassment, the poor kid. She always thought of him like a little brother, soft-hearted and sensitive, someone to protect. She never took her eyes off him as she waved at Petra dismissively. "Have Alex take that thing outside and burn it. Scatter the ashes, too. You go get me a wet washcloth or something." She paused, still reeling from the revelation that things like possession existed. It upset her entire mental framework. Then her strange dreams over the last several months all wanted to crowd into her head at once. Her heart started to flutter in her chest, an almost panicky feeling threatening to overcome her resolve to handle things. She stepped on it. Hard. But she did snap at Petra, "From now on leave me out of crap like this!"

Mal was ready to call 911 when Teddy finally lifted his head. He had blood everywhere and was nearly shaking himself apart but when Mal wiped his face and hands with the warm damp cloth there wasn't a mark on him, not even a lump where his head had bounced off the table and she'd seen it split. She checked his pupils with a little flashlight from her keychain and was satisfied he was probably physically alright, although she couldn't imagine how. Mal called his parents and waited with him until they arrived. She moved him gently to the bench along the wall so Alex could put furniture back where it belonged and sat with her arm around Teddy's shoulders for a while. She whispered to him softly, over and over, that he was going to be okay. Soon he came around more fully, saying he felt nauseous. When his parents pulled in she walked him out so she could talk with them, saying Teddy had gotten ill, had seemed to pass out, but he really honestly hadn't been drinking and everyone was worried about him. The Sullivans thanked her for calling and drove away; casting concerned glances over their shoulders at Teddy huddled in the back seat. He was clearly still feeling pretty rocky. Without bothering to tell Petra what she was doing, she climbed into her car and checked her phone. At least he'd texted back.

I'm sorry. Call me.

And then a few minutes later,

Please don't be mad.

Are you okay?

And finally just,

Mal please.

She thumbed the call symbol next to his picture. He answered before the end of the first ring, "Mal, you're alright."

"I … yeah. Are you home?"

"Yeah, I caught a ride."

"I was afraid you'd frozen," she said, her tone reproachful.

"It was stupid cold. I tried to text you sooner but I forgot my gloves." He couldn't add that he'd also been so scared he couldn't focus enough to do a spell to keep warm either and his newly acquired scar was still itching and burning from the cold, annoyingly resistant to his magic, a distracting uncomfortable reminder of a terrible promise.

"I'm glad you're safe." She teetered on the verge of tears.

He'd felt something powerful trying to breach the barrier between worlds, not some run of the mill demon either, and he'd felt totally helpless. He knew how it would have ended if he'd stayed but the tremulous quality of her voice made him feel like a coward for leaving. His own voice was taut as he asked, "What happened?"

"Something awful," and this time a sob slipped out. She'd managed to keep her cool until she was relieved of the burden of supporting Teddy, but she found now that panicky feeling wanted to come back, and she just wanted to curl up under a blanket, cover her head, and maybe have a good cry. "I just want to forget it and I don't want to stay here."

She could hear his concern, but also a little bit of a smile as he said, "So, come over. Stay with me."

Chapter 34

"Every mind was made for growth, for knowledge; and its nature is sinned against when it is doomed to ignorance."
~ William Ellery Channing

Ari glanced around the restaurant, unable to shake the slight sense of unreality hanging over their gathering. He hated lying to Mal. He'd be the first to admit he'd kept many things from her over the years but to look into her face and outright lie about an art show so he could come here and meet his friends just grated on his sense of being a decent parent. He knew they needed distance from her to gather safely but she was an adult and the idea of lying for her own good sat increasingly ill with him. His companions seemed much more at ease. Davi loved a gathering of friends and a good meal and was always the one to make everyone comfortable, see that everyone was at ease and had what they wanted, always ensured every detail came together as naturally as breathing. He was glad Mal had picked that up from Davi, because Ari much preferred a quiet book or canvas all to himself, and he would have felt badly if Mal couldn't realize her potential because he was a quirky single parent. Metatron was simply thrilled to be in this crowded place in his earthly form surrounded by people. He'd spent the early part of the evening at the bar, flirting, grinning, and doing shots of tequila. Now, he was on his second Hurricane and seemed like this was just the sort of business he could get used to conducting daily.

They talked casually until their food and another round of drinks arrived. Sometimes it was lovely to be able to travel in the old way, with no thought for time and space. Ari was unable to do that under his own power since he had assumed his mostly-human form but it was freeing to experience it again. He might be enjoying himself if he wasn't so on edge. There was a reason for this meeting and he'd be happier if they'd just come to a point.

Davidos smiled, putting down his pint glass. "It's good to be with you both tonight."

Metatron held up his glass in salute, "It certainly is. I've missed you. I've definitely missed visiting Earth with all its fun and its bare minimum of angelic bullshit." He drew out that last, casting his eyes skyward, and everyone knew he was referring to Michael.

Ari was intent on getting this part of the conversation going. "Yes, how are you managing above? Is Michael still pursuing this damned prophecy?"

"Like a dog with a bone. Actually, more like a nasty selfish child with a sticky lollipop."

"We have to do something. Eventually the obvious will to occur to him and even though they don't have all the information they have enough. It would be better if we moved on but I can't do that anymore without Mal knowing why. I won't have my daughter forced to be a weapon!" Ari raised his voice more than he'd intended and a few other diners glanced around. "I'm sorry. Maybe we should have met someplace private."

"Maybe we met here because I need you keeping tight control on yourself, old friend." Davi, who hadn't paused in his enjoyment of his meal, waved at them indicating they should eat, relax; this was just talk among friends. "Metatron, we're definitely pleased to have you with us. I'm glad to learn that Sandalphon and Gabriel are prepared to take Mal's part but it may help Ari to hear what made you decide not to inform Michael of Mal's whereabouts."

"I'm the Commander of the Guardians! Protecting her is my job as much as yours. More so! Michael doesn't see that she has a choice. To him this affair is another war declaration and she's his first draftee." Davi smiled at his vehemence. "Besides Davi, I've told you I dislike being put in a position of telling a child they have a place in someone else's plans no matter who's doing the planning," Metatron said drily.

"I do seem to recall it's not a job you take lightly or without some argument." Davi's voice carried gentle amusement. He took a long drink.

"Gabby and Sandy can be counted on to do the right thing, as they always have."

"Of course," Davi agreed. "I don't think Michael would try to force Mal, although if he could get her to agree, Ari's right, he'd undoubtedly use her for his own ends. He's unpredictable though. We need to be wary, but he's not my primary concern at the moment."

"There's the much more concerning matter of Hell to consider," Metatron suggested. "Lucifer would do anything to change his circumstances." He drained his glass and waved for another.

Ari sucked in his breath at the casual mention of Lucifer's name. He could picture Maggie's face the night Lucifer's underlings had found them and his appetite evaporated. Davi put a steadying hand on his shoulder.

"It matters little to Lucifer what Mal would prefer. He'll force her to do his bidding if he can find a way; and we know he has a distressing gift for applying leverage."

Ari blanched at the thought. "But Davi, what is it they want from her? Do we really know?"

"It's difficult to say. Michael keeps the prophet and his work closely guarded. I know there's a choice coming for Mal and the Gatekeeper is appointed to help her discover what that is and how to proceed. Have you revealed yourselves to each other yet?"

Ari sighed, leaning back from the table, "We have, but only briefly. He'd like to meet; perhaps with all of us would be best. It seems like her Guardian and her Guide should know one another."

Davi indicated his agreement, then carefully suggested, "We do have another ally in this matter; somewhat unusual, but entirely welcome."

Ari's stomach dropped. He had a terrible feeling Mal was in trouble and stood abruptly. Something had triggered one of the spells he'd set to alert him to danger.

"Ari, please. Mal's fine. She's just learning a little something about herself. My inner eye is with her for now, and I'm never far, not really."

Reluctantly Ari sat, looking back and forth between his companions who were studying him with something like pity. "Why don't you have a drink?" Metatron advised.

Ari shook his head, touching nothing on the table. "Ari, you might find this a little difficult to hear." Ari was not paying attention to Davi's words, his alarm and a sense of Mal's danger increasing. "Ari, she's alright. I need you to listen and to remember we are surrounded by humans and if you reveal us by acting impetuously or using some of the little power Heaven left you, you put Mal at risk, too."

Ari felt trapped but he knew it was the whole reason Davi had brought them here, to keep him roped in. As the threat he felt toward Mal receded, he considered what Davi was doing. Ari accepted that he was known to make rash decisions; he smiled a little when he thought of the one that had ultimately given him his daughter. He took a deep breath and nodded slightly.

"Her boyfriend's a demon." Metatron announced. Saying what was on his mind was an old habit that had no intention of dying, hard or otherwise.

190

Ari was about to stand again but Davidos held up his hand. He was sharply sarcastic, "Thank you, Voice, so much. I'm sure that made things easier for Ari. When will you learn to act like the oldest?" Metatron did his best to look innocent and then laughed. It had been a long while since he'd been in such pleasant company and he was thoroughly enjoying himself.

Ari numbly waited for an explanation. "Ben is a demon. But, that's not all he is. It's not even most of what he is." Ari did not look reassured. "On Christmas, when we were alone for a few minutes, I confronted him."

"And?"

"Ben loves Mal, wholly and absolutely. He's willing to endure terrible things for her sake, things with incalculable consequences, things he doesn't see a way out of, and he loves her enough that he doesn't count the cost."

"Are you sure?" Ari's voice sounded hollow, frightened.

"Not only did he put himself through some spell work that was difficult for even the old gods to endure, he did it just to hold her hand. You know what that's like Ari, to risk dangerous magic to just be with your love." Ari only blinked. "Besides, he let me look into his eyes."

"What did you see?" This peculiar power of Davi's was one Ari trusted implicitly. Although other angels possessed the ability to see into a soul, Davi saw the totality of them, not just the measure.

"His humanity is all there, complete. Hell has not managed to twist his soul. He's a survivor certainly, but his capacity for love, and for pouring that out for others, for Mal in particular, is a truly beautiful and precious thing, and he has no idea of his own value."

Ari was a confusing combination of angry and relieved; angry that his spells hadn't revealed Ben's demon nature, but relieved that his immediate impulse to like and trust him had not been misplaced. Now Ari reached for his beer and took a sip, asking over the glass, "Does she know?"

Davi chuckled, shrugging, "She will after tonight. That's the other reason I wanted to speak with you both." He paused, considering how to begin. "We all know things are in motion. Signs are lining up. It is only fair for Mal to have knowledge of her true power and some time to develop it, and since she's safe with Ben and I owe her a little privacy just now, it's a good time to discuss how to begin."

Ari agreed readily, relieved her Guardian had reached the same conclusion he had. "It's time to tell her the whole story."

Chapter 35

"The end may justify the means as long as there is something that justifies the end."
~ Leon Trotsky

Bhaal howled, a sound of mixed defeat and exultation. He lay gasping within the circle of fire and symbols on the altar in their secluded den in the deepest part of Hell. A sighing question went up among the gathering of gods. He hadn't expected the child to take him by the throat, and her command at the end had held genuine deadly anger, but it had been worth it. Bhaal composed himself as quickly as such an ordeal allowed and joined his companions.

"Well my friends, that was worth the effort. I stretched myself far and managed to slip into a friend of our target. He was part of a little group playing with dangerous toys and his thoughts and affection for her singular energy drew me like a beacon."

Exclamations and applause scattered around the room. He raised his hand and the assemblage fell silent. "I was cast out with true Heavenly authority. This Scion is something altogether new."

More gasping and applause rang around the chamber.

"Some names floated to the surface as well. Petra belonged to the place we were in and the boy I was stepping on was Teddy. Our target's name bubbled right to the top with nothing preventing me from discerning her identity."

"What is it, Brother?"

"Her name is Malin, but the boy was thinking 'Mal' over and over again. It was as though he knew she could help him. She was practically all he was thinking about while under my boot. Her light does not easily conceal itself in the presence of those who love her."

"What does she look like?" a deadly battlefield goddess asked, voice filled with hunger.

"I could not go deep enough to see her, Morrigan. Full possession was not possible. His soul was fighting back like a little honey badger." There was general amused laughter. "We are getting close. And now I have her friend's taste in my mouth."

"What about a location?" Moloch inquired.

"They were near the water and it was bitingly cold, but nothing specific, unfortunately."

"Shall we report this to Lucifer?" Tiamat inquired, getting to his feet.

"Don't be ridiculous! We've learned something much too important tonight to give any further consideration to Lucifer's pathetic little mission." They were mystified. "The child was *alone*. There was no angel by her side; some clever spell work, but nothing else protecting her." Bhaal felt he was leading them by the hand as they contemplated his meaning.

Finally Tiwaz smiled, "They are spreading themselves awfully thin."

Bhaal's wicked grin showed approval. "They are indeed. I am beginning to have a sense of what Lucifer meant when he said that God is not a factor." He paused letting his words sink in. "We can use this knowledge; negotiate our return. Before we approach Lucifer, we must consider carefully how it is to be done."

Chapter 36

"The highest compact we can make with our fellow is, 'Let there be truth between us two forever more'."
~ Ralph Waldo Emerson

Mal rolled onto her back, linking her leg around Ben's. You couldn't be the little spoon if the big spoon was dozing off and rolling away from you. He sighed comfortably, playing absently with her hair. She rolled over, draping her arm across his chest, her head on his shoulder, tipping her head up to kiss the corner of his mouth. His breath was deepening and seeing the softness of his features she knew he was nearly asleep. She began tracing the patterns in his tattoo with her fingertips and his breathing started to sound like the earliest stages of a snore. Mal's eyes narrowed and one corner of her lips quirked up as she sat up and trailed her fingernails over the hard muscles of his belly, having discovered earlier as they undressed that he was helplessly, almost hilariously, ticklish. She was immediately rewarded with Ben curling onto his side, his face half in the pillow, mumbling the obvious in a sleep-sodden voice, "Hey, that tickles."

She said with a distinct pout, "It's supposed to. I sort of want you awake."

Then she scratched her fingers lightly back up his side. He squirmed and peeled an eye open, loving the way the highlights in her tangled hair glowed from underneath in the soft lamplight, almost like embers. He grabbed her hands and kissed them, smiling sleepily. "Brat," he teased. Then he drowsily dropped them again. She lay back down but looked at him expectantly. He shifted a little, rolling onto his back again as he pulled the sheet up to his chest. He mumbled, "Mal, baby, if you want to go again, I totally will. But maybe we could just take a little nap first, okay?"

His eyes were already closing. She sat up again, leaned close to his ear, and whispered, "Ben ... I think I can tell you now."

Ben's eyes snapped open. He was jarred fully awake more quickly and thoroughly than if she'd doused him with a bucket of ice water. He stayed where he was, looking up at her uneasily. He swallowed hard and said, "Okay, I'm listening."

When she arrived, Mal refused to say anything about her experience. She'd obviously been crying in the car and he didn't want to push her, so they just sat on the couch holding each other for a long time. Whatever happened felt dangerous even from a distance, and Ben was just relieved she was still in one piece. After a while, hoping she'd at least look at him, he touched her cheek. Turning to him, she looked searchingly into his eyes for a long moment, and then kissed him passionately. She was suddenly astride his legs, kissing his face and neck, her hands running all over him, laughing a little when he wriggled away, and then stripping off his shirt. Once she'd peeled her dress over her head and wrapped herself around him, it was a pretty short trip down the hall to his bedroom. She was a pleasant combination of generous and demanding and Ben didn't think he'd ever been happier. As a demon he'd had many lovers but he didn't think he had ever really made love before tonight. He knew it was trite to even think, but he didn't care because it was also true. Whatever price he paid for their time together would be worth it a thousand times over even if this was his last night on Earth. The end he'd bought for himself would be worth it, too. He had this, her, now. He was somewhat surprised to find that it was enough.

Several vigorous and exhausting hours later, Mal recounted the events of the evening, sitting unselfconsciously in a pool of sheets. She began shivering and Ben sat up and grabbed a rumpled shirt off his nightstand and helped her pull it on while she spoke. He couldn't help admiring the picture she made wearing his oversized button-up open in the front and the high striped stockings that were the only things she hadn't taken off. How close Hell had come was an ominous development. He would have to do some work to discover how far they'd gotten through and what it might mean, but he'd need Chris's help. Doing the magic himself was a good way to get caught. She was about to reveal the creature's name but Ben, now lying propped on his elbow, interrupted.

"Don't. Don't say their names. Ever." She searched his face, brows beginning to draw together. "It's powerful. It can call them … Jesus; don't ever call one of those things. Don't ever be someplace where someone else might. I've been worried about something like this for a while. Petra doesn't take it seriously and she has some real natural talent."

Ben's face was ashen, having picked up the name from her thoughts. It was a damned good thing he'd left. Bhaal had spent eternity perfecting exquisite endless suffering. Ben's nightmares often revolved around the things he'd seen Hell's second in command accomplish, things he himself had suffered when he foolishly ran afoul of the Hell-god. The almost superstitious dread the name inspired made him cold all over. But knowing Bhaal's habit of practicing his craft on new souls and that he had been close to Mal and her friends, had crushed Teddy down, made him feel like he was on the edge of a cliff losing his balance. Mal's power must really be something if she'd booted *him* without any difficulty.

"How do you know so much about it?" Ben was keeping something from her. It was all over his face.

He knew he had to tell her, no matter how it made her feel about him. Now that he had the daggers and could protect her he had no excuse. Ben sat back up not quite looking at her, his expression guilty. "Shit, Mal … I should have told you before now … Definitely tonight before we …"

"Ben, you spill your guts right now. What are you hiding from me?" She looked so cross, with her eyebrows knitted together. Even though he thought this might be the worst moment of his existence he loved how her expressions always seemed so purely complete.

"Mal, I'm so sorry, but I'm … Oh fuck," his breath hitched. Knowing there was no way to dress this up he closed his eyes and said simply, "I'm a demon."

For a second she just sat on the bed looking thunderstruck and then it seemed to sink in and she scrambled away, panic-stricken, until she fell off onto the floor, continuing to back away until she was against the wall. He didn't move, didn't want her to see him as more of a threat than she already did. He stared down at the floor desolately and said with complete sincerity, "Mal, I would never hurt you for anything."

As her moment of initial shock passed she became furious instead of afraid and immediately got to her feet, determined to make him tell her the truth, all of it. She advanced on the bed, incensed, "You're telling me you're one of those things like was in Teddy?"

Ben only shook his head and whispered, horrified, "No, never like that. I swear."

"What, then?" she said more forcefully, grabbing his arm, pulling him toward her. "Are you here to knock up unsuspecting girls like me with nasty creepy demon babies? Because poking holes in condoms seems a little low rent even for Hell!"

Near tears, cringing under her stare, he whispered, "Mal, no, I promise." So upset his powers were nearly useless to him, he winced a little at how hard her fingers dug into his flesh. She immediately let go, but still looked angrily into his face. "I would never do anything that wasn't what you wanted from me. It's been killing me to keep things from you. Especially since Christmas."

Her eyebrows drew closer together. "What about Christmas?"

"Your uncle, he knows. I thought he'd tell you and I wanted you to hear it from me. Then I was just afraid of what you'd think. I don't even know ..." Ben had thought about telling her everything countless times, but when faced with the reality of it he found himself at an uncharacteristic loss for words.

Mal couldn't quite sort through all the things she was upset about at the moment. "What do you mean Davi knows? How the hell does he know anything about it?"

"Look, I can't. That's his stuff and your uncle is one guy I definitely don't want to cross."

"What about Dad?"

"I don't know if Ari knows. There're other things, but they aren't mine to tell." He was looking at the floor again, a portrait of abject misery. "Mal, *please.*"

Her voice softened a little. "Tell me your stuff then. Everything." She sat down on the bed again, arms folded, willing him to raise his head, to look at her, but he didn't. He hesitated, and then began speaking in a quiet voice laced with shame, all while he stared at some imperfection in the wood floor. He revealed more than he had intended about himself, but he didn't want to tell her more than he had to, especially about the prophecy and who she really was, and he was so distraught he couldn't think straight anyway.

After several minutes of talking in circles, he said, "I was sent to Earth because of this prophecy and I was supposed to find you, but all I was doing was taking a vacation from ... that place. I met Chris the spring before I started school and I just decided I didn't care what Hell wanted, I was going to help him. Then, I met *you.*" He ventured a tentative look at her, but didn't meet her eyes. "Nothing in this world or any other could ever get me to do anything but help you, protect you ... Love you."

She'd heard the 'L' word before in a few past relationships, but it was kid stuff, never more than something you tossed around lightly, like 'thanks'. There was real weight to Ben's words. A promise.

"Maybe I believe you. I want to believe you." She felt so torn, confused. "Are you even real, Ben? Or do you just disappear in a puff of smoke?"

Ben let out his breath in a way that was almost a laugh but was too bitter to be mistaken for one. "I wasn't always a demon. I was human a long time ago. This is a real body and it doesn't belong to anyone else. But there's magic to it, some power too."

"Magic?"

Still looking at the floor, he had an almost irresistible urge to smile, and he felt it tug one corner of his mouth a little. He hesitated, but Mal brushed his hand, almost reassuringly. "Yeah, like for example, even absent completely unsabotaged condoms, I've made sure I can't get anybody pregnant. Not even with a fork-tongued spike-tailed Hellbaby."

She nearly smiled in response, thinking that though the conversation was stranger than she could have ever imagined, this sounded like the person she'd been falling for, letting into her life. She decided she didn't want to ask any more about Hell because she found she simply couldn't give a kitten's whisker of a damn about it. He was Ben and she wanted to know *him*. Not even sure why, she got up on her knees and put her hands gently on either side of his face, turning his head toward her. He moved slowly until his whole body was facing her and looked up, unresisting, naked in every way that was possible. She felt a strange shift in her head and it was as though she were falling into his golden eyes, seeing all the way down into his absolute center, his soul. She saw brief confusing flashes of everything Ben had ever been, ever seen, ever done. In the midst of it, the kind of man he was became clear. An indeterminate amount of time later, she came to herself and he was still passively looking up at her, his expression unreadable, silent tears running down his beautiful face.

All her anger gone, a few tears spilling unbidden from her own eyes, she whispered, "My God Ben, I see all of you. Baby, how can you be from Hell?"

He shook his head, not even hearing her, staring up, altogether vulnerable. She moved so she could be next to him and stretch her arms around his shoulders. After a moment his head rested against hers. When his breathing felt less like weeping she made him look at her again so he could see she wasn't angry anymore, that she meant what she said, as she gently dried his tears with her thumbs.

"Ben, it's okay. You lied about being a demon. So what? Shit, it's not like I've always been completely honest about myself with people. It's hard when you don't think people will accept you for who you are, or you think knowing will hurt them."

He shrugged, feeling utterly unworthy of her forgiveness.

"I don't believe for one moment you've ever lied about anything important."

The relief on his face was total and it broke her heart a little. Another single tear spilled and he dashed it away with the back of his hand.

"You said there are other things. My family? Some prophecy?"

He bit his lip and nodded slightly, still not quite trusting his voice.

"Will you come home with me when my dad gets back?"

He gathered himself, took a deep breath. "Of course." He was quiet, thinking for a moment, not sure how much more he should say. "Could I call Chris and ask him to come? I don't want to unload any more on you without him, but he's part of this. Would it be okay?"

She hedged, "Sure, but ..?"

"When I said I was going to help him before ... He's in the prophecy, too." Her eyes went wide again, but she said nothing, just tilted her head, thinking. His breath caught again and his voice cracked when he said, "I just want to be able to help you as much as I can."

Mal couldn't stand the devastated look on Ben's face. Breaking the seriousness of the mood completely, Mal shoved him over and acrobatically straddled his hips. "You've already been helpful several times tonight."

He gave her a half-smile and rested his hands on her thighs, feeling all at once that they were okay. "Glad I'm good for something."

She slid down into bed between Ben and the wall, wearing a small secret smile. He moved over so he could be closer to her but was still looking up at the ceiling. She rested her hand on his chest, feeling the slightly raised edges of the scar hidden by his tattoo and the wild beating of his heart beneath it. "Ben, we don't have to talk anymore if you don't want, but I was wondering why you left tonight. If you'd stayed, couldn't you have just fought it?"

She heard a dry click as Ben swallowed and when he spoke he sounded unsteady. "Mal, I'm kind of nobody down there ... Well, no, that's bullshit; I've got some pull, but ... only a little. And I am definitely breaking the rules right now. Like all of them. Whatever came up would have known me, forced me to go back, and ..."

The thought of what would have happened if he had stayed chilled him to his core. Traitors were Hell's favorite public entertainment. He wasn't about to suffer that and what would surely come after without knowing Mal was alright, was through this. Once he was sure of her safety, he thought he could endure anything. Mal felt him shiver and pulled him closer, resting her head on his shoulder, pulling the tangled blankets over them as best she could.

He wasn't quite ready to admit he'd read her thoughts so he changed the subject, making a face, "And *those* things ... people think they're just for fun, but I can feel the magic. It pulls at me, makes me feel at someone's command. It's awful."

"I'm sorry, Ben. You've been through the wringer tonight haven't you?"

He gently traced the smooth curve of her hip with his thumb and managed to sound more like himself, "There have been compensations."

Mal wrapped herself more fully around him, her affection stamped in her eyes and every nuance of her expression as she leaned in, nipped his earlobe, and whispered, "I thought you were too tired."

He shivered again, pleasantly this time, and smirked, "Confession restores the soul, or so I've heard."

She bit her lip provocatively, threw the blankets off onto the floor, and was once again on top of him with her characteristic lithe grace.

When they were spent again, they lay in the dark, this time with his head resting against one side of what were, in his considered opinion, the world's most perfect breasts; the rhythmic beat of her heart and the warmth of her body next to his under cozy flannel sheets lulling him to sleep. Nearly dreaming already, the restful peace of truth finally between them, Ben confessed softly, "I really do love you."

Mal knew his words required no response, that he wasn't saying it to be answered. But she already knew how she felt about him no matter where he came from. He barely heard her whispered reply as he drifted off, "I love you, too, Ben."

For Ben, any chance of turning back ended right then.

Chapter 37

"That's the way things come clear. All of a sudden. And then you realize how obvious they've been all along."
~ Madeleine L'Engle

Chris had already gotten out of his car and begun picking his way over the uneven icy ground toward the house. Ben was poised to get out of Mal's car, but she just sat, both hands still on the wheel. He stopped, entirely sympathetic to her reluctance. "Can you do this right now?"

Her tension made her short with him. "Don't be a dumbass. Of course I can."

He reached out, removed her hand from the wheel and squeezed it. It was cold beneath his fingers even though she'd been blasting the heat all the way over from Chris's. "I'm serious."

She frowned, "How bad can this be? You told me you're a demon and all that happened was you got even more laid."

Ben smiled crookedly. "That and maybe a few unkind words regarding my character." She glared at him. Then his face held feigned outrage and he mumbled, "Demon babies."

She was instantly caught in a fit of nervous laughter and put her head on his shoulder, her arms going around him. He held her, thinking how she'd complained over the weekend about how her Uncle Davi and her dad could both be mercurial. He'd immediately thought, *Run in the family much?* Although he had to admit she'd accepted the revelation of his demon nature with remarkable aplomb, and even survived Teddy's possession with minimal consequences other than nightmares, which she admitted weren't new. She'd commented this morning that if you wanted to keep it together when everything was falling apart it helped to wake up next to someone who understood what you were going through, or who at least really wanted to understand. He'd had to agree, having enjoyed his first dreamless sleep in years, but was up at dawn worried about how she was going to react when the revelations she heard were about her.

When Ari called Saturday to say he'd be home early and had something he needed to tell her, he'd wanted to meet at church and go to lunch afterward. She'd snapped that she wasn't going to church because he knew damned well Ben was a demon, and after the difficult time he'd had telling her she wasn't just taking off someplace if he couldn't come. Ben was shocked when he realized Mal, even separated by hundreds of miles, had sensed that her father knew about him. The call ended amicably enough after she also admitted that she just wanted to meet at home because she wanted Ben near her for whatever it was Ari had to say. Ari immediately agreed, saying he understood, but Mal still let him know she was hurting. Realizing everyone who's important to you has been hiding things was kind of a cold slap.

Chris sat with her this morning while Ben had gone for a run in the forbidding cold. Chris had asked him to go, saying he wanted to talk to Mal privately, but really suspecting Ben had a rough time of it and could use the space. Although he thought Ben had felt better as soon as they confirmed that Hell hadn't managed to break all the way through, and he looked reasonably well-rested for the first time since Chris had known him. Chris carefully explained to Mal who he was and his apparent role; someone meant to help her understand an ancient prophecy. There was more, but she needed to hear the details from her family. This was some heavy shit, as Ben had put it, and no one wanted to tell her she was not only half-angel but the last in the direct line of God on Earth. It sounded impossible even to Ben, who knew it was not just possible, but true. Ben's head was much clearer after a few miles and he felt better prepared to help her through today, and whatever came after. When he had a moment to think, he realized he felt irrationally peaceful about his decisions in the last few years. He truly didn't regret the price he would pay to help her, to be with her, even for a short time. Besides, he'd had his chance at life. This was about Mal, and he'd done the right things to ensure she had a chance to come through this.

Ari opened the door and was speaking to Chris, looking over the Gatekeeper's shoulder at the two of them sitting in the car. She knew it was time, even if she didn't feel ready. Abruptly, she released Ben and looked seriously into his eyes.

"I'm sorry I called you a dumbass."

Ben shook his head and gave her a reassuring smile. "It's okay, Mal. You're upset. I know how crazy this all must be for you."

"It's not okay. You're trying to help." Her chin puckered and he touched her cheek. She put her hand over his. "I love you, Ben. I really do."

"Just tell me what I can do to make this easier."

"Stay next to me. Don't you let go of me."

"Whatever you need." Ben's face was full of concern.

"They know you're a demon, Ben! What if they try to hurt you?" She was a jumble of confused emotions and was almost sick with worry about what was coming.

"Mal, I don't think they'd do that. Your uncle's known for ages. And hey, protecting me isn't your job," he offered lightly.

"Everybody apparently gets to protect *me*, so it is if I say so! I decide what I do!" she snapped, in no mood for Ben or anyone else trying to insulate her from what was really happening.

Ben opened his door and climbed out, mumbling, "Okay, okay," under his breath.

Mal was around the car in a flash, holding his arm possessively. Ben heaved a loud dramatic sigh hoping to break her tension. She smiled, unable to help herself, and wriggled her fingers under his ribs inside his open coat, more than a little amused with her new-found ability to make him squirm defenselessly.

He pulled away, pretending annoyance unconvincingly. "Hey, cut it out. Brat."

"I'll try but, no promises." Mal smiled at his reaction, his obvious affection, glad he was with her. She turned and walked slowly toward the porch with one arm wrapped around him. "I'm not letting go of you either." She frowned and stopped about half-way there. "Ben," she didn't look at him, just moved closer, held him tighter, and he could feel her trembling. "I don't want to do this. I don't want to know."

"Mal, I know this is difficult, and we can leave if you want … but I think you should hear everything. I feel like when you're caught in a web like this, it's better to see all the threads. Then you're the one in control." She nodded and made her feet start moving again.

They climbed the steps and said good morning. Her dad was clearly worried, his eyes searching Mal's face. She didn't trust her voice, didn't even want to let go of Ben until she knew exactly what was going on. To break the tension, Ben extended a hand toward her dad, wondering if his offer would be accepted. Ari shook it warmly and gave them both a nervous half-smile. Ben relaxed visibly and he felt Mal sag against him just a little. She let go of him and hugged her dad. Ari tipped her chin up so he could look into her face and saw her tears were close; she felt backed into a corner and it made her angry and afraid. She definitely took after him in many ways. He'd always told himself her mile-wide stubborn streak came from her mother, though when he said so Friday evening his friends erupted into boisterous laughter. He supposed that was fair.

When they got into the living room her uncle was already sitting in the battered chair by the wall and some of the kitchen chairs were arranged around the coffee table. There was a vaguely familiar darkly handsome man sitting in one of those. Chris sat down next to him, looking like something was bothering him. Mal led Ben to the couch, wanting him close. Her dad joined them in the chair nearest Mal.

"So," Mal began. Everyone sat, mute, uncomfortable. "So," she said again, waiting. They all shifted uneasily. "Nobody wants to start, huh?"

Her dad began tentatively, "Mal, it's not that. It's past time for this. It's only that we all love you and this is going to be difficult for you to hear, for us to tell."

Ben's powers of discernment were on high alert. He wasn't sure quite what to expect either. All he could pick up was concern for Mal and regret this hadn't happened sooner. From Mal, there was a jumble of confused emotions, psychic static, so unlike her usual calm clarity; but he was hoping it was somewhat intentional after their work this morning.

"Then I guess *I'll* start with what I already know. I know about Dr. G ... sorry, Chris. I swear I'm going to remember to call you Chris away from school like you asked."

He gave her an encouraging nod. "Whichever you're more comfortable with. Okay?"

A smile flitted briefly across her face, "Thanks ... Chris." She looked around again. "You see, he's a good guy. And I already know he's a great teacher. I finally managed to learn some Latin! I actually kind of feel better knowing he's involved." Ben squeezed her hand.

"And obviously I know about Ben. I'm sorry I was so snotty on the phone when I realized you knew, too. It's just, I looked into his eyes, and ... I saw that he's a good person. I want everyone clear about that." Surprised glances were exchanged around the room. The ability to look directly into a soul had been thought to be a somewhat singular talent of full-fledged angels, usually Guardians or Shepherds. "I don't care where's he's from either. I love him, okay?" There were nods and mumbled assurances all around. Ben's uneasiness decreased further and she stopped holding him quite so protectively, settling for intertwining their fingers. Mal was trying hard to keep a lid on her emotions, but there was a slight crack in her voice as she continued, "Could you please tell me who you really are and why I'm caught in some stupid prophecy. There's just nothing that special about me ... I don't get it."

The man Mal couldn't quite place began, "You probably don't remember me, but when you were really little you called me Uncle Matt." She realized where she knew him from; he sometimes visited with Davi when she was very small. He winked and went on, "You hardly need anyone to speak for *you*, darling, but

I'm known as The Voice in some circles, or Voice, if they're being overly familiar. My name is Metatron."

Mal's mouth hung open. She knew that name, certainly.

He continued, "I'm an Angel of the Lord. Once upon a time, I was the Voice of God. Haven't heard from Him in a bit, and now there's this prophecy thing." He'd intended to be funny but she looked so dazed, he went on simply. "I'm here to help." There was a long silence as she stared at him blankly and he added, "We understand this is a lot to process. Take your time."

Chris was staring at him now, his face clear with recognition. Metatron glanced at him and nodded, offering a silent heartfelt apology. Seeing the stamp of his years in the man's eyes made the phrase *'just following orders'* feel even worse than it always sounded in his mind.

Angel of the Lord. She noticed his iridescent orchid eyes and knew this was the absolute truth. She slowly realized she could see a glow around him, white and lovely. Until you noticed it you thought he was just handsome, but once you saw it, you couldn't un-see it. She bit her lip and turned to her dad, hoping he was going to say something to make this all seem sane and then she saw it around him, too, a similar light; in his case very faint, but no less beautiful. Her breathing got rapid and her wide eyes revealed a mind close to panic. She shook her head. "Nononononono. What the hell is going on?"

They had talked all night about the best way to tell her. Since there was no good way, he was blunt. "I'm your dad, but I was once an angel; it's still part of who I am, in a way."

She drew a short, sharp gasp. Ben moved closer and put an arm around her. She closed her eyes and leaned against him.

Ari swallowed hard and continued. "Being an angel's not so much. Your mom though, she was special. I was her Guardian. I loved her so much I chose life with her over Heaven. She loved me enough that she didn't care what I'd been."

She opened her eyes.

"I understand about you and Ben. I did the same kind of crazy stuff to—" Ben's eyes widened in a pleading expression and he gave a tiny shake of his head. Ari tipped him a quick wink of understanding before clearing his throat and changing tacks. "Love can make us forget everything else sometimes. Even who the world thinks we should be ... But after everything that's happened, I'm afraid for you. Your mom and I, what we had was wonderful, but it was also dangerous. Because of the prophecy."

"What happened, Dad? Not the accident story, but for real?"

Ari sighed sadly, looking much older for a moment. Mal noticed for the first time with some distress that his hair was beginning to grey and it occurred to her to wonder how that even worked for an angel, or at least how it worked for him and whatever he was now. Slowly, unsteadily, Ari told them of meeting Maggie as she was starting college here, and then going away with her to graduate school, of them moving around as she worked on her doctorate in psychology and he figured out that he really was much better at art than at guarding anything. He told about their joy at having a baby on the way, about almost losing Maggie when Mal was born. Babies with an angelic parent had the potential to be both more and less than human, regardless of the steps they had taken, but Mal had been a beautiful good-natured little creature with too much curly hair. Everything seemed entirely normal. But something had been off, probably something to do with the magic that was part of both of them, or possibly it was simply genetic, but whatever it was, Maggie lost her womb to the bleeding after. Since they had Mal, and Maggie had recovered from the surgery quickly, it just didn't seem important. When they finally bought a house, ready to settle down, the Knights revealed themselves, claiming it was too dangerous to stay, their child was special, more so than anyone in the already celebrated genealogy she belonged to. There was a prophecy of grave importance concerning her, and since Maggie could have no more children, even if the prophecy proved false, she deserved extra care. They were determined to keep her safe so that she could preserve the Line, that she not be the last. Mal frowned, but stayed quiet.

Ari had never told Maggie why he was her Guardian, only that he had chosen her over his position and could now have a real life with her. She'd just assumed that everyone got a Guardian Angel, so she was stunned by the revelation, but their lives had seemed so perfect she had been quick to accept it. They talked through everything and then asked the Knights to leave. They only thought a life in hiding was not what they wanted for Mal and neither of them had any interest in someone else interfering with her future. Both of them felt there had never been a better time to raise a child who could make their own decisions and that she should have the freedom to do so. Besides, Ari could find no confirmation of the Knights' claim at all. Eventually Davi, the Guardian who set himself in Ari's place, heard a whisper of prophecy, but it was too late. Ari took a shuddering breath and told about the night Hell came for Mal, offering as few details as he could. When he finished, he took in Mal's pallor, and put his face in his hands. Mal got up and brought him to the couch. She held him, unable to keep back tears herself. Ben sat with them, face eloquent of distress, wishing he could do something to help.

After a little while, what everyone had been waiting for finally occurred to Mal, and without lifting her head from Ari's shoulder she asked all in a rush, "But Dad, who were those knights? What do you mean the last? The line? And why *were* you mom's Guardian? Wait, does this mean I'm some kind of mutant?

Some angel-hybrid? Am I gonna grow wings or something?" She looked ready to be sick.

Davi, who had been entirely silent up to now, said, "You're not a mutant anything, honey, just truly exceptional. Everyone this special gets a Guardian." Mal sat up, looking intently at her uncle. "If you didn't know before, you do now; I'm an Angel of the Lord. You've probably figured out that I hung around to be *your* Guardian. Those Knights wanted to help guard you, too. You're kind of important ... Do you know what a scion is?"

Mal wrinkled her face in pretended offense. "It means somebody's the descendent of an important family ... or it's a weird looking car." She tried on a laugh and found it felt natural enough, even if it sounded a little brittle, a little forced.

Davi smiled. "Any guesses what I mean if I tell you that you're *the* Scion?"

Mal's whole body went rigid and she began shaking. Ben tried to take her hand but she leapt to her feet. "Oh, wow. No freaking way. When you say *scion* ... No, uh uh. My mother had brothers and sisters. I never saw much of most of them, but I've at least met them. We've even stayed with my Aunt Bethany a couple of times!" She felt her face reddening. "*Of course* you're a freaking angel! How did I never see it?" Mal was furious, anguished, and she was trying to think her way out of this. "And Knights? You mean the Templars! I've been on the goddamned internet you know! I know about all that Holy Grail bullshit. *The Scion*? What kind of shit is that?"

Davi spoke calmly. "It's just one of those things, Mal. Power transfers according to rules and traditions, especially where magic is concerned. One brave wonderful woman chose to carry this gift, or burden ... depending on how you look at it ... and she was her family's eldest daughter."

She wandered the room aimlessly, wringing her hands. "Do you mean Mary Magdalene? Wasn't she a prostitute or something?"

Ben's eyes followed her, wishing he could help, his face at least as distressed as hers.

"People have been saying that about the daughters of the Line since that time certainly, but Mary," Davi smiled, "was the eldest daughter of a wealthy and powerful man. She was reviled for leaving that behind for her new family. And ... well, her husband wasn't all that popular in certain circles either," he added drily. He went on gently, "When your grandmother Rose passed away ... much too young, having a child that didn't survive either ... the power moved on to your mother, and then when your mother died, it passed to you."

Mal felt too hot, then too cold, like she had a bad fever. She thought of that thing calling her '*whore's child*', of her mother's full name. She began shaking her head again. "So all this bullshit? Like I'm supposed to toe the line here and be part of this stupid prophecy thing because I'm like the great-great-whatever of *Jesus*?" Her tone was disbelieving but her voice started to rise. "I'm nobody! If he's the son of God, he can fight his own fucking battles!"

Her dad gasped and stood, moving toward her, "Mal, honey …"

Her face was flushed and her volume was increasing, "Or maybe if he can't do that, he should have kept it in his pants!" Ari put his hand on her arm. She threw him off and shouted, "NO! I won't be part of this!"

She ran from the room, then out of the house into the cold. When she slammed the door the light on the stand between Davi and Metatron shattered.

Metatron smirked, "Well, I think things are going rather well, don't you?"

Ari moved to follow her, but Ben rose and stopped him. "I'll go. I think she might need somebody outside the family for a minute, and I don't think she's pissed off at me anymore. Finding out who you all are, who she is? That's kind of big." Ari smiled kindly at Ben, who had stopped to grab Mal's coat. He looked back over his shoulder as he went out the door. "As long as she stays Mal, she could be the Great and Powerful Oz, too, for all I care."

Davi turned to Chris as Ari rejoined their group, slumping onto the couch. "You've been awfully quiet, Gatekeeper. How much have you already told her?"

"She knows who I am." He shook his head. "I told her there's a prophecy involving her and that I'm meant to try to help, but little else. She already knows me so I think most of that was relatively easy to accept. I felt the rest should come from you."

Ari was trying to concentrate on what was being said but every time he spoke about Maggie his sorrow was like an open wound. He missed her every day and now that this was all becoming so real for Mal he felt guilty about nearly every choice he'd ever made. He still felt responsible for Maggie's death, and now for the danger Mal was in, not to mention how upset she was. He let out a long slow breath. He knew what he was about to say was a bit of a speech, but he felt if he didn't just get it out all at once he might break down. "First, we'll have to let her know about the prophecy and what we are doing to determine its meaning, our next steps, then we need to work with her on not getting overly focused or worked up about anything. She may not be ready for the magic part of things, but I can't be with her to keep up the protection spells all the time now. She's a grown-up. She's earned her space."

He stopped, looking out the window at the two figures sitting on the picnic table facing the water. Ben's sturdy form was obvious, his arm wrapped around a huddled figure in a huge coat, his head resting against the lumpy hood. Ari sighed.

"Her personal wards are powerful enough to repel all but the most determined demons … I'm a little worried other demons may have stumbled to the old magic though." He paused, thinking he would have to try to get Ben alone later to apologize for almost letting things slip about the magic he had done. That was personal and if he wasn't ready to share it, it wasn't up to Ari to interfere. "If they have, some of them are bound to have survived." He paused, frowning. "And angels are more difficult. The results are much less predictable where they're concerned."

His eyes continued to explore the familiar room, thoughtful. After a few long breaths, regaining his composure by mentally reinforcing the warding spell, Ari went on. "She's relatively safe here regardless, but I don't want her drawing some monster to herself anywhere." Ari's face wrinkled in freshly remembered loss.

"Well, the exposition will be our job, certainly." Chris chuckled. "But Ben is already working on teaching Mal some protective magic. He was up ridiculously early this morning worrying about it. I've never had a more elaborate breakfast. As soon as Mal got up he told her he knew about magic Hell was using that could make any intense focus dangerous, that there're ways to make her thoughts safer. She trusts him, and he's a good teacher; patient, intuitive."

"What makes him qualified?"Ari wanted to know, beside himself with concern.

Chris looked thoughtful for a moment. "Apart from being quite the talented mage and having a number of useful powers, diffusion is natural to Ben. He doesn't focus unless he puts himself out to do it. He's willing to go to ridiculous lengths to help Mal and he believes this can only end badly for him. I think, no matter what he says about it, the idea overwhelms him. Focus just highlights those feelings. Diffusion is easier …" He paused and could see they were all wondering about Ben. "When he needs to focus it's like a laser. Otherwise, it's a bit like living with a big ravenous squirrel."

Despite his concern for Ben's future, an affectionate chuckle bubbled up from the most unguarded part of him as he pictured Ben's habit of frequent pacing and almost constant fidgeting, jumping from one task to another in a need to be constantly busy. Given Ben's manner and easy likability it wasn't hard for any of them to envision. Ari even smiled and managed to collect himself to go make tea.

Sometime later, as they sat deep in discussion, the front door opened and closed softly. Mal shuffled in wrapped in her heavy coat, her face puffy and tear-stained. Ben followed, red-cheeked and doing all he could not to shiver himself to bits, which having been hit by the cozy air of the kitchen was harder by the second. Through chattering teeth he mumbled something under his breath and warmed visibly. He'd obviously been focused on shielding Mal from the elements while they were gone since she didn't look like she'd even been outdoors. Davi smiled. It was good to know Mal had something of a protector when he couldn't be with her, at least until she got a handle on her own powers. Mal stood in the doorway looking at them soberly.

"I'm sorry I stormed out like a little kid. It's just … this doesn't … fit in my head."

They were all sympathetic. Metatron's admiring expression revealed that he thought she was absolutely heroic. Ben touched her elbow and she moved into the living room, taking off her coat and tossing it onto the arm of the couch, sinking back down next to her dad. She felt like maybe she was in danger of tears again if she just jumped back into this, so as Ben sat down next to them, Mal ventured to speak, "Hey, could someone get Ben a cup of tea or something? The nut job didn't wear his coat when he came looking for me and it's ridiculous out there."

Ben put a warm hand on her leg to reassure her, "I'm alright, Mal."

She saw no remaining evidence he'd just spent better than a half hour sitting in the freezing cold. "Wait, how did you warm up so fast? You were an ice cube!"

"You know I can do magic and stuff."

"Why the hell did you let yourself get all frost bitey then?"

"You didn't need the cold distracting you. But the spell takes a lot of energy and the field's small." He waved his hand like his comfort was the least important thing in the world.

"Ben, you can look out for yourself, too! You brought me my coat."

Ben smiled apologetically at her reproach. She had conquered any selfishness he might have had, but if he was honest he'd always been prone to those sorts of impulsive grand gestures. He just didn't think before he acted sometimes. He'd have to learn not to step on her toes though. He'd never cared much for the 'damsel in distress' type anyway, and he'd never once met anyone less damsel-y than Mal. His smile broadened a little. He'd have to remember to tell her that later. He thought she would take it as a high compliment, and it would probably make her laugh.

"I … I'm embarrassed. That was quite a tantrum." She rolled her eyes.

Davi laughed, "Others have done much worse with similar news." Mal saw only sympathy and approval in the faces around her.

"Where's Dad's lamp?" she asked, confused by its noticeable absence on the end table.

Metatron, who had picked up the many little shards of carnival glass and deposited them in the trash, looked at her affectionately. She was doing awfully well. "Mal, everything we've told you lets you know this whole thing comes with responsibilities, but I don't think we've much mentioned it comes with some power as well."

"I broke it when I was mad? Just by accident?"

Ben gave a little snorting laugh, "I told you this morning, magic is going to come naturally to you. The rest of us kind of have to work at it."

"Ben! You didn't tell me I could just break stuff!" She was indignant.

"Well, how do I know what your powers are? I just knew you'd have some. Actually, I'm pretty sure about healing." He looked at Davi, "Right?"

Davi couldn't have been more proud as he said, "She's probably done it many times out of natural love and concern."

"That's what I thought." Ben was a little smug.

Mal looked at Ben, her brow furrowed, "You mean like when you had a headache yesterday? That wasn't a '*Mal gives good shoulder massages*' thing?"

Ben grinned. "Well you do, but I don't think that's what fixed it."

"Why do you even get headaches, Ben? You told me your magic kind of protects you and you can't get sick. If I can just fix stuff I will, but you get them all the time. Why?"

Ben was thinking he was glad she didn't remember his fabricated flu back before Christmas and that it didn't occur to her to ask about how he was hurt enough to need stitches, when Davi answered, giving Ben something else to think about. "Some of it may be a human tendency after so much time back on Earth, but I believe it's at least partially Ben's demon nature pulling at his true soul. While they're bound to be unpleasant, given how you obviously feel, fixing either cause should be easy for you, Mal."

"That must be how I helped Teddy, too. I love the hell out of that kid and I thought his face was going to be hamburger." Mal's mouth snapped closed.

There was a moment of silence so complete Mal could hear her own blood, supposedly so special, rushing through her veins with the hammering of her heart. Mal looked at Ben and gave a little shake of her head, indicating he should tell it, that she didn't want to.

"Friday night Mal did something incredible," Ben offered to the other curious parties in the room. "She cast out a powerful possessing spirit like it was the morning trash." Davi was nodding, smiling a bit. Mal remained silent, so Ben explained everything she'd told him. He paused, wondering if they needed to know everything. Then, even though he knew she'd probably be angry with him, he went on. "Look, I didn't mean to, but I heard Mal thinking the name of the thing trying to break through. It was a Hell-god. They're getting seriously intense about this."

Mal spun angrily to look at Ben. "You read my goddamned mind?"

Ben looked down at his hands, trying to decide how to explain. "I didn't. Not really." He heard her irritated puff of breath and forced himself to look up at her and take her hand. He spoke quickly, hoping she would believe him, that she wouldn't be too upset. "I can't read minds. It's more like … not telepathy or anything, but like being a real empath, sensing feelings and intentions, things like that. Sometimes words just kind of bubble over. That's what happened, I swear." She was frowning, and he was wondering how to make it up to her. "I could teach you how to do it; I can tell you'll be good at it, because you already always know what kind of mood I'm in even if I don't want you to." She smiled a little at that. "I promise you I'm not rummaging through your thoughts. I didn't even mean to hear the name. But even if you hate me for it, I'm glad I did … Shit Mal, the thing that had hold of Ted was massively dangerous. You all need to know about it."

As he spoke, Ari got increasingly upset. "That was the danger I sensed, Davi? How could you not let me go to her?"

"She needed to begin to see her power. And she did." He paused. "Besides, Ari, few but the Archs are a match for one of those creatures. And I don't want Michael knowing Metatron is with us just yet." He was calm.

Ari, by contrast, was completely incensed, didn't care at all that if confronted with such a being he would face the final death as surely as Ben. "Davidos, a Hell-god said her *name*."

"And she humiliated him for his trouble!" Davi opened his hands, "We've always recognized they know more than we'd like. Something Hell just learned is that she's not to be bullied or trifled with. I'm her Guardian, Ari! I wouldn't have let anything happen to her." That seemed to make Ari feel marginally better, but his arm had gone protectively around her.

Mal frowned at Ben but he didn't think she was mad at him, now; well, not as mad anyway. "So you really can't just read my mind?" He shook his head, still feeling awful about the expression on her face. She was thoughtful for a minute, considering everything she was still learning about him. "How come you said you were too cold to text me back Friday? You could've just done your magic-y thing."

Ben reluctantly admitted, "Honestly? I was terrified. For both of us." He flushed and looked away. "I couldn't focus enough to pull the spell together."

Mal, smiling at his sweetly vulnerable expression, took his hand. After a minute, she spoke, "I can't wrap my head around everything at once ... Can somebody tell me more about the prophecy?"

Everyone turned to Chris, who was named in all of this too, as the person who would guide her through it. "The whole thing is awfully complicated, Mal, although my part is much easier than yours. All it asks of me is to keep doing what I do; be your teacher." She smiled again and he proceeded to detail what they knew so far. He shared the breakthrough on the older text, giving Ben due credit, and Ben flushed again at their approbation.

Mal flashed a genuine smile and elbowed him playfully. "I finally know why your nose is always buried in a book!"

"A gentleman and a scholar. See? You hit the jackpot." He succeeded at sounding like his usual droll self. He was relieved she was starting to see this as just part of her life. It would make diffusion easier. An unperturbed Mal meant less worry about drawing Hell's unwanted attention.

Chris continued, "You see, Mal, there's not a question it's talking about you. Holy, royal, angelic. However you want to put it, people like you don't exactly happen every day. In fact, you're literally one of a kind." Mal was horrified at the idea there was truly no one on Earth like her, that she could be the only one the prophecy meant.

Ben leaned in and kissed her cheek, "I've been telling you how special you are for ages."

She managed another smile, reclining against him, "Oh, everyone knows what you think." Then Mal was serious for a moment, "Dad, I've got to ask. What's with you and church? You gonna try to tell me God's Catholic?"

Her dad shook his head, almost embarrassed. "No, but your mom was, wanted to raise you that way. It just got to be a pleasant habit, I suppose."

She felt relieved; the idea of a particular religion being the '*right*' one had always bothered her, and a lot of what the Church said just pissed her off. *No birth control? Who the hell did the Pope think he was? And the Templars? Just showing up and telling people what to do with their kid?* Mal was working up a pretty good rant in her head when she came back to herself and what was in front of her. "I know you guys are still working all of this out and there are all these versions and whatever, but what does it mean, '*choice*'? What am I supposed to choose? When? How?"

Davi and Metatron spoke at the same time; then Metatron deferred to Davi. "We're trying to learn more from the prophecy's author, but it's not easy. He's well-guarded and a bit mad. We know it's something about Heaven and Hell. If we're right, it appears it will be a choice between Lucifer and the Archangel Michael in some way."

Ben's face was screwed up in silent displeasure as Mal asked, "What about God?"

"God hasn't spoken on any of this. Everything we've seen points to some manner of disagreement between the brothers. But this is not about good and evil, no matter what they may try to tell you. They are nearly equals, with equally suspicious motives," Metatron offered.

Mal was thoughtful, "So somewhere, for some reason, I'm going to have to choose between Lucifer and Michael?" Names previously known only from church felt strange on her lips.

Ben made an exasperated sound but was trying to hold his peace. Davi wouldn't let him, "Go on Ben, what is it?"

"It's just such bullshit, cornering Mal between the two of them like that. From what I've heard, all they do is fight like kids, over something that isn't even theirs. So this big prophecy is just trying to decide between the lesser of two evils? That's not how choosing works, no matter what any dusty old scroll says." His face flushed. "This is more complicated than that!"

Chris had heard all this before and had come to agree with Ben's philosophy. Everyone else was waiting for his explanation; especially Mal. Ben shifted in his seat and took something out of his pocket. It was a little eight-sided diamond-shaped pendant dangling from a delicate chain. Ben held it out and Mal took it, feeling its weight, turning it over in her hands and looking at it carefully, noticing the little symbols on its faces.

"I was going to wait and give this to you for graduation but I thought today was a more meaningful occasion. It's a coin. But, not exactly."

"Ben, this is beautiful. It's solid gold. Where'd you get it?"

His expression was guarded. "I made it."

She knew his semi-guilty look. "Is this the coin we gave you for Christmas?" His eyes cut away from her face for just a second, confirming her suspicion. "You can't give me your present!"

"If it was a gift I can do whatever I want with it!" She shook her head at the stubborn edge in his voice. He took a deep breath and when he continued he was more subdued. "It's a symbol like I wanted, but I did some protective magic, too. I needed something important to me to do the spell and … you gave it to me." She indicated he should continue by brushing his arm, now waiting patiently for his explanation.

"Like I said, it's a coin. Seems everybody in the whole damned universe wants to reduce every choice to a coin flip. Good versus evil, liberal versus conservative, freaking tacos versus pizza, I don't know … If you think about it for even a minute, it's obviously a load of crap." Ben extended his hands, indicating a scale. "There are almost always degrees of good and evil, politics aren't just liberal or conservative, and if the only things I got to eat were pizza or tacos, this body wouldn't be worth the trouble." She laughed just as he intended as he pointed to the necklace in her hands. "This coin is to remind you it's not all one or the other. No matter what happens I want you to promise me you'll remember that. Don't let anybody force you to choose between a rock and a hard place. That's not a freaking choice at all. You stay *Mal*. And you make *Mal's choice*."

Mal put on the necklace, touched the pendant one more time and then dropped it down inside her collar so she could feel it against her skin, still warm from being in his pocket. Ben's face got extremely serious and for a moment Mal could see the man he would be years from now, if only she could figure out how to give him that chance. She'd thought about that a lot the last couple of nights. How could she fix things so Ben could just be Ben and they could just be together? She didn't care how silly it was either or even if he believed it was possible. If the rest of this craziness could be real, so could helping Ben break free from Hell, be really human again.

As he looked in her eyes, some of her thoughts bled through and he blinked slowly, determined not to acknowledge it. "Besides, choosing the lesser of two evils is still choosing evil. Don't let them make you do that."

There were thoughtful nods around the room and Ari looked at Ben with almost fatherly affection. Ben could see that Mal felt much less trapped, more in control of what she was feeling, and he thought she had let go of her ideas about their future, for the moment at least. She was finally ready to hear more of what it meant to be her, that one of a kind her that put her in the way of this prophecy. She sat between Ben and her dad, no longer looking quite so vulnerable, and no longer reacting from the panic she had felt earlier. She was just focused on what she needed to know.

"Okay, so I'm the Scion. Please tell me what it really means."

Chapter 38

"There are no secrets to success. It is the result of preparation, hard work, and learning from failure."
~ Colin Powell

Lahash sat within the circle, candles flickering. It was becoming increasingly difficult to use this power, not for lack of ability, but for her frustration at so many years among the human vermin with no more results. Lilith was slouching around the dark room like some monstrous ancient evil, further pulling at Lahash's focus. She wondered briefly if the magic Lilith had been working would be reversible when this mission was over and she would return to her former terrible beauty, or if perhaps this was the harvest one reaped from years of wantonly dining on the innocent.

There had been this bare golden thread of thought Lahash had been trying to pick up for several days, but every time she thought she had it, the ends frayed and disappeared. This was her third hard effort in as many days and soon she would need a break from it. It might be another month before she could try again. Her head snapped up. She had heard it as clearly as if the girl had spoken in the same room with her. *I'm the Scion.* They were so close! She tried to pick up the thought and follow it but was so exhausted by her efforts it slipped away from her again. She collapsed to the floor. Lilith knew something significant happened and was at her side immediately.

"What have you found, Sister? Where is the girl?"

"I have nothing specific. But she is near. Please contact Lucifer; tell him we need some of the shielded demons. We are close enough to begin our search in earnest." Lahash slowly drifted off then, dreaming of the day they could return to their true place, triumphant. All it would take was convincing some little slip of a girl to agree.

Chapter 39

"Actions are the seed of fate; deeds grow into destiny."
~ Harry S. Truman

Ari had spent the next few days doing a great deal of soul searching. Nothing would ever make him regret his time with Maggie or their decision to marry, to have a child together, but the danger, the decisions Mal was facing were weighing on him heavily. He was relieved when his doorbell rang Wednesday morning. He answered, smiling warmly. "Thanks for coming. I thought it might be good to sit down together, Cartaphilis."

The name came as an unpleasant shock. "Just Chris, please."

"I'm so sorry. I meant nothing by it. It's just force of habit from brooding over this damnable prophecy, I suppose."

Chris waved off the apology. "It's fine. Just … that man ... I buried him long ago. I only speak of it now because that's the tie that binds us together, so to speak. You understand."

Ari nodded. "I suppose it's a bit different for me, since I chose my fate, but bearing a curse from the Lord must be a terrible burden." Ari preceded him to the kitchen table where the two of them sat facing each other.

"Actually, to be honest with you Ari, I haven't felt cursed in a long while. I feel the weight of my years certainly, some days more than others, which I'm sure you can appreciate. But more and more, I feel as if I truly have a purpose."

"Like you've been chosen and directed," Ari hedged.

"Not so much that." Chris became thoughtful. "I feel more like I've been given choices. And I've made the correct ones."

Ari had never heard anyone named in any kind of prophecy say they felt they had any choice. He knew Mal viewed it as someone trying to hijack her life. "What do you mean?"

"Only that through my decisions, I'm not only meant to be a guide to Mal, but I'm actually prepared to do it. I just don't believe any of this is as simple as fate." A line formed across Chris's forehead as he considered how to explain himself.

Ari's face creased as well, prompting Chris to continue. "You see, I could easily have gone a different way. In fact I spent an inordinate amount of time early on trying to die, just drunk and angry, hoping to outsmart God. Young and stupid is young and stupid no matter when it comes around, I suppose." Chris shook his head.

Ari, who certainly had his own version of that, smiled a bit. "But it's obviously not a path you stayed on. What changed for you?"

"The Apostle Peter found me, spoke with me. He told me about denying the Lord and, more importantly, being forgiven. He offered me hope the same could be true for me … I met the risen Lord once, and He told me forgiveness is always possible at any moment, but for people it doesn't always feel so easy, that we have to feel we've earned it. Since then I've devoted myself to helping others find knowledge; to stamping out ignorance and fear. To earn it, I suppose." Ari smiled. "I could have just as easily spent my life selling my sword to whoever would have it, inflicting pain on anyone in my way. But I was shown kindness and decided it was a much better way to spend my days."

Ari was thoughtful. "That makes me think of Ben and his friend. I had questions after we all spoke but Ben took Davi to meet her. He said she'll be a powerful ally. Every evil act she has been forced to carry out by her circumstances hurts her. Mal is a bit keen to meet her. She's feeling somewhat protective of Ben just now." Chris smiled, thinking they were exceptionally protective of each other. Ari smiled back. "We're quite the extraordinary group. I feel as though we're moved by the hand of God."

Chris's lips pressed into a colorless line. "I would tend to disagree, but when I first learned of his nature, Ben said something remarkably similar." Chris paused, thinking that for someone who insisted on the concept of free will, Ben seemed convinced all too thoroughly of his own fate. Chris wished he could find a way to get him to be more hopeful. He suspected the spell in Quebec had something to do with Ben's increased brooding; the boy would say nothing about it though. "This can feel awfully contrived if you don't keep perspective."

Ari frowned. "I'm not sure what you mean."

"We've been given choices, and our actions, our reactions to these forks in the road that have brought us here. Any of us could have done differently at any point. None of this is coincidence perhaps, but nothing has forced our hands."

"But what do you make of the prophecy then?"

"If the prophecy is truly divinely inspired then I suspect its true author knows our hearts and trusts us to make the right choices. To be worthy."

"Thank you." Ari gave a bright genuine smile. "I needed to hear that. I know you'll do right by Mal. She already trusts you completely, but I'm enough of an over-protective dad that I needed to, as well." Chris returned Ari's smile, glad they could be friends, knowing Mal would need all of them, united. "Now," Ari stood, "can I offer you some tea?"

Chapter 40

"The meeting of two personalities is like the contact of two chemical substances: if there is any reaction, both are transformed."
~ Carl Jung.

Mal had waited impatiently all week for this evening. She could sense Ben's distress and was sorry, but not so much that she was willing to withdraw her request. She felt she had a right to know everyone involved. Davi had met Aife and approved. When Mal suggested she should meet her as well, her usually eloquent Ben had gotten charmingly tongue-tied. She had pried out of him that Aife was a demon and had been his occasional lover for centuries; he had even confessed blushingly that Aife had been his last lover before Mal. She'd tried making him feel better by saying she was still friends with a few ex-girlfriends, boyfriends, too, and that she didn't think it was a big deal at all. He'd just shrugged and turned a slightly darker red. She thought Ben's discomfort was silly, but his worry that his past would somehow hurt her feelings was yet another oddly appealing demonstration of his love for her.

They sat around the apartment chatting casually. Ben showed way too much interest in Chris's new research project because anyone could see hearing about it bored him to near tears. His curiosity about her volunteer position at the hospital and her LNA course didn't seem particularly genuine either, since when she talked science and medicine he often got a glazed look or flat out wrinkled his nose in disgust. They were moving on to weekend dinner plans when a soft knock at the door interrupted their debate about which local pizza place was best. Ben was tense as he went to answer the door and Chris sat quietly smirking behind his book. No amount of artful persuasion could have moved him. Ben was usually so smooth. His self-consciousness made this terribly intriguing.

When Ben led Aife into the living room, Mal's breath caught. She didn't react from shock or jealousy but because she understood the attraction immediately. Aife was almost petite and kind of deliberately curvy, with skin like fresh cream tinted with rose petals. Her green eyes were sparkling peridot, set off by a smattering of freckles the same beautiful color as the tangle of soft flame-red waves falling past her narrow waist. She was definitely a woman who had seen better than three decades in that body, but Mal thought all age had given her was an elegant self-assurance. She couldn't fathom why Ben was embarrassed. They were both gorgeous. *What else were two beautiful demons with eternity in front of them going to do?* Mal had a few ideas about what she would do if she were going to live forever and was presented with a companion this lovely and if she didn't think it would render Ben permanently speechless she would have told him so.

Ben moved to make an introduction, saw Mal's open appreciation, and blushed. She decided he needed to be teased out of this unfounded embarrassment. She also thought he probably needed to see for himself that she really didn't think this meeting was a big deal. He was always so worried about her feelings, her comfort. She wanted him to relax a little so she held up her fist to him. "Wow, Ben, you definitely weren't punching above your weight or anything, but still … You must bump this. Respect."

"Aw, Mal, c'mon." He plucked her hand out of the air in front of her and squeezed it gently. "Don't." His voice was nearly pleading.

Mal grinned mischievously and turned to Aife, repeating the gesture. Aife, amused by Ben's expression, started to raise her hand, but he stepped between the two of them. Aife caught the widening of his eyes that he directed her way that said very clearly he hadn't accepted her reassurance over the phone that she wasn't worried about Mal touching her, that she was sure she could tolerate whatever the evening had in store.

"Knock it off, you guys." Ben's tone was less of a plea this time, and had an imperious edge that Aife associated with orders he resented having to give.

In spite of Ben's disapproving glare, Aife was caught in a fit of giggles; that one gesture all she needed to know she liked Mal a great deal. Ben's deer-in-the-headlights expression caused them both to dissolve into genuine laughter.

He was flustered into near silence and wouldn't look anyone in the eye. He stood between the two of them like a wall but, caught up in the basic formality of an introduction, Ben sighed and offered grudgingly, "Mal, Aife. Aife, Mal." He flushed redder, up to his ears, stuffing his hands into his pockets, and could barely look at either of them. "There. You've met. Now let's get this over with."

Mal raised her eyebrows, but lowered her lids, "Well, hello, Aife."

"Hello yourself, beautiful," Aife flirted back jokingly, entirely comfortable.

"Okay, that's enough!" Ben snapped, beyond put out.

The picture of innocence, they replied together, "We were just saying hello!"

Ben shook his head and sighed deeply, holding his hands up in surrender. "You guys are all cool and whatever. You've made your point. Must you make me suffer?"

Mal winked and quipped, "Only if there's a safety word."

Ben reddened even more. "Jesus, Mal!"

Chris put his book down, and said, in a remarkable impersonation of Ben at his worldliest, "Wow, you're a real book guy, huh?"

Didn't the man ever forget anything? "Goddamnit Chris! That's enough!"

"Are you sure? I feel like an accurate impression of you should include some swearing."

Mal laughed. "I think I'd like to see that! You don't ever swear, Chris!"

"I was a soldier. I could probably come up with a few that would surprise even Ben. Just half the time I forget I'm not at work. And when I'm with Ben, he does it enough for both of us."

Aife chuckled affectionately. "He does have a tendency to pepper his sentences with creative invectives."

Ben was indignant. "Since when is ganging up on me so much fun?"

Chris got up, smiling not quite apologetically at Ben. Aife stopped, taking in Chris's broad shoulders and well-proportioned height. Her eyes gleamed with an almost predatory sheen. Not even glancing at Ben, she scolded him softly, "Darling, you've been holding out." An inviting smile spread across her face as her eyes ranged over Chris. "Hello, Benjamin."

Chris didn't know if she was quite Mrs. Robinson, since physically she had maybe five years on him. Chris moved toward the little group, thinking it was about time someone observed some of the basic rules of etiquette. He offered his hand to Aife, who took it and more clasped than shook it. His mouth dropped open and her eyebrows went up at the almost electric feeling that passed between them. "Well, hello."

"Hello, Aife," Chris stammered, looking more like a boy than the immortal soldier and scholar he was. Her effortless sensuality made him feel like an awkward kid. "I was thinking of getting us take-out," Chris managed, so disconcerted he didn't realize he hadn't followed through on his intention of introducing himself properly. His amusement at Ben's discomfort was quickly forgotten in an attraction so palpable he could barely formulate a coherent sentence. "Any thoughts?"

"Just get Chinese." Ben was curt, still uncomfortable.

Mal was agreeable, "Sure, I love egg rolls."

Aife smiled, "I could go for some *Italian*, although if I have to settle I suppose I can cope."

Chris nodded, mumbled indistinctly, fumbled for his keys, and made a hasty exit.

Ben, as self-conscious as he'd ever been, was reproachful, almost stern. "Aife! Seriously?"

"I never joke about my appetite. I love Italian … and he looks positively scrumptious." Aife brushed past him and sat gracefully in the chair Chris had vacated.

Mal followed and sat on the couch so Ben could join her. "I don't get it. Chris is like … kinda old." Aife somehow didn't strike her as old, though she knew better.

"Oh honey, you're only saying that because he's your teacher. He's not even half old by my count. He's just a big handsome puppy." She sounded positively wistful.

Ben gave a deep roll of his eyes. "Can we just get down to business? Stop with all the … sex stuff?" He looked so affronted it made them laugh again.

"I told you, I'm up for anything. But you know that about me, Ben." Aife purred, enjoying his discomfort, if only because she was a little irritated with how protective he could be sometimes.

Ben looked ready to dig a hole, climb in, and pull it over himself.

Mal was starting to feel sorry for him, wondering why this had him in such a twist. He'd told her as a demon he'd had a lot of partners, and she had laughed saying she'd had a few herself and didn't feel like they needed to tally things up. As far as Mal was concerned practice made perfect, and she was glad he'd had practice. She'd said so. His reaction to this meeting was as surprising as it was strangely sweet. "Ben, baby, I'm sorry. I never expected you to get embarrassed over this. It was just demon stuff ... just sex even. Honestly, all I'm thinking is '*go you*'. I've never had an orgasm friend half as cute as Aife!"

Ben sputtered, "*Orgasm friend*?" He fidgeted and only half-met Mal's eyes, offering a somewhat inarticulate explanation, "Look, I … sex … demons … I figured …" He ran both hands through his hair, his pinched expression consistent with someone having severely stubbed a toe. He nearly whispered, "I've never done this before. I don't know if I know how to … relationship."

His confession made her wonder, not for the last time, about his human life. She felt a little badly for having provoked this uncharacteristic response so she kissed him, holding his gaze for a moment, and assured him, "You're doing fine." Then she giggled. "At relationshiping."

He laughed quietly and shook his head, mostly at himself, still blushing faintly.

She turned to Aife. "We should probably quit harassing poor Ben." She paused, "He said he already told you why I wanted to meet. I know it's weird. Is it really okay?"

His discomfort momentarily forgotten, he glanced anxiously at Aife. He hadn't worried about Davi, but was concerned about Mal and the effect the magic around her might have. Aife wasn't nearly as powerful as he and didn't have a best friend capable of performing the kind of dangerous magic that made Mal's wards tolerable. The night he'd confessed everything, including the shielding spell, Aife had cuffed him in the back of the head and chewed him out for a good ten minutes about risking himself like that for a roll in the hay. They hadn't spoken for days and their relationship had remained strained until a couple of weeks after Christmas. She had called him out of nowhere, apologized for minimizing his feelings for Mal, telling him that she'd learned more about that spell and anyone who'd suffer it willingly must be either madly in love or completely off their rocker. He laughed and said it probably had to be a bit of both. He hadn't really wanted to ask her to come over and do this. He'd risked a lot to spare her suffering in his life; the idea of purposely letting someone inflict it on her, even if they didn't know they were doing it, made him feel a little sick. He'd apologized about a hundred times on the phone this week, saying he felt bad but Mal needed the reassurance. Aife had told him dismissively it was fine, that she wasn't worried about Mal's magic; she had a high tolerance for that sort of thing. She wasn't quite ready to tell him why. She thought when he learned her reasoning she might see a new level of frustratingly protective come out.

Aife nodded. "Of course, sweetie. Anything you need."

Mal stood, put her hand on Ben's shoulder and offered a smile, then went and stood in front of Aife. Her presence was almost soothing, and her natural attraction was incredibly flattering, given what a lovely young woman she was herself. Without speaking, Mal put her hands gently on either side of Aife's face and began peering into her eyes. Aife drew in her breath sharply and Ben flinched in sympathy. The look on Aife's face didn't say Mal hurt her though. He felt like a bit of a wimp for how her magic had knocked him for a loop, but then he reasoned that Mal hadn't been intentionally using her powers when she had hurt him and her focus on learning what she needed to know might be dampening her wards or something. He might have given it more thought, but he was distracted by the scene in front of him. Aife seemed so peaceful; it gave Ben the most peculiar feeling. Had he looked the same way when Mal used her extraordinary power on him? Tears began slipping down Aife's cheeks. When Ben looked into Mal's eyes like this not long ago, all he had seen was a stormy sea of blue-grey but now he saw all of her. Mal looked so strange, inhumanly still, seeming not even to breathe; and her face ... God, it made him want to cry. There was such compassion there, such love. *How could anyone look at this woman and not love her beyond reason?*

She released Aife after a few moments, handed her a tissue, and sat back down next to Ben wearing a strange thoughtful smile. Aife composed herself, waiting for Mal's reaction. Mal nodded reassuringly. "You're like Ben. No scary Hell stuff. I'm so glad you're with us."

Aife managed to smile back. She didn't know what to make of Mal's pronouncement, only that if it were true she had Ben to thank for rescuing her before Hell could ruin who she was. Ben wanted to ask after her, but not in front of Mal. The idea of Mal knowing the pain her wards caused or about the awful magic that allowed him to be near her bothered him. She was already under so much pressure. He was afraid it would upset her and add to it. When Ben told Ari that's why he wanted it kept quiet for now, he'd agreed, saying Ben was probably right. One shock at a time.

When Chris returned with the food they were all grateful for the diversion. Mal was not lying about her love of eggrolls, putting away three on her own, and easily keeping pace with Ben on everything else. She laughed at everyone's expressions, expertly using chopsticks to grab another dumpling and saying now they knew why she was a runner; if she didn't work out, her love of food would turn her into a marshmallow. When Aife felt she could reasonably excuse herself, Ben walked her out to her car to gain a moment alone.

"Are you alright?"

Aife gave a regal wave of her hand that Ben interpreted as being told molehills were not, in fact, mountains. "Of course, other than being quite irritated with you for hiding that delicious old Roman away from me all this time. I'd have been more helpful sooner if I'd known there was a door prize."

Ben shook his head. She was almost as gifted as he was at steering conversations, garnering agreement, and distracting people from their own points. "You're really okay? Mal's magic stuff ..."

Aife cut him off, "I'm fine, Ben. Honestly." She almost told him then, but instead decided to leave well enough alone and just gave him an affectionate, if slightly exasperated smile. "You just tell that roommate of yours I'm off on Tuesdays, won't you?"

Ben manufactured a dirty look, then smirked and nodded. She stood on tiptoe, kissed him on the cheek, got in her car, and left. Ben found he had no idea what had happened tonight, but realized since everyone seemed alright, and he'd survived feeling more awkward and embarrassed than he could credit, he was just as happy to be in the dark.

Chapter 41

"The moment you have in your heart this extraordinary thing called love and feel the depth, the delight, the ecstasy of it, you will discover that for you the world is transformed." ~ Jiddu Krishnamurti

The rest of the winter was something of a whirlwind. Several months flew by that none of them could ever properly remember in detail. For Ben and Mal it could have just as easily been a few weeks as the plodding bitter cold surrendered to a misty and magical spring. Some of it was just how intoxicated they were with each other's company, but perhaps it was more easily explained by how busy and chaotic their lives were. With everyone working together to discover the best approach to what was coming, what defensive magic to use, what Mal might need to learn, and keep up with the mundane aspects of daily living, time seemed distorted, like there was never enough of it. Davi and Metatron popped in frequently to let them know what they were finding, or at least trying to find. Everyone was totally focused on discovering what to do, where to go. Between that, working with her to develop her abilities, teaching her magic, and maintaining his status as a student athlete, Mal didn't know how Ben could do it. Some of it was probably his power as a demon, but most of it was just how Ben felt about her. She thought he might walk a hundred miles barefoot over broken glass if he believed it would help. She worried over the way he looked in quiet moments; such a strange expression, so bittersweet and lonely. She couldn't explain it. But it made her resent anything that kept them apart.

Ari was in and out of her life right now, too, often disappearing to chase down some lead or work on some complicated spell that required isolation. Even though she and Petra had reconciled somewhat and were acting as tag-team besties for Teddy, Mal never stayed anywhere but Chris's when her dad wasn't around. She'd wondered if her dad or Chris would make some weird parental-type objection to the amount of time she and Ben spent in bed, but neither of them treated her as if she were anything other than an equal, for which she was extremely grateful. She appreciated the opportunities to be close to Ben or to curl up with his pillow if he was away. His bed was small, but neither of them minded. If they were together, they usually chose to be touching anyway. She preferred being the big spoon, her back pressed against the wall and her front to Ben, to the emptiness when he was gone, but it always smelled like him, like sunshine and fresh air, the clean scent of his shampoo, so she slept better regardless. Ben often stayed at her house, feeling downright spoiled by her big double bed and her dad's expensive choice of dryer sheets. She had a hard time sleeping if Ben wasn't there, so she and her dad often just zonked out in the living room with the TV on.

She would have thought everything she was discovering about herself would be the most taxing part of her life, but it turned out that it was prom season in an unanticipated and totally teenaged way. Prom had been something she'd let herself want when they moved here and now it was ruined. No one who graduated was allowed to attend, not even the Saint Thomas's kids, half of whom had gone to St. Auggie's, and many of whom were dating its juniors and seniors. Mal was livid. Some freshmen were her age! She'd grumbled for hours and nothing anyone said talked her down.

She'd more or less decided not to go. When Ben showed up with Chris that evening for dinner he changed her mind. She wanted to be indignant on his behalf, but he tried to make her feel better by joking about it. He would have been more than happy to take her, but if the rules said he couldn't, he was probably dodging a bullet. Didn't she know it was going to be some crappy buffet table and sub-par speakers, or worse a shitty band, kids sneaking around with peach schnapps in pocket flasks, puking behind the bleachers, and sucking helium out of balloons?

At first Mal was a little annoyed even though he was being pretty funny. "You jerk. I just wanted to get all dressed up together, and dance with you, and kiss you, and be stupid and romantic like normal people. I need some normal, okay?"

He'd gotten up from the table, pulling her along, and spun her around the kitchen a few times in a skillful, although silent, waltz. "Anytime, Mal Sinclair. If you say the word, I promise I'll be there, and I'll be as normal as possible."

"The word," she said emphatically, and he laughed.

Once she was a little less upset, Ben suggested she take Teddy. The poor kid had hardly left his house since February for anything other than school or the endless stream of parentally-mandated doctor's appointments and therapy sessions, and if he'd been quiet before, he was practically mute now with anyone other than Mal or sometimes Ben. Teddy still considered Petra a friend, but she acted so guilt-ridden when they were together it made him uncomfortable. At first Mal resisted the idea, but she'd eventually seen the sense in it. She could help Teddy have a good time, she'd still get a senior prom, and Ben promised to meet her afterward to say good-night, maybe stay over, if she wanted.

She decided if she was going, she was going to get the full experience. So the following weekend she dragged Petra, Ben, and a reluctant Teddy, out to help her choose a gown. She'd never bought a real formal in her life, and was kind of a thrift shop junkie who favored comfort over style. Petra was making a half-assed effort at finding a new dress, but her parents dragged her to so many fancy functions, her closet was already brimming with taffeta and sequins. At one point when Petra was in the dressing room helping Mal with about a million satin-covered buttons on a dress Ben despised on sight, he saw Teddy sneaking furtive glances in his direction. Ben concentrated for a minute, pretending to look at the book he had opened on his tablet. Poor kid, he'd better let him off the hook. About everything.

"I'm glad you're going with Mal to the prom," he offered. He knew Teddy nursed a small silent crush on Mal, so this would probably be the highlight of his young life. Ben smiled. "She was so disappointed when I couldn't go. Now she's getting to go with one of her best friends and she's cheered right up." Teddy smiled shyly back at him.

"Thanks, Ben. I'm glad you don't mind. It's weird to go with a girl who has a boyfriend I guess … I didn't want to go at all. Some of the kids who were there that night … either they're scared of me or they give me a lot of shit about it. I don't even remember much." He became busy studying the backs of his hands.

"That's really unfair." Teddy ventured a hesitant glance and Ben quickly went on, his face and voice reassuring. "You didn't do anything wrong, Ted. Most people don't think Ouija boards are a big deal. How were you supposed to know?"

Teddy's eyes narrowed with the memory of pain and his freckles stood out a little more brightly than they had a moment before. "It was awful. It hurt a lot." He stopped, his eyes distant. "It felt like I was being crushed, or maybe torn apart, but I could feel myself saying awful things, there were terrible images in my mind … and … I saw the …"

"Don't think about it anymore. Dwelling on it's bad. It could've happened to anybody." Thinking about it was dangerous, could keep the door open, and Ben wanted him to stop. "You just got unlucky. Fortunately for you someone who doesn't know how to back down was there, too."

"How come *you* left?"

Ben decided his honest answer was exactly what Teddy needed to hear. "Because I was scared shitless, dude."

Based on Teddy's skeptical expression, Ben thought it was obvious the kid hadn't gotten a good look at him before he'd bailed. If he could've taken Teddy back in time and shown him Big Ben shaking like a puppy in a lightning storm he would have.

"You? How come?"

Ben took a moment, deciding how to respond, since the whole truth was out of the question. "Well, you know I study a lot of different stuff … There's all kinds of cases like what happened to you, so I knew Ouija boards could be bad news. I didn't want it to be my bad news, you know? Plus I just had a bad feeling about it. I trust those."

Teddy sat processing the idea that Ben had been scared, too, that it was nothing he had done wrong, that there were good people who still wanted to be his friends. He sat up a little straighter. "Thanks, Ben. Seriously."

"Anytime, Ted."

Mal and Petra came out of the dressing room and Petra was in raptures over the fluffy atrocity she'd convinced Mal to try on. It was awfully frilly given Mal's usual tastes, which generally ran to sweaters, leggings, and Chucks. It made her look like a different person. Ben just said, "That's a nice one," in as neutral a fashion as he could. After all, it wasn't his night, and if he was honest, Mal looked lovely no matter what she was wearing. Besides anything was an improvement over the beautiful cream-colored satin she'd tried on first. It had sent Ben's brain into surprising and utterly forbidden contemplations involving organ music and flowers. It made him feel almost lightheaded. She'd seen the look on his face and given him a small knowing smile, saying she thought it made her look pale so she'd rather find something with some color.

Teddy had taken one look at this new dress and given what Ben thought to be a shockingly honest and helpful answer. "Jeez, Mal, you look like a big pink cupcake."

Mal growled at him playfully, knowing he was right. She waved off Petra's help and headed back for one more try, grumbling good-naturedly. Petra sat down in the little half-circle of chairs to wait, casting frequent remorseful glances at Teddy, who after a few minutes, rolled his eyes, got up, and said he was going to get a soda. Ben thought this was a fine opportunity to get Petra sorted out. He'd wanted to talk to her about things for a long time. It seemed like here and now was as good a place and time as any.

"How've you been, Petra?"

"Hmm? Fine, thanks," she said distractedly, pretending to look at her phone. Ben's focus was already sharpened, so he got right to it.

"I'm glad you and Mal have gotten over whatever was between you." He let that float for a moment.

Petra snapped, "You know what happened at that party. Don't pretend she didn't tell you."

"Of course she did. You want to talk about it?"

She glanced in the direction Teddy had gone, dismayed. "It was stupid. Magic is stupid. I'm stupid."

"Only one of the things is true." He grinned at her. "Any guesses?"

"Mal's right. You make it sound like nothing is a big deal. But this *is*. I was an idiot."

"Well, playing with magic you don't understand *is* dumb. You could've gotten somebody killed. Like that little ginge you keep chasing off with your guilty looks."

"Oh thanks, rub it in! Poor Teddy!" He could see that she was already punishing herself more than anything he said ever could. Time to offer her a better way.

"Teddy's gonna be okay. No permanent harm done. Get him out of his own head as much as you can. He'll come around eventually." Ben's own uncertainty crept into his voice and Petra gave him a withering look over the rims of her little round glasses. "It would help if you stopped looking at him like you ran over his cat." He turned on the edge of his chair to face her. "Look, magic isn't stupid and neither are you. Magic is mind-bogglingly cool, and you, whether you know it or not, have real natural talent."

"Oh, how would you know?" She was dismissive.

"Because I take magic seriously. If you took it seriously, too, you could be a genuine help to someone." He was thinking of Mal, that he had no idea what the future held, and no matter what, she'd need all the help she could get.

"From the kind of thing I'd been reading, I wasn't doing anything wrong."

"Yeah, well you're reading shitty pop-culture garbage. If you don't want to walk away from your beliefs and your gifts, you need access to better information."

"What's wrong with my stuff?"

"Ever work a love spell?" He knew the answer, but it made his point exactly.

"Sure; couple times."

"Did you have permission from the subject?" He was at least a little proud of himself for not using the word '*victim*'.

"Well, no ... but I was just helping friends and the spell was in a book I bought at the mall, so it was no big deal!" Somewhere, deep down, this natural witch knew better than her haphazard actions implied.

"That's black magic." She opened her mouth to protest, but he pressed on. "Controlling someone against their will, even a little, is black magic. Maybe not raise-the-dead evil but it's a damned slippery slope. Kind of *'come to the dark side we have cookies'*." She smiled slightly at Ben having picked up Mal's habit for constantly dropping geeky pop-culture references. "Not too many people today know enough to practice magic safely and effectively, or have access to decent books on the subject. What you need is a mentor to help keep you on track."

"A mentor for learning real magic? I wouldn't know where to start."

Smirking, Ben leaned toward her, extending his hand, "Hi, I'm Ben, do we know each other?" She shook it, amused. When they'd met she'd been somewhat intimidated by how good looking he was but, although she sensed a serious streak and it seemed like he worried a lot, when he was relaxed and just being himself, he was about as intimidating as a bunny rabbit.

"You know magic?"

"Sure do."

"And you'd teach me?"

"I'm teaching Mal, a little. I'd work with you, too."

"That'd be cool. Maybe we could work together, the three of us."

"Three's a good number for a lot of things in magic, and even if it's not the number you're aiming for, it never hurts to have some extra players on the bench."

Ben was thinking of a complex spell for uniting energies he'd recently found and it required all the cardinal points. Chris and Aife were willing to help, but they needed another fourth because Mal's aura sometimes overpowered the others and broke the circle. He had some regrets about introducing Aife to Chris. Too many areas of Ben's life were overlapping.

Teddy returned from his trip to the soda machine and they heard him breathe, "Well, da-amn."

Ben and Petra glanced up and Mal was standing there looking like a wood nymph in a long slinky crushed velvet dress. It was a rich mossy green that was absolutely her color. It was off one arm and shoulder completely and the other sleeve had fabric fashioned into pointed leaves tight along the arm and then draping into an uneven leaf-shaped cuff. The leaves were part of the dress all the way down to the hem and wrapped around at strategic points to highlight the wearer's shape, in Mal's case delightfully shapely. It hugged her body all the way to the floor and had a daring slit up one side, trimmed with more leaves. It was definitely worth the two-syllable damn. Ben didn't realize the expression on his face until Petra reached over and used two of her fingers to close his mouth. Mal giggled at the look on his face and Teddy and Petra quickly joined in.

Ben got to his feet and walked with Mal over to the mirror so she could see how gorgeous she was and hopefully excuse his awed expression. The two of them were so obviously happy, their smiles so completely spontaneous and unreserved, she wished she had a picture of it. Ben never looked that contented and relaxed, even in bed. Everyone agreed that was the dress. Teddy, seeming more himself than he had in months, joked that Ben was a fool to let him out on the town with such a beautiful woman. He might have to convince her to elope. Ben was pleased he'd gone with them. Reality was barreling down on them like a freight train. Mal deserved something special before it hit. All he wanted was for her to have a nice time.

When the night finally rolled around, she did have a nice time. She managed to be caught up enough in the silly magic of prom night that she wasn't even mad that Ben couldn't be there anymore. Well, not too mad, anyway. She had glared at the Headmaster and given him a substantial piece of her mind when they'd gotten there though. He'd sputtered as his eyes had gotten rather large, and he'd actually mumbled an apology about policy affecting her evening. The whole exchange reduced Teddy to near hysterical laughter and he'd sneakily taken a picture of the Head's face and immediately posted it online. After that, Mal was able to just enjoy herself. The kitschy lights, the little flameless candles on all the tables, the disco ball and glittering dancefloor were charming in their own way. Ben had been right about a lot of things; the schnapps, the balloons, the terrible cover band. But the pictures, the singing loudly on the dancefloor, the random hugging and kissing of people she might never see again in another month, plastered an elated smile on Mal's face she thought might be there for days.

At one point she lost her impossibly high heels, little gold ones that went with the pendant Ben had given her. She never took that pendant off. Her heels, on the other hand, were four inches high and narrow. They made her absolutely tower over Teddy and they pinched uncomfortably. They were fine for going out to dinner but for dancing bare feet were better. Maybe Ben and her dad were onto something with their refusal to wear shoes anywhere they didn't have to. Teddy found them under someone else's table where he was scrambling for his boutonniere for about the tenth time. He took them out to Mal's car for her and left his flower there, too, fed up with trying to keep track of it. Mal's own flowers were attached to pins Petra had spent all afternoon working into her hair piled high on her head with artful tendrils pulled out at strategic points until, like magic, she appeared to be growing little pieces of vine and tiny pink tea roses out of her curls.

She and Teddy hardly sat out a dance, and when they did Petra joined them with her flavor of the month tagging along. Once when she and Mal were alone, Petra had tried to apologize for what had happened at her birthday, but Mal had just hugged her and told her not to worry about it. They were going to be classmates at Ben Brody's School of Witchcraft and Don't Mess Up or I'll Make You Run Laps, so everything was fine. Petra laughed, relieved things seemed truly normal between them again.

When Mal had finally dropped Teddy off it was well after midnight and her feet were killing her. She drove home barefoot, with the heat on and the window cracked, laughing at herself a little for all the times she'd picked on her dad for doing the same thing. He and Ben had been working on some new spell this evening. She knew how tiring magic was for pretty much anyone other than her, so she'd told Ben she'd be home by eleven or eleven thirty and she wouldn't be mad if he just crashed if she was late. It was after one so she figured he was probably asleep, hopefully upstairs so they could at least wake up together. He had a habit of falling asleep on the couch if she wasn't with him, but she thought she could wake him up; he never seemed to sleep all that well. The idea of being able to crawl into bed next to him made her think that there couldn't possibly be a more perfect ending to the evening. Then she turned into their parking area and caught her breath. The apple trees flanking their porch were strung with twinkling lights, and in their soft glow Ben leaned against the porch railing wearing a tux jacket, starched white shirt and bowtie, matched with a beautiful tartan kilt with red, black, and gold, high socks, shiny shoes, and some other accessories that she couldn't name. He stepped toward her, devastatingly handsome in her headlights. She parked and got out of the car. The air was cool and pleasant, the sky sparkling and clear. Music played softly from the steps.

As she stood, Ben made a formal bow. "May I have this dance?"

"What are you doing?"

"You said '*the word*'. I always keep my promises, Mal."

She took his hand. He pulled her close, smiling at the delight dancing in her eyes. "How did you do all this? I thought you were doing magic with Dad."

"What? Didn't I?" His pretended offense made her laugh. "Your dad helped. We've been conspiring for weeks. Neither one of us like seeing you not getting what you want. Regardless of anybody's rules."

"So that's why you two have clammed up every time I've walked into the kitchen since Easter!"

"Well, yeah … What do you think?" he asked tentatively.

"I've never danced with a boy in a skirt as nice as mine before."

"Hey, this is how my people dress up. Don't you like it?"

She giggled into his chest. "You definitely have the legs for it. I *strongly* approve." He laughed softly. "Are those your family's colors?"

"I ... no ... well, I suppose they are. This pattern belongs to the Brodies. They're my family now, thanks to Aife and her paperwork. Makes me a highlander, which I guess is close enough for me. I like their whisky anyway." He looked almost shy. "Seriously though, do you like it?"

Mal studied him, eyes moving up and down. "I do. A lot. Although, I could do with the accent, too."

He laughed again and drew in a breath like he was about to speak.

She put her fingers to his lips, "Wait. I'm just teasing. I like everything about you, just as you are."

Mal went back to the car and got her phone so she could get a picture of them together, the one she'd wanted all along. She got a nice one on her first try but took a whole string of them anyway then put her phone down on their picnic table while Ben turned up the music. It was an old song, one Mal recognized from a box of CDs her dad couldn't bring himself to throw away. It was sad, and lovely, and just about as romantic as you could want. She put her arms around Ben's neck, savoring what he'd given her, the two of them together, this song about the book of love, a life shared, of ecstasy and pain. Her eyes sparkled and he gazed back at her, his love radiating like heat. She thought she had never seen someone look so happy and sad all at once. Maybe that's how you knew you loved someone; it was the good as well as the bad, and the fact that you went through it together was what made it mean anything. He kissed her softly and mouthed *Love you* and she leaned against his shoulder and whispered it back, wanting this to last forever.

For that perfect moment they were just a couple of kids in love, holding each other under the stars, and neither Heaven nor Hell existed.

Chapter 42

"In a heart, there are windows and doors;
you can let the light in, you can feel the wind blow."
~ Warren Zevon

"Hello, Ben." Aife answered her phone sounding exhausted and like she needed another task about as much as a hole in the head.

"Um, actually it's Chris." His voice sounded nervous and tentative even to him. He couldn't believe he was doing this. If Ben came out of his post-run shower while they were on the phone he was expecting to be glared at all day. Honestly, he was trying to forget that he knew Ben and Aife had a past and had decided to adopt Mal's attitude that it was just something demons did to pass the time. Of course, he'd also gathered from Ben that Aife was somehow technically his subordinate and he didn't want to get her in trouble. Since Ben typically waved off any mention of Hell these days, he probably shouldn't be worried. He'd never suffered from a case of nerves talking to a woman in his life. Until today.

"Well then, what are you doing calling from our Ben's phone?"

"He wouldn't give me your number. Told me I'd be getting in over my head." He laughed nervously.

"Isn't he a dear?" Aife spoke with the affection of someone who knows another's faults, and likes them because rather than in spite of them. "To what do I owe the pleasure of this clandestine phone call, Centurion?" Unlike Ben, Aife bore no grudge against Rome. She just liked having the upper hand.

Chris laughed nervously. "That was an awfully long time ago, and I never served on the Isles myself."

"Relax. I'm just having a go at you. But honestly, day I've got ahead of me, I shouldn't be spending time exchanging pleasantries with you."

Chris hurriedly apologized. He was almost relieved he had an excuse to back out before risking rejection. "I'm so sorry. I'll let you go."

Aife laughed. "Nonsense. I'm just complaining. It's the end of the month, you see. I don't know how much Ben has told you, but Hell is nothing more or less than the universe's biggest bureaucracy. So much paperwork!" She gave a resigned sigh.

Chris, given his profession, was sympathetic. It certainly explained the exhaustion in her voice. "You have my condolences. Since I teach at a private school it's not quite as bad for me, but even there the job comes with its own unnecessary deforestation."

"While your sympathetic ear is appreciated, I shouldn't take too much advantage of it, or there'll be Hell to pay." She chuckled ruefully over her small joke. "What can I do for you?"

He tried unsuccessfully to sound casual. "Nothing earthshaking. Actually, it's fairly mundane. I was wondering if I could take you to dinner some evening."

"You fancy a date with me, do you?" He could hear the warm smile in her question, loved the soft lilting quality of her speech. His face heated up just talking with her on the phone.

"Well, yes ... I mean no ... um, well ..."

Aife thought she could hear him blushing and smiled warmly. The evening they'd met she'd flirted with him, assuming his long life made him more than a match for her, but he'd flushed crimson up to the roots of his dark hair. Her demon nature didn't seem to bother him at all and he was absolutely her type. She'd made that rather clear. And the prospect of a man who wouldn't just pass out of her life as he aged was quite appealing. Besides, he was tall, fit, and most importantly smart. She could leave off either the height or the build, or both for a man who was smart, good to talk with, but not the other way around. There was Chris, the whole delightful package, and he was funny, too.

"Oh, so I'm not good enough to date you then?" she asked, pretended hurt in her voice.

Chris's laugh was tense, but appreciative. "Ben said you were quick. Warned me, more like." He cleared his throat. "I'm actually working on an article dealing with your general time period. I'm interested in your impressions of the Roman Empire as it pertains to its treatment of indigenous populations. We both know I can't ask Ben and keep my head." Aife laughed knowingly. "The fact that you are an intelligent and beautiful woman is to be counted as a rare perk of the job."

He'd recovered fast and his flimsy pretext for seeing her was nothing shy of adorable. She liked both. "I'm free tomorrow night, once all this cursed paperwork is finished. I believe I mentioned my strong preference for Italian." She pictured him blushing and smiled. "I like lasagna. Ever been to Bove's?"

"I have, and it's a date." She could hear his satisfaction, and a rather large measure of relief. "You see what I did there?"

Aife gave a musical little laugh. "I do, and I like it."

Chapter 43

"Perfection is not attainable, but if we chase perfection,
we can catch excellence."
~ Vince Lombardi

"Oh, quit your whining and try again," Ben dismissed Petra's complaining. "You had it for a second. You're just too easily distracted."

Petra thought that was rich coming from Ben, captain of Team ADHD, and her irritated expression said so. "I'm tired and I'm getting a headache. I should be studying for finals."

The petulant tone she was using gained no traction with Ben. This wouldn't be so hard for her if she'd done the training exercises he assigned last week. She claimed that she had, of course, but her struggles spoke more loudly than her half-hearted protests possibly could. It probably made him a terrible person, but he was enjoying pushing her like this. He lounged on the couch casually, using magic to light and snuff a candle on the coffee table, attempting, albeit a little smugly, to reinforce the lesson that practice was important to proficiency.

Hanging upside down in Ari's lumpy orange chair, enjoying watching Ben torment Petra, Teddy had to throw in his two cents. "Oh please, Harvard girl, you were early decision. Plus, your parents throw enough money around, it's not like it was a question. Finals," he snorted.

"Teddy, too mean," Mal commented absently without looking up from the textbook she was lying on the floor with.

Teddy shook his head. "Just mean enough. I didn't get into any of my first choices, 'cause I bombed this semester." He frowned and said sullenly, "Wonder why that happened."

"Teddy!" Mal looked up this time and her tone was as sharp as it ever got with him. "We agreed; no more blaming. Petra didn't know it was dangerous either."

"Ben did," he grumbled. Then he sighed and mumbled an apology.

Petra was so caught up in what she was trying to do that she'd only half heard them. She was going to get this spell right and wipe that smug smirk off Ben's face if it killed her.

Ben was distracted by Mal and Teddy almost arguing, even more so by the amusing scrunching and smoothing of Petra's face, and he accidently lit the candle with a little more force than he intended. It popped and sparked impressively.

"Show off." Petra scowled.

"It's not showing off when you're this good." He smiled crookedly.

Ari walked in from the kitchen, stepped over Mal and put a plate of sandwiches on the coffee table for them. He pointed at the candle and grinned at Ben. "That is definitely showing off, kid."

Ben crossed his eyes and stuck out his tongue, and then snuffed and lit the candle again with more precision. Ari went back into the kitchen, where he was planning on sitting down with his own book, laughing and shaking his head. Teddy sat up and grabbed a sandwich with each hand. Ben grinned. It was good to see him eating without someone pestering him to do it.

"Ben, how come you can tell when she loses it? It just looks like Petra sitting there making screwed up faces to me."

"You mean more screwed up than her usual?" Petra had about enough of Ben's teasing and tossed a pillow at him. It bounced off his head, messing up his already tousled hair, and sent Mal's cat scrambling toward the stairs.

"Sorry, Petes. That was mean," he apologized, laughing a little. "I don't know how to explain it, Ted. When she's holding it this protection spell is kind of like a tight golden web and it moves and shifts so nothing can get through it. But then she starts to lose focus, and it gets holes kind of punched in it by, whatever, interference. Then it falls apart like a wet tissue."

"Yeah, but how come you can *see* it?" Teddy was genuinely curious.

Ben was mulling over what to say carefully. Telling Mal's friends about real magic was one thing, but for safety's sake they'd decided not to reveal anything else. Not yet, anyway.

Before the silence could stretch out long enough for more questions to surface, Mal jumped in, "It's like any other talent. Some people can just do it and some people can if they practice. Ben practices a lot."

Petra was trying to pull the spell back together, chanting softly. Mal rolled onto her side, her book forgotten, looking up at Ben. She liked the expression he got when he was working some little spell or power of his. It was a look that said he was amused, confused, and it was peppered with what passed for concentration on Ben. He caught her looking and winked.

"That big book gonna study itself?" His teasing tone and wide smile told her this study session wouldn't last much longer and then she could take everyone home. Little did Ben know that Chris was going out to dinner with Aife again and they'd have his place to themselves for a while this evening. The idea of surprising him with unexpected privacy fueled her secretive grin, not to mention her interest in teasing him a bit. He looked pretty mellow today and she wanted him to stay that way.

"Please. I already passed AP Bio. This Anatomy and Physiology book is just for fun. Besides, I've been accepted into my top three, and then some. I've got my pick of schools." She smirked.

"I'm sure it's a terribly difficult decision for you."

"Yeah, really tough. I mean, Boston College has access to an unparalleled music scene and there's certainly something to be said for what BC offers academically ... Although I think the Jesuits take scholarly pursuits a little too seriously for my taste."

He grinned. "So Boston's out?

"It would appear so." She paused and gave him a long slow blink that made him feel warm all over. "Then there's NYU. It has New York, which means everything plus pizza. I could go there and have Famous Original Ray's like every day."

"What about Original Famous Ray's? Won't he get jealous?"

"You're right. I can't do NYU. I could never keep the pizza men happy."

Ben shook his head, smiling. She was stringing him. And he liked it. *Damn.*

"And then good ole St. Tommy's has ..."

"Me?" He threw her his most winsome smile.

"I was going to say a great relationship with the medical center, but you do make an excellent point."

Ben was distracted from their playful flirting by Petra, who had finally nailed the protection field. He held up his hand to let the others know to be quiet. He barely whispered, "Petes?"

Eyes closed, lips moving, she responded with a slow careful nod of her head.

"You've really got it, really well. But I want to try something to see if it holds up. It's a little risky. Is that okay?"

Without breaking her concentration, Petra acknowledged him by giving a thumbs-up. Ben rubbed his palms together and began to focus, building a charge. Teddy's eyes grew round and even Mal was enthralled. A little ball of blue lightning grew from a spark to over an inch in diameter, suspended between his hands. "Petra, do you feel the strength of what you've built?" She dipped her chin slightly. "Do you feel its flexibility?" Her soft chanting became slightly more audible as she nodded again, and Ben encouraged her, "Feel it totally. You're doing great."

Without any warning Ben let go of the tiny lighting ball. Mal could see the field when the lightning struck it, for just a second, then the energy bounced back and hit Ben's hand before dissipating into the air. "Ow! Sonofabitch! That hurts!" He snapped his stinging hand vigorously, as though it would help, laughing in spite of it. "Way to go, Petes! That was fan-freakin-tastic!"

Petra let the field collapse, looking incredibly pleased, though a little tired. She smirked at Ben, "Your hand okay, Coach?"

Mal immediately got up and knelt in front of Ben and reached for his hand. There was a nasty burn across his already-scarred palm. She held him gently by the wrist, looking at the burn carefully. She moved to touch it and he flinched involuntarily, but the moment she made contact the blistering was erased. She kissed his palm and then let him go and sat on the floor between his feet and he began absently rubbing her shoulders in gratitude. He thought that was awfully nice of her. He'd kind of been asking for it.

"I'm fine." He held up his hand for a second so Petra could see it was unmarked. "You did an incredible job. I feel like I need to give you shit more often. We might just turn you into a proper witch." His voice was proud now rather than teasing.

"So, no running laps today?"

"Not even one. Gold star."

"Good, I'm beat. Besides, you running people are crazy. Twenty-six miles for fun. Someone should examine your head, Brody."

Ben grinned. He had been training for his second local marathon and thought maybe it was becoming something of a tradition. Mal wasn't interested in that kind of distance, but she'd been running with him for some parts of his training, and promised to be as inspiring as possible on the sidelines this weekend, cheering like a lunatic. He'd told her the other night he'd find it more inspiring if she could maybe jump up and down a lot. Because she thought he'd been entirely too introspective all evening, she had responded by unhooking her bra under her t-shirt, pulling it out through her sleeve, throwing it at him, and asking wryly, "Would that help, too?" When he'd responded with an amused shrug, she climbed onto his lap and paralyzed him for a full five minutes by tickling him into a half-assed breathless apology for expressing such a transparent preference for a single part of her body. She'd grinned down into his red face when he'd finally managed to catch hold of her wrists and told him he could try fighting back. Wasn't he even curious whether or not she might be ticklish, too? He'd told her there was no way he was going to invite retaliation like that; he was way too easy a target. She'd given him a provocative wink and said he'd have to find another way to pin her down then. He'd responded by scooping her up off the couch, and saying with an amused shake of his head, that all she'd had to do was ask. As she'd hoped, he'd stopped looking so damned distant and serious.

The rest of them finished their sandwiches in companionable silence while Petra dozed, leaning against the couch, exhausted from the effort of maintaining the spell. Soon, impatient to have Ben to herself, Mal woke Petra and announced, "Okay, time for everybody to go home. I need Ben to help me study."

Her friends' collective eye roll told them that '*study*' was no longer a good euphemism.

Chapter 44

"There is nothing more deceptive than an obvious fact."
~ Sir Arthur Conan Doyle

Michael sat at the head of the table, looking at Uriel and Raphael, knowing they were depending on him to have a plan, at a loss as to how to proceed. Today he sorely missed the counsel of his other siblings. Michael took a deep breath, about to speak, and then stopped again, uncertain. He had to say something. "Metatron knows something and he's doing his best to keep it from us."

Uriel, her voice husky and purring, entered the discussion "I agree, but pursuing Metatron is a dead end. Even casting rank aside, The Voice is first amongst us."

Michael scowled. He knew what Uriel said was true, of course. Metatron was the first. He was the eldest and the wisest. These facts, even separated from his status as the Chosen Voice, meant Metatron alone could set aside Michael's commands and wishes. It was particularly vexing since Metatron had always been quick to point out when he thought his little brother was being rash and selfish.

Sensing Michael's darkening mood, Raphael, hoping to be reassuring, offered, "Brother, set aside such thoughts. Even if Metatron is hiding something from us, we know he is the last angel in all Creation who would be in league with Lucifer. Even if he is not assisting in our cause, he is not assisting in the Adversary's efforts either." Michael appreciated Raphael's confidence that their situation was salvageable, and part of him wished he thought he could tell his brother the whole story. He continued, "Michael, we are not without resources. We are the obvious choice. We will find the girl and I am sure she will see the wisdom of your arguments. Enoch has said ..." Raphael's words were cut short as Gabriel entered the room, a young herald in tow.

"Oh don't get up." She waved at the table casually. "I didn't mean to intrude." Her blazing violet eyes narrowed slightly. "Well, perhaps I did a bit. I wasn't aware we were holding a council today." Her implication that there was something untoward about their gathering was hardly subtle.

Michael could only sigh. This was all becoming so exhausting, not at all what he'd intended. Heaven was becoming so factional, so fractious, and he was to blame. How did one repair this? How did God manage it?

"No council, Gabriel. Just talking amongst ourselves," Uriel offered, hoping to placate her sister.

"Mmm." Gabriel's face was appropriately skeptical. "That's good. I'd hate to miss anything important all the archangels should be privy to." She pointedly faced Michael who could not hold her gaze. "Since I'm not interrupting, I'll just get down to business. I have news."

The reaction was immediate and satisfying. Michael, usually so tightly controlled, was half on his feet before the words were out of her mouth, "Of the girl?"

"Perhaps," she hedged. "We have word about some of Hell's forces gathering, focusing on a small area of Earth."

"Where?" The urgency in his question belied the face he was presenting to the rest of the Host outside of this room.

"Vermont. Which is funny when you think about it; the name almost literally means emerald hill," Gabriel said, almost lightly, quashing her irritation with her brother's maneuvering, her resentment at this situation.

Michael, who failed to see the humor in Gabriel's observation, rose and paced the hall. "They must have some type of lead. Lahash again perhaps."

Gabriel opened her hands, acknowledging the possibility. "I'm sure I don't know, but thought you might find it encouraging. It bears watching, certainly."

Raphael stood, "I could go now. See what I can discover."

Michael raised his hand, "Not yet, but all of you watch. If the Fallen flush her out we must be prepared to move. Lucifer cannot be the one to reach her. He will leave her no real choice in the matter at all." Michael's fist slammed down on the table in complete frustration. "I hate being in this position, only reacting, never taking independent action! She's so well hidden. Not a hint other than to almost lose her in almost nineteen years! We must be the ones to find her!"

Everyone was quiet in the face of Michael's anger and frustration until the young herald cleared her throat. Michael, with his eyes flashing, snapped "What?"

"Begging your pardon, but what of the Church? The Templars have been, well, if not answering to the Pope, at least awfully friendly for generations now. Their whole job is to guard the Line. Certainly they must know where the girl is."

Michael's face grew deeply red, as his jaw tightened.

The silence was deafening.

Chapter 45

"I, not events, have the power to make me happy or unhappy today."
~ Groucho Marx

Driving home to shower and change, Mal truly felt like her old self for the first time in ages. She had an imperturbable smile she just couldn't seem to shake. The weight of Creation had been dropped on her shoulders a few months ago and had made those random easy smiles all too rare, but today it felt like gravity had finally shifted back in her favor. She always felt good when she was with Ben, but when they were apart she had become almost used to thoughts of what might be in front of her dominating her attention, and she was catching his bad habit of getting broody about it. She'd desperately wanted to find something that allowed her to think more positively about all aspects of her future. Mal had enjoyed volunteering at the hospital enough that she'd taken a night class and was now a licensed nursing assistant, but in spite of satisfying paid work several nights a week that she knew was helping her develop important professional skills, she had no interest in giving up her other volunteer position completely. Working in the kitchen of the homeless shelter, feeding hungry people, going out to the tables and talking with kids, always made her feel inexplicably light and happy. Even though it had been a school service project that had long ago been completed, Mal still went back once a week eager to help. The thought that maybe it ran in the family actually bolstered her spirits today.

Most important to this feeling of lightness was probably that she had finally graduated, this past Wednesday, with honors, thank you very much. The best part was, with a word in the right ear, Chris had managed to get her a full ride at St. Thomas's and she had already secured a spot on the cross-country team. She'd always known that was what she wanted, but the scholarship made everything easier. She knew pre-med wouldn't be a walk in the park but she found the human body fascinating and was a confirmed science nerd from way back. She breezed through the nursing assistant's course effortlessly, so she was really looking forward to a challenge. Her growing healing abilities made her earlier decision to enter medicine seem almost destined. Ari had signaled his approval by making her graduation present a particularly nice Littman stethoscope and several sets of scrubs. Besides, going to her mom's old school felt right, and the fact that she and Ben would see each other every day, even run for the same team, was the icing on the cake. She had casually mentioned the possibility of getting an apartment together and he seemed more than agreeable. Everything was coming up Mal.

She was excited for tonight, too. Her friends and their families had been organizing a cookout on the waterfront for weeks to celebrate everyone's accomplishments. Mal was planning on meeting them at Battery Park after she got herself cleaned up from work. She had suggested the location, mostly because it was Ben's favorite spot, but it was also conveniently close to Petra's for bathroom use and keeping extra food and ice, and the atmosphere made it seem like a good place for some good-byes. Everyone wanted this last responsibility-free night together before they went their separate ways.

Teddy had been right of course, Petra was Harvard bound, although for what she had no idea yet. Her parents were Harvard alums, and since they were paying, she wasn't going to complain, although she'd wanted to stay here and go to UVM like her brother. But Alex's reasoning had been a starting position on the hockey team, and she had nothing so grand to argue for a change in the family plan. She would have been happier if Mal was going to Boston, too, but Mal finally had a real home, and Petra thought she'd have to be dragged kicking and screaming to ever leave it.

Teddy couldn't quite face the idea of college yet and had decided to take a gap year. He was leaving after his birthday to work on some conservation projects in Central America. Chris had used his connections to find a placement he thought would be a good fit, had even arranged housing with a family he knew from his time there that he was sure would look out for the young man until he was ready to be on his own. Teddy was expecting his parents to be upset, but they were so pleased that he seemed to be more himself they were thrilled. They'd run the kid through every medical and psychological test under the sun, and the best explanation they had for his strange '*illness*' and the difficulties that followed was perhaps an isolated seizure from which there seemed to be no lasting damage.

Emily was the shining star of their group. She had excelled in every advanced placement class she tried throughout high school and had withdrawn socially somewhat after the events of Petra's party. Always an excellent student, all the extra time studying had resulted in her managing valedictorian by a wide margin. After this weekend she was heading to England to spend the summer with relatives before she began her studies at Oxford.

Mal turned into their long driveway, singing softly. Ben had absolutely cheated and given her another graduation gift even after the pendant he'd made her over the winter. Her new iPod, fully loaded with music she loved, and Bluetooth speakers were a nice addition to her drives back and forth to town, and it made her laugh a little when she thought of her dad referring to it as their generation's version of a mix tape. As she turned the last bend, The Magnetic Fields came on and she felt a familiar overwhelming floaty happiness when she thought of how Ben had surprised her after the prom. She turned over softly iridescent memories of swaying in his arms, of falling into bed exhausted, waking up the next morning, her head resting on his chest, and seeing him looking at her, of wondering how long he'd been watching her sleep with that sweet smile playing on his lips. He kissed her forehead then, and sighed. When she'd asked him what he was thinking, he'd said, "I don't know, Mal. Sometimes I feel like my whole life, just thousands of years, has been leading up to this. That I've always been meant for you." It had made her feel strange, but incredibly happy. She didn't think too deeply about it, but felt it was meant, too.

Her blissful feelings evaporated when she pulled into their parking area. Several strange cars were parked haphazardly all over the grass. There were a number of armed men in odd-looking uniforms patrolling around her house. Just what was going on here? She felt a brief moment of panic, but after a few careful breaths, was back in control. She was grateful for the years of martial arts classes her dad had insisted on as well as what Ben had been teaching her; it all made maintaining at least an outward appearance of composure much easier. One of the men, seeing that she was making no move to get out of her car, approached her slowly, showing her his open hands. She hesitated for a moment, and then put down her window a few inches.

"Miss Sinclair." This man knew who she was by sight. "I am Father-Captain Francis of the Order of the Temple of Solomon." Mal's eyebrows drew together. The Knights. She should have known. What the hell did they want? "Your father and our Bishop-General are waiting for you in the house."

When she remained still, he indicated the house again.

Annoyed, she demanded more, "What's the deal?"

"We are a spiritual and military order, created to protect the …"

She rolled her eyes and got out, gratified to see she was taller than this man, and he had to look up at her to meet her eye. "Yeah, Knights Templar, blah blah. What are you doing here?"

"Miss, if you'll just go inside, everything will be made clear, I assure you."

"What if I say no, just get back in my car and leave?" Her voice carried the hard edge of a challenge.

The man tipped his head in what she could only interpret as a bow. "That is certainly your prerogative, Miss Sinclair."

"You're not going to try to force me?" Mal asked, unconvinced and wary.

He quickly held up his hands. "We wouldn't dream of it, Miss! We serve the Line."

She narrowed her eyes, trying to sense his thoughts and emotions. He was totally closed off. That made her more nervous than if she'd sensed some malicious intent. You couldn't fight what you couldn't see. Mal told herself that members of their order were probably just very magically disciplined. She nodded at him grudgingly. "Fine. But call me Mal. And knock off that weird bowing thing."

He gestured for her to follow him. Into her own house. Oh, that was irritating. She stopped for a moment and took another deep breath. The last time she'd let other people set her off, she'd accidentally exploded her dad's favorite lamp into about a million pieces. There was no reason to get worked up, no reason to blow all of the hard work she and Ben had been doing on diffusing her thoughts, as long as her dad was okay. Somewhat resentfully, she followed him. Inside she found more armed men stationed at various windows, and her father along with a kindly looking man of late middle age, seated at their kitchen table, talking over tea. The man rose, about to speak, as she entered. She spoke first.

"Dad, are you okay?" She scrutinized his face trying to discern even the slightest indication he was being coerced. He gave her a small, sad smile.

The Bishop General spoke, "Miss Sinclair, it is an honor."

Mal had no interest in formalities, only explanations. "What is all this?" She leaned against their stove and folded her arms waiting for his reply since she could get nothing from his mind either.

"I am Bishop-General Roy of what you might know as the Knights Templar."

"That's what Captain whoever said. But what's going on? I thought you people were suppressed by the Church now. If that's true, this is a stupidly bold move." She was daring him to explain himself.

He pulled out a chair for her as he spoke, "A popular story, certainly, but one we have perpetuated as a convenient cover. While we are an independent organization, our relationship with the Church is most beneficial." He indicated she should sit but Mal didn't move. "We went underground voluntarily after we discovered the Grail, which is to say your family. We have devoted ourselves for centuries to protecting the Legacy of Christ."

Mal was half listening as she scanned the room, and beyond, out the windows into the parking area. "How thoughtful," her voice was dry. It felt petty, but she couldn't resist a small dig. "Obviously, your consideration has meant a lot to my family. Like my mother … I mean maybe that angel would have found us anyway, but I doubt it." Her father winced, but didn't contradict her. The Knights probably hadn't known about Lahash's power to sense divine intent. Ari had known her before her fall and it never even occurred to him. But, from Mal's point of view they were responsible. She'd said so more than once since she'd heard the whole story. Mal's voice grew even harder, "Go ahead and explain why you've been following me. Actually, I think *'had me under surveillance'* is more accurate." She turned toward her father, "Dad, did you know about this?"

Ari spread his hands, about to speak, but the Bishop cut him off. "We have to be close."

Mal's annoyance was growing, particularly at the Bishop's dismissive tone. "Yeah, you've been *really* close," Mal began methodically scanning the faces around her and then pointing. "He was the janitor at my school." Ari's eyes widened a bit. "He's the assistant manager at QCB." The young man, who Mal knew as Joe, gave her a little waving salute. They had certainly seen enough of each other in the last year, had seen each other this morning, in fact, when he'd handed her a Red Eye with a smile, asking how her job at the hospital was going. She'd gone straight from an overnight to the shelter and just assumed he was reminded about where she'd been working from the scrubs and the name tag, but now, knowing how much he probably knew about her, it kind of gave her the creeps. Then she noticed the woman who'd helped her find all the books for her senior capstone paper and scowled with true irritation, "And she works in the library … Wait. She?"

The Bishop smiled at Mal's momentary distraction. "We are somewhat more evolved than the Church on certain issues; women are a valuable part of our Order. We also employ a wide variety of sub-contractors to meet all of our needs. And yes, some of our people have been close, to protect you should the need arise, which given your current situation it almost certainly will. We have been unable to be as close as we would prefer."

Mal's jaw tightened. "Dad, seriously …"

Ari stood up and moved next to her so he could look into her face, "Mal. I knew the Church would help keep you safe at school, but I didn't know they'd planned all this. Nor would I have agreed to it. When I said I told you everything, I thought I had."

Mal composed herself and leveled her gaze at the Bishop-General. "So, what *exactly* are you doing here now?"

"Miss Sinclair, Mal, all the signs indicate the time has come for you to once again embrace the safety that travel has to offer."

"Beg your pardon?"

"Put simply, you've had your fun. It's time to return to your old life until something can be done about this prophecy. You must be protected to carry on the Line."

Mal looked from her father to the Bishop General, her face utterly calm. "No," she said flatly, and then made a contemptuous face. "And as if I'd go around having babies because somebody else thinks it's a great idea. I've been on the Pill since I was sixteen. It's the Twenty-first Century. Please."

Bishop Roy was confused by her reply. Ari shifted, uncomfortable. He didn't want this, had no interest in the Knights' agenda, especially since Mal had always been certain, at least until very recently, that she didn't want children, but the Bishop made a good case for what might happen if they stayed. Metatron and Davidos had found some troubling signs as well. Ari's eyes were sad as he spoke, knowing she needed to hear this, but disliking it all the same, "Mal, it's not just them. I should've told you before, but I wanted to wait until all your celebrations were over ... There've been other signs. Hell's agents are gathering close by. The eye of Heaven has been pulled this way as well. For your safety ..." He stopped, knowing that was not enough to cause her to reconsider. "For the safety of innocent people, we should go." She shook her head stubbornly, her lips pursed. "Mal, please. There's too much at risk. We just don't know what they'll do, honey."

Mal asked them coolly, "What's your evidence that I'm really in danger here?"

Bishop Roy began, "Various divinations, signs ..."

Mal rolled her eyes, not about to disrupt her entire life for something as unreliable as magic. Even in her short foray into the strange world of the mystical, Mal had learned to regard spells as notoriously untrustworthy. Chris was ancient and worked all the time to get better and his success rate with anything complicated was, as he put it, spotty. Even Ben, who had been practicing for longer than Chris and had all kinds of powers, too, could only count on about eighty percent of his spells going completely as planned. And Chris said Ben was a man of iron will, ideally suited to working magic. She cut him off. "I'm sorry, but I've said no. I have a life here. A job, a boyfriend, a freaking full scholarship! A future! I'm staying." Those who had been assigned to be close to Mal responded only with raised eyebrows. They'd gotten to know her over the last year and her reaction wasn't surprising to any of them. But her father and the Bishop both seemed prepared to resume their arguments. Before they could speak, she said, "Please excuse me. My friends are expecting me. Dad, I hope you'll still join us."

Mal brushed past her father and the Bishop, pretending not to see the people in the living room by the windows. She was going to get out of here as quickly as she could, maybe shower at Petra's. As she had planned all day, she packed an overnight bag for the party, grabbed a change of clothes so she could ditch her scrubs, and headed out of the house. She nearly stopped in the kitchen to say something more to her father, but whether he had known about this before or not, she was still unhappy with him. He was taking their side; without even talking to her first. She decided it was better to keep trying to diffuse her thoughts and not say anything. She simply left. She was surprised no one tried to stop her, but glad because she felt if anyone had put their hands on her she might have hurt them. As she was pulling out of the parking area she saw her dad come out onto the porch, worried and lost. *I'm sorry, Dad, but I'm not going anywhere*, Mal thought. She tried not to keep replaying the look on his face in her mind, but it was difficult.

The Bishop joined him as she turned the corner for the main road, and found Ari running his hands through his hair, like it would help him clear his head. "Well, that was a disaster." Ari reluctantly deferred to the Bishop. "What do you suggest?"

"Don't worry, she'll come around. She's a bright young woman. In any event there are people following her and waiting at the park. There's a device we've attached to her car." Ari frowned in momentary confusion. "We can simply track her, in case this meeting has changed her plans. You can come along. Perhaps you'd feel better if you had eyes on her yourself?"

Ari's eyes widened and his voice rose sharply. "You *lojacked* my daughter?"

"It's only her *car*. And it's for her safety." The Bishop was indifferent.

Ari shook his head, walking down the steps. "This is all so high-handed. No wonder she's upset. Take me to her. I want to try to talk to her again before this escalates."

Not far away, Lahash's face broke into a shark-like grin. She hadn't even had to work the spell and a thought had come to her with almost painful force.

"What is it, Sister?" Lilith demanded.

"It's the girl. She is close. Her thoughts are gaining momentum. It will be today." Lahash's smile of anticipation would have frozen the blood of anyone but her current companion.

"I will alert our troops and inform Lucifer." Lilith cackled with glee.

Chapter 46

"Things fall apart; the centre cannot hold; mere anarchy is loosed upon the world, the blood-dimmed tide is loosed, and everywhere the ceremony of innocence is drowned." ~ *William Butler Yeats*

Ben was helping set up the new portable grill and had just pinched his fingers for about the millionth time, when he heard Aife laugh softly. Chris made some quiet comment as he dipped into the cooler to hand her a soda. Ben saw her touch his arm lightly. Chris approached to help Ben with whatever caused him to settle on Chinese for today's instructive profanity.

Ben, who had been sucking on his thumb and what was bound to be a blood blister, took his hand out of his mouth. "So, it's official. You and Aife, huh?"

Chris responded with an elaborate frown. "I have no idea what you're talking about."

Aife walked up behind Ben and dumped a handful of dripping ice cubes down the back of his t-shirt. "Whatever do you mean?"

"Aww, Aife, what the hell?!" Ben yelped, untucking his shirt and trying unsuccessfully to shake the ice out as it melted unpleasantly down his overly warm back. He shook his head, "C'mon, we're all friends here. I can't know you guys are, like, closer friends?"

"Such an imagination. I don't know what we'll do with you," Aife said primly. They were grinning and blushing like teenagers, obviously in high spirits. This was a game. They couldn't wait to tell him they were an item. Today was a good day for such revelations. The crowded park was filled with a party atmosphere already.

Aife was making short work of the grill top that had been trying to sever Ben's fingers. In a vain effort to dry his shirt by waving it around and to ignore the now-wet waistband of his boxers, Ben said in pretended indignation, "Fine, don't tell me. I'll mind my own business."

Aife and Chris laughed, holding hands. "We're sorry, Ben. We wanted you to know, but it's still so new. We're not sure of anything ourselves, only that it feels kind of right," Chris assured him.

Aife stopped, looking momentarily worried. "Is it a problem?"

At first, Ben could hardly think what she meant. Then he realized not only did they have a history, which had been strange for him until he saw how unimportant nearly every aspect of his life as a demon seemed to Mal, but, regardless of how human either of them felt or appeared, in their other lives he was her liege lord and could forbid their association. Ben smiled.

"Two of my favorite people in the world are finding a way to be happy. What kind of asshole would have a problem with that?" He thought for a second. "Except no ganging up on me with your lecturey parenty voices. I'm technically older than both of you!"

"You and your technicalities." Chris grinned at him. "I'm making no promises. I kind of like having an ally to talk sense to you." He and Aife laughed.

A smirk was the only appropriate response. *Subject changing time.* "So, Chris, you going swimming with us this afternoon?"

"Very funny. I'll pass; thanks." Chris shifted uneasily and Aife gave him a confused look. "I don't care for the water. Long story." She saw his discomfort and her arm went around him in an affectionate squeeze that told him she wouldn't ask. Not until they were alone anyway. Then she resumed proving how handy she was at a cookout.

Ben did his best to find someplace else to look as Aife, victorious with the errant grill cover, expected Chris's affection as a reward. They did look well together. Searching around, Ben saw Mal striding through the crowd. "There's the guest of honor. I'll be back."

Ben headed in her direction at a jog. He passed Teddy and Petra settling onto the grass. They seemed to be having a nice time and Teddy looked almost like himself today; his color was good and he'd maybe put some weight on. That was reassuring. Mal approached him in the crowd, looking lovely in a white shirt with the sleeves rolled up, sandals, and denim shorts, damp ringlets framing her flushed face. He could see her expression was troubled. No, that wasn't right; she was angry. He arrived at her side, expecting their usual embrace, but instead she put her hands on her hips, looking both furious and conflicted. She was breathing too fast and looked ready to explode or burst into tears.

"Mal, what's wrong?"

"Oh, it's nothing. It's all fine. Just my Dad and some glorified priests with delusions of grandeur planning out my life for me! Again!"

Ben took her hand and led her to a nearby bench and they sat facing each other. He was worried. He could feel her thoughts tripping away a mile a minute. A litany of *iwontgoiwontgoiwontgo* drummed painfully into Ben's mind. She needed to get through this so she could release her focus as soon as possible.

"Tell me what happened."

Mal rehashed the conversation for Ben. He listened, with no questions or interruptions, and when she was done he closed his eyes for a minute and took a deep breath. His expression was reserved, and pain not unlike one of his worst headaches was starting to pull at the corners of his eyes.

"Mal, do you think maybe they might be right?"

She let go of his hand. "You've got to be kidding!" She gestured around at all the people, friends laughing, kids running around, music playing. It seemed like everyone in the city was here to celebrate something. This was the least dangerous her life had ever felt and she just couldn't accept giving it up because something might happen, maybe, because magic said so.

Ben took her hand again, knowing this was the last thing she wanted to hear, but recognizing the familiar fluttering in his chest and sinking in his stomach telling him bad things were on their way. "No, Mal, please, I'm serious. I don't believe we've even recovered half the prophecy yet. If you're traveling, it's harder for any of them to get a fix on you."

He was so obviously heartbroken. Mal's immediate reaction was to try to make him feel better. "Ben, even if it is true, it should be fine. I'm warded like crazy."

If anyone knew that, it was Ben, but he shook his head. "I know, but Mal, you know about the angel who can home in on divine intent and …" There were starting to be funny black flashes in the periphery of his vision, but he was too caught up in talking to Mal to process that he was seeing the little rifts in the fabric of reality that signaled demons in their natural state punching through. Part of him must have detected it, because he began to nervously chew his lip.

"That's why we've been working so much on my learning diffusion!" They had been working hard, but it seemed all their labors had gone out the window this afternoon.

Ben acknowledged her efforts with a nod. "But Mal, you're awfully focused right now and it's scaring me a little. Since you can't stay on top of it all the time, moving might be better …" He trailed off again, looking almost wounded.

"Oh Ben, not you, too! I'm tired of being some kind of crazy nomad because it might be safer. You have no idea what my life was like. This is home. *You're* home."

Her words were so sincere, so intense, it hurt all through him. He tried giving her a small smile. "So, I'll go with you. You know I'd follow you anywhere."

"No, we have something real. *Here*."

His face fell. He knew what she was thinking. "Mal, don't. We should just go."

"Ben, how can you ..?"

"This feels so dangerous. I just … I love you."

"And I love you! We've started a life here. We can go to school together. I don't know, maybe …"

Now Ben looked like he was in danger of tears. "What? Get married? Have kids?" He closed his eyes, trying to quell his wayward emotions, to be rational. "No, Mal … I wish I could give you that, but …" Ben ceased his soft, almost sobbing, whisper before any other forbidden thoughts slipped out.

"Ben, stop. I know you want …"

Ben interrupted, eyes downcast, "Well, I don't every time get what I want. Jesus, Mal … I …" Ben wanted those things as badly as she did, maybe more so, but he knew in the deepest darkest part of his heart how this all had to end. His certainty that they would get none of what they wanted, the effort of holding his feelings in check, choked him and reddened his face.

She touched his cheek and he forced himself to meet her fiery eyes. "I just don't accept that, Ben. If I'm the Scion, it's got to be worth something. I love you. I'll fight Heaven and Hell together if I need to for that life. For us."

The air grew chilly as all the color drained from Ben's face, and his eyes went wild with panic. From behind Mal came a voice, cold and terrible, "That can be arranged."

Mal was quickly on her feet and when she turned she saw the same hideous creature that had dragged Ben into the pit in her dream at Christmas. It had long thin razor-like teeth, a blood stained mouth, grey skin hanging from its frame, and bizarre reptilian eyes. Its companion was a sharply attractive creature who was looking at Ben with unsettling amusement. "My goodness, but we are in trouble, my little Lord Ronoven. This is going to be delicious fun."

Mal could see their auras now, grey and black, like filthy smoke. These could only be fallen angels. "Leave this place!" Her voice had the unmistakable ring of command that had driven Bhaal from Teddy that night in February. She figured it had worked once and right now she had nothing to lose.

The grotesque creature laughed and the sound made Mal feel as though she had swallowed a bellyful of writhing snakes. "I don't think so. I am Lilith, and this is my sister Lahash. This can be quite simple if you'll just come with us."

Mal shook her head. "No, I'd much rather not." Poised to flee, she said, "Ben, run!"

Before she could even turn, Lilith laughed again, "Don't be silly, child. He can't do that unless I release him."

Mal spun around. Some force had pulled Ben to his knees. His arms were bound behind his back by invisible ropes of thought; the pain lining his face was unmistakable. Whatever they were doing to him, they were making sure he suffered as much as possible. He was trying to fight back but Lilith was too strong. The more he struggled, the more she hurt him. He choked out the barely intelligible words, "Mal, run." Then she could tell from his gasping beleaguered breaths that he was unable to speak further.

"Let him go! NOW!"

"My dear, don't be ridiculous. He'd only get in the way, and I'd prefer no one interfere with our little *tête-à-tête*. Besides, the filthy little traitor has this coming to him." She made a stabbing motion with her hand and Ben collapsed onto his side, twisting helplessly in agony. She was clearly looking for a muffled scream or maybe some pleading, and Ben was sweating, clenching his jaw. Nevertheless, he resisted the urge to make a sound. He just stared steely death up into the face of the creature binding and tormenting him.

Not far away, Aife noticed the nip come into the air and the quickly darkening sky, angry clouds scudding across the bright blue surface out of nowhere. She shuddered as a chill seized her. Chris saw her face and moved to put his arm around her. She shook her head, pointing in the direction Ben had left, her hand shaking. Chris followed her gesture, unable to quite take in the nightmare unfolding not a hundred feet away.

"Chris, we've got to try to get these people out of here."

"Aife, what's going on?"

"The Fallen have come for Mal. Hell's out in the open. It's going to get bloody. Fast."

Chapter 47

"And the only solution was to stand and fight and my body was bruised and I was set alight but you came over me like some holy rite and although I was burning, you're the only light." ~ Florence and the Machine

Lilith and Mal sized each other up. Mal was working to find her center, knowing she was the only way out of this for Ben, trying not to think of him being tortured, writhing on the ground near her feet. There had to be some way to gain an advantage. Wasn't Hell breaking the rules by trying to force her? She looked at the fallen angels steadily and thought with complete focus and no small measure of desperation, *'Sure could use a Guardian about now, Uncle Davi. Like right now. Anytime now would be super. Okay? Just please. Okay?'*

Lahash smiled, moving closer, picking up on her intention quite clearly. "My dear girl, that's a complete waste of precious energy." Mal's eyes narrowed. "Summoning is tremendously complex magic." She sensed Mal trying not just to summon angelic help, but to alert her Guardian specifically. "Child," she crooned, "that's not how that arrangement works. Guardians can only sense when you're in danger. You can't possibly perform a summoning. And since you're in no danger from us? That means no Guardian." She stuck out her lower lip in mock sympathy, and gave Ben a sharp kick in the side. She wanted him making noise; that would break the girl. He grunted but that was all. He wouldn't allow himself to be used against Mal if he could prevent it.

"I won't go," Mal said with a deadly icy calm.

"Perhaps not at first, but you will agree." Lilith smiled her bloody smile, tightening her invisible chains on Ben, finally eliciting a muffled sound of pure torment.

Mal shook her head, her mouth set into a stubborn line. "Never gonna happen."

Lahash got close, trailing a long finger down Mal's cheek, ignoring the smoke rising from its tip. "I think it will. I'm unusually convincing." Mal glowered at her. "Let's see what we can do with your demon lover." Lahash gave Ben another kick, harder than before. "I'm looking forward to sending the little turncoat back to Hell for what he deserves, but this will do for now."

Lahash kicked Ben again and this time a breathless whimper escaped his lips. He was now barely holding onto consciousness. Mal was unsure of what to do. His eyes were shut tight, his breathing shallow and rapid. She knew what he'd say to the idea of bargaining with them, but she'd just heard at least one of his ribs snap like a green twig, and all she wanted was to free him. It must have shown in her eyes because then Lahash decided to really needle her.

"Was it love, little girl, or does whoring just run in your family?"

Her rage was instant and perfect. Mal acted without thinking. She dropped back and threw a punch with all of her might, connecting with Lahash's cheekbone and sending her flying, skidding to a stop on the grass nearly ten feet away, where she lay motionless. Mal thought it was a good thing she'd never been that pissed off at Krav Maga, and also knocking that creature unconscious was about the most satisfying thing she'd ever done, even though her hand now hurt more than she'd expected it to. Sparring and fighting were two different things, she guessed.

Lilith pulled a terrible face, "Impressive, child. But you're wasting time." She smiled slyly, raising her arms over her head and beginning to invoke Hell's power, "Only you can stop this. Just say 'yes'."

Lilith's chanting coincided with the darkening sky and thunder pealing so loudly it shook the whole waterfront. Steam rose from the water and the stench of sulfur filled the air. Across the park, twisted demonic abominations rose from everywhere, materializing out of those half-seen rifts Ben had almost noticed earlier, leaping into immediate destructive action, as ten of the fiercest Fallen appeared outfitted for battle. Mal looked around helpless as Hell's growing numbers wreaked havoc in every way possible, destroying property, tearing panicking humans to pieces. She could see their dark forms spreading out, could hear the screams in their wake. It took her a moment to notice that all of them carried heavy chains. They weren't really going to negotiate with her, they meant to wrap her up and drag her to Hell. She broke out into a cold sweat, and for a moment there was only Mal and her fear; pure terror at the idea that someone could take away her freedom like that, and would do it cheerfully. Mal hadn't known it was possible to be this scared and keep your feet, and with that thought alone her legs wanted to buckle under her. Then Ben's hoarse cry of rage and pain brought her back to herself, and that the danger was to everyone here. She was their target, but her friends and neighbors were in their way. Some invisible force now pulled Ben's limbs in opposite directions, and he was struggling to free himself from it. She gaped in horror and thought only that she should have called Ben when the Knights showed up. They could have left then and prevented this. *How the hell am I going to get everyone out of here?*

Mal was scanning the chaos looking for a straw to grasp at when she heard a familiar voice right next to her, "I'm here."

Over the clamor of battle she heard her father's voice, although she couldn't make out what he'd shouted. She saw him fighting alongside the Bishop General and several other Templars, trying to break through a line of demons.

Without even turning her head, she asked, "Uncle Davi, what do we do?"

All Mal wanted now was to get them out of here alive.

"That depends on our friend here." Mal saw his hands flex, his aura shimmering with power. "What say you cut your losses, Lilith? Go back to Lucifer with your head still attached while I'm feeling kindly disposed?"

Whatever Davi was doing, Mal was relieved to see Ben able to start struggling to his knees, finally released. He said her name, barely a whisper, and she bent to help him stand, held him close while he steadied himself. She wanted to just take him and run, but there was nowhere to go, and his breathing had a distressing wet sound she wanted to stop before he moved much more. She put her hand gently against his ribs and he drew in his breath sharply at her touch, then swayed for a second before resting his head on top of hers.

Lilith hissed, "You are powerful, Davidos, but we are many, and we're guarded against your usual nonsense. We relish this fight,"

Davidos smiled, almost carelessly. "Oh, Lilith, holy fire isn't my only weapon. Besides, I didn't come alone."

She cast a glance at Mal, who felt her skin crawl as the creature's eyes moved over her. "Best get back, child. Wouldn't want anything to happen to you."

Metatron appeared, sword drawn and all of the Fallen took a step back. None of those present had ever seen a righteous Archangel prepared for war. His aura glowed so brightly, was so resplendent with Heavenly power, that many of the demons began to smolder just from his proximity and a few actually burst into flame. Metatron surveyed the carnage already accomplished by the unchecked demons loosed on the city, his face grim. He stared Lilith down, the dare clear in his eyes. Lilith chanted and summoned perhaps a score more of Hell's most savage warriors.

"You can still turn back you know. Send this legion back to Hell and return home."

When Metatron spoke, even though he had done so quietly, the entire battlefield stilled.

Lilith appeared to consider the offer. Then, she drew her own weapon and raised her cadaverous voice to order Hell's militia forward. Davi and Metatron were immediately set upon.

Mal's efforts had righted Ben enough to act, and although his ribs still ached like a rotted tooth, he was no longer rasping and struggling against the dimming around the edges of his vision. He saw his moment and untangled himself from her arms, motioned for her to stay close. From a sheath concealed under his shirt, he drew a short slightly curved black blade, forged at a high price in the cold Quebec winter for this exact purpose. It was such a natural movement Mal suspected he had practiced it a thousand times. He moved them away from the main action of angels and approached Lahash struggling to sit, her face burned black where Mal had struck her.

Lahash croaked, "Come to try to surrender, you treacherous coward?"

Ben, holding the blade up along his forearm to slash, flipped it easily in his hand so it was an extension of his arm. He didn't bother with words, didn't have the breath for it. He dropped to one knee and grabbed a handful of Lahash's hair, pulled her head back, and thrust the blade up through her chin until the point was visible out of the top of her head. His face was emotionless, but his eyes burned with fury. Mal's own eyes grew wide as Lahash thrashed for a moment, a black oily mess bubbling from her mouth and her wounds. Ben withdrew the blade with a yank and her body convulsed and began to flake away in floating black wisps, turning to ash and smoke. Wiping his weapon on the grass, Ben stood, reached into his pocket, and through a hole cut in it, drew his second dagger from where he had hidden it strapped to his leg. He turned it carefully in his hand and passed it reluctantly to Mal, grateful for Cain's advice about their size and scope and his own habit of carrying them everywhere over the last month or so. "Come on. Let's find a way out of here." Then he paused, "Be careful using that; don't get cut with it. It's death for angels. Poison." Her eyes widened but she nodded and joined his search for a way out.

Across the park, Aife and Chris were doing their best, but faced with scores of slobbering, glowing-eyed demons in their most twisted Hellish forms, fully armed for war, it was an uphill battle. Aife was breathing heavily, bleeding from several deep wounds, including a demon bite, already festering, and when she paused to catch her breath she caught sight of Mal and Ben in the midst of the melee. She pointed, drawing Chris's attention, and shouted, "Over there! They need our help! I won't see Hell win after all this!"

Chris bent to retrieve a sidearm from a fallen police officer and moved toward Aife. He handed her the baton he had grabbed as well. "Right. Let's go ... Wait ... have you seen the other kids?"

Aife just shook her head, and Chris noticed for the first time her eyes glowing like antimony salt in a flame. He looked around desperately as they ran to join the fight at the side of the Scion. He had already seen too many of his students destroyed today, on the cusp of discovering who they were, of beginning their own lives. His anger at this waste steeled his resolve, blunted his sadness, for now. He was not about to let Mal or Ben fall to this violence on top of everything else. He cocked the gun he'd picked up. He knew the bullets were of little use against the demons since they weren't silver or filled with consecrated salt like the weapons of the Templars, but he could hurt them, move them out of their way. Aife appeared deadly with any weapon in her hands. He'd always thought she moved with the grace of a dancer, but now he finally saw some of her demonic power as she fought; agile, acrobatic, and inhumanly strong. She was a warrior goddess, beautiful and terrible, as they waded into the fight together.

In the bushes overlooking the water, so choppy and grey it looked like the sea in a storm, Teddy had lost all the progress he had made since the night Bhaal had violated his soul. He stared blankly, tears running down his face, arms wrapped around his knees, rocking, breathing in ragged sobbing gasps. Petra held him, her eyes closed, focused on chanting to build the protection spell Ben had spent so much time teaching her. The dense branches dug painfully into her back and side, but their cover was working. So far they had gone unnoticed.

The battle unfolded around Chris and he became more aware of the implications of the curse Ben had once explained. He was amazed he'd never noticed before. Aife outpaced him, her speed now that she had called on her power startling, and mildly frightening, to watch. She cast aside the now-broken baton in favor of a wicked looking knife she had taken off the body of a demon. Her eyes glinted with triumph as she surveyed those she vanquished. Chris thought briefly he was glad he had never been called upon to campaign in the Isles. Seeing Ben in the distance and following Aife as she cut a swath through the demons, he thought their people fought like they didn't value their own lives. She and Ben were ferocious and brave, utterly calm in the face of countless attacks, heedless of their wounds, eyes always on the next line of enemies. Maybe it was the power they were imbued with, but Chris doubted it. He remembered Ben saying once that his powers were mostly more of what he had been. Watching now, he really believed it. Then there was Chris, no slouch in a fight himself, but realizing Ben had been right about his curse. It seemed he could take no missteps. In myriad events amounting to dumb luck, his life was spared. It was almost a farce as demons advanced to attack him. One demon slipped in what could only be the entrails of some other creature. Chris suppressed a shudder, telling himself they weren't human. At one point, two demons with bladelike hands charged at him from either side, he tripped over an unrecognizable corpse, and as he fell they managed to behead each other. Whatever the reason, he was glad it got him through the battlefield and near Ben and Mal.

As he and Aife approached this central fight, he could see his friends were pressed on all sides. Ben was fighting with his enchanted blade, which was as deadly to demons as it was to angels. He was obviously hurt enough that it was keeping him from fully accessing his powers. Chris could see his breathing was ragged and he bled from multiple wounds. In spite of terrible injuries, he kept his feet; his look of determination an inspiring thing in the midst of all this destruction. Mal wielded the dagger Ben had given her as though she were born to it, and when the blade failed her, she was smiting demons with her fists, setting their flesh smoking. She didn't look like a girl in the midst of her first fight. She looked like a creature native to battle. She was nearly a match for Ben and Aife, her years of martial arts and newfound power showing their effect. She was learning something of her power today. If Hell had no fury like a woman scorned, Chris thought Lucifer had miscalculated rather badly and had better watch his step if Mal got her hands on him.

Then Chris saw Aife fall to the ground. He slid down next to her, unable to stand.

"Aife? Honey?" He was trembling badly.

She opened her eyes a little. "I'll be okay," she managed weakly. "Go to them."

He and Aife were just beginning. The deep wound in her side might as well have been his for the pain it caused him. Eyes locked on Aife's face, his hands on her shoulders, he was trying desperately to think of some way to save her, prevent whatever would happen if her wounds overtook her. He was certain that if this body died, she would be forced back to Hell and they would kill her for good and all there, just like Ben was always certain would happen to him. For the first time Chris really felt the weight of what a final death meant. He sensed a lull in the immediate fighting around him as Ben dropped to his knees beside them, looking worse than Aife, and Mal sank down next to them, exhausted.

Ben managed, "Is she ..?"

"I'm fine, ya big baby," Aife said, almost jokingly, but didn't open her eyes this time. "Okay, I'm hurt some. Maybe," she allowed. Ben gave a little sobbing laugh that made him narrow his eyes and press his hand to his side as Mal put her hands over Aife's most serious wound and closed it. Aife immediately exhaled with relief. No matter how tolerable Aife had claimed they were, Ben had expected Mal's wards to interfere with her ability to heal Aife, but she'd done it quickly, easily, with no obvious pain.

Aife opened her eyes, touched Mal's hand, "Thanks, sweetie."

His own wounds forgotten for the moment, Ben frowned at them. "Want to tell me how that's a thing, Aife? Mal just healing you like it's no big deal? Something's going on with your magic."

Aife sighed. She could hardly put this off any longer. "I was subjected to that godawful spell you discovered months ago. Hell's orders."

Ben's mouth dropped in horror. "Why didn't you say anything, damnit?"

"Figured you knew, you being so clever."

"Bullshit. You knew I was worried sick about you when Mal ..."

"Alright! I didn't say anything because I didn't want you making the face you're making right now," Aife snapped, and then she made a small pained sound as Mal closed a wound on her arm with her fingers before healing it with her magic. "There was nothing you could've done to stop it, Ben," she offered in a more subdued, reassuring tone. As Mal finished helping with the worst of things, Aife sat up slowly and lifted her hair, displaying the tiny dark mark nearly hidden in the fire of the curls at the nape of her neck. "It was ten shades of awful, love. I didn't much feel like comparing notes."

Mal was so focused on helping Aife that she only half heard them but her tone was suspicious. "What's she talking about?"

Ben eyes closed briefly. "Nothing, just some magic. It's no big deal."

Mal filed that away for future consideration. At the moment she was too frightened and exhausted to try to draw Ben out about anything, and they still needed to get out of this mess.

Aife scowled at him, climbing to her feet and looking expectantly at the rest of them. They rose slowly, looking around. Ben held his side as he stood. Mal tried to get him to stand still so she could heal him, at least the more serious wounds that were basically gushing blood, but he was too busy, desperately searching for a clear path out.

Demons lost interest in the park and were starting to move along the waterfront and into the city on an orgiastic rampage of destruction. The group looked on in horror as one creature was using long clawed talons to scoop people off the ground and, with its grey bat-like wings, haul them up to the level of the roof of one of the waterfront hotels and fling them off, laughing with an awful chortling howl as they splattered on the pavement. Another being, with eight limbs like pointed stilts that appeared to be all bone and sinew, was skittering back and forth through the panicked crowd skewering people and flinging them out into the water, where they bobbed like gruesome screaming buoys, until they went under. Others worked in groups, eating their fill of, what one snarkily called, free-range organic human. That particular ball of bloody fur and teeth had an obvious preference for children. Bodies and parts of bodies littered the ground and blood made the grass slippery and stained the pavement. The coppery stink of death filled the air.

Not far away the angels were engaged in their deadly dance. Metatron and Davi fought back to back, their swords gleaming and magnificent. With some careful maneuvering they managed to get their backs to a building. It seemed like the Fallen and their demons had managed to corner them, but all they had done was allow room for Metatron to perform a spell to try and break Hell's wards against holy fire while Davi fought them off from the front. The moment the wards were weakened, Davidos sent a shining wave of power through the lines. Many of the demons were immediately consumed; even a few of the Fallen were scorched. Those it didn't touch were infuriated, but although they dug in to fight harder, reducing their numbers was all the Guardian and the Archangel needed to begin to gain the advantage.

Mal's eyes scanned the chaos. For once her use of magic seemed to hit her as hard as it did the others. She didn't know what to call the power she had sent through her hands to injure the demons attacking them, and it had worked like a charm on every one of them she touched, but she felt weirdly tired, almost dizzy. And she knew, looking around, that this was nowhere near over. She couldn't quite process what she was seeing. Mal felt a surge of relief as she heard Ari's voice call to her. He approached them, alone and bleeding. She saw that not a single Templar remained standing. Such was the brutality of the Fallen and their demonic allies.

Ari embraced his daughter with his uninjured arm. "Thank God you're alright," he breathed like he hadn't dared to hope it was true. He glanced around at the small group. "We've got to get out of here. This group is determined to take Mal to Hell, along with anyone else they can drag along."

Ben grimaced. "That can only have been the first wave. And if grabbing me at the get-go is any indication, Lucifer hopes to use us, to blackmail or terrify her into compliance however he can." Ben finally stood still for a moment, putting his arm around Mal. "I was afraid when they had me you might … I don't even know … but you didn't. You stood your ground. You were incredible."

Mal blinked at him like she couldn't understand why he was impressed. "No, you were."

"You were so brave." He let go of her so he could face her, look in her eyes so she could see his sincerity. "There is nothing they can do, any of them, to make me want you to go with them. No matter what, remember that. Don't let them scare you into agreeing with their bullshit."

As if triggered by Ben's words, the ground began to shake, and they turned and saw a horrifying sight rising near the band shell. Ben's head shook violently, irrationally, instinctively pulling Mal back, "Goddamn it!" Ben shouted.

His face was close to panic, so different from the fierce calculation of battle, Mal stammered, "Ben, what is it?"

Ben, pulling himself together, looked significantly at Ari, hoping the name would mean something to him. "Real trouble. Moloch; a Hell-god. He's not allowed to be here in his own form. It violates all the rules. Not just Hell's. Heaven won't stand for this."

More beings materialized around the terrifying form of the angry monster.

Ben gasped, grimacing as he drew in his breath, "Those are his minions, twisted souls of his earthly followers." His eyes were wide, glowing. He shook his head in disbelief. "More powerful than demons."

Mal and her companions watched in horror as Moloch's full form unfolded, standing at least twenty feet tall. Its face was a mask of pure hatred incarnate, its head crowned with blue flames and striking serpents. The god roared, brandishing its claws, bearing its thousands upon thousands of teeth, shattering the remaining glass in the buildings on the waterfront. It began to throw large flaming balls of brimstone at the city, into the crowd of survivors in the park, seemingly conjuring it at the speed of thought. The city was burning, buildings collapsing, people wailing.

Mal shook her head. This was on her. This was her fault.

Chapter 48

"The Creator has not thought proper to mark those in the forehead who are the stuff to make good generals. We are forced, therefore, to seek them blindfold, and then let them learn the trade at the expense of great losses."
~ Thomas Jefferson.

Michael sat across the table from his brothers and sisters. He had called this council to discuss the girl. His scouting party had found the place where she lived, but she and her father had not been home. He frowned. Metatron was conspicuous by his absence. "Sandalphon, what of your twin? Metatron has not answered my summons. Tell me why." Michael's voice was contentious and full of irritation.

Sandalphon could not have appeared less interested as he picked up a glass of wine and the book he had brought with him. "Well, you know our Voice. Perhaps he had better things to do." He smirked, knowing Michael felt this subtle challenge to his authority deeply.

Michael's pinched face betrayed his annoyance. "It makes no matter. We've found the girl, or rather, we know where she resides. Raphael will go now and wait for her to return. And we have this young one among us to thank," Michael inclined his head to the young herald.

"Pardon me, my Lord, but why wait?" she offered in her charmingly confused manner.

Michael barked, curtly, "Explain."

Her sweet face was apologetic. "Well, it's just I would think the Templars would know exactly where she is at all times. They are known for being the best at what they do. And what about her Guardian? Surely one of our number is charged with looking after her?"

Once again, Michael was at a loss. Why did he have such a blind spot? And why was it so large where the Scion was concerned?

Sandalphon cackled, more amused than he'd been since watching that drunk Noah try to build a boat to contain early quantum state phenomena. "Oh, I love it! I'd nearly forgotten about Davidos, myself. It's almost as though I've been encouraged to forget. Just what kind of magic does the Scion have at her command?"

Michael slammed his fists into the table. Of course, Davidos, but how? His thoughts were interrupted when a herald entered the room.

"Brother Michael, news from Earth. A number of Fallen and hundreds of demons have surfaced."

"Where?" Michael barked, almost unnecessarily.

"Near the home of the child, my Lord."

Michael cursed under his breath and sighed. Lucifer; somehow he had managed to get to the girl first. His face tightened. "How many?"

The herald bowed, "Perhaps thirty or so of the Fallen. Demons by the hundreds. Also, my Lord, Metatron and at least one other angel are present."

Michael barked, "Very well. Clear this room, all but the Council of the Archangels."

When the room was cleared, Uriel spoke first. "Girl or no girl, our little Morning Star goes much too far."

"Agreed." The consent was unanimous. All the archangels were on their feet, prepared to aid Metatron and save the city; unanimous save one. Michael stood, his hand raised, staying their action.

"Hold. Metatron is more than a match for such a number."

Sandalphon pushed his chair back, purposely knocking it to the floor with a clatter. "I will go to him."

"No. Your judgment is clouded. If you insist on sending aid, Uriel will go."

The doors burst open, all protocol forgotten, the herald almost out of breath gasped, "Moloch has manifested on Earth. He fights with Hell."

Michael's eyes narrowed. Was Lucifer trying to advertise Hell's plans? They must have the girl or be fairly certain of victory. He decided to put an end to this before everything was revealed. His voice rose, assuming an air of battlefield command as if it were the sole reason for his creation.

"Uriel, go there. Cut out that blight on the Earth and sanitize the scene. No half measures, Soldier."

"At once." Uriel spoke curtly, rose and disappeared.

Sandalphon and Gabriel were enraged. What Michael was calling for would kill thousands, destroy half a city, not to mention potentially put their brother to the final death and eliminate the Scion. *Why was this not being brought before the Almighty? Why was Michael behaving as though his word were supreme?* Their ire was readily apparent.

Michael stared down his brother and sister, so close to insurrection.

"Sit. Both of you. I may have to tolerate this insubordinate nonsense from The Voice, but I'll be damned if I'll listen to it from you. Not for a second."

His glare let them know the precariousness of their current position in Heaven. Michael glanced at Raphael and ordered, "Brother, go to the girl's home. If she survives Uriel's wrath she is bound to return there. Bring her to me."

He walked away dismissively, calling over his shoulder for anyone who cared to hear it.

"This council is ended."

The door slammed behind him.

Chapter 49

"You may have to fight a battle more than once to win it."
~ Margaret Thatcher

Mal stood, immobile, staring in horror at Moloch and his dreadful entourage.

Ben looked at Ari, Chris, and Aife; he avoided Mal's eye. "If we can get close enough, I think the blade would work on him, too."

Ari thought about it; then nodded his agreement. Chris stepped forward, prepared to join him. Aife puffed out a long sigh and held her hand out to Mal, obviously expecting to be given the other knife. "Give it here. You get under cover."

She shook her head, looking at them like they were crazy, "We can't fight that thing!"

In confirmation of the futility of standing against a Hell-god, the creature roared at the lake and it stirred into a massive waterspout, destroying all the boats in the harbor, along with the returning ferry barge. Ben reached out for her knife now. "We have to try ... look at what it's doing. It's going to win and then ..."

Goddamnit, she was not going to let her friends commit suicide right in front of her by charging that thing. She looked him up and down and snapped, "You are practically dying already."

Ben shook his head, "I'm alright."

"Sure you are ... Couple of knives against *that*? No way."

"Mal, please, just ... hide until it's all over. We've got this."

She stubbornly held onto the knife. "Show me then. Do some power thingy."

Ben tried. He managed some heat, but no fireball, then a spark, but no lightning. He couldn't even lift a torn baseball cap from the ground with his power. He was just too hurt, too tired. *Shit.* "We're going have to fight our way out the old-fashioned way," Ben hedged, looking like he couldn't fight his way out of a wet paper bag. "We don't have a choice."

Davidos had joined them while they were distracted by Moloch. "No more fighting is necessary. I can take us to safety."

Of all of them, he was the only one who bore no signs of having been in the battle, although they had all seen him fighting. The bodies of the Fallen littered the ground, seeming to burn from within. In the midst of the chaos, Lilith remained alive, on her knees, bound by angelic will. Ben couldn't help being pleased that Metatron meant to make an end of her.

"Oh, go on, Voice. Do it," she sneered. "Voice of no God. God's gone. God's dead. You have nothing," she spat, looking for a reaction.

She certainly got one. Her head bounced twice after it hit the ground, her body crumpling as her eyes blinked their last several feet away. Metatron didn't bother to clean or re-sheathe his blade as he walked toward them, looking almost bored. He motioned with his chin toward the forces gathering at the apex of Battery Park. Moloch had picked them out of the crowd and started advancing toward their position. Metatron sighed with irritation, stepping in front of them to put himself between Mal and an old enemy.

"I suppose I'd better see to all this. Davidos, would you mind ..?" The rest of his words were cut short by a blazing light in the sky and the loudest thunder a living mortal ever heard. Metatron glanced at Davidos. "On second thought, I think it's time to go."

Mal felt her body and mind pulled from a thousand directions. The pain was pervasive, like it was meant to put an end not just to her life, but to every bit of her existence. Her thoughts were on Teddy and Petra and her arms reached out to Ben whose face was fixed into an expression capturing everything she was feeling. The last thing she saw was what appeared to be a woman plummeting toward the park, standing inside an exploding sun.

Chapter 50

"The woods are lovely, dark, and deep.
But I have promises to keep, and miles to go
before I sleep."
~ Robert Frost

The tiny group found themselves on a clear cool mountaintop in the light of the late afternoon's pleasant sinking sun. Most of the group was scattered on the ground. Mal felt a dizzying wave of nausea, but Davi put his hand on her shoulder and after a few deep breaths it passed. Mostly. They couldn't have gone far. This still looked like home to her. Smoke in the distance told her Burlington was not far away, but she shied away from the idea that the dark smoldering spot to the west could be her city. To have gone from the middle of battle and all that devastation to this peaceful airy place in an instant was disconcerting even for angels, and for humans it was traumatic and painful. Mal quickly became distracted from the feeling by her concern. Her father was on the ground, bleeding from his shoulder. Chris was using cloth torn from the edge of his shirt to staunch the flow of a deep slice through his calf. Teddy lay on his side, whispering to himself and weeping. Petra was on her knees beside him, throwing up; shock overwhelming her thin body. Teleportation wasn't normally as hard on Ben and Aife as if they'd been fully human, but injured as they were, it winded them badly. Aife stood slowly, favoring her right leg, blood oozing from a wound in her thigh. Ben, obviously hurt more than a little, got up with deliberate carefulness, first to his knees, and then cautiously to his feet, bleeding freely from an indeterminate number of wounds. He looked so fragile and human as his eyes searched Mal's uncertainly. She stepped toward him, thinking only to help, and he almost stumbled back from her, looking miserable.

"Ben?" She reached for him again, "Baby, come here. Let me help."

This time he moved close, taking her hand, not thinking about his injuries at all, only contemplating what he had to say, and knowing it would hurt her. There was nothing he wanted less. "I'm so sorry, Mal … I just … ran out of time."

He wiped some blood off her face with his thumb and absently wiped his hand on his shorts. She hadn't known she was hurt and noticed with strange satisfaction the bleeding in his hand seemed to stop instantly. He couldn't find any more words, was afraid that if he kept talking he might break down, so he just shook his head. She wrapped her arms around him gently and leaned her face against his chest unsure of how to begin helping him, not wanting to hurt him, only wanting him to be alright. As Mal held him, Ben felt the strange sensation of most of his wounds closing. He felt the weird itching of his badly broken ribs knitting. The few deeper cuts, Mal had to close with her hands first. Ben gritted his teeth and kept still, resisting making even the smallest sound because she was so obviously distressed that she might cause him pain. When she finished, he hesitated, then pulled her close, buried his face in her hair, appreciating his ability to take a full breath again. He could feel Aife hovering at his elbow and he knew what they needed to do. He still didn't want to have to tell Mal, although he was sure on some level she already knew. Now she would have to face how angry and afraid she was, for him, at him. And he knew she'd hate it. He was feeling all that himself, truly. If only those Knights hadn't set her off, triggered her focus, they might have avoided Hell long enough for him to get clear, to get her out of the city where the legions caused so much damage. *Damn them all.*

Aife put her hand on his arm nervously. "Ben, we have to go."

He shook her off. "I know it." He needed explain, maybe make a plan for a change. "Gimme a minute." He felt Mal tense. She pulled back to look at him.

"What do you mean? We got away." Even though her words denied it, anger sparkled in her eyes.

Davidos put his hand on her shoulder. "We saved you from Lucifer's hunting party, from Heaven's response, but this isn't over. Both sides are still looking for you." He spoke to Ben then, but Ben's eyes never moved from Mal's face. "What are you going to do, Ben? You're clearly going to report to Hell, to try and maintain the deception. If you do, you know you may be going to the final death at Lucifer's hand."

Mal's face blanched but Ben spoke with calm certainty, looking into her eyes. "That won't happen. I can work this. Buy some time." She started to protest, but Ben pressed on, "Besides if we don't go, he'll summon us. I can't prevent that. I haven't found a way out from under. I have to try this."

Metatron stepped forward and interjected a further caution. "If he finds out what you've been up to, Ben, I think you might look on the final death as a kindness, particularly after his losses today." Ben swallowed hard. "He's always been a bit of a sore loser. You'll have to be very clever."

Ben forced a little smile. "I know. But, that's kind of what I do."

What he wanted more than anything was for Mal to stop looking so utterly devastated. He'd move Heaven, Earth, and Hell, too, to get back here just to see her smile again, even for a moment. He thought his words must have helped, at least a little bit, because Mal reached out to Aife and absently healed her last real injury, barely thinking about it. Aife was starting to get more visibly nervous. "Ben. Now. If you make him rip us from here with a summoning, we have no chance at all."

"I know! We're going, damn it!" He gazed into Mal's face, wanting to lock the memory of her stormy eyes into his heart. "Mal, I *will* come back and then you can have all of my life that's mine to give. I'm so close. Just a little more time. I'll figure it out."

Ari finally spoke, feeling awfully protective of Mal and not caring for the idea of losing Ben himself. "What's your plan, Ben?"

The effort of holding his composed expression fixed in his eyes, Ben answered, "I don't have one … Shit, when have I ever had a plan?"

Ben sighed in resignation and closed his eyes for a long moment. This was nothing but pain and terror for any of them. Heaven and Hell had both revealed what they were capable of today. There was nowhere to turn for help but each other.

Chris, who had rejoined the group silently, stepped forward, his injured leg plainly worse than he wanted to let on. He put his arm around Aife, looking shattered. His words were more to reassure himself than Ben and he knew it, but he found he needed to say it anyway. "Ben, you can do this. Hell can't know everything. I'm sure you've talked yourself out of worse positions."

Ben assumed his cockiest façade and flashed his most disarming smile. "Of course I have. Master of Expression, right?" His expression changed like the flip of a switch as he stepped back from Mal and took her by her shoulders, looking earnestly into her face. "I. Am. Coming. Back."

A tear slipped down her cheek. This was all too much, but she wasn't selfish enough to make this more difficult if she could help it. She hadn't been sure what real fear looked like on him. Even when the Fallen were torturing him he'd held fast, and in the heat of battle he'd worn the belief he could win like armor. Now she could see from the way his eyes darted around the clearing, despite his veneer of confidence, he was truly afraid and stubbornly trying to hide it from her. If that's what he needed, she would give it to him.

"Okay." She breathed, and then said firmly, "You damn well better."

If Lucifer harmed Ben, she thought she might burn down Hell itself. She was crying silently, unable to help it, tears washing streaks in the dirt and blood all over her face. Ben wiped his own face with the back of his filthy hand. He gently hooked his fingers on the chain of her necklace and pulled it out, held it. "Stick with your family, with Chris. Look out for Teddy and Petra. Don't let those angelic creeps push you into anything. Much as I'd like to tell the world you belong to me, you belong to yourself. You decide."

Mal's hand closed over his as she gave him a watery smile of agreement. Her dad stepped closer to them, put a hand on each of their shoulders and Ben glanced around at everyone. "You guys, you help her. Never lie to her, even if you think it's for her own good. Heaven and Hell have both decided to declare war and on our side she's the General. No … she's the Commander in Chief."

Deciding Hell could spare him another minute, he gathered Mal into his arms again and they kissed passionately, their eyes locked on each other. When he thought about it, they almost always kissed with their eyes open, and he thought vaguely it might be strange. In her arms, that blessed place where time stopped, he could almost believe they could all come through this and he and Mal could have the life they wanted, regardless of where he'd come from or anything he'd done. When they finally broke apart Ben rested his forehead against hers and whispered, "I will always come back to you. No matter what it takes. No matter how lost in the dark I am. I promise. Always."

Mal took a deep breath and gave him another whisper of a kiss. "And I'll always leave the light on."

Chris stepped forward, extended his hand to Ben, who took it, and found himself pulled into a rough hug. Ben could feel Chris's tension, could tell that he was very close to breaking down, and feeling every inch the disappointing worrisome son, bit his own tongue to keep from weeping openly. Chris released him after a few moments, face lined with concern, voice husky. "You get yourselves back here so you can help her, too."

Full on dad voice. Ben's affection tugged the corners of his mouth into a reluctant smile and he blinked quickly to keep the moisture in his eyes where it was. "Count on it."

Then Chris and Aife were locked in a silent embrace Ben would not interrupt for anything. When she drew back, Ben motioned for Aife to join him as he drew a circle in the soft earth with his toe. "Follow my lead," he ordered. "Don't say anything unless you absolutely have to. This is our only play. I'm damned well going to make it work."

Aife only looked back at him numbly, certain they were headed to their deaths, or worse. She gazed at Chris, putting everything she felt into her eyes.

Ben and Aife bowed their heads and started softly chanting the incantation. The air around them began to shimmer like the crest of a hill on a hot day. The angels and her father stood with Mal and she welcomed their presence even though part of her still felt completely alone. Heat baked outward from the circle and Mal couldn't stop herself. She stepped toward him and cried out in a desperate voice, "Ben! Wait!"

He raised his head, almost reluctantly. She had to say it. And not like when you say it a hundred times day but in a way that means forever. What if she never had another chance? "Ben! I love you!"

He smiled for her then, a beautiful smile, but it didn't quite touch his eyes. "I love you. More than my own life. Goodbye, Mal."

She told him once never to say goodbye, her life had been too full of goodbyes, and there was such a resigned finality in his voice, she wanted to make him take it back. But at that moment Davidos stepped forward abruptly, something seeming to occur to him, and he raised his hand. He said only, "Let me," and Ben's grim expression evaporated as a thin sliver of hope lit up his whole face. There was a terrible sucking cracking sound and they vanished with a flash. The only evidence they had been there was a small scorched circle of earth.

Mal, her eyes wide, barked at her uncle, "What did you just do?"

"It's better if it looks like they were thrown back by magic outside themselves. They can't show up in Hell under their own power. It would look too suspicious. Lucifer is a lot of things but stupid isn't one of them. Ben will know how to use this to their advantage."

"Oh go to Hell yourself then!" she shouted, completely overwhelmed by their losses, the devastation she had witnessed, not to mention how much of the responsibility fell on her.

If she hadn't been so stubborn, if she'd just left, things would be fine. She turned and ran toward the edge of the woods, then crumpled to the ground on the soft green earth. She had never asked for any of this. The battle had been truly terrible. There were so many people dead, so much destruction left behind. It was all her fault. And now Ben and Aife were gone to Hell, literally Hell. She wept, feeling about as helpless as a person can. Her father, The Voice, and her Uncle Davi gave her space, choosing to sit on some rocks and talk quietly. Her friends sat near them on the ground, in silent shock. Chris limped around, casting sympathetic glances at her every so often, clearly in anguish over Ben and Aife and everything else that had happened.

She wept quietly for a while. Then, when it almost seemed like she might be back in control of herself, another wave of images replayed itself in her head, of the battle, of her nightmares of the things that could happen to Ben in Hell. It seemed to fill her up and destroy everything that she was. She screamed and rolled on the ground pounding the earth with her fists. She just wanted out of this whole damned thing, wanted it all to go away. She cried until there was nothing left and she felt empty, clean. How was this even real? Angels and demons both had done terrible things today. As though choosing either side made any sense.

As she rolled over, she felt the pendant Ben had given her slide against her breast. With her eyes still squeezed shut she pulled it out of her shirt, clutching it hard in her hand until she felt it grow warm. Somehow that seemed to make it easier to calm down, to pull out of the nightmare world of memory and imagination. She thought of his words when he'd given it to her, his conviction that none of this was as simple as fate. She felt like she had wept out the last childish bit of herself, and a cool certainty came to her. She was in charge of her own destiny. She got up, dusted off as best she could, wiping her tear-swollen face with her shirt. She could go on. Because she had to.

She walked calmly to what was left of her companions. Teddy and Petra might need some help to come around. Teddy was staring blankly and Petra was absently wiping her mouth with the back of her hand, looking like she might throw up again. Chris was pacing, trying to walk some of the stiffness out of his bleeding leg. She'd have to see to it for him. Metatron just sat, his eyes closed. Her father and uncle were both about to say something, but she held up her hand. She felt the need to speak first, to feel some modicum of control and autonomy. Besides, this was the worst she'd ever felt and anything they said would only add to it. Chris limped toward them and she gave him a small smile. He understood. He was as devastated as she was.

She stuffed her hands in her pockets when she realized she was wringing them. "We need to go, keep moving right? Figure this out. What to do next. Does *anybody* have any kind of plan here? Because I can't even think right now."

Ari sighed. He was suffering for his daughter, what she had witnessed, what had happened, for Ben and Aife. "Davi and I have discussed it. We think we know what we can do, for now. Chris has a few ideas, too … Of course, it's up to you." He paused. "I should have told you everything, put this in your hands a long time ago." He took a shuddering breath.

"Dad, don't second guess yourself. You did the best you could."

He smiled. That was Mal; always trying to make things alright for everyone. He began again, "I'm just so sorry … and Ben … I …"

She cut him off. She couldn't talk calmly about today. She was back in control of herself, but it was tenuous, at best. "Dad, don't. You tried." Mal stepped away, looking off into a distance only she could see, "And Ben … He'll be back," she said firmly. "He promised."

She was now determined if there was a way out for any of them she would find it.

And she would do what Ben had said.

She would make her own choice.

"Now this is not the end. It is not even the beginning of the end. But it is perhaps, the end of the beginning."
~ Winston Churchill

Thank you for taking the time to read this book. If you liked it, please consider telling your friends or posting a short review on Goodreads or the site where you bought it. Word of mouth is an author's best friend and much appreciated.

About the Authors

Keith and Jess reside in the beautiful mountains of Vermont with their two children, three cats, a dog, and an immortal guinea pig. Jess has worked in newspaper and art publishing, freelance writing, cake decorating, and presently works as a special education teacher. She enjoys playing the ukulele badly, reading, and binge-watching unhealthy amounts of TV. Keith spent many years as a chef and business manager and now runs a quaint country store. He can often be found writing poetry, reading, or cooking something amazing. They love to cook together, go hiking around the gorgeous terrain Vermont offers, and spend time together and with their boys. They also enjoy working together to create a world with interrelated but independent compelling stories.

demonsrunlit@wordpress.com

https://www.facebook.com/jkf.demonsrunlit

Twitter: @jk_demonsrunlit

CPSIA information can be obtained
at www.ICGtesting.com
Printed in the USA
BVOW11s0900060717

488534BV00008B/193/P

9 781681 604466